A dangerous alliance in the desert...

"DeStar, will you help me?" Dina's words surprised herself.

He appeared to study her. "Ten minutes ago you said you would rather...what was it? 'Choke on the dust of this planet' than ask me for anything. Now you not only have questions, you want my help. And yet, I sense your request is sincere. What changed your mind?"

She kept her eyes on him and didn't reply, mostly because she didn't have an answer, but partly, she had to admit, because he fascinated her. She told herself it was because she had never seen a *dens* before. She took in the full mouth, then followed the clean, angled lines of his jaw to where the exodite stud flashed at his ear. How could a *dens* look like this?

Dina sucked in a quick, deep breath that caught in her throat. The investigation, of course. She had to do everything and anything to further the investigation. But somehow she sensed that there was something more, but something she couldn't, or wasn't prepared to, put into words. She felt confused, and it scared her. She wondered if the *dens* was playing with her mind. Damn him! How was she ever to know?

"I'm sure you know the answer to that better than I do." Her answer left a sour taste in her mouth.

Rayn did understand it better than she did. It was his power. It seduced people, even the strong-willed and clear thinkers. And while his plan of seduction had originally involved a sexual conquest, nothing more, he had to admit to the pleasure he felt at her unsolicited request. He had given her but a tiny taste of his mastery of the mind, and already she wanted more. *And you will keep coming back for more, little girl, no matter what your feelings for me are.*

This is dedicated with love to Dorothy and Roland,
who always supported me in every crazy thing I ever
tried to do, to Linda K. for her encouragement and faith,
and to Linda G. for her invaluable assistance.
Also, to the men and women I worked with on The Job,
who were always there to back me up.

Rainscape

***

Jaye Roycraft

RAINSCAPE
Published by ImaJinn Books, a division of ImaJinn

ISBN: 1-893896-31-5

10 9 8 7 6 5 4 3 2

Books are available at quantity discounts when used to promote products or services. For information please write to: Marketing Division, ImaJinn Books, P.O. Box 162, Hickory Corners, MI 49060-0162, or call toll free 1-877-625-3592.

Cover design by Patricia Lazarus

ImaJinn Books, a division of ImaJinn
P.O. Box 162, Hickory Corners, MI 49060-0162
Toll Free: 1-877-625-3592
http://www.imajinnbooks.com

CAST OF CHARACTERS

Mondina "Dina" Marlijn - A rookie investigator with the Interplanetary Investigation Bureau, and a telepath

Karjon "Jon" Rzije - Dina's partner

Rayn DeStar - a telepathic *dens* from B'harata, leader of the Desert *Dailjan*

Myrr Chandhel - Minister of the colony on Exodus

Maris Iridino - Minister Chandhel's assistant

Avvis Ranchar - the first Minister of Exodus

Kaz Katzfiel - Commander of the Aeternan Enforcement Agency

Kim Khilioi - A Corporal of the Aeternan Enforcement Agency

Hrugaz - a Sergeant of the Aeternan Enforcement Agency

Jalena Lumazi - a doctor

Gillique Samek - a miner, the latest homicide victim

Dais Johnter - a miner, the first victim

Kilist Marhjon - a miner, the second victim

R'ke Kai-Men - a miner, the third victim

Jai Hwa-lik - Mother Lode Mining's Executive Director

Rum Ctararzin - Mother Lode Mining's Operations Manager

Faitaz Chukar - Mother Lode's Attorney

Quay Bhelen - Mother Lode's Chief Financial Officer

Karsa Hrothi - Mother Lode's Chief of Security

Kalyo Rhoemer - a Mother Lode Security Officer

Rukhyo Nastja - a Mother Lode Surveyor, now off-planet

Kindyll Sirkhek - an ex-miner, now a *Dailjan*

Trai Morghen - en ex-dock worker, now a *Dailjan*

Raethe Avarti - an ex-miner, now a *Dailjan*

T'gaard Kai-reudh - a *Dailjan*

Alessane Sorreano - Rayn's *Dailjan* woman

Xuche - a *mantis*, captured and deported from Exodus

Gyn T'halamar - a *dens*

Ryol - Rayn's brother on B'harata

Flyr - Rayn's brother, deceased

Daar - Dina's former lover on Glacia

Roanna - Dina's former partner, killed by a *dens*

GLOSSARY OF GLACIAN AND B'HARATAN WORDS

agherz - dawn
al - beyond, after
albho - white
angwhi - snake
bhel - flame
chayne - chain
dailjan - desert dweller, literally "leftover"
dens - mental force
dher - to muddy
dheru - truth
ghe - gate
ghel - glass
gwer - mountain
kap - haven
kathedra - chair
kel - mine
kewero - north
krek - derogatory term, literally "fish spawn"
mercari - merchants
merkwia - twilight
m'riri - reflection
pelag - basin
pur - fire
spithra - spider
uz - leader
wespero - west
wiara - twist
yegwa - power

ONE
THE ARRIVAL

Something shattered the calm, but there was no sound.

Awareness was the intruder, Dina's relaxation the victim, and she didn't like it one little bit. She called tired limbs and senses to alert, and her now open eyes widened further when she saw the cause of the disruption. The man staring at her was hardly someone Agent Mondina Marlijn expected to see in the spacedock's quarantine module high in geostationary orbit over Exodus.

He was dressed in neither the dark blue uniform of dock personnel nor the pale green tunics of the medical staff, but rather had the appearance of an escapee from the brig. Long, inky hair fell from either side of a sharp widow's peak, like the wings of a crow, and black stubble shadowed skin already darkened by the sun. A brown leather vest half covered a bare chest, and soot-colored leggings that hugged the skin vanished into high, well-worn leather boots. Brown bracers on his forearms trailed long suede fringes that snaked past his wrists to tease his fingertips. The lean-muscled body thus revealed lacked only a weapon in hand to complete the outlaw image.

Dina rose slowly to her feet, curiosity and caution banishing the wake of exhaustion left by the final two frenetic days of spaceflight.

"Who are you? What are you doing here?" she challenged.

The man's only answer was a cocked smile and a deep bow from the waist which climaxed with a flourish of upturned arms, sending the bracer fringes undulating in a silent dance.

Dina was about to call for Jon, her partner, to join her from the examination room next door, when the stranger winked an amber eye at her and was gone.

She stepped forward and cast her gaze around the small waiting room. There were few places to hide behind save several chairs, a table, and a narrow bed. She tried the door leading from the quarantine module to the curving corridor accessing other modules strung on the circular dock, but the door, as expected, was locked. The only other door was to the room where Jon was being scanned for infectious microbes.

Dina keyed the door and poked her head into the room, sweeping her gaze from wall to wall. Both Jon and the quarantine assistant raised their heads and looked at her. There was no one else in the room.

Dina pasted on a smile. "Excuse me...much longer?"

"As I said before, Agent Marlijn, a couple hours. You'll just have to be patient," replied the assistant.

Her smile jerked upward. "Thank you."

She closed the door and paced the waiting room. It had not been a dream. Tired as she was, she had been awake. Nor had she imagined the man. He had been too real. A thought came to her. Spacefever. Sleeplessness, disturbing dreams when sleep did come, dizziness, and hallucinations were all symptoms of the "fever" that plagued men and women on spaceflights not made in hypersleep.

She drew in a deep breath. She should report the hallucination to Jon and the quarantine master. It was required by Rules and Regulations. But if she did make the report, it would mean more tests. A longer quarantine. Planetfall would be delayed. The start of the investigation would be delayed. She released the long breath slowly. No one had seen the image of the man but her. The investigation was too important to her. There could be no delays. There would be no report.

***

Rayn DeStar felt his consciousness spiraling downward at a speed to rival that of the fleetest star cruiser. Elation, wonder and anticipation swirled around him in a vortex of pure emotion. Uncontrolled, the feelings sang to him like the keening of a fierce wind, and Rayn rode the storm with abandon until his ethereal self reached his physical body, slowed, and reentered it.

Whole again in body and mind, he took a deep breath and raised his arms, not only to stretch cramped muscles, but to celebrate. The experience of an out-of-body projection always gave Rayn a sense of freedom that was impossible to achieve encased in his physical body, but this projection had been especially sweet.

A telepath! And a female, at that! After more than five years of projecting his etheric self to the spacedock to look over new arrivals, his travels had finally paid off. He had all but given up on another *dens* coming to this world. He had waited patiently for the bans to be lifted that forbid his people to travel to Synergy Worlds, but knew in his heart that the bans would most likely outlive him. There were many more telepaths in the galaxy than just the *dens*, though, and Rayn had held out hope that some day one would come to this godsforsaken sand heap.

Some day was here! This barren world had finally sent him a challenge. Oh, it was true that just surviving in the desert day after day was a formidable task, but he had mastered survival years ago. No, this challenge was worthwhile, and one that made his blood run hot.

His race had been bred to control, born to dominate, and even though he had shunned his home world of B'harata, he couldn't change the blood that gave him life. Yes, he had sorely missed the sweet satisfaction that surrender to his power gave him.

Who was she? Whoever she was, she would provide gratification. She had the ability. She was receptive to the energy of thought in a way that no other visitor to Exodus had been for many years. Once on the spacedock, his ethereal body had felt it immediately. Her powers were undeveloped and undisciplined, but the gateway to her mind was there for him to enter whenever he desired.

***

Mondina Marlijn had arrived, in every sense of the word. Her booted feet—her very tired booted feet—were finally on Exodus as her ship, *Justitia*, had berthed at the spacedock above the city of Aeternus the evening before last. Her head, though, in spite of her exhaustion, was in the heavens, where it had been since she had gotten the word she would be assigned to field duty with Karjon Rzije, Specialist *extraordinare*. It was a promotion, a chance to travel to places she had only dreamed of, and best of all, she was with Jon.

It had been *al-merkwia*, past the twilight, when Dina and Jon's shuttle landed at the city's port, but there was no lack of light. After the low light of the ship's interior, Dina found herself squinting at the floodlights that adorned the outside of the port facility. The two moons of Exodus—Foraii and Egnis—hung low in the sky, adding their radiance to the night.

It had been a relatively short trip from her home world of Glacia, too short for hypersleep, and Dina had been busy every waking moment. But even so sleep had been elusive. And now, as much as Dina tried to forget the stranger in the "hallucination," she hadn't been able to. She was hoping that with the end of the flight and her feet planted firmly on the ground she would be visited by no more disturbing images.

All the pride and nerves of an actress stepping on stage for the first time fizzed through her body in an adrenaline rush when Dina's heels rang against the stone-paved outer entrance to the port facility, and the cool night air snapped around her like applause. The fact that she had been without sleep for more than two standard days was lost in the rush that elevated her. She beamed in the spotlight of her enthusiasm until a young liaison officer strutted toward them. Colorful flags, rippling languidly in the glow cast by carefully hidden ground lamps, bordered each side of the walkway that stretched before her and framed the approaching officer as if he were a work of art.

He rivaled the flagpoles in height, color, and pomp. His smooth, tanned face was as bright and shiny as his polished sable boots, and his lustrous, dark hair reflected their rich color. He sported a tan military cap, its glossy visor pulled low over his eyes, loose tan trousers and a matching shirt that shone almost silver in the night light. A burgundy sash slashed his chest from his right shoulder to his left hip, where a similar circle of color banded his trim waist. The ends of the sash were fringed and danced from his left hip. Gold insignia flashed from his cap, his shoulder sash, and the front of his shirt. A long tan coat, paled to pearl by the moonlight, draped perfectly from his wide shoulders, the buttoned-back lining of red darkened to the color of claret. The man's booted legs were impossibly long, and his white teeth gleamed in the bright light of the city night.

"Good evening, sir, ma'am. Corporal Kim Khilioi of the Aeternan Enforcement Agency. Assigned to be at your disposal for the length of your visit."

"Evening, Corporal. Karjon Rzije, Specialist First Class of the Interplanetary Investigation Bureau, and my partner, Mondina Marlijn, Specialist Second Class. We appreciate the efficient docking and unloading protocol. If you could show us to our quarters, we'd like to get some sleep before meeting with the administrator tomorrow. It's been a long trip."

"Understood, sir. However, I must ask you to come with me to the Medical Center. Minister Chandhel and the Commander are waiting there for you."

"Corporal, can't a meeting wait 'til tomorrow? It's been a very tiring trip."

"Apologies, sir, but no. There's been another incident."

Jon's thick eyebrows drew together, almost touching. "Another homicide?"

"Yes, sir."

"Let's go."

Once, Dina would have sighed, but not now. It was always this way. What was needed for the job always took precedence over personal considerations. Little things like exhaustion and hunger simply didn't matter. Besides, she was on Exodus, and she was with Jon.

Her fatigue forgotten, Dina braced herself for the unpleasant task ahead of her as she matched the men's strides to the all-terrain hugger. Watching Jon's broad shoulders and the slight swagger he had to his walk, she smiled.

Her gaze slid to the Aeternan officer, and something familiar about his expression shadowed her enthusiasm. It was a look she had seen countless times—a smile as bright and cold as artificial light, and eyes as unreadable as dark ink spilled on blank paper.

Except for the brief "ma'am," he hadn't acknowledged her at all.

Dina reached her mind out, feather light, and touched Khilioi's, and the smile that had risen at the joy of her arrival deflated quickly as she felt the unmistakable disdain. Whether it was because she was a female or simply IIB, Dina wasn't sure, but it was nothing new for her. That never made it easier to bear, though, and Dina's head suddenly felt too heavy for her neck, her boots too heavy for her feet.

Unbidden, a memory from four years before, as if newly experienced, surged to the front of her mind. It had been just three weeks before the end of academy training, and she recalled how high her confidence had been. The most grueling training was behind her, graduation was clearly in sight, and she had thought to be accepted by her classmates. She had especially looked forward to that day of high-risk training scenarios, not only as a welcome change from the classroom lecture, but to reinforce her feeling that she was as capable as, if not more so than, anyone else in the class.

But then she remembered how those positive feelings had drained away as she stood and waited for another recruit to choose her as a partner for the exercise. It seemed like an hour, but it had taken only seconds for the males in her squad to partner up with each other, laughing in anticipation and slapping each other on the back. She remembered turning, at last, to Roanna, the only other female in her squad, who was also standing alone, and seeing her own humiliation mirrored in the other girl's eyes. She remembered shrugging and smiling, as if it made no difference—male with male, female with female— but she had cried herself to sleep that night, asking the gods for the hundredth time why she was different.

Dear Jon. Even though he was her superior, he treated her like an equal. For years females had held the same positions as males did within the Bureau, but there was still, and probably always would be, a trace of prejudice toward female members. Overt prejudicial comments and actions were, of course, prohibited by Rules and Regulations. That didn't stop many from making their feelings clear in subtle ways. She normally didn't dwell on such matters, but tonight her tired mind had no power to keep the memories at bay. Not with Khilioi beside her, turned only toward Jon. Making small talk only to Jon.

It certainly didn't take any telepathic power to sense the

contempt of such men, but Dina was especially aware of their attitudes, since her telepathic abilities had rated the highest in the Academy for five years running. She never bragged about her ability, in fact, made it a rule of hers never to mention it to other bureau members. In this way her telepathic power had become one of her strongest assets. Jon, of course, was well aware of her ability. It was one of the reasons she had been chosen for this assignment.

As the hugger jounced forward on its wide tires, the fairy city before her spun its enchantment and lifted Dina's mind from its somber musings. She was nearly blinded as a myriad of mirrors flashed their faces her way, as though the prospect of new adoring admirers was not to be ignored. Crystal pyramids, glass bubbles and mirrored cubes, all lit from both within and without, vied for her attention. The effulgence enveloped her, bound her, and she heard not a word of what the corporal said.

At last the hugger rolled to a stop before a sparkling bronze cubic structure of mirrored glass and gleaming metal. She reluctantly refocused her attention on Khilioi's narration, and with a final pulsing glimmer, the luminous energy of the city released her. Dina heard him say that this was the Aeternan Medical Center and was adjacent to the Visitor Center, where she and Jon would be housed for the length of their visit on Exodus.

Once inside, Khilioi, the metal taps on his boots echoing a drumbeat off the walls, escorted her and Jon into a large white office where two men and a woman waited. The first man was older, of medium height, with an abundance of silver hair which he wore partially tied back behind his head. The hair at the nape of his neck was worn loose and hung below his shoulders. He wore a loose white shirt and trousers. A gold sash around his waist was the sole indicator of his stature as colony administrator. His brown, weathered face reminded Dina of a rose petal, dried and faded, yet still retaining a trace of its original robust color. His eyes, though, were anything but faded. Of a shade just darker than a sea at dawn, they radiated the strength that had once been present in every aspect of his physical being.

The woman, middle-aged, had honey-blonde hair styled in a simple but impeccable coif, and rich hazel eyes that showed intelligence. But her expression was stern, and her mouth was the only straight line in a face of gentle curves.

The second man, younger and sporting short, dark hair, was dressed in a similar manner to the corporal, except that an embellished silver sash, instead of burgundy, adorned his chest and waist. No warmth or compassion was apparent in his face. He looked more like a carefully drawn portrait, studied and precise. The mouth wore not even a sham of a smile, and his eyes had a disturbing quality to them. Glass cold, they were as colorless as his sash.

The older man greeted Jon and Dina. "I am Minister Myrr Chandhel. Welcome to Exodus, and thank you for responding to my request so promptly. This is Commander 'Kaz' Katzfiel of the Aeternan Enforcement Agency, and Dr. Jalena Lumazi, our chief biotech engineer. I regret bringing you here so soon after your arrival, but there's just been another...incident...and we thought it best you be brought up to speed immediately. Come. Doctor, if you would."

Dr. Lumazi led them to another room. Upon entering, Dina felt a chill slither snake-like down her body from the base of her neck to her toes. In the dull-white room, the only thing that relieved the tallow walls, metal equipment and lights that hung from the ceiling like so many giant silver bulbous-eyed insects, ironically, was the body of their latest victim.

The corpse, enclosed in a clear case, reclined in the middle of the room, a grotesque trophy under glass. Dina studied the man's face. It was impossible to tell if he had once been handsome or not. Death in his case had not only taken his vitality, but had destroyed all semblance of the person.

The eyes were mercifully closed, but the features were contorted in pain and something else, as if in the moment before his death, he had seen horror beyond words. The mouth was open, and Dina could almost hear the scream of agony that surely must have echoed through the mine's tunnels. The skull was misshapen, as if squeezed in a vice. She had seen corpses before, but never one like this. She felt the bile rising in her throat, but she fought it down and averted her eyes from the body to regain her composure.

The doctor spoke matter-of-factly. "His name is Gillique Samek, a miner at Dheru Kel. He was found near the mines three days ago. Blunt trauma to each side of the temporal area of his head resulted in skull fracture and subdural hematoma. He died almost instantly. We're not sure what caused the massive head trauma. No weapons, no evidence, no witnesses have been found. The other miners died in a similar manner."

Jon and Dina kept their questions to a minimum, and thankfully the briefing was short. She was glad to leave the white room of death and even happier to leave Commander Katzfiel's presence. His pale eyes unnerved her. When the black pupils shifted in his restless eyes, she thought of tiny black bugs skittering across the chalk-white walls.

When the meeting was over, Khilioi led Jon and Dina across the road to the Visitor Center. The outside air was cool and ice bright after the closed antiseptic air of the Medical Center. This quickly deepened to a dry chill, however, and the change in temperature, coupled with her exhaustion and the memory of the dead miner, threatened again to send her stomach into revolt.

Upon entering the building, Dina felt relief as the warmth of the heated air washed over her, but still she fought to keep from getting sick. Building security heartened her, though, and both she and Jon patiently endured the thorough scans and procedures. Upon completion, both Jon and Dina received key discs from the corporal.

The corporal explained their use. "Long as you're here, you can come and go into any secured building with a sec level of three or lower using the key discs. They also allow you access to the desert way stations. This building is sec level three, but your rooms, as well as the storage bay to the rear, are sec level four, so you'll need retina scans as well to get into those areas. Know I don't have to remind you to be careful with these keys."

Jon glanced sideways at Dina, and she gave him an answering look. For all his deference, Dina suspected that the corporal resented the Bureau's interference in local affairs and doubted their ability to solve problems they had no first-hand experience with. As the security door whooshed open, Dina gave Khilioi a smile dazzling enough to rival his own.

Krek, she thought, as she followed him down the corridor. It was an old Glacian word for the spawn of a lower life form.

Their rooms were on the second floor, side by side. Dina entered her suite and, unable to control her nausea any longer, bolted for the bathroom and retched into the sink. At another time she would have been pleased to find a small but comfortable bedroom with a kitchenette, a dressing room, a bathroom, and an inside door connecting the two suites, but for now she was thankful only for privacy and that the day was finally over. Almost. As she leaned over the sink, afraid to move, she heard a soft knock at the connecting door.

"Just a moment," she called. She quickly rinsed her face and took a small sip of water. She opened her door and, in spite of her exhaustion, felt the familiar jolt of pleasure being face to face with Jon always brought.

Strands of his shoulder-length hair, normally neatly kept, strayed over his green eyes. He was leaning against the doorjamb, and Dina could detect fine lines around his eyes and mouth that weren't normally there. She realized, with a start, that he was tired, too. Oddly, his appearance didn't lessen the attraction she felt for him, but served to remind her that he was as human and vulnerable as she was.

"Some arrival, huh?" Jon said. "There should be time to unpack tomorrow. Right now, just get some sleep. I'll call you at seventh hour mark zero."

Dina gave him a small smile, nodded, and closed the door. Much as she longed for sleep, there were some things she had no choice but to do before retiring. She logged on to the room's computer, identified herself, was voice-printed, and assigned her verbal command access code. As always, she used *pri* as her computer code.

Pri was the endearment her father had used to address her and her mother when Dina was young. He was a wise man and a loving, supportive father, and using his pet name for her as her VCAC always made Dina feel close to him, even when she was far from her home world.

Next she gave verbal commands to program room air and water temperature, wake up time, light levels, and breakfast selection. She laid out an outfit for the upcoming meeting, and when she finally dropped onto the bed, she thought, a little sadly, that she was too tired to even dream about Jon. But she dreamed anyway.

She was lost in the Sea of Glass, floating on an air current high above the sand, buoyed by the heat, mesmerized by the light that shot arrows at her from all directions. She heard faraway laughter, as if the sun, the mighty golden ruler of the sky, were sitting back, safe in his heavenly lair, content to let his desert warriors do his cruel bidding.

With a burst of energy, she broke loose and fell, spiraling slowly to the earth. The sinuous curves of the dunes, like ivory arms, beckoned her, and she settled, like a child at its mother's bosom, between embracing barchans of glittering sand. Shielding her eyes, she ventured a bold glance at the sun, only to have the light blocked by an object which dropped from the sky and wafted languidly down to her, riding the shimmering waves of heat until it came into focus.

Silhouetted by the sun, the huge eagle floated just above her, bolstered by the heat rollers, then descended to the dune sea's surface, its powerful wings drawing up against its body. Dina watched as the eagle transformed into a man, a man whose face she couldn't see. A golden mask covered his face. Bronze silk trousers, his only other apparel, billowed around his legs like the red fire of a dying sun. The lone figure seemed to outshine the day star, the sand, and the mirages that melted and reformed in the periphery of her vision.

He called to her, and she answered with a challenge, nevertheless drawn to him. She tried to take a step forward, but the sea held her tightly, and in its grip, a ribbon of fear wrapped itself around her as well.

The man removed his mask and circled her so that the light illuminated his features. The hot breeze lifted mahogany hair away from his face, revealing piercing golden eyes. She called out to him again and tried to move, but the sea sucked at her feet. She heard his laughter once more, rich and ringing, and he glided toward her with the ease of a snake over sand, until he stood before her.

A scythe of shiny hair arced over one amber eye, while other strands caught in the sheen of sweat at his temple and lay trapped against his skin.

Desire and fear clashed within her. Beasts fighting for domination, they butted and twisted until they became one, feeding off each other. Her desire heightened her fear, and her fear sharpened her desire until she could feel hot blood racing through every limb.

He raised both hands to brush the hair away from her face and run the pads of his fingertips down her cheek to her chin. He held her head gently but in such a way that she could look nowhere except at his face. A line of sweat zigzagged past one eye and crept down his cheek, and she had an overwhelming longing to reach out and touch it.

She slipped an arm up between them and touched his hot skin, rubbing a fingertip across the trail of moisture. His lips parted, full and sensuous, and his face slackened with his need. Her fingers skated upward, and as her hand rose, so did her gaze, until she stared straight into eyes that burned so hot she thought she would burst into flames. Instead, she shivered in the heat, caught by a power in his gaze she didn't understand. She tipped her head back, still held by his hands, and his hungry mouth fed at hers, sapping her will until her lips parted for him. She clung to him, one hand clutching a fistful of his long hair, the other running over the muscles of his back.

His mouth released hers at last, leaving her gasping for breath. No man had ever made her feel like this, chilled and enflamed; consumed, yet whole; afraid, but fearless. When he removed her tunic, she didn't protest. Nor did she try to stop him when she felt his hands, cool against the warmth of her breasts. Her body tightened at his touch, her back arching, her nipples hardening when his hands cupped her.

She closed her eyes, and he touched her in a way she had never before been touched. Then she felt his will, more insistent than his lips or hands had been, and suddenly her fear untangled itself from her desire and rose to warn her. What he wanted was too much. She would not submit in that way.

"Mondina..." She vaguely heard her name from somewhere high above.

He commanded her and compelled her, but she pushed away from him, screaming at him with words that blazed in the heat, were consumed to ash and lost on the wind.

***

Rayn's ears rang with her outcries as he withdrew from her mind. He laughed long and easily, knowing Dina would no longer be able to hear him. The test had been an unqualified success.

His mind had injected images into hers that she would interpret as nothing more than a dream, and he was surprised and pleased to find not only such clear reception on her part, but strength of will. He had the power to overcome such will, of course, but she had enough power of her own to make a grand game of it.

Controlling her mind would be a challenge. Her body was another matter entirely. If the dream was any indication of what her physical response to him would be, she was already his.

TWO
EXODUS

"Mondina...Wake up, Mondina. The time is sixth hour, mark zero. Wake up, Mondina..." lilted the pleasant female voice of the computer. Dina awoke with a start as the lights in the room came on and brightened gradually. Though the room was programmed for a comfortable sleeping temperature, Dina's body was bathed in sweat, her heart still pounding with the memory of the dream.

She pulled her hair back and rubbed her face. It had been the stranger, the man she had seen on the spacedock. There was no doubt about that. But why? And how had he made such an impression on her that she would dream about him in such an erotic manner? Could this be another symptom of spacefever? This had been a dream, albeit one more realistic than she could ever remember having, but still a dream, not a hallucination. Still, the manifestation of disturbing dreams was one possible sign of fever, and this one was definitely disturbing. She tested her door. It was locked. She was in a secured building. No, there was no way it could have been anything other than just a dream.

Though the erotic dream had been new for her, nightmares were not. While she was working on a case, she usually had work-related ones every night. She chased and was chased. She was fired upon, and she fired at others. Yes, this dream was different.

As she slid out of bed and took a warm shower, she struggled to scrub the images of the man from her mind. She'd anticipated this day for a long time and was eager for it to start on a positive note.

She took the dark bread, fruit, and juice out of the food selector and ate slowly, concentrating on the morning's itinerary. There would be, of course, the meeting with Chandhel, Katzfiel, and whatever other officials the Minister deemed necessary. She hoped it would be a small group. Too many people would distract her and make it more difficult for her to probe those present.

She took extra time in dressing. She and Jon would be sizing up the Exodan contingent, but it went both ways. She checked herself in the mirror, pleased there were no lines in her face to betray the previous night's exhaustion. She styled her long hair into a twist and saw clear eyes reflected back at her. The dark circles she had feared would collar her eyes were thankfully absent.

She dressed not in a uniform, but in a suit the color of steel with gold accents, grateful her exercise regimen on board *Justitia* enabled her to slip perfectly into the fitted jacket and trousers. As a final touch, she slipped her exodite ring onto her middle finger. The marquise cut stone was bezel set horizontally into a band that generously shouldered the top and bottom of the gem with gold. The exodite gem, blazing with silver fire, almost overshadowed the small black pearl burnished deep into the band below one of the points of the gemstone, like a tear to the exodite eye.

She had owned the ring for several years. Her father had presented it as a special gift upon her graduation from the Academy, telling her the stone reminded him of her eyes, fiery and alive, yet far too sad. She had first worn it because it reminded her of her father and made her feel that he was nearby supporting her, no matter how far away she was. Gradually, it had become her anchor for confidence, a directive to her subconscious whenever she began to doubt herself. At those times she would close her eyes, finger the ring, and think of her father's faith in her. Now, after years of using the ring as her anchor, all she had to do was to look at the exodite eye, and she instantly felt better equipped to tackle whatever problem was at hand. She twisted the ring on her finger now and felt confidence and strength swell inside her.

She smiled again as she thought of the irony. The exodite mines on Exodus were, in fact, the focal point of her assignment. Her token stone the heart of the mystery. She shook her head and glanced one last time in the mirror. She hated to admit it, but she had also dressed with the hope Jon would be pleased with her. She wanted as much to make a good impression on him as on Chandhel. She quickly chided herself. No time now for fantasies.

The computer softly chimed. "Mondina, you have a call waiting from Jon Rzije." She could feel her pulse race. So much for suppressing fantasies.

"*Pri*, answer with visual."

Jon's handsome face immediately appeared on the monitor. His long, light brown hair was neatly combed for a change, so did not detract from the clean-shaven features. Dina sighed. *Dear gods, but he was gorgeous.*

"Good Morning, Dina. Are you ready?"

"All set, Jon."

"Good. Come in, and we'll compare notes before we call for our escort."

"On my way. *Pri*, log off." Dina took one last look around the room, picked up the slim case containing her notebooks and recorders, and rapped at the connecting door. Jon opened it with a quick verbal command and motioned with his head for her to come inside. He held a steaming cup of mocava in one hand and a sweet twist roll in his mouth, but even so, Dina didn't miss the attention his eyes paid her, or the slight lift to his brows.

"You look very nice. And very professional," he said, taking the twist out of his mouth.

Trying to suppress a grin, Dina took in his appearance as well. She never tired of looking at him. He was tall and well-built, but none of his attributes could compare to his eyes. They were the purest green she had ever seen, no touch of hazel or gray, so translucent she swore she could see through them. They were set off by thick lashes and brows several shades darker than his hair, and this morning Dina was glad to see their sparkle back. She was more pleased by Jon's remark than she was willing to admit, even to herself.

"Thanks. Let's hope Minister Chandhel is suitably impressed as well." She sat down opposite Jon at the small table and leaned forward.

"You've run diagnostic tests on your recorders?" asked Jon between sips of his mocava.

"Yes, of course."

"Good. It'll be interesting to see who else we meet. So far, the checks on Chandhel and Katzfiel show them coming up clean. Neither has any documented telepathic ability, so you should be able to discreetly probe both of them. I'll try to do most of the talking to allow you to concentrate on the probes. Let's hope there are no surprises."

Dina nodded, but had a feeling that surprises were inevitable. When the AEA had first contacted the IIB, only the basic facts regarding the murders had been forwarded. Therefore, research aboard their ship had focused on the study of Exodus, its history, the mining of exodite, Mother Lode Mining Consolidated, and their contacts, Chandhel and Katzfiel.

"Nervous?" asked Jon, with a smile.

"A little, I guess. Mostly excited."

"That's natural. I remember my first out-planet assignment. I was excited, too, then proceeded to make one mistake after another. It's a wonder that case was ever cleared." He laughed, and the famous Rzije dimples popped into view. "Hey, mistakes happen. Let's just try to keep them to a minimum, okay? Well, any questions?"

"Nope."

"Then we're ready. I'll call the good corporal."

Fifteen minutes later, the ever-smiling Corporal Khilioi arrived, and they followed him to the hugger. The sides of the clear bubble roof glided over them, and Dina felt strangely closed in. She leaned forward. "Corporal, can we travel with the top open? The temperature seems pleasant enough."

"As you wish. Tolerable now, but don't be fooled. Temperature increases rapidly during the morning hours. Here, hang on to these while you're on Exodus. You'll need them any time you're outside during daylight hours; otherwise, you'll burn." Khilioi handed them sunshields, opened the top, and accelerated the hugger smoothly.

Dina took the offered sunshield, put it on, and enjoyed the soft morning light before she turned her attention to business, hitting the environmental data button of her recorder. She quickly scanned the readings. Outside air temperature was much hotter than Dina was used to on the temperate world of Glacia with its many oceans and lakes. There was some wind here, but not strong, and humidity was extremely low. Dina knew from her research that this was an enhanced atmosphere, boosted to acceptable human levels by the original colonizers.

They passed the same structures they had the night before, but the feeling of the city was completely different in the soft morning light. Mirrored walls that faced east blushed orange and yellow and winked at the rising sun.

They arrived at the Aeternan Administration Center, a cubic building with a large triangular entrance of pink glass brick. They went through the usual security checks and were shown to an antechamber that contained chairs, two small tables, and a reception desk. An attractive woman with short dark hair stood and greeted them.

"Welcome to Exodus. We've been eagerly anticipating your arrival. I'm Maris Iridino, Minister Chandhel's personal assistant. Can I bring you some iced mocava?"

"Yes, thank you, Miss Iridino," replied Jon, his dimples showcasing white teeth that flashed when he smiled at her.

Her pasted-on professional smile widened, even ascending to her eyes. "Call me Maris, please," she breathed.

Maris, draped in a jade sleeveless dress which brushed the floor, glided from the room. Dina glanced at Jon, whose eyes had followed every move Maris had made. Dina smiled to herself. He was good, no doubt about it.

Dina slid her gaze from Jon and glanced around the room. The walls were cream, the chairs a dark champagne gold. Bright panels of silk in green, burgundy, cream, and gold hung from one wall, and a framed floral depicting large burgundy blooms hung on the wall over the desk. Constructed completely of glass, it was unlike anything Dina had ever seen.

Maris floated into the room balancing a tray on one arm, and with a sweep set it noiselessly down. As Jon reached for the drinks, Dina lightly probed the woman's mind. The probe was quick and not deep, but Dina detected nothing incongruous with Maris's outward projection.

Years ago Dina had addressed the moral questions raised

by probing the minds of others. After a period of soul searching, she had devised a set of guidelines she followed to this day. She was still unable to answer the question of whether probing the mind of another without his or her knowledge was morally right or wrong, but the guidelines enabled Dina, without guilt or remorse, to probe others as part of her job.

"Dina's Rules," as she had come to think of them, were simple. She never probed deeper than was necessary. Other than to a partner such as Jon, she never discussed with others what a probe revealed, and even then she discussed only what was relevant to the assignment. Her final rationalization was that her ability aided her job performance, which was to solve violent crimes and bring criminals to justice, and therefore was a necessity.

Jon took one of the cups for himself and handed one to Dina. She sipped at the sweet, refreshing drink.

"Very good," she said to Maris, smiling.

"I noticed you admiring our artwork. You'll find some of the finest glasswork in the galaxy on Exodus. We have silica in abundance here, and not only a large glass factory in the city, but true artists, too. I also see you have one of our stones. That's quite a good quality stone, and an unusual setting."

"Thank you," Dina replied. The woman didn't miss much, she thought, glancing again at Jon. She didn't have to probe him to know the same thought was running through his head. That was her last "rule." She didn't probe partners unless an emergency dictated it.

The console chimed. "Excuse me, please," said Maris, again wafting from the room.

Dina put her mocava down and prepared her mind for the mental connection she would soon make. There was no time for her full preparation exercise, so she made do with the abbreviated version. Normally she did this when she was alone, but she trusted Jon and knew he wouldn't interrupt her. She closed her eyes and began breathing slowly, deeply, and deliberately.

Next, she visualized a ray of red light, concentrating with her mind's eye until the color was clear, bright, and exactly the shade she wanted, not tinged with yellow or blue, but clean and pure, like light through the finest ruby. She imagined each color of the spectrum in turn—orange, yellow, green, blue, indigo, and violet. The process took three minutes, and by the time Dina finished, her mind was clear and relaxed, and she knew she had achieved her basic psychic level.

A moment later Maris returned and motioned for them. "Please come this way. Minister Chandhel is ready for you."

Dina and Jon followed her into the next chamber, a conference room which, despite its lack of windows, was airy and bright. Pitchers of ice water and tall, fluted crystal goblets graced each side of the large triangular table that dominated the room. A glass floral arrangement similar to the one on the anteroom wall decorated the center of the table and trailed crystalline tendrils. One wall held a large map of Aeternus, the opposite wall a map of the desert and mountain areas of Exodus surrounding Aeternus. The wall behind the point of the triangle was as white and blank as a diary page yet to be written.

Minister Chandhel and Commander Katzfiel rose as Jon and Dina entered, and formal greetings were exchanged. Each in turn gave a small bow, their hands held over their hearts.

"Please sit and be comfortable," said the minister. "If there's anything you require, let us know."

"Specialist Rzije, Specialist Marlijn, we are at your disposal," said Katzfiel in a brusque tone which almost negated the meaning of his words.

Dina's feeling of discomfort deepened to dislike, and she decided to probe him first. Jon and Dina sat at the base of the triangle, Minister Chandhel and Maris occupied the second side, and the Commander sat alone along the third.

Chandhel spoke first. "I know you were briefed when you received this assignment, and I realize you learned much last night, but allow me to sum up all that has transpired. As you know, this is primarily a mining colony. Construction of the city and the mines began twelve years ago after enhancement of the atmosphere was completed. Originally the Synergy meant this to be a penal colony, but discovery of exodite during the primary geological surveys quickly changed that. The Synergy granted mining rights to Mother Lode Mining, who, of course, pays for these rights. Mother Lode handles all mining operations, including the hiring of all mining personnel."

The Minister halted, looked down, and took two sips of water before continuing. "A little over seven months ago, a miner was found murdered outside Kewero Kel, the northern mine. The miner, Dais Johnter, had his skull fractured. As with Samek, there were no witnesses found, nor has a motive been discovered. Since then there have been seven more murders, two of which have happened since you were contacted. All the victims have been miners, and all were found with their skulls crushed, just the way you saw last night. Immediately following the discovery of the first victim, the spaceport was closed to outgoing departures. Shipments of goods, including exodite, have continued, but no one has been allowed to leave Exodus."

As the Minister spoke, three-dimensional images appeared against the screen of the blank wall, first of exodite—both raw and cut and polished—then an exterior view of Kewero Kel, followed by a holo of Dais Johnter. The image was startling in its realism. He was a middle-aged man, with short salt-and-pepper hair and slate blue eyes which held a humor and intelligence apparent even in what was obviously an ID holo. The holo was projected only an arm's length from Katzfiel, and Dina, shifting her gaze between the two, was hard-pressed to tell which man was alive and which man was not. The holos were distracting to Dina's probes, and she wished Chandhel hadn't opted for the elaborate media presentation.

"As you can imagine, Mother Lode protested very strongly to the Synergy, alleging the Synergy has been negligent in its administration and has not provided adequate security for the colony's protection. In addition to the murdered miners, Mother Lode has lost quite a few other employees. Many miners, especially those with families, have broken their contracts and quit. The company has had difficulty hiring new workers, even with the promise of large sign-on bonuses. With fewer miners, less exodite is exported, and Mother Lode's profits go down."

The Minister paused. "Mother Lode's Executive Director, Jai Hwa-lik, has informed us that if the murderer is not stopped by the end of the current year, they will bring a suit against the Synergy. The suit will no doubt be for millions, and given our history, they have a very good chance of winning. That gives us about thirty days. Commander, if you will fill our friends in on the investigation."

Commander Katzfiel leaned back in his chair, as if to give himself the broadest view of his audience. There was nothing at the table in front of him to distract him. "All details regarding the investigation are, of course, at your disposal. We've done extensive background checks on all the victims. Autopsies were performed on each, of course. Dr. Lumazi can give you that information. Feel free to contact her any time. We've interviewed everyone connected with Mother Lode who is on-planet, including all miners."

Dina watched the Commander's eyes as he spoke. The colorless orbs continued to disconcert her. Like a doll's, she thought, staring but giving no clue to what they were seeing.

"Excuse me, Commander. How many AEA personnel have you on-planet?" asked Jon.

"We have eighteen altogether. They've logged hundreds of hours of overtime on this investigation."

"The question was not a criticism, Commander. I'm sure your people have done everything possible."

Katzfiel glanced at Chandhel, who shifted in his seat and reached again for his water, downing the liquid this time in a gulp instead of a sip. Could it be that Katzfiel had that affect on everyone? Or was there something more, Dina wondered. The Minister cleared his throat and continued. Dina shifted her probe from the Commander to Chandhel.

"There were several developments on Exodus prior to the start of the murders which may be relevant. We are not proud of what happened, but have done our best to make amends. The first minister of Exodus, Avvis Ranchar, was a greedy man. He filled most positions in his administration with friends and relatives who paid him smartly for his favors. Many of these men were also greedy, and corruption quickly spread. Contraband was smuggled in, undeclared goods were shipped out."

Chandhel hesitated, as if reluctant to continue. "Worst of all, procedures for approving and clearing arrivals of outworlders became very lax. Word quickly spread amongst neighboring worlds, and soon every undesirable with nowhere to go came to Exodus. Some were on the run from enforcement agencies. Some just wanted the opportunity to get rich quick from any illegal means possible. But, by far the most dangerous were the dark outworlders—those banned by virtue of their dangerous genetic predispositions, or the ideology of their homeworlds."

Dina looked at Jon and caught his eye. She looked back at Chandhel. "Minister, who do you mean specifically?"

"It consists of a broad group, including shapeshifters, the cannibals of Onipherus, the *dens* of Deorcas Tron, the *mantis* of Etesia..."

"Excuse me, Minister. Do you have knowledge that individuals from the specific groups you named actually arrived here?" asked Dina.

"Yes. Let's see...we captured several of the Onipherans and *mantis*. Of those I named, the shapeshifters and the *dens* would be most difficult to apprehend. We have only suspicions they are here."

Gods, thought Dina, *dens* here on Exodus. Her gaze flicked to Jon again. It was a possibility she hadn't previously considered. She knew relatively little about shapeshifters, Onipherans, or the *mantis*, but she knew a great deal about the telepathic Deorcan *dens*. She hated the *dens*.

She looked at Jon now with eyebrows lifted ever so slightly. He gave her a small smile and squeezed her hand below the table's surface.

Jon asked the next question. "Minister, why was the situation as such on Exodus tolerated so long? Surely a new colony is scrutinized more closely?"

"We're talking about a relatively short period of time. Ranchar knew how to beat the system, so to speak. Reports were sent on schedule, and Mother Lode was showing profits. It took a while to determine there was a problem, then an investigation was begun to determine the root of the problem and how far the corruption had spread. By then the damage had been done."

Dina had been gently probing Chandhel. Thus far he seemed to be what he appeared, a conscientious man in a difficult position, trying to do his best. Yet Dina sensed he had not told them everything.

"Minister, you stated there were several developments which may impact our investigation. Is there more?"

Chandhel adjusted his robe. He glanced at Katzfiel, who sat leaning back in his chair with his arms folded across his chest. The strange, pale eyes stared from beneath hooded lids, and his mouth was drawn as taut as a tightrope.

"Yes...there are the Desert *Dailjan*," said Chandhel, looking back at Jon and Dina with a sigh.

Dailjan? It was an old Glacian word, the meaning of which was just out of Dina's reach. Too many surprises. "Who...what are the Desert *Dailjan?*" she asked, trying to keep her voice neutral.

"It's an old word, meaning 'leftovers.' Someone coined the phrase years ago, and it stuck. Even the *Dailjan* themselves use the term, somewhat haughtily, I think, given its derogatory connotation. 'Leftovers' is an apt term, indeed. They're the misfits of Aeternan society, living where no decent person would choose to live, in the desert. The *Dailjan* are a highly organized and very efficient band of men and women who live beyond the mines. Unfortunately, we haven't been able to find out much about them. That is to say, we haven't found out much reliable information. Rumors, on the other hand, abound."

Chandhel paused and fixed a baleful eye on Katzfiel, who returned the minister's cool stare with his own ice water gaze.

Dina's eyes flicked back and forth between the two men, their interaction as interesting to her as their words.

Chandhel cleared his throat and turned to Jon and Dina. "The *Uz-Dailjan,* their leader, is said to be some sort of sorcerer, who is looked upon as very nearly a god by the people of the desert. The AEA has sent numerous agents into the desert to question members of the *Dailjan,* but the agents return with little information."

Katzfiel's expression remained unchanged, his blanched eyes showing supreme indifference.

"Who are they exactly?" asked Dina. "The *Dailjan*, I mean. The undesirables who arrived during Ranchar's reign?"

"We don't know precisely. We suspect it's a varied group, consisting of some of the dark outworlders, deserters from the mines, and those who, after the change of administration, found themselves without a job and nowhere else to go."

Jon's eyes met Dina's. "These Desert *Dailjan* sound like a significant group. I don't quite understand how it is you know so little about them," he said, turning back to Chandhel.

It was Katzfiel who answered. "As I said before, we have a small number of enforcement personnel here. The *Dailjan* are not quite the bloodthirsty outlaws you seem to perceive them to be. They trade fairly for food and supplies, don't raid settlements, set upon travelers, or sabotage the mines. They are, in fact, quite peaceful. Since there have been almost no complaints made against the *Dailjan*, it has not been a priority to send a large force out into the desert to round them up."

"I'll want to see the reports made by those AEA agents who did attempt to locate and question these people."

"Of course, Agent Rzije."

The Minister addressed Jon again. "Please see Corporal Khilioi at your convenience. He will issue you skimmers, maps, clothing, supplies, and anything else you may need for the desert. We have a vast amount of reports and information available which can be accessed from your room computers. Anything you cannot locate, you have only to ask. Have you any other immediate questions?"

"Not at this time. Mondina?" Jon glanced at Dina.

"Yes, I have a question. Mining operations traditionally have a high level of security. Who provides security for the mines, and what does their security consist of?"

Chandhel looked to the Commander, who, ignoring Dina, turned to Jon and directed his answer there. "Mother Lode provides their own security. They employ very stringent security procedures, and punishment for smuggling raw gems is severe. After the first murder, and subsequently, their complement of security personnel was increased dramatically.

Unfortunately, it hasn't helped. I'm sure their Chief of Security, Karsa Hrothi, can fill you in on any details you require."

Dina struggled to keep her calm exterior lidded tightly on the brew of anger and humiliation that Katzfiel's obvious slight had set to boiling. Jon turned to Dina, and their eyes met. Dina knew Jon was aware of her feelings and understood. Once again, her eyes relayed "thanks" to him.

"Anything else?" he quietly asked her.

"Not just now."

Jon stood and bowed first to Chandhel, then Katzfiel. "Thank you, Minister, Commander."

The farewells, some of them cold, to be sure, were completed, and Maris escorted Jon and Dina out. Khilioi drove them back to the Visitor Center, this time with the bubble top in place, and reminded them that he would be available whenever they were ready to take delivery of the desert supplies. Jon and Dina thanked him, then ascended to their rooms. In the hallway, Jon whispered to her. "Meet me in my room in five minutes."

She nodded, and once inside her room, leaned against the coolness of the metal door. A line of sweat had glued her white T-shirt to her spine. She pushed away from the door, shrugged off her jacket and stripped the white top off, tossing it to the bed. It hit the edge, slid to the floor, and pooled like spilled milk. She left it. In the small bathroom, she rinsed her face with a fresh cleansing cloth, and wondered what had contributed to her discomfort more, the burning embarrassment she had felt at Katzfiel's treatment, or the news there may be *dens* on Exodus. She slipped on a clean top, ordered a spiced juice drink, and thought about what had been said during the meeting.

She had been hoping for few surprises, but had been genuinely shocked to hear about the possibility of *dens* on Exodus. Jon was aware of the *dens'* powerful telepathic abilities as well as the fact that Dina had no love for them, but she doubted he realized just how deep her hatred of the *dens* actually went. After all, in her profession, she wasn't supposed to display prejudice against any type of human or creature. Though human in form, she definitely put the *dens* in the "creature" category. She didn't want to lie to Jon, but she would have to be careful in discussing the *dens* with him.

Dina knocked at the connecting door and entered upon hearing Jon's reply. "Make yourself comfortable. Want anything to eat?" he asked.

Dina noticed that Jon, too, had removed his jacket and wore a short-sleeved gray T-shirt with his loose fitting matching trousers. Dina couldn't help admiring the powerful biceps and pectoral muscles thus revealed. She wished, certainly not for the first time, that she could just relax with Jon instead of discussing a case.

"Not just yet. I'm still trying to calm down a little."

Jon nodded his head and sat on the bed, stretching one long leg out in front of him. "This job will always spring surprises on us, no matter how thoroughly we prepare. I think we have a number of issues to discuss before we go see the good corporal and formulate our plans for the next few days. First, did your probes reveal anything other than the fact that Commander Kaz doesn't like us in general and women in particular?"

Dina laughed. Jon always had a knack for putting her at ease. "Well, if he likes them, I'm sure it's for serving his needs and warming his bed, not working beside him. I don't like him, but no, my probes didn't pick up much else. I think he resents us and sees us as a threat to his authority. Whether or not he resents us enough to try to compromise our efforts wasn't clear, but we should definitely keep an eye on him. Minister Chandhel appears sincere in wanting us to solve the murders. I get the feeling he laments the fact that his administration will go down in history as being as bad as, if not worse than, that of his predecessor. He and Katzfiel are not the best of friends, as I'm sure you could tell. I even probed Maris. She thinks you're cute."

Jon smiled. "Next issue. What do you make of the possibility any of the 'dark outworlders' Chandhel referred to had anything to do with our murders?"

Dina took a deep breath and finally dropped into one of the

room's two chairs. "Well, the Onipherans are flesh eaters. Since the autopsy reports show that the bodies were intact, we can probably eliminate them. The *mantis* are diviners. Prophets if you like. They're generally harmless, but many have been known to be great orators, influencing large numbers of people to a cause or ideology which, of course, fits their 'vision' of the future. Depending on what their 'cause' is, they can be dangerous. This *Uz-Dailjan*, who is supposed to be worshiped by so many, could be a *mantis*. I don't know much about shapeshifters. Obviously they would be almost impossible to apprehend. And the *dens*..."

Dina hesitated. "If there are *dens* involved, we'll have our work cut out. In addition to their powers, they're cold-blooded and known to hire out as mercenaries. Our murderer could very well be a *dens*."

Jon leaned forward on the bed. "If you should encounter a *dens*, you'll know him for one, won't you?"

Dina stood and walked to the room's one small window. She didn't want to think about this. "Yes, if I survive the encounter. Jon, my abilities are no match for even the weakest *dens*. I was born with a gift, but the *dens* have evolved genetically far beyond most humanoid species."

"Just what exactly are they capable of?"

"Besides the obvious ability to communicate with each other telepathically, they can compel others to do just about anything. They can induce short-term memory loss, or they can completely destroy one's mind."

Jon rose and joined her at the window. When he spoke, his voice was soft. "All right. Let's not panic over this. We don't even know that any of them are really here. I want you to research all these groups."

Dina took a deep breath. "Okay. What's our agenda for the rest of today?"

"Let's see what toys the corporal has for us. Then we should tour the city. I don't know about you, but last night I was too worn out to pay much attention to Khilioi's prattle."

Dina laughed. "I thought I was the only one being lulled to sleep by his little speech. You have no idea how much I was thanking you for your well-timed responses. I was too tired to even nod as he pointed out one building after another."

Jon gave her another of his warm smiles. Dina loved to see them. His smiles were genuine, creating little lines that flowed outward from the corners of his eyes, and a large dimple just to the left of his mouth.

"After that we'll eat, start accessing the computer files, then I think it would do both of us good to catch up on sleep. Tomorrow we'll make our first trip into the desert. We'll need to view the mines, talk to Mother Lode security, and, of course, see where the murders took place."

"And the *Dailjan*?" Dina asked.

"First we'll see what's in the Commander's reports, then we'll take it from there."

"All right."

"Go back to your room and get whatever you'll need for our tour. I'll call Khilioi. Say, fifteen minutes?"

"I'll be ready."

Jon nodded, and Dina slipped back to her room through the connecting door. The investigation was finally underway, but her excitement had waned. She could brush off her anger toward Katzfiel, but the dread over the possibility of *dens* on Exodus just wouldn't go away.

THREE
THE DARK OUTWORLDERS

Corporal Khilioi led Jon and Dina to a secured room on the first floor of the Visitor Center.

"This room has been stocked especially for you and should contain everything you'll need for safety, self-defense, and survival in the desert. We've provided a skimmer for each of you for transportation. Small, fast, and light, but unfortunately don't enclose the rider. Of course, that should please Agent Marlijn, but it makes for a hot ride for the rest of us. You're familiar with their basic operation?"

Though the question was addressed to both of them, the corporal's gaze swept Dina up and down like the bristles of a well-worn broom. She stared back at Khilioi, straddled the skimmer easily, and expertly pushed several buttons on the console. The machine came to life with a steady hum and rose a bar in height off the floor. With just the right amount of pressure from her right hand, then her left, the skimmer spun like a top in tight circles. With the touch of another button, she settled the machine gently to the floor and turned it off.

"Yes, Corporal, I think I can handle it."

She wondered if all of the AEA personnel were like Katzfiel and Khilioi. But then again, she thought, Exodus was a hot, ugly little rock, and a posting to this colony was certainly not a plum job. Maybe high quality candidates had been hard to find for the jobs here.

"Fine. Let's continue." The corporal seemed neither impressed nor nonplused and continued his narration. Khilioi grabbed a cooling vest and held it up. The vest was constructed of large, soft plastic fibers "woven" into an open, diamond-shaped pattern.

"These vests are filled with a liquid which, after being frozen or cooled, will remain cold for up to ten hours. The vests can be reused simply by refreezing them."

Dina tilted her head and shifted her feet, her eyes wandering impatiently around the room. Gods. He sounded like a damn salesman.

Khilioi, ignoring Dina, continued with his presentation. "After I get your measurements, I'll see that several weather suits are delivered to your rooms. And don't neglect to wear one of these in the desert." The corporal picked up a hood with an attached sunshield. "The inside of all our hoods are lined with detachable cooling mesh, and there's a small supply of water and oxygen built in. Oh, and keep in mind that sunset is currently at the seventeenth hour. After the sun sets, the desert cools off quickly, and temperatures at night in the desert can drop well below freezing, so plan your excursions into the desert accordingly. In case you're in the desert *al-merkwia*, there are heat packs and a blanket in the skimmer's cargo bags."

Khilioi continued with his explanation of the equipment, relayed Jon and Dina's measurements to the stores officer, then led them outside to begin the tour of the city. The corporal wore a short-sleeved shirt rather than the long coat she had first seen him in, but he looked no less smart. His leather visor was canted low over his eyes and hid the top half of his mirrored sunshields. Lightweight cloth panels in a reflective, bronze-colored material extended from the sides and back of his cap like the headdress of a desert god. Tanned arms with biceps that stretched the material of his sleeves were decorated with a golden commband on one wrist and a gold bracelet the color of melted butter on the other.

They settled into the hugger, and with the bubble top in place, the ride was comfortable. Khilioi pointed out the greenhouses, the power plants, the recycling plants, and the glass factory. Though attractive in their clean, efficient lines, it was the architecture of the various housing facilities for the city workers, the food courts, the recreation halls and the port facility that caught Dina's attention. Each of these was unique and stunning in its design, the various shapes, sizes, and colors like shiny baubles. Pretty lures, she thought, to attract workers to this blistering sand heap.

The one building that stood out even among the other jewels was the Mother Lode building. It was shaped like a pyramid, with numerous small steps creating extra facets to reflect light. The front face of the pyramid was silver, the remaining faces iridescent. It was obvious the architects had tried to give the building the appearance of a giant exodite stone.

Near the western edge of the city, Khilioi pointed out two tall columns, one on either side of the road. On top of the columns pulsed bright lights which Dina could see easily even with the beams of the late morning sun glaring down on them.

"The western gate, Ghe Wespero on the maps. Beyond the gate is the Albho Mar. There's a road of sorts across the mar to the mines, which are about forty decbars out, due west. Mines are at the base of a crescent-shaped range of rocks called the Chayne Gwer, and beyond the mines and within the crescent is the Ghel Mar. On the edge of the Ghel Mar, hidden in the caverns of the Chayne, is where we believe the *Dailjan* live. What possesses anyone to live that far out is beyond me." It was the first time Dina could remember the corporal expressing a personal opinion.

"And beyond the Ghel Mar?" Dina asked.

"Al-Ghel Mar. Beyond the Sea of Glass. Don't know. More sand and rocks. The area has been surveyed and charted, of course, but apparently nothing of importance was found out there. I suppose someday more cities will be built, but for now, I've never heard of anyone, even any of the *Dailjan*, living that far out. The conditions would be intolerable, and it would be a long way from any source of supplies."

Dina looked southward from the western gate and noticed numerous small buildings, some of them crudely built. "What are those?" she asked, nodding toward the structures.

"The *mercari*. Small tradesmen and merchants. Sell mostly to the miners on their way to or from the mines, but they also trade with the *Dailjan*. The *Dailjan* are far from being self-sufficient. They have to trade for just about everything."

"Corporal, can we take a closer look? I'd like to see the stands and what they're selling," Dina injected.

"Leave it to a woman to want to shop, eh, Rzije?"

There was no answering smile on Jon's face. "I don't think that's what my partner had in mind. If you would comply,

Corporal?"

"Of course, Agent Rzije."

Khilioi moved the hugger into the hot mixture that sizzled, day after day, at the desert's rim. Dina's mouth turned downward in a sardonic acknowledgment of the ugly side of every city, present even in this newly created paradise. Every flap of tent canvas, every bawdy shout, every defacing sign, seemed to mock the beauty of the rest of Aeternus. There seemed to be little permanence to the structures, and most of what Dina saw resembled a seedy traveling show forever on the verge of pulling up stakes. The cants of the merchants broke through even the bubble top of the hugger.

"Corporal, I'd like to get out and walk around."

"As you wish," he replied, in a tone which seemed to imply that he wouldn't miss her company.

Dina hopped from the hugger and strolled past several of the tents. Food, drinks, clothing, jewelry, glasswork, tools, and novelties were all in evidence. Children ran after her and plucked at her tunic, but she firmly told them "no."

She reached the end of the row and looked around, trying to decide whether to continue or head back to the others. As she scanned the tents across the road, her gaze lit on a man who was staring directly at her.

She froze. He was dressed in a loose khaki desert suit, with a long scarf that wrapped around his head, covering most of his hair and the lower half of his face. Standing in the shade of a tent awning, he had removed his sunshield, and the narrow eyes that riveted on her were hard enough to scratch glass. A chill seemed to pass straight through her. There was something both unsettling and familiar about his eyes and the way he looked at her, as if she knew him, and he her.

But how could that be possible? She had just arrived on Exodus and had met no one save Aeternan government employees and AEA personnel.

The answer started her heart pounding. It was the man in the dream. Just as quickly, she chided herself. It wasn't possible. It had been just a dream, for gods' sake. The image of the stranger had been too much on her mind. It was just a coincidence.

Why, then, was this man looking at her as though he knew every thought in her head? She stared back at him, as unmoving as he. Thick strands of dark hair escaped from beneath the scarf and fingered the low, shawl collar of his tunic.

A new thought came to her. *Oh, gods...* Minister Chandhel had said there were dark outworlders on Exodus. Could this man be one of them? She had to get help from Jon and Khilioi, fast. She spoke into her commband.

"Jon, I'm just north of you, at the end of the row of tents. Get over here. Now."

She had only taken her eyes off the man for a few seconds, but when she looked up again, he was gone. *Damn!* She crossed the road at a trot, but the man had once again performed his vanishing act. Jon and Khilioi ran up to her.

"What is it? Are you all right?" asked Jon.

"I'm fine. Sorry. It's nothing. I saw someone I thought you should check out, but he's gone."

"'Check out,' Miss Marlijn?" parroted Khilioi.

She felt her face redden, feeling foolish. She was sure that beneath his mirrored sunshield, the corporal was arching his brows. "The man made eye contact, then fled."

Khilioi laughed. "This is not exactly the high rent end of the city, Miss Marlijn."

Dina ignored him. She approached the merchant at the tent where the man had been standing. "Excuse me, do you know the man who was here a moment ago? The man in the headscarf and khaki suit?"

"Sorry, miss, I didn't recognize him."

"Come along, Miss Marlijn. You're wasting your time. Won't get any cooperation here," interjected the corporal.

Frustrated, she knew it would be fruitless to pursue the matter. She turned and headed back to the hugger with Jon and Khilioi. She tried to pick up the thread of their previous conversation.

"If the *Dailjan* do that much business here, I would think the tradespeople would be a good source of information about them," Dina said.

The corporal snorted as they stepped once more into the coolness of the vehicle. "As I said, you won't get much cooperation there. The *Dailjan* are good customers. These people won't risk losing their business."

"You're the law here," stated Jon, obviously trying to keep the impatience from his voice. "I would think it would be easy to put some pressure on. Threaten to revoke their trade licenses. They won't lose business. From what you tell us, the *Dailjan* have no choice but to get their goods here."

"All due respect, sir, you don't understand the complexities. First of all, the *mercari* are very competitive. They struggle to make a living here. Won't do anything that threatens to reduce any edge they have over their competitors. Secondly, Mother Lode is the most influential power here on Exodus, not us. They wouldn't stand for any threats or pressure put upon the *mercari*. *Mercari* keep the miners happy. Right now, Mother wants more than anything to keep their miners happy."

Dina concentrated on what the corporal was saying, which wasn't easy considering the ire that rose at his condescending attitude. "Why all these small independent tradespeople? Why not a single supply post run by the city? Seems like that would simplify things and eliminate problems of competition."

Khilioi shook his head. "What you're suggesting is exactly how Ranchar ran things. He had one centralized trading post which had a monopoly on everything from bottled water to play chips. Ran the prices on everything so high that the miners finally protested enough for Mother to step forward and put pressure on the administration to allow free enterprise."

"The *Dailjan* obviously don't work in the city. How do they get the goods or credits to buy or trade for so much of what they need?" asked Jon.

Corporal Khilioi shook his head. "Damned if I know. They produce some jewelry and artwork which they trade, but that doesn't come close to accounting for the amount of supplies they acquire. You'd be surprised how well equipped they are. Most likely there's some 'Avs' among the *Dailjan*."

"'Avs'?" asked Dina and Jon together.

"Don't know much about our proud history, do you? Avvis

Ranchar and his network of corrupt officials? Well, back then there were the 'Avs' and the 'Av Nots.' Either you were part of his network and getting rich, or you were victimized by his system and starving to death." Khilioi laughed, but neither Jon nor Dina saw much humor in the remark.

"I thought that all of Ranchar's cronies were found out and prosecuted," said Jon, frowning.

"Oh, sure. Most were, most were." Khilioi turned the hugger around and headed back into the city. "Detailed maps of Exodus with exact coordinates for all known structures and settlements should be in your rooms. As I said, the Albho Road is pretty heavily traveled with miners. Lots of ground markers along the way, and way stations every five decbars that are kept well stocked with water and supplies, should a skimmer or transport break down."

Jon and Dina looked at each other, each one knowing that one raised eyebrow hung behind the sunshields of the other. Khilioi snickered.

Dina turned and glowered at him, but it was a wasted gesture, lost behind anti-glare lenses.

"Oh, a precaution only. Our machinery and equipment here are of the highest quality," continued the corporal, his snigger reined in to a mere smirk. Dina suddenly felt sticky beneath her weather suit and silently rejoiced when they arrived back at the Visitor Center.

"Your maps and weather suits should have already been delivered to your rooms. If there's anything else you need, just call me," droned Khilioi, tiredly slipping back into his role as the proper and professional liaison officer.

"Thank you, Corporal. We will," said Jon, equally proper. He lowered his sunshield to the tip of his nose and winked at Dina. She suppressed a small smile, noticing that in the strong sunlight, Jon's hair appeared to be streaked with gold. Hot and sweaty as the man was, there was no mistaking the twist she felt in her stomach when she looked at him. Khilioi, on the other hand, reminded Dina more and more of a sleek and smug rodent.

***

Rayn sat on his skimmer in the shade of the first desert way station and smiled. He shaded his eyes toward distant Aeternus, the lights of Ghe Wespero glinting on the horizon like a large exodite.

His excitement mounted.

The woman he had seen had taken his breath away with her beauty. But it had been much more than that. He had had lovers on this world before, all of them lovely to look at—including Alessane, his latest, who was sweet and willing to please—but none of them had provided what he truly needed. Sport, and the resulting victory.

He had made the first move. The connection had been formed. His eyes had challenged hers, and when her gaze had squared off against his, she hadn't been able to mask the recognition on her face.

He smiled again as he took off his headgear and drank from a flask of water. She would remember her "dream," and would wonder about him. Her mind would search for a logical explanation of his appearance, and the puzzle would give her no rest.

He put the water away, pulled his hood back on, and powered up his skimmer.

Little girl, the next move is yours, he thought, shooting his skimmer westward toward the mountains of the Chayne Gwer.

***

An hour later, refreshed and fed, Dina joined Jon in his room and sat beside him at the table. Jon had already started organizing the reports and files he wanted to view. Though eager to begin studying the files on the *Dailjan*, Dina knew she had to start at the beginning. They reviewed the facts surrounding the actual murders first.

The victims were eight males, all miners in good standing in the employ of Mother Lode. Five were from Dina and Jon's home world, Glacia; two were Dreinen; and one was a Feoht. All were relatively young and in good health until they were found, their skulls crushed, in little-used or abandoned crosscuts of Kewero Kel and Dheru Kel, two of the three Mother Lode mines. Thus far, no victims had been found in Sawel Kel, the third, and newest mine.

The first victim, Dais Johnter, a Glacian, was found by a co-worker seven months and four days ago. The second victim, Kilist Marhjon, another Glacian, was found three weeks later. R'ke Kai-Men, a Dreinen, was found next, six weeks later. The eighth victim, the Feoht Gillique Samek, was found just three days before Dina and Jon arrived.

The facts themselves were unremarkable. Nothing reportedly was stolen, no gems were unaccounted for, there were no witnesses, and no physical evidence had been found. A background check on all the victims revealed little. All the miners were members of the Miner's Guild, but had signed on at Exodus at different times. None of the victims apparently knew each other before arriving on Exodus.

Jon rubbed his face with the palms of his hands. Dina knew he was still as tired as she was. "All right. I know you're itching to look at the *Dailjan* file. Go through that material while I look at the interviews of the captured dark outworlders."

Dina nodded and returned to her room where, with renewed enthusiasm, she opened the first file on the *Dailjan*. She raised her eyebrows. There was a lot there. She was bound to find something useful. The AEA had actually made quite a few attempts to learn the identity and location of the *Dailjan*. AEA personnel, both uniformed and dressed as civilians, had questioned suspected members of the *Dailjan* at the Wespero marketplace numerous times. The *Dailjan* questioned were reported to be cooperative and polite, always removing their hoods and presenting their ID chips. Thus, there were several names, photographs, and holos on file, but all such identified were legal residents of Exodus.

One, Kindyll Sirkhek, was a miner whose contract had expired. Rather than renew his contract or return to his home world, where he reportedly had no remaining family, he had chosen to remain on Exodus and live the simple life of a *Dailjan*. He would have his contract fulfillment bonus, Dina thought. So much for Khilioi's silly "Avs" theory. Here already was a logical explanation for some of the *Dailjan's* wealth. When questioned about the "leader" of the *Dailjan*, Sirkhek had been vague. He had stated that there was no single leader, that everyone participated in the decisions that had to be made and the work that had to be done.

Another *Dailjan* questioned was Trai Morghen, a former dock worker who had hurt his back and had decided to "retire" to the desert. He, too, gave no information regarding the leadership of the group, and both Sirkhek and Morghen gave the location of the *Dailjan* main settlement to be "north of the Ghel Mar, south of the Pur-Pelag."

Another ex-miner, Raethe Avarti, had had his guild membership revoked. Dina sat up straighter and re-read the entry. Basically, this man had been fired, but worse still, could no longer work as a miner for any company requiring good standing in the guild. A reason to hold a grudge against Mother Lode or individuals who had contributed to his revocation? All her fatigue now forgotten, she pulled up the detailed Mother Lode file on Avarti. The charge had been "failing to safeguard confidential company business while off company premises." The incident had occurred a year before, but the revocation hearing had taken place only nine months ago. Before the killings started. Rum Ctararzin, Mother Lode Operations Manager, had signed the revocation order. A hearing, thought Dina, probably meant that witnesses testified against Avarti. A motive for revenge? Dina made a note to find out more about this man.

She didn't believe for a moment that the *Dailjan* had no single leader. *And he's very, very clever*, she thought. He only sends members who are legal into Aeternus to trade. The illegals and dark outworlders, if any, stay well hidden in the mountains.

Dina opened another interesting file detailing the results of AEA officers attaching a homing device to Morghen's large cargo skimmer. They had tracked his progress into the desert following a large supplies purchase. A simple tactic, Dina mused, but not so effective in this case. The AEA had tracked Morghen's skimmer to a cavern near the base of the Chayne Gwer. There they found the skimmer and some supplies, but nothing more. The AEA had tried staking out the cavern on several occasions, but with negative results.

The AEA had even tried infiltrating the *Dailjan* by having an undercover officer pose as a disgruntled city worker anxious to join the desert band. Dina hunched forward, her gaze riveted to the holo file.

The officer, mingling with the *mercari*, approached a legal *Dailjan* at one of the stands. Dina smiled as she recognized the officer as Khilioi, wearing a rather poor disguise which included a head scarf, narrow sunshield, and the loose shirt and trousers favored by the desert dwellers. Dina watched him stroll casually up to the tall *Dailjan*, who was closely examining a pair of rare, knee-high leather boots.

"Afternoon, friend. Cygian leather, are they not? Finest in the galaxy," said Khilioi.

The *Dailjan*, wearing a hood and sunshield but no mask over the lower part of his face, looked up, but did not reply. Dina could see only tanned skin and a severe expression below the sunshields.

Khilioi tried a new tact. "Listen, friend, don't mean to bother you, but I know you're *Dailjan*. I was told you might be able to help me. Was terminated from my job last month, and I can't find work in the city. I'd like to join you. Almost out of funds."

"We're not a charity group," said the *Dailjan*, the frost in his voice apparent even through the recording.

"Willing to work. I'll pull my share, I promise."

"Do you have a skimmer with you?"

Khilioi nodded. "Over there."

"Come with me."

Dina watched as the holo continued with Khilioi and the tall *Dailjan* waiting on their skimmers at a place which was obviously well into the desert. The white sand whirled in tiny dust devils about their skimmers while a second *Dailjan* approached on a one-person skimmer, halted the machine, and dismounted. The holo showed the second *Dailjan* as a man of medium height and build, dressed in a weather suit with a full hood. Nothing at all of the man's skin or hair was visible. His voice, distorted by the faceplate, would be difficult to recognize. Dina waited patiently while Khilioi again made his appeal to be accepted into the desert band.

Khilioi finished his speech, and there was silence as the second *Dailjan* apparently considered his reply. When the *Dailjan* did speak, it was with a voice that was as chilling as any she had ever heard.

"The commitment to the desert and to the *Dailjan* is not one to be made lightly, and certainly not one to be made as a last resort simply because one cannot find a job in the city."

Dina shivered, spellbound by the man's voice. For a moment she forgot she was viewing a holo.

"You will not be accepted as one of us. I suggest you go back to Aeternus and evaluate your life and the choices available to you. The desert life is one of hardship, deprivation, and above all else, dedication. The willingness to embrace all this is something I doubt you have now, or will ever have."

Dina could see that Khilioi's face had reddened, whether from the sun or from anger, she couldn't tell. Khilioi tried to protest, but the *Dailjan* ignored him, vaulting onto his skimmer and powering the machine away.

Either he's very cautious, or somehow he spotted the officer for a ringer, she thought. She would love to meet this man and probe his devious little mind. Already a plan was taking form in her mind as she envisioned herself as the down-on-her-luck civilian attempting to join up with the *Dailjan*. If only Jon would approve it. But she also knew better than to ask him right away. They still had a lot of basic legwork to do before trying a scheme like that.

Dina started the next holo, which once again showed Khilioi in his disguise approaching a *Dailjan* at the marketplace. Dina smiled as Khilioi used the same opening line, admiring the boots the *Dailjan* was looking at. This *Dailjan*, more affable than the last, in turn admired Khilioi's own. Dina watched the corporal brush the red dust from his high leather boots and boast about the deal he had made to purchase them.

Her eyes tiring from the strain of viewing the holos, Dina was glad to hear Jon's soft knock on the door. "Come in."

Jon poked his head into Dina's room. "How about we share some dinner? I know we have a lot to do, but I think both of us could use a break."

"Let's try the commissary below. It'll get us out of these rooms, and we can stretch our legs. If it's not too crowded down there, we can swap some information."

"Sounds good."

A few minutes later Dina and Jon shared a secluded booth in the commissary, their plates filled with succulent raw fruit slices and a lightly seasoned mixture of grains and vegetables. As they started eating, however, they noticed a number of people file into the room, and the low hum of conversation became apparent. Jon thought it best to wait until they were back in his room to discuss their findings about the *Dailjan* and dark outworlders. Dina agreed, and relaxed for the first time all day. She forced herself to eat slowly, but all too soon the break was over, and they were back in Jon's room.

"One of the dark outworlders captured was a *mantis* named Xuche," Jon began. "No other name, just Xuche. He was found living in a small cavern in the Wiara Gwer about eight months ago."

"Wiara Gwer?" Dina was trying to remember from the study of her maps where that was.

Jon reached for his map and pointed out the area. "It's a range of winding dunes north of the Albho Mar. I take it it's a pretty isolated area, not really close to where the *Dailjan* are thought to be. Anyway, Xuche was found on an anonymous tip to the AEA. And he was found alone. From what I know about the *mantis*, they rarely, if ever, live alone. That would be in complete opposition to their...What would you call it? 'Mission?' 'Calling?'"

Dina shrugged. "As good a term as any. I know what you mean. So what did Xuche say when questioned?"

"This is interesting. He said he had been the *Uz-Dailjan*, but that his teachings over the past few months had become more and more unpopular among his followers. They came to a mutual parting of ways, and Xuche was in the Wiara Gwer trying to establish a settlement he could bring a new following to. When questioned about the other members of the *Dailjan*, he refused to give any information."

Dina shook her head. "Doesn't sound right to me based on what I know about the *mantis*. They thrive on challenges and overcoming them. Giving up a following voluntarily...that sounds all wrong. Unless the truth is that he was forcibly ousted by someone more powerful."

"Another dark outworlder perhaps?"

Dina looked into Jon's eyes. "Perhaps. I don't know. We still don't have any concrete evidence that there are any on Exodus. But whoever it is, he's very cunning." She related to Jon what she had found in the files on the *Dailjan*. When she finished, Jon stood up, turned away, rubbed his temples with the heels of his palms, then ran his hands through his hair. He turned around to face Dina, and quietly said, "No."

"No, what?"

"No, you aren't going to pose as a discontented city worker, and you aren't going to try to be recruited by the *Dailjan*," stated Jon.

It was eerie. An outsider would tell her that Jon was telepathic, too, but Dina knew it was just a rather common phenomena amongst partners. They often came to know each other so well they could anticipate what the other was about to say before they said it. Dina felt a swell of pride and pleasure that Jon was getting to know her that well.

"Why not? I have a distinct advantage over the other officers who tried it. And chances are they won't suspect a woman."

"It's too dangerous. If a *dens*, or someone equally as powerful, is behind all the strange doings in the desert, your disguise won't hold up for two seconds."

"Even if it doesn't, what's the worst that could happen? He'll deny me and tell me to re-evaluate my life."

"The worst is that he could kill you."

"I don't think he'll do that."

"No. Now forget it. We have lots of work to do yet."

Dina was frustrated, but she knew Jon was right. They did have a lot to do. But she didn't intend to forget her plan. "All right. What's next?"

"Go over the information available on the dark outworlders that Chandhel mentioned, and study the maps for tomorrow.

Khilioi made an eighth-hour appointment for us tomorrow, so we'll have an early start. I don't think either of us have had a good night's sleep for a while, so knock off early and make sure you're rested."

Dina nodded her agreement. "What time should I be ready?"

"Let's meet at the seventh hour, mark zero. It won't take long to make the trip to the mine, but I want to make sure we have plenty of time."

Dina nodded again, picked up her reports, and started for the connecting door.

"Dina."

She stopped and turned back towards Jon.

"Good work on your first day," he said quietly, giving her a wink.

Dina beamed. "Thanks." Jon's opinion of her meant more to her than anything, and she felt her exhaustion dissipate, as if she had been wearing a heavy cape on her shoulders that had just been lifted off by invisible hands.

Back in her own room, she instructed her computer to link with that of *Justitia*, which was still docked at the Aeternan port. She then downloaded information on the *mantis, dens,* shapeshifters, and cannibals to the room computer. She requested the *mantis* file first, and at her command, the room dimmed, the computer projected three dimensional images, and the computer voice recited the basic information Dina had requested.

Dina learned that the *mantis* originated largely in the Cyg Etesia system, but now came from various worlds. Many of the *mantis* claimed to be "true" by virtue of actual divine intervention. Those claiming to be "true *mantis*" often repudiated others of their kind as being false and using trickery, guesswork, and mind-altering drugs as substitutions for divine inspiration. True divine inspiration was a difficult thing to prove, and even those forsaken as "false" were often able to cultivate large followings. The "divine" messages of the *mantis* varied, but most embraced a simple, austere lifestyle, stressing spirituality and downplaying, though not totally abandoning, technology.

An idea started to formulate in Dina's mind as she listened to the dissertation. Trickery. She thought about the *dens*. No, she thought, she should stick to the facts. But the idea wouldn't go away. A *dens* who could use his powers on an unsuspecting group of people, picking up their thoughts and feelings, then relaying that information to a *mantis*. Even a false *mantis* could easily appear to be truly prophetic. It was definitely a possibility. An unscrupulous *mantis* in league with an unscrupulous *dens*. Perhaps Xuche had been in league with a partner and had been forcibly ousted when the partnership went bad. The various possibilities continued to spring forward, one after another, and Dina gave them free rein. Perhaps Xuche had resented being a "puppet" figure. Perhaps another *mantis* had ousted him. Then a new idea formed.

This "leader" was clever and seemed to know every step the AEA makes. Perhaps he was a former AEA officer. Dina made a note to check with Commander Katzfiel to see if any former members had resigned or been terminated.

Dina took a short break, ordered a hot mocava, and dutifully viewed the files on shapeshifters and cannibals next. Though interesting, there seemed little chance either could be involved in the murders. Shapeshifters primarily used their ability for personal survival and were not known for hiring their talents out. The cannibals of Onipherus were an extremely primitive people, very fierce, who fed from the dead bodies of their enemies. If not for the fact that the autopsy reports revealed the bodies of the victims to be intact, Dina might have believed an Onipheran to be the killer. But she doubted that one could kill and then resist feeding on the body.

She had purposely saved the file on the *dens* for last, not especially wanting to view images she knew would upset her. She opted to take another break first to clear her head and peered out the small window of her room. Confined to the ship for so long, Dina craved fresh air. She looked at the time, then glanced out the window again. The sun had dipped toward the horizon and sat balanced on the roof of the building to her west, throwing spikes of light upward and outward like a blazing crown of thorns. The temperature would be comfortable, but she picked up a light jacket just in case and knocked softly on Jon's door.

He opened the door right away, dressed in the same clothes he had been wearing before. Dina noticed that Jon's eyes once again had the weary look they had had the night before, and thick strands of hair hung down over his forehead.

"Hi, partner."

Dina couldn't help smiling. "I'm still working, but I need some fresh air. I thought I'd go outside for a walk around the compound. I figured I'd better let you know, or hopefully, that you'd want to join me."

"You sold me. Come on in."

Jon's computer was on, and there were maps and files covering the table and a good portion of the floor. There was a half-eaten piece of fruit bread and a steaming cup of mocava on the corner of the table. Jon instructed his computer to mark his place in his file and to close it. He then picked up a jacket and followed Dina out the door. Moments later they were outside the Visitor Center.

The Exodan sun had slid further still, so that it was secreted behind the larger buildings. They ambled westward, the flashing rays playing hide-and-seek as Dina and Jon wove their way past the jewels of Aeternus.

She took a deep breath and looked around, seeing a number of people making their way from building to building. Not unlike any other city, she thought. People were walking, a few riding in huggers or skimmers, as they moved from the food court to their quarters, or from their quarters to the recreation hall, or from their place of business to their place of rest. Some were talking, laughing in pairs or groups. Some were alone. Some were strolling, as if they were lovers who had a forever, and some hurried, as if time was their biggest enemy.

Somewhere out there, somewhere, is the real enemy, she thought. *A killer...* Dina shivered as the temperature began to drop noticeably. She put her jacket on.

"Jon, let's walk over to the recreation hall. It's nearby, and we don't have to stay, just take a peek inside to see what it's like."

"Dina, this isn't a vacation. We still have a lot of work to do."

"I know. But it'll only take a few minutes. And it will be a help to us if we get to know the city and the people a little."

Jon gave her a look that said she had won this battle, but to be careful.

They picked up their pace and soon beheld the Crown. A round, two-story building, it sat perched not far from the Ghe Wespero, its crenulated roofline adorned with an overabundance of white lights. A giant glittering tiara, it drew patrons like a magnet, and a narrow stream of people, many of whom seemed happy and animated, were already being sucked inside. Jon and Dina joined the throng, and in five minutes passed through the large double doors.

A large entrance hall fed the crowd to the various establishments within. To the left, skirting the outer edge of the building, was the Mocava Cave. A glance inside showed cozy seating areas for drinks and conversation. To the right was the Opaline Oasis, a beautifully decorated sun room for reading or contemplation. Between the two, leading deep into the windowless center of the building, was the Furnace. A thick double-paned black glass door covered with dancing neon flames beckoned patrons to enter. Most of the people making their way to the Crown at this time headed straight for the Furnace, and every time the door opened, Dina could hear music and laughter.

Dina pulled Jon towards the Opaline Oasis instead and, once inside the quiet room, her gaze quickly fell on a couple seated on a cushioned bench next to a decorative water fountain. The man hunched over the woman, stiff as a fortress, his arm and bent head ensconcing her from the world. The woman's head was lowered as well, her curtain of hair hiding her features. Dina watched the woman's fingers pluck at the hem of her shirt.

The man spoke in low tones, and the woman's head bobbed gently, her hair rippling with the movement. Her fingers moved faster, the hands telling a story no one else could hear.

Dina couldn't pick up their voices, and, not wanting to intrude, did not tune her mind to them. But suddenly the man squeezed the woman's arm, she threw her head back, and the toss of her hair revealed a smile brimming with hope and joy.

The corners of Dina's mouth lifted in response, and she glanced up at Jon's face. His eyes weren't on the couple, but were scanning the room methodically like a security camera. Dina's mouth flattened with the reminder of who she was.

Jon caught her eye, and his voice was soft as he spoke. "Come on, let's head back. Our work for tonight isn't done yet."

Dina only nodded and reflected once more, as she had many times in the past, on the strangeness of her job. She worked all hours, and when the average person's work day was done, hers was often just beginning. There were no holidays and no relatives nearby. Danger was a constant. Unpleasant conditions were a given. And her only friend was her partner.

Dina wondered for a moment why she couldn't be like the woman on the bench, or the many like her. If she were someone else, perhaps she would be here with Jon as her lover, his arm protectively around her, his head bent to hers so he could brush her silky hair with his lips. They would have come here to be alone, to savor each other's company, perhaps to make plans for the future.

But as she headed back to the Visitor Center with Jon, the moment passed. Dina was different. She had always been different. And her career was a conscious choice she had made. Jon seemed to sense her mood, and they walked back to the Center in silence.

Was it possible that Jon had the same feelings she did? Surely he too craved the closeness only a lover could provide. If only he would think of her as more than just a partner.

She paused outside the Visitor Center, and Jon stopped beside her. She knew he was impatient to get back to work, but the western sky wouldn't let her go. The last rays of light reflected fire off the glass on the west sides of buildings, while the eastern sides were already shrouded in shadow. The sun was just sinking below the edge of the world, a final bead of orange there, then gone. The sky was snaked with shades of crimson, purple, and blue smoke.

The street was quiet, and Dina stood silently, feeling a part of a worship service. As she watched, the colors of the sky shifted, deepening, until only a glow above the horizon gave evidence of the vanishing day. A chill shiver skated down her spine.

Once inside, Jon and Dina paused outside her door. Dina searched the depths of the beautiful green eyes, but saw only kindness, perhaps affection, and she wished again for what was not. Did an absence of passion in his eyes mean he felt none? Or just that he hid it well?

"Be ready at seventh hour, equipped and dressed for the desert. And get some sleep," he said.

Dina nodded. "Thanks for taking the walk with me."

"You're my partner."

Dina smiled and felt a little better. Inside her room, she took a long drink of water, cleared her mind of thoughts of Jon, and ran the computer file on the *dens*. There wasn't much she didn't already know. Their laws were strict, but many *dens* were nevertheless destroyed by those more powerful than themselves. They were banned from numerous worlds, but many found work as mercenaries on other worlds in spite of the bans.

When she had first become aware of her ability, she had read, viewed, and listened to every piece of material she could find on the Deorcans. At first she had hoped to feel a kinship with others who had abilities similar to her own, but she soon discovered the Dark Star *dens* were a ruthless and hated people.

When Dina was still a child, the other children in her neighborhood, upon learning of her ability, had taunted her, excluded her from their group activities, and sometimes even hurt her. Dina's father was forced to move his family on more than one occasion. As Dina grew older, she had learned to fiercely guard the secret of her ability, the loneliness and isolation far preferable to the pain.

Even as an adult, Dina had been reluctant to form relationships, fearful that her secret would become known, and she would once again be the object of hate. There had been few boyfriends, and only one lover. The relationship had come to a disastrous end when Dina admitted the existence of her ability to him. Dina had applied for the Bureau as soon as she had been old enough and had immersed herself in her work.

But the worst had been yet to come. It was only a year ago that disaster had randomly struck her life like a lightning bolt. A lightning bolt in the form of a d*ens* from Deorcas Tron. A killer *dens*. If Jon had known there was a possibility of *dens* on the small colony of Exodus, would he have brought her on this assignment? Did Jon even know how strongly she felt about the *dens*? Dina knew he was well aware of what had happened to her that night a year ago, but they had never talked about it.

He had simply accepted her from the first time they had met and hadn't questioned her feelings or discussed his. He was a private man, but up-front with his friends and co-workers. What you saw with Jon was pretty much what you got. Unless you were a suspect, and then you got the famous Rzije act, complete with dimples, charm, and crinkles around his eyes that convinced you he was your best friend.

Yes, Jon knew about her ability and accepted her nonetheless.

Enough, thought Dina, wearily instructing the computer to exit the *dens* files.

She quickly programmed the following morning's wake-up time and breakfast selection, then took a warm shower and lay down on the bed. Now she was sorry she had saved the *dens* file for last. As she closed her eyes, she prayed that the computer images of the *dens* wouldn't take residence in her dreams. She needn't have worried.

She was in the shadow world again, alone in a hall of mirrors. Her reflection flashed back at her from every angle, and she spun around and around, sensing no escape. Then she stopped spinning, and one by one, the reflections began to melt and reform. Instead of herself, she saw strangers in the mirrors. They were shadowed, and the more she strained to see their features, the more indistinct they became. All of them beckoned to her, each more insistently in their turn. The first merely stood, waiting for her, while the second called to her in a voice without words. The third reached out his arm to her, and she shrank back, confused. She turned again to the first and tried to call to him, but he gave no answer, and she found herself spinning once more, faster and faster, until the images blurred into one...

FOUR
THE KELS

"Wake up, Mondina. The time is the sixth hour, mark zero. Mondina, it is time to wake up..." announced the computer voice. Dina awoke with a start, the mirrors having shattered as the computer announced the time.

Another disturbing dream. The man in this dream, however, had been faceless. She couldn't even tell if there had been three different men in the mirror, or if it been one man and mere reflections of him. Was it the stranger from her first dream? Dina had tried not to think too much about the erotic eagle-man, but he persisted in invading her mind, as did the man from the marketplace. Were they indeed one and the same? Had the vision in the marketplace simply been another dream?

As she got out of bed and bathed the sweat from her body, she focused on evicting the troublesome images from her mind. She had slept longer than the previous night, but it didn't seem to be enough, especially given the manner in which she had awakened. However, this would be their first foray into the desert, and that thought alone spurred Dina to dress with enthusiasm, putting on a cropped undershirt, a rose beige weather suit, and lightweight, knee-high boots. She pulled her hair to the nape of her neck and fastened it with a small gold clip.

She checked her equipment, grabbed a vest and hood from the cooler, and knocked at Jon's door. As she did, she could feel her heart racing as always when she was near him. He answered promptly, looking well-rested and refreshed. His just-washed hair was still damp, and his clear green eyes fairly sparkled.

"Good morning. All set?" he asked.

Dina nodded, and smiled as she noted the rare absence of the cup of mocava in his hand. Jon was indeed ready. "I see you are, too. Let's go."

Equipment in hand, they descended to the storage bay and thoroughly checked their two skimmers. Satisfied that food, water, first aid supplies, rez guns, blankets, and recorders were all present and in good repair in the storage compartments, they set their trail finders for the Dheru Kel. Exiting the bay doors, they kept their speed in check through the city until they arrived at the Ghe Wespero, where the *mercari* were well into their brisk morning business. Loud shouts vied with sing-song proclamations as merchants competed for customers.

Once through the Ghe Wespero, Jon and Dina opened the throttles, and the machines sped smoothly through the desert air across the Albho Mar. Dina watched the undulating waves of white sand move beneath her and felt almost mesmerized as the endless patterns of light and shadow passed. She took note of the small way stations that appeared every five decbars, like silent sentinels, and, remembering Khilioi's warning, forced herself to keep her line of sight high and to keep shifting her gaze to prevent the hypnotic effect of the waves of sand from distorting her perception.

For all her dislike of Khilioi's condescending ways, she was grateful he had taken the time to explain "desert hypnosis" to her and Jon, and had given them tips on how to prevent it. Moving her head slightly and skating her eyes across the landscape gave her a good excuse to watch Jon. He was a little ahead of her and to her left, and rode his skimmer with a relaxed seat, as if he had been born to the desert world. Dressed in a white weather suit, he looked strong and sure of himself. She had to force herself to shift her eyes to the trail finder, the skimmer controls, and the horizon, but her gaze always seemed to fall back to Jon.

Soon she could see that the skyline was no longer flat, but humped with the tops of white and gray peaks, like the sails of giant ships that sprout on the horizon as they approach the observer. As she neared the tall crests, they seemed to multiply, like an armada spread across the sea. They teased her vision, seeming, through the wavering heat shimmer, to extend endlessly in either direction along the horizon. But as she neared the base of the Chayne Gwer, she saw that the range of low mountains diminished to the south and extended only to the north.

Dina knew from the maps that the mines were at the foot of the Chayne, dead ahead, and that the low mounds snaking their way north, like large naked children crawling over the sand, made up the range known as the Wiara Gwer. As they approached Dheru Kel, Jon and Dina cut back on their throttles, easing the skimmers to a slow drift. They could see a large metal structure built flush against the gray granite mountain. Signs announced "Dheru Kel, Operated by Mother Lode Mining Consolidated, Access Beyond This Point Restricted."

Jon and Dina parked their skimmers in an area where numerous other skimmers, huggers, and a large transport were also parked, set the parking braces, and strode to the structure's entrance. Dina, for one, was eager to get out of the sun. At the door an amplified voice requested their ID chips and audio identification. After a moment, the door slid open, and a man wearing a gray uniform sporting a "Mother Lode Mining Security" patch beckoned them in. After the security check was completed, another man, similarly dressed, approached.

He was of medium height, with cropped brown hair and eyes so dark she couldn't see their color. It was difficult to guess his age, for though his features appeared young, black circles collared his visage, making the dark eyes appear almost unholy.

"Agents Rzije and Marlijn, welcome to Dheru Kel. I'm Kalyo Rhoemer. Chief Hrothi is aware of your arrival. However, he asks that you have some time to freshen up from your trip before you see him. Follow me, please."

Jon and Dina followed Rhoemer to a comfortably appointed room stocked with water, cleansing cloths, weather suits, and various pieces of miner's gear. Restrooms were off to one side, and private dressing rooms were on the other.

"If you plan on a tour of the mines, you'll need a miner's hood. Choose one that fits, and please avail yourselves of anything else you need. When you're finished, ring the buzzer." Rhoemer indicated a button near the door, and left.

Jon was just about to touch the button several moments later when his hand froze in mid-air.

"Hold on. My comm is sounding." Jon paused. "Yes,

sir...We just arrived at Dheru Kel, sir," Jon answered into his commband. He listened, and Dina waited. Finally, with a final barrage of "yes sir, no sir, yes sir," Jon disconnected the call.

Dina didn't like the look on his face. The green eyes glowed like light shining through emerald, and tight lines played with the corners of his mouth, pursing it, relaxing it, then twisting the curve of his lower lip up and down. "That was Chandhel. Something's come up. Something important. He's requesting— no, ordering—us to meet with him immediately at his office."

Dina let out a long breath, not realizing she had been holding it while she waited for Jon to speak. "How can they expect us to make progress this way?"

"I know, I know. But we can't ignore his summons."

"Jon, do both of us have to go? What if you go and I stay to tour the mines? This is important. If I at least stay, we won't lose valuable time."

Jon hesitated before answering, lowering his head. Finally he raised it and nodded. "All right. But I want marks every half hour. And safety, I repeat, safety, is your number one concern. You don't go anywhere alone. Do you understand?"

"Yes, I understand."

"Get someone from the mine to escort you back to the city."

"Yes, if I can. Don't worry about me."

"It's part of my job to worry about you."

"You'd better get going."

"Not before I see you set your commband for those marks."

Dina let out an exasperated sigh, but did as Jon requested, revising the setting on her commband to remind her, through both a tone emitted through her earpiece and a vibration on her wrist, to send a mark to Jon every half hour.

He put a hand to Dina's shoulder, then pressed the button to summon Rhoemer. Jon explained the change in plans, and Rhoemer escorted him out.

Dina was on her own. She drew a deep breath, and faced the security officer when he returned. "Tell me, do the miners use the areas we've been in?"

"Oh, no. The miners have a separate entrance and facilities for clean-up and refreshment. This area is reserved for visitors and administrative personnel only. This way, please, Agent Marlijn. Chief Hrothi is waiting."

Dina followed Rhoemer to the rear of the building and stopped before a door that was marked "Chief of Security." Rhoemer announced them, a door slid open, and they passed through an anteroom to an inner office. A tall, middle-aged man stood and came forward to greet them. He was handsome, with dark gray hair, long silver sideburns, and clear cerulean eyes.

"Thank you, Kal. Agent Marlijn, please come in and sit down. I'm Karsa Hrothi, Chief of Security for the Mother Lode mines here on Exodus." Hrothi continued speaking as Dina made herself comfortable. "We've been awaiting your arrival with great anticipation. I'm prepared to answer any questions you have and to cooperate fully with any request you have. Too many good men have died, Agent Marlijn. The matter needs to be resolved before anyone else loses his life." Hrothi made a gesture with his hands. "Please, I am open to your questions."

"First, tell me about your security measures, both for the gems and for all personnel. Then I'd appreciate a tour of the mining facility."

"Of course. Historically, Mother Lode has had very few problems with theft, or with its personnel. All miners hired are members in good standing of the Synergy Mining Guild. Mining is a hard job, but for those who don't mind the travel or being away from family for long periods of time, it's a good-paying job. All miners sign a contract for a particular job for a particular length of time. The contract-fulfillment bonuses are quite high. Punishment for theft or smuggling of gems is very severe. Anyone caught with even a single stone in his possession illegally is subject not only to criminal prosecution, but forfeits his fulfillment bonus and good standing in the Guild. Administrative personnel are screened just as carefully for hiring."

"Can you give me the specifics of your security here at this mine and Kewero Kel?" asked Dina.

"Certainly. All mine personnel go through a security check upon arrival similar to the check you went through, and an even more stringent one when they leave. Visitors and administrative personnel come in the front entrance, the one you came through. The miners have their own entrance on the north side of the building."

"Is there any other way into the mine except through these entrances?"

"Not into the active areas, no. But there are numerous tunnels, shafts, and crosscuts—especially in Kewero Kel, the original mine—that are worked out and abandoned. Originally the abandoned areas were of little concern. There is a negligible amount of gem-bearing rock there. The miners have no business there and know to stay out. However, since the murders, we have made attempts to close up as many of these areas as possible."

"'As many as possible.' That sounds rather vague. Do I understand you to mean that it is still possible for an unauthorized person to gain access to one of these abandoned areas undetected?"

Hrothi met Dina's gaze without wavering. His reply revealed no discomfiture or annoyance. "The fact is, either someone working for Mother Lode is responsible for the murders, or, yes, an unauthorized person has found a way to gain access. I can't rule out the second possibility completely."

Dina paused before answering, her eyes still locked on those of Hrothi. "I appreciate your frankness, sir."

Hrothi inclined his head ever so slightly in acknowledgment. "We have a tour waiting. Perhaps it will answer many of your questions."

Dina had expected him to call for Rhoemer or someone else to take her on the tour, but to her surprise, Hrothi rose, picked up a miner's hood, and indicated that Dina put hers on. He gave her a very leisurely, complete tour of the mines, describing the mining procedures and answering all her questions.

The tour over, they unhurriedly made their way back to Hrothi's office, the Security Chief casually chatting about exodite's merit compared to other gemstones. Dina looked up, and from the far end of the corridor saw a tall, striking man approaching them. The man had brown hair that gleamed with red highlights each time he passed beneath a ceiling light, and as he came to a halt before her, she saw that he had eyes the color of the richest mocava.

"Agent Marlijn, this is Rum Ctararzin, our Operations Manager. Rum, Agent Mondina Marlijn of the IIB. She and her partner, Karjon Rzije, are here to help with the investigation."

Ctararzin greeted Dina with a very proper bow. "Excellent. Welcome to Exodus and the Albho Mar. I trust your trip across the desert was not too uncomfortable? The desert sea can be a little daunting to those not used to it."

Rum Ctararzin. The name was familiar. This was the man who had signed the revocation order banning the miner Raethe Avarti from the Guild. "Thank you, sir. I fared well."

Ctararzin nodded, a small smile on his face which he promptly dropped. "This is a tragic, tragic situation. We're family here at Mother Lode. These are honest, hardworking men. That they should be taken in this senseless manner is intolerable. I blame the government for their laxity in keeping this colony safe, especially the desert. Everyone knows there are dark outworlders and illegals roaming the desert at will, and yet nothing is done about them. I hope you and your partner can truly do something to stop this insanity."

"We'll do our best, sir."

With another nod, this time of dismissal, Rum put a hand on Hrothi's shoulder. "Karsa, if you have a moment..."

"Surely." Hrothi turned to Dina and extended his hand. "I hope I was some help. Rhoemer will see you out. Good day, Agent Marlijn."

Dina thanked Hrothi for the tour, and Kalyo Rhoemer arrived seconds later. Dina watched as Hrothi and Ctararzin ambled down the corridor, their heads close and their voices low. She couldn't pick up their conversation.

At the front entrance, Rhoemer offered to send an employee back to Aeternus with Dina as an escort, but she declined. The road back to Aeternus was well traveled, and Dina was armed. Standing close to Rhoemer, she could see that his eyes were actually blue, but a blue so deep that it was like the color of the deepest ocean. A light probe picked up no malice, but a guardedness that made Dina wonder what he was shielding.

She left the building and thought about the other people she had just met. She had liked Hrothi. It had been difficult to probe him while asking him questions at the same time, but she had picked up strength, integrity, and intelligence as well as a disturbance that Dina couldn't pinpoint. It was part fear, part hatred, and had been very strong. Dina had also picked up a strange feeling about Ctararzin. Though his words had meant to sound sincere, his speech had sounded trite and prepared to her. She wished she had had time to probe his mind as well.

As Dina left the mine and approached her skimmer, the full force of the sun at its zenith hit her, sending a wave of heat over her. Even with her hood on, Dina felt dizzy, and her head started to pound. She stood at her skimmer for a moment, waiting for the feeling to pass, but it didn't.

She leaned on her skimmer, the silence of the Kewero seeming to beckon her. During the tour, she and Hrothi had traveled to the rim of Kewero Kel, but the labyrinth of abandoned crosscuts and tunnels spread far north of where they had traversed in the hugger. She mounted her skimmer and, vaguely aware that she was disobeying Jon's orders, slowly skirted the perimeter of Dheru Kel. Her head still throbbed. The sun didn't usually affect her this much, but today it was as though the yellow heart was beating all around her, sending pulses of fire straight to the back of her eyes.

Something was here. Something important. She wove her skimmer through the carcass of Kewero Kel, passing the scars of sealed adits, that, like wounds under a surgeon's care, had been carefully closed. Farther on, though, the wind whistled through punctures in the hillside that remained neglected, open tunnels and shafts that had no more than a warning sign posted. Like silent open mouths, they seemed to be alternately screaming in silent terror and shouting soundless warnings to her.

She slowed her skimmer at the gaping hole of a long abandoned tunnel entrance on the far northernmost Kewero rockface. This was it. Something vital to the investigation was here. She knew it. She also knew she should return to Dheru, or at least summon assistance, but she couldn't. Dust rose in lazy ribbons around her skimmer as she dismounted and approached the adit. She realized she had left her rez gun on the skimmer, but she couldn't turn back. She had to move on.

The pounding in her head blossomed like an explosion, and the desire for the shade of the entrance overwhelmed all else. She stumbled forward, and as she lunged from the blinding blood of the sun into the black breath of the shade, she fell into the arms of a man swathed in full desert regalia. She tried to adjust her eyes to the shadowed interior, but none of her senses or reflexes were as swift as the stranger's, who snagged both her arms and held her as if she were nothing but a doll.

Dina tried to speak, but she seemed sapped of both strength and will in this man's grip. Brief, disjointed images were all that flashed through her mind. Power. Blackness. A malevolence. All as tangible as the brawn of his muscles. A helplessness that was foreign to her drained the strength from her legs.

She sagged in his arms, seeing nothing but the visor of a dark sunshield, its shiny surface ringed by layers of a colorless scarf that hid all identifying features. He jerked her closer to his body, and she gasped. She heard laughter, and felt a red-hot heat radiate from the man straight through to her bare skin. A dagger seemed to pierce her skull, laying her bare to her soul, and she collapsed, moaning.

The man said nothing, but with two efficient tugs stripped her of her commband and utility belt. He then shoved her into the murky depths of the tunnel, and the last thing she knew was a fear and vulnerability greater than anything she had ever experienced.

The fear lasted only a heartbeat. The force of a stun gun blast drilled her, enveloped her like a shroud, and sent her into a world of blackness where not even dreams lived.

FIVE
DARK STAR

Mondina's conscious mind struggled to take control, but she couldn't move her head or limbs. She felt disassociated from her body, as if she were floating high on the desert air currents, looking down. Just like the dream. The dream with the eagle-man. The pleasant thought was the first to filter through the clouds of her dazed mind, but the blistering air that scorched her throat as she gasped for breath quickly told her otherwise. Her mind fought harder as she realized that her body was indeed helpless, and that this was no dream.

The echo of the resonance blast that had sealed her in the mine tunnel resounded again in her mind, and every pulse told her that if she couldn't escape, she would be the killer's ninth victim.

Panic welled up, and with it, stinging tears. The irony swam before her. She, the hunter, had now become the prey. Dina squeezed her eyes shut and forced the fear down with an effort. As she did so, her academy training kicked in. She knew if she surrendered to hysteria, she would die in this dark pocket of hell.

No. An Interplanetary Investigation Bureau agent would *not* be a victim.

Her training mantra sang to her mind. *I will never give up...never give up.* The familiar words, recited over and over again in the Academy, shielded her mind from the panic, and her thought processes went to work. She had to get help, that much was obvious, but how?

Review your options, she thought. She forced her eyes open, but in the belly of the rock-ribbed desert beast called Kewero, she saw no more than a black haze that swam before her like the secrets of the dead. Did she still have her commband? Not able to see it or to move her arms to feel it on her wrist, she shut her eyes and replayed the attack in her mind, trying not to let the terror strip her memory of the facts.

She saw the faceless stranger in her mind's eye. Cloaked

in the shade of the tunnel entrance, he had seized her before her eyes could adjust to the darkness and had torn off her commband and utility belt before propelling her deeper into the bowels of the abandoned mine. The commband was gone. She couldn't contact Jon, and she had sent her last mark to him just before she had left Dheru Kel, just before she had made her foolish decision to view the Kewero mine on her own. Why hadn't she thought to tell someone of her plans?

Jon. Once Jon failed to receive her next scheduled mark, he would immediately begin tracking her via the small transmitter surgically implanted in her thigh. Yes, her partner would come, but too late. It would be more than an hour until Dina could expect help from Jon, and the mine's air, already below optimum standards, would not last that long. She had a small supply of oxygen in her hood, but the effects of the stun charge held her hands and arms in thrall, reducing them to traitorous minions that would refuse the orders of her mind until time released them. She had no way to position the small oxygen mask and open the valve.

She felt a bead of sweat glide down her temple, followed one upon another until they ran into the track of her tears and merged with the salty trail. The stifling heat of her trap invaded even her desert hood, reminding her that she was quickly running out of time. Her skimmer. It was parked outside the tunnel, and it was equipped with a distress beacon. What had Corporal Khilioi told her about activating it? She blinked her eyes, as if clearing her eyesight would clear her mind, but the small effort did help. The memory of the haughty voice arose. "'...the beacon can be engaged manually, from your commband, or will activate automatically if the skimmer is damaged...'" Damn! The commband again. Without it she was without communication.

No. Her ability. She had her ability as a telepath. But Jon was not telepathic. Nor was anyone she knew on this small colony. Her eyes fluttered, and in the cloud of dust beyond her eyeshields a memory reached out to her. Minister Chandhel had said there may be telepathic *dens* on Exodus. If they had indeed infested this colony during the past administration, chances were good they were still here. A *dens* would be as impossible to capture as mist in a bottle. To say they were a cold, self-centered people would be kind...or naive. Even if one heard her, would he help? A *dens*, help? No.

She almost laughed. It was a ridiculous thought. A *dens* would never help her, and even if one did, she would not owe her life to such a creature. No. There had to be another way. But time pressed her. She couldn't just wait and hope that her body sloughed off the stun gun paralysis before she consumed the remaining oxygen. Even if the stun did wear off in time, the sealed tunnel was like a coffin encasing her—no air, no water, no light, no hope.

She sucked in a long, slow breath, thankful for the small blessing of the hood's nose filter which kept most of the dust out, and focused her mind on finding another option.

Ah, but I am an option, little girl.

The voice in her mind was as great and unpleasant a shock as she had ever had.

Shocked, are you? Well, imagine my shock to find a telepath on my doorstep, and a little spitfire at that.

Get out of my head, whoever you are! Sweat trickled down her spine and between her breasts, the uncomfortable sensation seeming to mock her inability to wipe the moisture away.

I can hear you, but I can't understand you. You need to do two things. You need to calm down, and you need to focus your thoughts. Try it again.

Damn you, you can understand my meaning well enough. Get out!

Now, is that any way to talk to the man who's going to save your life? Would you rather I left you to die?

No. She wouldn't die. Her survival training overcame her pride. *If you must do something, get help for me from Dheru Kel.*

There isn't time for that, so I'm afraid you'll have to settle for my help. I need you to calm yourself, so I can pinpoint your location.

His response filled her mind, as if he were lying right beside her, but his presence felt more like an invasion than a comfort.

Even so, she knew what she had to do to survive. Her visualization and relaxation exercises, practiced almost daily for as long as she could remember, were as second nature as the skills she had learned in the Academy. She did it now, without thinking about it.

In a heartbeat, she was no longer in the tunnel, but standing on the Road of Time, gazing at the Field of Forever. She saw the undulating ripples of golden grasses, stretching, peaceful and unbroken, to the horizon. The image was like a hand that wiped all else from her mind, and she suddenly felt a relaxation descend all around her, shutting out all her emotions, so that only a calmness remained. When next she projected her mind, it was with a certainty that he would understand her.

I'm in a closed tunnel on the north side of the Kewero Kel, number six, north.

I have it. I'll be there soon. You must remain relaxed. It's the most important thing you can do. It'll conserve oxygen and make it easier for me to understand you. What's your name?

Never mind my name. If you're going to help, get on with it.

Your obstinacy is of little matter...Dina.

She shuddered in spite of the stifling heat. His Voice was a part of him inside her, and the simple sounding of her name touched her in a way she had never been touched. She had never interacted with another telepath before. She not only heard his Voice, but it was so tangible she felt it. The word was a drop of ice water that condensed behind her eyes, hung on, then slipped away like a cold-blooded creature slithering over sand, leaving a slimy trail in its wake. She fought to erase the imprint from her mind, but the diminishing oxygen stole command of her thoughts and provided the tranquilizer for her distress. She suddenly wanted to let go. She closed her eyes and curled, like a paper in a flame, against the rock wall of the tunnel.

Dina! Can you hear me? I need you to keep projecting. Not a lot, I need you to save your energy, but keep projecting. Tell me if you're all right.

I'm all right...but... What was it she wanted? It was hard to remember.

Rayn was already on his skimmer. He estimated he was only three decbars from the north face of the mine, as many minutes away. *I'm on the way. I should be there in less than five minutes.*

Not enough oxygen for five minutes...

Yes, there is. Dina, you're going to be all right.

He accelerated the skimmer as if a race had begun, but his only opponent was the passage of time, an unwanted passenger clinging to him. When Rayn saw the adit, long moments later, his chest felt tight, and he knew with a certainty more time had elapsed than he had estimated. A tumble of broken rock blocked the narrow opening.

Dina, I'm at the tunnel entrance. Keep projecting!

Hurry...

He rocked the skimmer to a halt and snatched a small survival kit from the cargo well. *Get as far away as you can from the cave-in. Shield your face.*

He marked the passing of a half-dozen heartbeats, but felt no response reach for him. He couldn't afford to give time any more of an edge. He aimed a small silver resonance gun at the rocks that flowed like a frozen waterfall from the head of the entrance to his feet. Stepping back, he squeezed the trigger pad, holding his free arm in front of his hooded face. The rocks started to vibrate, then burst and spit stones and dust back at him. He fired twice more, praying that he wouldn't start another cave-in, until a hole large enough for his body gaped at him.

Dina! Can you hear me?

No answer came to him. Rayn flicked the switch on his rez to the illuminator setting, and flashed the powerful, narrow beam through the opening he had made. He scuttled through, and the tight circle of light fell on a silent golden form huddled against the black rock. He quickly tore the front of her weather suit open and, placing one hand on her chest, felt a tenuous rise and fall. He yanked her hood off, opened the survival kit, snapped an oxygen mask out, and held it over her nose and mouth, opening the valve.

"Come on, Dina, breathe!" He uttered the words aloud at

the same time he threw his mind to hers, delving far into the darkness of her unconsciousness to instill the commands her physical senses couldn't register or transmit. *Breathe! Dina, you must live. You must do as I say. Come on, Dina!* His mind held hers, and his compelling telepathic voice injected the commands deeper and more forcefully into her.

Finally, in frustration, he withdrew his mind from hers and vocalized a long string of unrelated profanities, learned over many years on many worlds.

The body in his arms was still, then jerked like a puppet on a string. Her breathing deepened, and Rayn closed his eyes in thanks to whatever gods had been listening. But the gods had not prepared him for what was to come.

His silent litany was cut short by a fit of coughing accompanied by arms that lurched upward and hands that scrabbled at his. Awkward as she was from the lingering effects of the stun, he was amazed at the strength in the slender limbs that tried to rip the oxygen mask from her face. He caught her wrists and held her arms securely.

"Easy, Dina, you're going to be all right. Come on, now, be a good little girl and stop fighting me."

Mentally he commanded her to relax. He continued his hold on her arms, but he could feel the resistance drain away as her mind acquiesced to his. Her coughing subsided, her breathing steadied, and the steel in her arms melted into soft, pliant flesh. He shut the oxygen valve off, pulled the mask from her face, and in doing so, was hit by a more potent stun than that which had hit her.

His ethereal self had seen her, his mind had recreated her image in the dream sequence, and he had seen her in the marketplace with her sunshield on. But he had yet to see her this close in the flesh. By the light thrown from the rez's illuminator, he saw that she had eyes like living, polished exodite set in a luminous face framed by hair the color of summer lightning. He stared, spellbound.

Dina's eyes blinked and stared back at the man, but the faceless image that registered in her dazed mind reawakened her fear. She tried to push herself away from him, but the wall gave her no escape. She scooted sideways along the rough stone toward the tunnel opening, but the man turned, too fast for her, his arm a striking snake. Slender, tanned fingers protruded from white leather half-gloves and tightened on her wrist. Dim light from the opening at the tunnel entrance fell on half his face.

He squatted before her like a hooded bird of prey. A cowl of white hideskin covered his head, and slanted mirrored eye slits reflected her gaze back to her. A v-shaped faceplate over the man's nose and mouth and a single white feather that hung low from the back of the hood tangled with his long hair and strengthened the illusion of a man-beast. A loose white tunic, pale tiger's-eye brown trousers, and dark leather boots the color of old, polished wood, completed the man's attire.

"Easy, little girl. It's just a desert hood. I'm not going to hurt you."

The spoken voice was so soft and rich that she almost wanted to believe the lie. The sound of it, tinged with the barest trace of an accent, somehow matched the Voice she had heard in her head. She went perfectly still. She was vaguely unsure whether it was because of his grasp on her arm, his voice, or a fear she was loathe to admit to.

"You're a *dens.*"

"How keen you are."

She felt the grip on her arm loosen. "I suppose I should thank you."

"Don't tax yourself."

She tried to shake her arm to free herself, but all she managed was a small tug. It was enough. The man opened his hand and released her as one might let go of a wild animal.

Dina sat stock-still and waited, concentrating on her breathing and giving her scattered senses a moment to gather. Turning her face toward the tunnel entrance as far as she could without taking her eyes off the man, she drew deeply of the fresh air that teased the breach formed by the man's rez gun. Hot dust still burned her throat, but she ignored it and savored the sweet oxygen instead. She picked up the threads of her thoughts and tried to lace them together.

The man, balanced on the balls of his feet, was as motionless before her as a predator, the glint from the mirrored eyes the only movement she caught.

She took a final deep breath and let it out slowly. "Thank you. Now, *dens*, who are you?" she asked, her voice sounding small, raspy, and hardly commanding. She hated feeling weak before this creature, but it was the best she could manage until more of her strength returned.

When he didn't reply, Dina glanced down self-consciously at the front of her weather suit, ripped open to the waist. She wasn't naked beneath the suit by any means, wearing a mesh cooling vest and cropped tank top, but sweat had glued the brief top to her like a second skin, and she felt her pale face flame as she tried to pull together the torn tunic.

The mask and the man beneath were utterly still. Finally, after an eternity of seconds, the man spoke.

"I had to make sure you were still breathing." The voice was still soft, but there was a huskiness to it that even the mask couldn't hide. Before Dina could reply, he continued. "Don't try to talk just yet."

Though the words and the voice were mild, they left no door open for argument. She was quiet while he removed a small flask from his belt and did a step-drag to bring himself closer to her. Though his position should have made the movement awkward, he moved with the ease of an animal born to sand and stone. As he closed the small gap between them, he went down on one knee, trapping her between the rock wall and his body, the leather of his left boot pressed along her right side, his right knee on the ground in front of her. She remained still, her knees drawn up to her chest, as he flipped the top open with the flick of one finger and offered the flask to her. Her eyes followed every move his hands made. Long white fringes from the fingerless glove swung back and forth in unison.

"Drink," he commanded in the same soft tone.

Even in her weakened state her sense of caution battled with her desire to obey the honeyed voice. She struggled to shake her head and brush the flask aside, but he would have none of it. Pressing closer to her still, he held the back of her head with one hand and lifted the mouth of the flask to her lips.

Drink, but slowly now.

The words resounded lightly in her mind like a splash of cold water, and she felt them flow down the length of her spine to her core. She had no choice but to obey, drinking small mouthfuls of the warm liquid. Just like his voice, damn him, floated the languid thought, smooth, rich, but with a bite.

Taking her fill, she paused, aware suddenly that his hand, no longer needed, remained where it was. The span of the hand cradling her head was broad, the slender fingers long, and she sensed rather than felt the strength in the possessive touch. It was an intimate touch. Too intimate. She shuddered and shook her head, fighting an urge to spit the last mouthful back at him.

"Get your hand off me."

His hand slipped from her head, but not before his fingertips feathered her hair to beyond her shoulders, and Dina had no trouble imagining a leer beneath the mask.

The man stood. "Come on, let's get you out of here." This time there was an edge of something harder around the liquid flow of sound that was his voice. He replaced the flask on his belt. When Dina didn't move, his words coursed smoothly once again. "Are you injured? Can you walk?"

"No, and I don't know. I was hit with a stun gun. And you didn't answer my question. Who are you?" Her own voice, though louder this time, sounded strange to her, as if someone else were speaking the words. She guessed that her throat was still a little hoarse from gasping the mine's hot, dusty air. What else could it be?

The man didn't answer, but picked up his rez gun, holstered it on his belt, slung the survival kit over his right shoulder, and reaching down with his left arm, grabbed Dina under her armpit. He lifted her effortlessly to her feet. Though still feeling boneless as the dead, she was able to walk, albeit with his hand securely on her arm and her left hand clutching a fistful of his tunic. When she exited the tunnel, she immediately brought her free hand up to shade her face from the blinding fire of the desert sun.

"Can you stand?" The mirrored creature-eyes flashed sparks

of silver at her.

"I can stand." This time her voice sounded normal to her. Her strength and mobility were returning, but there was still the problem of the creature holding her. She would have to be very, very careful.

Rayn had no trouble hearing the defiance in her three words. Well, she would have to wait for the answer to her question of his identity. He wanted to savor her discovery. He released her arm and jogged to the skimmer cargo hold, where he deposited the survival kit and pulled out a hood. He felt the feather that hung on a thong from the nape of his neck twirl in the shimmer of the heat and wrap around his neck in the hot breeze. Unlike the hood he wore, the one he pulled from the skimmer was unadorned and strictly utilitarian. He turned, and in the oven of the Kewero Valley, felt as if his feet had frozen to the desert floor.

In the tunnel her unusual coloring had struck him. Here, in the spotlight of this forsaken stage, he was spellbound. She was a magnet for the sunlight, her hair drawing all the white-gold radiance to it and reflecting it back at him a hundredfold. As the hot breeze lifted stray blonde tendrils off her shoulders and spun them around her head, he imagined they spun around him.

Gods, he thought, *what have you done to me?*

Inhaling a deep breath, he stepped back to where she stood and held out the hood. "Here. Yours was left in the tunnel. Put this on."

She pulled the hood on, and he soon saw her chest expand with a deep breath of clean, filtered air. Rayn turned back to the skimmer, straddled the machine, and reached out his arm to her.

"Come on."

Her head tilted, and he didn't need to see her face to know that her mind was beginning to function again.

"No."

"No?"

"I'm not going."

Rayn dropped his arm. "You need fluids and to get out of

this heat. Don't argue."

She circled, and Rayn knew she was positioning herself so that the sun was no longer directly in her eyes. He smiled. Her quick mind was indeed back at work.

"My partner will be here soon."

"Your partner."

"Such excellent hearing. Yes, my partner. So I have to stay."

He laughed. "You're not on Glacia anymore, little girl."

"What's that supposed to mean?"

"This isn't the tidy, civilized world you're used to."

"There's nothing civilized in what I deal with. I was attacked. This is now a crime scene. You and I both need to stay here. That clear enough for a primitive like you?"

"The scene will keep." The words were patient, as to a child. "You won't."

"How's this then? I don't know you. I'm definitely not letting you take me gods know where."

Rayn swore softly to himself, his hands on his hips and his head thrown back, as if the heavens could send him a response to her obstinacy. Being a witness at a crime scene in front of half the Aeternan Enforcement Agency was not a desirable option. This lightning storm needed to be controlled.

He dropped his head and turned toward her again, the mirrors on his mask flashing sparks of sunlight into her eyes. *The lord of the desert will help you, but you must seek him out...the Uz-Dailjan.* Rayn planted the suggestion carefully in her mind, covering it with a layer of warmth and good will. More than a suggestion, it was a compelling command. She would obey him.

Dina swayed in the heat, unbalanced by a shimmer of dizziness. All she saw was two wavering spots of white flame in front of her eyes. She widened her stance.

Damn stun, she thought. Maybe he was right. She did need to get out of the heat...and Jon would find her no matter where she went. She thought quickly. Maybe she could salvage something useful from this day after all. "All right. I hear that the Desert *Dailjan* have a camp near here. I assume you're one of them. Take me there. I wish to speak to the *Uz-Dailjan.*"

"And what makes you think you'll be safer with him than with me?"

"You're a *dens*. I'd be safer with anyone than with you." As soon as she said it, she was sorry. She did owe her life to him, but it was too late to take it back now.

He sat motionless for a moment, staring at her with the mask's eyes. "A strange thing for someone with your powers to say," he said in a neutral voice.

Dina's voice rose in volume. "I don't manipulate people with my mind. I don't destroy minds. And I don't use my powers to commit crimes."

"And you've decided I do all of those."

"You're here, on Exodus, illegally, and you've evaded capture for what I would imagine to be quite some time. That indicates you've done at least two of the three."

The mirrored eyes rolled like mercury away from her, and his head swivelled, as if he had heard something, but there were only the silent scars of the mines to the west and the white shimmer of the Albho Mar to the east.

Dina side-stepped further so she wouldn't be blinded again when next he turned his face her way.

The white mask slowly cocked toward her, like a bird alert to danger, and was so still for a moment that she wondered if he was indeed looking at her.

"Then you know what I can do with you now and that you would be powerless to stop me." The voice that had poured like warm honey only a moment before seemed to chill and congeal around her.

"I know what you can do." Damn him. She wondered what she could do.

Rayn stared at her, his hidden smile now as flat as the horizon over the Sea of Glass. Never could he get away from it, no matter how far he traveled. It seemed he could never outdistance the hate. It was a parasite, always clinging to him, but his control, as it had so many times in the past, drove the emotions back into the darkest recesses of his mind.

"Do you, now," he replied, drawing the cold words out like a dagger from a sheath.

"Yes. And you need to know I don't respond well to threats."

Rayn fought the powerful urge for quick domination and satisfaction. He was glad she couldn't see his face. She tasked him, no doubt about it, but so much the better. *When you finally submit, little girl,* he thought, *you will respond with a passion like none you've ever known.* But for now, threats wouldn't serve him.

"No threat, Dina. Simply fact. The *Uz* will want to speak with you. He won't take it kindly if I hurt you." Once more he extended his arm out to her, the white leather fringes dancing beneath his upturned hand. His voice warmed again, and he felt his features unlock. "Get on, then. I'll take you to him." She would not refuse.

Dina hesitated, but still under the influence of the compelling command, could not resist. She eased her leg over the seat to ride behind him, ignoring his outstretched hand with the curled, upturned fingers that reminded her of a spider.

He dropped his arm. "Put your arms around me and hold on tight. This machine wasn't made for two." He had turned his head to speak, but Dina was painfully aware that the gesture was superfluous. She knew she would have heard him regardless. The thought irritated her.

Dina slid her reluctant arms around the man's waist, hoping he was lean enough for her to interlock her hands in front of him. The thought of touching a *dens* repulsed her, but she was too slow. He leaned forward to power on the skimmer, and the motion pulled her against him, causing her to flatten her palms against his abdomen for balance. He retracted the parking braces and idled the machine a moment, giving her time to realize, with embarrassment, that her hands had found the narrow gap below his cooling vest and above his waistband. The thin material of his tunic did little to prevent her fingers and palms from feeling the contours of his hard muscles. Heat pressed against her palms like hot sand against bare feet. She wanted to jerk her hands away, but in that instant she felt his Voice inside her again, holding her.

Hang on.

As it was, the soft command was unnecessary, for as he

flicked his wrist, opening the throttle and shooting the skimmer forward, she instinctively tightened her grip. She tried to focus her mind on where he was taking her, what she would say to the *Uz-Dailjan*, and what she would say to Jon, but the assault on her senses of the desert, the skimmer, and the man she held cut her concentration. Her thoughts unraveled again.

He eased the skimmer back and forth through shallow, gray gulches that rose to shadowed gorges so deep and narrow they sliced the landscape like knife wounds. Dina soon lost her sense of direction in the twists and turns. The smooth rocking motion as the man banked the vehicle through the serpentine path soothed her, but did nothing to help her gather her stray thoughts.

All she could think about was that she was flattened intimately against his back, and, in spite of the furnace blown rush of air stinging her body she could feel the heat from the man's body radiate through the thin layers of cloth to her breasts. Beneath her hands, his muscles, for all their lean hardness, felt relaxed, as if transporting a strange woman across the desert was an everyday event for him.

She was thankful her hood prevented her face from touching the dampened strands of dark hair that escaped the bottom of his mask-hood and clung to the base of his neck, but even through the filter of her nose vent his strange mixture of hot sweat and leather, spiced with a faint aromatic scent, filled her nostrils. The feather snapped in the rush of air in front of her, teasing her as much as the thoughts of him that taunted her mind.

She wondered what he felt. He was a *dens*, she reminded herself. A ruthless manipulator. If anything, he was most likely thinking how he could turn this situation to his best advantage. She couldn't let him take the upper hand.

She had never met a *dens* before, and wondered what he looked like beneath the mask. She leaned her head back and squinted to try to view the dark hair that streamed down his neck and lapped the collar of his tunic. The *dens* were known to have long life spans. There was no gray to the hair that she could see, but that didn't mean he hadn't been around a long time. She imagined a craggy, time-worn face and black, glittering eyes with no soul, but the image somehow didn't match the Voice that had permeated every crevice of her mind.

The slowing of the skimmer nudged her back to attention. The man hovered the machine, threaded it through a narrow eye in the rock wall, then opened the throttle. The vehicle's exhaust blew a final kiss at the Chayne Gwer range, the acceleration melded the man's torso to hers, and the skimmer caressed the smooth dune sea before them.

Dina turned her head away from the glare of the midday sun and beheld a shimmer of gold extending from the Chayne as far as the horizon. Unlike the Albho, or White Sea, with its many transverse dunes, this sea was as unmarred as a nude lying on a beach. Only gentle swells and distant folds relieved the citrine stillness. She tried to remember the maps she had seen of Exodus. Was this the Ghel Mar, the Sea of Glass?

If so, she was west of the mines, further from the city than she had yet been. How far would this man take her? She shouldn't have done this, she thought. She didn't trust him. Yet there was no denying that he had saved her life. Why? What did he want from her?

The direction of her questions increased her awareness of the heat from the man's body once again. The thought of such intimate contact with a hated *dens* revolted her, but her body strangely seemed to feel no such revulsion. Before she could chide herself for her foolish thoughts, the skimmer slowed. The man turned them from the skirt of the dune sea back into the hidden canyons of the Chayne, and soon eased the machine to a gentle hover in a small valley sheltered by high cream- and white-banded rock formations.

He set the skimmer down, turned it off, and set the wide braces. After a moment he spoke, his voice hardly more than a purr. "You can let go of me now."

Dina, embarrassed, was doubly so because she had no trouble hearing his soft whisper. She couldn't pretend she hadn't heard, and she knew he knew it as well. She loosened her viselike grip on him and slid off the skimmer. Her feet planted firmly on the ground, she drew a deep breath. She could feel the tank top, damp with sweat, clinging uncomfortably to her, but she shivered, in spite of the heat. Forcing herself to concentrate on her situation, she shifted her focus from the *dens,* cast her gaze to the rocks before her, and finally saw that what first appeared to be a shadow was actually an opening in the wall.

Several men suddenly appeared at the entrance, all dressed in a fashion similar to the one who had rescued her, and all armed. The *dens* motioned to the nearest *Dailjan*, who jogged easily toward them. Dressed in a pale gray weather suit with slate blue boots, the man was stocky in build and no taller than the *dens*. He stopped beside the *dens*, and while it was clear he waited for instructions, it was just as clear, though his face was hooded, that his full attention was on Dina. The *dens* spoke once again in his smooth, controlled voice.

"This woman was trapped in one of the mines. She is under our protection and wishes to speak with the *Uz*. See that she has food, drink, and an opportunity to clean up. Oh, and keep an eye out for her partner, who will no doubt soon be coming to her rescue. I'm sure he'll also want to speak with our leader."

The *Dailjan*, still looking toward Dina, nodded once. "Done," came his voice from beneath his hood.

The *dens* addressed Dina as the three stepped into the shade of the entrance, where the others waited patiently but with the wariness of soldiers. "These men will take care of you. You have nothing to fear from them."

Dina pulled off the hood the *dens* had lent her, causing her disheveled hair to fan out in all directions.

"But wait! I need to know who you are."

"Gods," breathed the *Dailjan* in gray and blue as another one knocked him hard on the arm, but neither Dina nor the *dens* looked at the others. Their attention was solidly riveted on each other.

"I thought you wanted nothing more to do with me."

"I need to know your name." She swallowed, the dryness in her mouth only too apparent. "I need to know who saved my life."

"I'm sure the *Uz* can satisfy your curiosity. If you'll excuse me, I have matters to attend to."

Dina started after the *dens*, but the *Dailjan* in gray caught and held her arm, gently but securely. She felt an unexplainable loss as she watched the *dens* disappear into the depths of the cavern. She didn't know who he was or what he looked like, and she certainly didn't trust him, yet she felt a cold sensation now that he was gone. He had not been what she had expected from a *dens*.

Totally ridiculous, she told herself. It was the stress of almost dying, nothing more.

The *Dailjan* in gray released her arm. "Don't you mind that one, lady. He's just naturally high-handed. Always giving orders like he runs things around here." The other *Dailjan* chuckled from beneath their hoods. "The *Uz*, now," the one in gray continued, "I don't know if you'll like him any better. They're two of a kind." More laughter.

The men led her inside to a large well-lit chamber comfortably furnished with colorful rugs, flowing ceiling-to-floor drapes, and numerous bright cushions, pillows, and blankets surrounding a long, low table. An exquisite looking woman with gleaming, ebony hair came up to Dina and the *Dailjan*.

"That's enough, you misfits. Take yourselves off, now," she said. Facing Dina as the *Dailjan* reluctantly turned around, the woman spoke again in her clear, almost musical voice. "My name is Alessane Sorreano. Come with me. I'll show you where you can clean up without all those brutes staring at you."

Dina followed the young woman to a small, partitioned corner of the chamber where there were water, cleansers, scents, and cloths arranged neatly on a low table. A round mirror reflected Dina's disordered appearance back to her.

"The water's fine for drinking. Take your time. I'll bring you something to cover up with before I take you to Star. He'll have more food and drink for you."

"Star?" *The Uz? Was the Uz indeed a mantis? A mantis called Star?* Dina tried to think, but she had trouble focusing her thoughts. The young woman only smiled and turned away. Dina took a long pull of the cool water, scrubbed her face, combed her hair, and dusted off her suit. As she stepped around the heavy drape, Alessane again appeared, a clean tunic in hand.

"Put this on and follow me. Star's waiting."

Dina trailed Alessane to the entrance of an adjoining chamber which was appointed even more comfortably than the first. The furnishings ceased to be on Dina's mind, however, when the sweep of her gaze fell on two men at the far end of the room who were conversing in tones too low for her to hear.

It was the man of her dream.

Dina's sharp intake of breath nearly choked her. As if sensing her shock, the man's head snapped up, and his eyes found hers. The corners of his mouth lifted in a slow, smug cat-grin, and Dina felt more exposed than she had in her torn tunic. A knot formed in the pit of her stomach, and as images of the erotic dream flashed through her mind, the knot sank lower. The man's smile widened, and Dina's chin came up before she tore her gaze away.

She looked at the other man, finally noticing him even though he was physically more imposing than her dream partner. She canted her head. Which of the two men was the *Uz-Dailjan*? The taller man was powerfully built and wore his long hair pulled severely back and tied just beneath the crown of his head. The expression on his face, hard as the bulging muscles of his biceps, was a sharp contrast to the easy elan of his companion.

Dina studied both men, trying to reconcile their appearances with what she knew about the great prophets and orators, the *mantis*. She frowned. The *mantis* relied on the power of their spoken words to influence people, and were not known to be warrior-like in appearance. Something was wrong with her assumption that the *Uz* was a *mantis*. The larger man was clearly not a man of words, and the man with the mesmerizing eyes, who had invaded her mind on two occasions, was more likely to be...

"Welcome to Sanctuary, Dina. Come in and join me."

...a *dens!*

If there had been any doubt, the man's hypnotic voice dispelled it. It was the voice of the man who had saved her life, the Voice that had violated her mind. The man before her was her savior, the *dens*, and the man who had visited both her conscious and unconscious mind.

Dina crossed the chamber and halted before him. He said something under his breath to his companion, and the taller man nodded and left the chamber through a rear exit. The *dens* rose to meet Dina's steady gaze.

"You're the *dens*."

"Very perceptive. But I expected nothing less of you," he said, with an almost imperceptible trace of sarcasm. "Sit down."

"You saved my life."

"You keep stating the obvious. I forget my manners. Please...take whatever you wish." The man motioned to a table which was laid with bread and fruit. She continued to stand.

"Am I that much of a surprise to you? Perhaps you expected three eyes and head spikes? That is, is it not, how Glacians describe us to their children when telling horror stories?"

Dina felt herself redden. She couldn't bring herself to deny it, as she had heard the portrayal herself as a small child, and couldn't think of a polite response. Instead, she sat, and he did likewise.

There was a quality in his voice that held her, as it had in the mine tunnel, and for a moment she couldn't think straight. His voice was low and soft, but beneath the softness was something she couldn't define. His Glacian was very good, with just the barest accent. Yet the accent wasn't it.

To avoid answering his question she helped herself to a chunk of the brown bread and slowly spread it with a sweetened fruit paste, all the while appraising the man before her. He was indeed a surprise, but one she wouldn't admit to him. She noticed first his eyes. Far from the black she had envisioned, they were light brown, almost golden, set off by thick black lashes and brows. Next she noticed his mouth, full and sensuous, sculpted into serious lines very nearly resembling a pout.

Arrogant bastard, came the automatic thought. His features were strong and regular, with prominent cheekbones and an angular jaw, but it was a much younger face than she had expected. Thick dark hair hung forward in lazy arcs on either side of the prominent widow's peak. He wore a small exodite stud in his left ear and a gold chain around his neck which held an odd-shaped pendant. Only the pendant and a brown cooling vest adorned him from the waist up. She had been fooled. He was clearly not the largest man she had seen here. That coupled with the youthful face had indeed led Dina to believe he was anything but the group's leader.

As Dina slowly chewed the bread, she continued to study her host with an eye for detail that served her well on the job. He joined her in partaking of the brown bread, and Dina noticed he had a habit of running a hand through his hair in a vain attempt to control it, but like an oar through black water, the smooth waves reformed as if nothing had disturbed them. But the gesture had allowed her to glimpse the corded, muscled neck that had been camouflaged by the curtain of hair. Her gaze dropped, and she noted his biceps and forearms, equally developed. He didn't look at all the way she had imagined a *dens* to be. They were supposed to be physically unimposing as a race, but this was obviously a powerful man, mentally and physically. She would be imprudent to let his soft voice and sensual beauty lull her into forgetting that. No, she would not be fooled again.

Her composure restored, she put the bread down and spoke. "Forgive me if I appear dull to you. It's been a trying day. Who are you?"

"Rayn DeStar, evil and blackhearted *dens*, at your service," he stated, and stood, bowing more deeply than good manners dictated, one side of his mouth cocked higher than the other. He performed the traditional greeting of his home world, swinging his upturned palms to either side, but the gesture was done with a flourish bordering on mockery. She could see that he still wore the tiger's-eye trousers, only slightly lighter in color than his eyes.

"Not your real name, I assume. Where are you from?"

"Of course not my real name, but as good as any. I am, as I'm sure you've guessed, from B'harata, third planet of what you call the Dark Star, Deorcas Tron. Now tell me who you are and what you're doing here."

"You *dens* are all-knowing. I'm sure you already know my

business."

"I prefer to have you tell me."

"I'm Agent Mondina Marlijn, Interplanetary Investigation Bureau. I was sent here to investigate the homicides in the mines. I'm sure you're well aware of those incidents."

"And what do you want of me?"

"Your assistance, cooperation. An exchange of information."

"Exchange for what?"

"I don't know. What is it that a *dens* craves? Besides power, I mean." She knew she shouldn't have said that. After all, he was her host, and she owed him her life. More importantly, she knew she needed him for her investigation. She couldn't afford to anger him, yet she couldn't seem to help herself.

His expression shifted ever so slightly. The good-natured arrogance seemed to sink below the surface, drawn deep inside him, leaving a mask that revealed nothing. "I would think that to be an effective investigator one would need a more...'open mind' than you seem to have. You have nothing I need."

Her eyes rolled upward as she realized her mistake. How could she have been so stupid? She was saved from having to reply by the arrival of the tall, powerfully built *Dailjan* she had seen with the *dens* earlier. The *Dailjan* approached DeStar and whispered into his ear, cupping the side of his mouth with his large hand. Rayn nodded, and raised his hand ever so slightly. The large man went out the way he came in, without a further word or gesture.

"Your partner's been spotted. He'll be here soon. After you assure him that you are uninjured and quite safe in the hands of the *Dailjan*, I will talk to him in private. I'll need his...word...that he will not betray us to the *angwhi* in Aeternus who purport to be the law there. I can trust that the word of a Glacian is good, can I not? My business with you is concluded."

Though still soft, there was a cold, sharp edge to his words that chilled her and inflamed her at the same time. Her own voice again failed her.

Alessane appeared at Dina's side as Rayn turned and exited through the rear.

"DeStar, wait! We have more to talk about," Dina cried out, but he was already gone.

"Come," said Alessane gently, putting a restraining hand on Dina's arm. "One does not argue with Star."

"No! I need to talk to him!" No sooner than she spoke the words two *Dailjan* appeared, one on either side of her, to escort her to the entrance. As she waited for Jon to arrive, she fumed, hardly able to believe that she had jeopardized the most important investigation she had ever been on just because of her hatred for the *dens*.

Her gaze jumped from the rocks to each of her escorts to her own restless hands, plucking uselessly at the torn front of her tunic. There had to be a way to salvage this, she thought. She'd swallow her pride and crawl on her hands and knees to that rogue, if need be, but she'd pick up the pieces of this disaster. She couldn't imagine a more humiliating experience than apologizing to a *dens*, but then again, nothing about this job was easy.

After a moment, her eyes picked up the movement of a man on a skimmer. The skimmer popped to a stop about a decbar away from the cavern entrance, and the rider dismounted quickly, taking cover behind a jutting granite formation, his long rez gun in hand.

Dina turned to Alessane. "He won't come any closer until he knows it's safe. I'll have to go out to meet him."

Alessane called quietly to the *Dailjan* nearest to her, who nodded, left, and returned a moment later mounted on a two-person skimmer.

"Get on. I'll take you to him. Don't worry, I won't hurt you. DeStar would have my hide if I did."

Dina hesitated, then swung onto the skimmer behind the lean, hooded *Dailjan*. He cruised the skimmer to within ten bars of Jon's location, and coasted the machine to a gentle halt. Dina dismounted and ran to Jon while the *Dailjan* returned to Sanctuary. As Jon ripped his hood off and grabbed her, she saw the sweat run down his forehead, only to be caught by brows that were angled sharply into a *V*, below which smoldered green eyes glinting with moisture. From worry, she wondered, or from the heat?

"Gods, Dina, what happened? Are you all right?" He took her by the shoulders, then ran a hand across her face, looking for injuries.

"I'm fine. I'm not hurt, really. I was attacked at the mine, but..."

"Attacked! Damn it, Dina! I told you to be careful at the mines." The look of relief that had been on Jon's face changed swiftly, and the soft creases of worry reformed into tight, angry lines. His eyes hardened to emerald shards.

"Jon, listen to me! It was the killer, I'm almost positive. But a man saved me and brought me here."

"What man?"

"His name is Rayn DeStar. He's the *Uz-Dailjan*. He wants to talk to you."

"And I want to talk to him. Which one is he?"

Dina looked at the men and pointed to a figure to the right of the entrance. Though hooded and dressed similarly to the others, she knew it was DeStar. She wasn't sure how she knew, but she did. "That one. At the far right. He wants to talk to you in private." When Jon hesitated, Dina added, "We should be all right. It doesn't seem to be their intention to hurt us." She wished she could believe her own words.

***

Rayn escorted Jon inside to the private chamber before removing his own hood. "Welcome to Sanctuary, Officer. Rayn DeStar, leader of this humble band of strays, at your service." As he had with Dina, DeStar gave an exaggerated bow.

"Specialist Rzije, IIB. Let's dispense with the foolishness, shall we? Tell me what happened at the mine."

"I was near Kewero when I heard the whine of a rez gun."

"What were you doing near the mines?"

"I was on my way from Bhel Kap, one of my supply caverns, to the Albho Road. The way takes me past the mines."

"What happened when you heard the rez?"

Rayn met Jon's eyes with a gaze so steady his eyes didn't blink. "I know Kewero Kel is closed, so I went to see what had happened. I saw a cave-in at the tunnel entrance, then heard a call for help. I used my own gun to open the entrance, got the lady out, and brought her here."

"Did you see anyone else at the mines?"

Rayn was already growing bored with the questions. Time to end this, he thought.

"No, I saw no one." *After you leave here you will know me only as Rayn DeStar, leader of the Dailjan. You will not question my identity beyond that. You will not reveal this location, or my identity, to the Aeternan Enforcement Agency.* "We are a simple people, and mean no harm to anyone." *Dina has nothing to fear from me or my people.* "Agent Marlijn told me about your investigation. We will be happy to cooperate any way we can." *You will allow Dina to come here whenever she wants to come.* DeStar cast each compelling thought to Jon's mind, then, with a small smile, hooked Jon's mind and set the suggestions deep.

"And now, I think it would be a good idea if you got Agent Marlijn back to the city. She might deny it, but I think she's a little shaken up."

Jon blinked and shook his head. He looked at Rayn and extended his hand. "I have no doubt she'll deny it. Thank you for what you did."

DeStar grasped Jon's hand, and one corner of Rayn's mouth lifted higher still. "Come. I'll escort you out."

At the cavern entrance, Jon asked Dina about her skimmer.

"It's still back at the mine."

"Okay. We'll double up 'til we get back there. I want you to show me exactly where this attack happened."

Dina nodded.

Rayn stood next to her, his smile still in place. She could nod to her partner all she wanted, but it would be his bidding she would do. He burned her with his gaze until she reluctantly turned to acknowledge him.

If you want any cooperation from me, you will do as I say. Tell your partner the same story I told him. I heard a rez whine, saw that the tunnel entrance was blocked, and heard your call for help. You will not tell him, or anyone else, what I am.

I won't be dictated to.

Let's just say it will be to your advantage, and your partner's, to do as I say.

Ah, your true colors at last. Blackmail.

Call it what you will, but you will obey me.

Dina didn't reply, just returned a stare as cold and even as DeStar's. She tried to control the torrent of thoughts that sprang to mind, knowing he would be able to pick them up, but it was difficult. A heartbeat passed, and Dina looked back at her partner. "Jon, just get me out of here," she whispered.

Jon pulled his hood back on and reached into one of the cargo compartments for a second hood, handing it to Dina. "Get on, and hold on," Jon said as he mounted the skimmer.

Dina straddled the vehicle quickly, slid her arms gladly around Jon's waist, and tightened her grip as they surged forward. The journey back to the mine was quick, and all the more so as Dina's head spun. She tried not to think about the *dens*, concentrating instead on how good it felt to be holding Jon, her arms locked around his waist and her head against his back. She wished she didn't have the hood on so she could feel him next to her cheek.

Her savior, she thought, but as she did, her thoughts tangled, and as they drew close to the tunnel Dina had escaped from, her contentment at being close to Jon was replaced by unsettling memories of her attack and rescue.

Once at the mine, Jon called Security Chief Hrothi via commband, and before the sun could move in the clock of the sky, countless mining officials and AEA personnel arrived on the scene. They were careful to land their hovercraft away from the tunnel entrance to avoid disturbing any evidence, and within moments, the area was cordoned off. A scanning crew swept the entrance and the interior of the tunnel, but only Dina's discarded hood was found. There was no trace of her commband or utility belt.

Dina sat in the cool interior of the hovercraft and related her story to Hrothi and Corporal Khilioi. Hrothi's heaven-blue eyes seemed to invite trust, but even so, she kept the knowledge that the *Uz-Dailjan* was a *dens* to herself. Her rage at DeStar's parting thoughts still fresh in her mind, she had been tempted to divulge all his secrets, but something held her back. She wanted his cooperation. She certainly wouldn't have it if she betrayed him. She also wanted time to think and a clear mind before she took the step that would most likely mean a dangerous confrontation between a deadly dark outworlder and law enforcement officials.

When asked about the location of the *Dailjan* camp, Dina was vague, citing her dizziness and the sun's high position as reasons for her confusion, and when the trail finder on Jon's skimmer was checked, the data pinpointing Sanctuary was gone.

"No matter," boasted Khilioi. "Our technology is far superior to that of the desert waste. There isn't anyplace they can hide we can't find them. We'll flush them out."

Jon entered the hovercraft and caught the young man's final words. "Corporal, I would prefer you allow us to conduct the investigation," he stated, his mood clearly fouled by the events of the day.

"Of course, Agent Rzije," replied the corporal, his white teeth flashing through his smile.

Jon looked at Dina, and his expression softened. "Time to get you out of here. Are you sure you can ride? I can arrange for another hovercraft."

"I can ride. Let's just go." Impatient now to get back to the city, she forced herself to remain alert and in control on her skimmer.

Jon kept his machine at a prudent but steady speed across the Albho Mar, and Dina could see that his gaze constantly shifted her way. Dear Jon, making sure she was all right.

It was easier now for Dina not to think about what had happened. The sun was still high, and the shadows of the waves of sand, so prevalent and mesmerizing in the early morning light, were gone, replaced by a flat sea of blinding white, above which shimmered waves of heat. It took all her concentration to keep her perspective and to control the machine.

At last they arrived at the Aeternan Visitor Center and parked the skimmers in the storage bay. As soon as Dina shut off the machine, she felt the dizziness return with a vengeance, washing over her. She wondered briefly if she could get off the skimmer, and realized as she fell sideways that the answer was no. The last thing she remembered was being caught in Jon's strong arms before she hit the floor.

SIX
KATHEDRA KAP

It had been only two days since she arrived on his world, and so much had happened. She shuddered as she thought once again how close to death she had been. Dead, but for a *dens*. Propped up on the hospital bed, Dina wriggled to relieve the stiffness and glanced at the clock on the wall. It was late in the afternoon, and she knew she should be spending this time resting, not thinking about all that had happened, but it was hard to stop her mind from replaying the images. Besides, she thought, the dreams hardly allowed her any rest. In the end, she called for a medical assistant to give her something to help her sleep.

When Dina woke later in the evening, thankfully not remembering any dreams, another quick series of tests were run. Finally, satisfied with the tests, Dr. Lumazi released her. Back in her room, Dina cleaned up, then plopped to her bed with a sigh. She still had a lot of thinking to do before talking to Jon, and all of it involved the *dens*.

Dina was sure that DeStar knew what was going on in the desert. He might even know the identity of the killer. The trick would be to pry the information from a man who was a master of mind games. Could she do it? Could she outwit such a creature? It would be dangerous, possibly even deadly. The *dens* hadn't struck her as a brutal man, but she couldn't assume anything. Did she dare do it? If she did, and succeeded, it would make her career.

Her career. Thoughts of Jon stirred. If Jon knew that DeStar was a *dens*, he would never allow her to interview him. More than that, Jon, ever a straight arrow, would probably try to take the dark outworlder into custody. Dina had no doubt that in such a confrontation DeStar would have no compunction against destroying an opponent.

It seemed to Dina that her only choice was to try to con both men. She didn't like it. She had never lied to Jon before. Being truthful was not only part of her professional code of ethics, but part of her personal code as well, and she was closer to Jon than she had ever been to anyone, save her parents.

Yet she couldn't risk Jon's life. Nor did she want to lose a golden opportunity to move the investigation forward, perhaps even solve it. Like it or not, the *dens* was a key she was loathe to let go of.

Her mind was made up, and as soon as she realized that it was, she felt the burden of indecision lift from her. In its place, though, she felt an unseen shadow glide over her. She shivered again, but this time not because of fanciful notions, but because she knew she had made a dangerous pact. She was going to bargain away her integrity to try to keep two men alive, one of whom was but a chameleon-like creature housing thoughts and motives she couldn't even guess at.

Dina took several deep breaths, then checked her appearance in the mirror. She put on a little makeup and tied her hair back at the nape of her neck, allowing a few long strands on either side of her face to escape. She took one last deep breath, then called Jon on the room computer.

"Dina. It's about time, you slacker. Get in here."

As she opened the connecting door and entered Jon's room, Dina resolved to be as truthful with him as she could without betraying DeStar. *I can't believe I'm going to lie to Jon.*

***

Sleep, always an eager caller before this assignment began, deserted her again that night like a spurned lover. Her mind, her most powerful asset, betrayed her, replaying the incident in the tunnel over and over. DeStar had saved her life. She tried to think of something, anything else—his arrogance, his cutting words to her—but her mind returned each time to the tunnel. She remembered how his voice had sounded in her head, first like a caress from the dead, chilling and repulsive, then like an edict from the heavens, compelling her to live.

She owed him her life. A *dens*, damn him! But each time she damned him, she saw him pull off the white hood and saw the molten eyes beneath the arrow point of dark hair. As dawn approached, exhaustion weakened her, and surrender finally dropped her into a troubled sleep. Her last thought had been his parting words to her. *You have nothing I need.*

When she awoke soon after, she felt tired and shaken. She stood in the shower and let the hot water cascade over her, wishing she could as easily flush thoughts of the *dens* out of her mind. But the water soothed her, and she took her time dressing, even allowing extra time to perform an abbreviated version of her favorite relaxation exercise. By the time she met with Jon for their morning meeting, she was confident he would detect nothing amiss in her appearance or expressions. During the meeting, however, Dina caught Jon looking at her several times with his brows drawn together. He said nothing, and Dina chalked it up to concern following yesterday's incident.

Last night she had relayed to Jon more of the details of the mine tour with Hrothi, her ill-fated decision to view the abandoned tunnel, the attack, and her rescue by DeStar. Dina followed DeStar's story that she had called audibly for help, and that DeStar, happening to pass close by, heard her. As she told the tale, it sounded horribly contrived, but Jon had seemed to take no notice, only nodding his head as he sipped his mocava.

Jon had given her the results of the investigation of her attack. No witnesses had been found at the mines, and there had been no surveillance equipment at the abandoned tunnel where the attack occurred. No physical evidence had been found. Jon had made no further mention of DeStar.

As she expected, Jon had berated her, though gently, for ignoring his order not to wander off alone. He had also explained what Chandhel had wanted that was so urgent he'd called Jon away. Mother Lode had decided to move up their date for filing suit against the Synergy. That meant there were ten fewer days than there had been to solve the case. Chandhel had emphasized once again the urgency of the situation, as if Jon wasn't already aware of it.

They now outlined their plans for the day. Jon would continue interviewing the miners, and Dina would again try to talk to the *Uz-Dailjan*. After last night's speech on the dangers of being alone in the desert, Dina had expected strong opposition to her suggestion she try interviewing the *Dailjan* on her own. Surprisingly, Jon argued the point very little and merely cautioned her to be careful and to send him marks via her replacement commband.

Dina still wanted to interview Katzfiel to find out if any AEA personnel had been terminated in the past few months. Even though she knew DeStar was the *Uz-Dailjan*, she was better off knowing from a source other than a *dens* who else might be in the desert. To this, Jon also cautioned her, warning her to tread lightly with the Commander. Before they parted, Jon gently grabbed her arm. She looked up into the warm eyes and again saw the clear look of concern.

"You know I trust your judgment," was all he said.

She smiled, her first of the day, and put her hand on Jon's arm. "I know. Thanks." She wished she could communicate to Jon how much his trust really meant to her, but the simple gesture would have to do.

Back in her room, Dina spent time using relaxation techniques she had learned years ago. Snuggling into a comfortable position on top of the bed, she dimmed the room lights with a quick verbal command, shuttered her eyes and drew five deep breaths, inhaling through her nose and exhaling slowly through her mouth, each puff soft as a blown kiss.

Dina lifted her arms out to her sides until they were parallel to the floor, fists closed, then uncurled her fingers, palms upward. She visualized a glowing orange fireball in the palm of her right hand, a ball that spun in her hand, the rotating force casting tails of yellow and gold to arc around the sphere. The fireball lifted, spinning slowly, and rose, warming her arm, shoulder, and neck. The tiny sun paused at its zenith, directly over her head, and showered rays of heat and light onto her upturned face, to cascade over her cheeks and hair to her shoulders, strengthening her aura. Strung on its invisible arch, the fireball again moved, continuing in its descent over her left shoulder and arm, still bathing her in its radiance, until it settled gently into the cradle of her left palm. Dina yet waited, feeling the heat soak downward through her body until it reached her toes.

The total relaxation of her body and mind generated the alpha and theta waves needed for her performance with Katzfiel.

She raised the light level, called him, and requested a brief meeting. To her surprise, the Commander didn't put her off, but told her that he would be available if she could come to the AEA Center right away. Dina arrived within moments, but found herself waiting for Katzfiel for the better part of an hour. She tried to remain calm while she waited in an anteroom and again practiced her relaxation exercises. Although she was sure the delay was intentional, she told herself she mustn't reply in kind. She knew Katzfiel already had a poor opinion of her, and that yesterday's incident had only served to reinforce that opinion.

Finally, the door opened, and Dina looked up at the sound. She heard a whisper-soft "later, Kaz" float to the doorway. Seconds later, Maris Iridino swept into view, her tall frame almost boneless in its grace. Her short, dark bob was perfect, and a wide smile immediately lit her perfectly made-up face.

"Agent Marlijn. How nice to see you again. I heard what happened to you. How are you doing?"

Dina wondered if Maris was concerned about her health or the investigation. "Fine, thank you, Miss Iridino."

"I'm glad. Call me Maris, please. Oh, the Commander should be with you shortly. I have to run. I'm sure I'll see you again."

Maris glided from the room, still smiling. Dina wondered what business Maris had with Katzfiel. Chandhel and Katzfiel hadn't seemed to like each other much. Perhaps Maris was a go-between.

When the Commander finally instructed her to enter his office, he made no apology for keeping her waiting, but pointedly glanced at a large time display on the wall.

"Well, Miss, I have about five minutes. What is so important it couldn't wait?"

"Thank you for seeing me on such short notice, Commander. I just have a couple questions. Can you tell me if any of your AEA personnel have been terminated or have resigned in the past year?"

Katzfiel frowned, and the harsh face took on an even more unpleasant appearance.

"Now why would you ask that?"

"In viewing the files on the interviews the AEA made of known *Dailjan* members, it occurred to me that the *Dailjan* seem to know a great deal about how the AEA operates. I was wondering if it were possible there are any former AEA members among the *Dailjan*." Dina hadn't intended to be quite so candid, but, as had happened with DeStar, her diplomatic skills failed her. She found it impossible to completely ignore the resentment she felt at Katzfiel's obvious slights.

The Commander didn't reply at once, but sat staring at Dina. The beady black pupils seemed to vibrate against the silver irises. A person of lesser strength would have wilted under such scrutiny, but Dina went on the offensive and took the opportunity to quickly probe the man. It was apparent from her probe that Katzfiel felt insulted that Dina would imply that any AEA members, former or otherwise, would degrade themselves by associating with the desert garbage. She also picked up the dislike and disdain he felt for her. No surprises there.

"No. Since no one for quite some time has been allowed to leave Exodus, it would be an obvious breach of security to terminate someone at this point, knowing they would have the run of the colony afterward. Any changes in personnel will be done after this investigation is completed."

"'Keep your enemies closer than your friends,' Commander? What about the reverse? Have any new AEA members been hired in the last year?" Dina asked, realizing she was already disobeying Jon's order to "tread lightly."

Katzfiel took his time in answering. "No. All my people have been with me longer than that," he replied at last, glancing again at the time display.

Dina took the not-so-subtle hint. "I won't take up any more of your time. Thank you, Commander."

"Miss Marlijn, let me be blunt."

Dina had to force herself not to laugh. Varying degrees of bluntness seemed all that the Commander knew.

"I'm disturbed by what I've observed the past two days. Poor judgment and questionable reasoning are not what I expected from the IIB, and they will not be tolerated by this agency or by Aeternan Administration. I hope you understand the gravity of the situation. I can only hope Agent Rzije is pursuing more productive lines of inquiry. Good day to you."

"Commander, to do my job properly, I need as much information as possible. If you feel I have offended you by asking the questions I did, understand that was not my intention. I will not hesitate to question anyone on this colony about anything I feel is relevant to this investigation, and in doing so, I expect complete cooperation. Good day, sir, to you." Well, she had done it again. But she'd be damned if she'd apologize to this bastard.

Katzfiel's impassive face had flushed to an angry shade of purple, but Dina barely saw it as she turned and made her own way out of his office. She didn't much care what he thought of her, but she knew this would get back to Jon, and the thought of Jon's disapproval worried her.

Back at the Visitor Center, Dina forced herself to relax and forget about Katzfiel. She closed her eyes and concentrated on her breathing, inhaling deeply and exhaling slowly, until in her mind she saw the long road, stretching endlessly in either direction, and the expanse of golden field that filled her view as far as she could see. After a final deep breath, eyes still closed, she projected as forcefully as she could. *DeStar. I need to see you.*

A moment passed with no response, and Dina began to despair. She hadn't considered the possibility that he wouldn't answer her at all. Had she angered him that much? She tried to remain optimistic. Maybe it was simply that she hadn't projected so he could hear her. After all, she wasn't used to contacting other telepaths. She took another deep breath, stood on the Road of Time, and tried again. *DeStar.*

I heard you the first time. What do you want?

The reply that sounded in her head was so cold that icy shivers raised goosebumps on her arms. Several thoughts, none of them complimentary to DeStar, rushed forward, but she halted them before they could form. She couldn't afford to anger him again. *I would like to meet with you again. It's important.*

Important to you, not to me.

What I have to tell you could very well be important to you and your people. Besides, I never thanked you properly for yesterday.

'Thank yous' and 'I'm sorrys' are meaningless words and are foreign to my world. You merely took advantage of an enemy to survive. I respect that. In turn, I'm sure I would never be able to convince you that my motives were any less selfish. So let's leave it at that. I told you before, you have nothing I need.

He caught her off guard with that. There was too much truth in his statement for her to deny it. She had accepted help from a *dens*, a creature she normally wouldn't give the time of day. What could she say now? How could she reach him? She could, of course, threaten force. She was sure that the AEA could make short work of the *Dailjan*, but she really didn't think DeStar would respond well to a threat of force. No, she would just have to continue pouring the honey.

'Thank yous' may not be important to you, but they are to me. I believe you're an honorable man. Show that you are, and meet with me.

I hardly think these platitudes are any more important to you than they are to me. What do you really want of me?

She felt her temple start to throb with pressure, but she couldn't give up now. She replayed his initial response in her mind, and latched on to one word. Enemy.

Perhaps what you say is true. But enemy? I don't even know you.

No, you don't. But you're a Glacian, and I'm a B'haratan. We are born enemies, no? And even if we were not, I'm an outlaw. That alone puts us on opposite sides of the table, does it not?

What he said was true. How could she argue it? Yet, she had to. She frantically cast around for the right words. *I'm the one willing to talk. You aren't. If anyone is assigning labels here, it's you.*

Really? I hardly think you're either willing or wanting to put aside our differences. Your thoughts are showing definite signs of stress. Perhaps it is the strain of telling such lies. I ask again, what do you really want?

Dina felt her patience vanish like spit in the sand of the Exodan desert. *I thought charm was second nature to the dens. How is it you're so lacking in it?*

Another one of your many misconceptions about us, I'm afraid. But I'll make a deal with you. Tell me one honest statement—if you can—and I'll agree to meet with you.

All the nasty thoughts Dina was keeping reined in surged forward. *You're an arrogant, manipulative son-of-a-bitch, and I would rather choke on the dust of this damn planet than ask you for anything, but the fact is that I need your cooperation for my investigation.*

That's more like it. If you had said that to begin with we could have dispensed with all this foolishness. But then again, I would have missed out on your very entertaining performance.

Dina steamed at the laughter she heard in his Voice. *I can see why you keep the company of outlaws, deserters, and illegals. Who else would put up with such conceit?*

Insult me all you wish, but take a care when you speak of my comrades. Each one of them is worth a shipload of your kind.

Dina didn't have to feel the flatness in his Voice to know she had gone too far. But how else could any rational person respond to such contempt? She was a professional, trying to do a job, and he had made her feel like an idiot. *You may not accept apologies, but I apologize to your friends. Now, will you meet with me?*

Very well. Meet me in an hour at these coordinates, 42.3d west of Aeternus, 6.8d south. I trust you can find your way?

I'll be there, don't worry.

Until then.

His parting two words slithered through her mind, a mockery of an endearment. For the second time in two days, Dina fumed. He obviously felt nothing but disdain for her, and like Commander Katzfiel, saw her not as a highly trained professional, but as a silly female. Except that DeStar was worse.

The *dens* looked upon her as someone that he could amuse himself with. What angered Dina the most was that he had made her lose her temper. She had always prided herself on her ability to talk to people of different races, cultures, and worlds. And he, in a matter of seconds, had provoked her to profanity and name-calling. But then again, Dina hadn't anticipated encountering a *dens* on this planet.

***

From the beginning Rayn had had every intention of meeting with her again, but she had indeed angered him, and it had amused him to see how far she would go with her act of beseechment and humility. He knew her true feelings were far from her honeyed words. He smiled to himself as he thought how badly she must need him to suffer such an act, and laughed even more when he remembered her angry words. That was more like Little Miss Summer Lightning. If it meant honesty, he would suffer the prejudice. Rayn had once admired honesty above all else.

***

She checked her supplies in the storage compartment of her skimmer, pulled on her hood, mounted the vehicle, and made her way once more into the desert. She programmed the coordinates DeStar had given her into her finder and followed the now familiar Albho Road westward.

As before, she had to concentrate in order to prevent the soporific waves of shadow from giving her "desert hypnosis." She pushed her skimmer beyond the end of the Albho Road and skirted the mines south of Sawel Kel, happy to put the siren sea of white with its mesmerizing shadow dance behind her. The low mountains of the Wiara Gwer loomed before her like giant beasts sleeping in the midday heat.

She slowed her skimmer and frowned, studying the finder. To reach the coordinates Rayn gave her, she would have to cross the Wiara to the heart of the Chayne. As she approached the first windswept dune, she saw that the Wiara was not a single mountainous range, but a series of twisting mounds and valleys. She wove the skimmer back and forth through the shallow canyons until the appearance of higher, rockier formations announced her ingress into the Chayne Gwer.

The red dot of her skimmer's trail finder changed from a

steady glow to a pulse, confirming her arrival, but she saw nothing but numerous gray granite tors, ancient sentinels of the desert, now bent with age and silent with sleep. She was well beyond the mines, but by her reckoning, not as deep into the mountains as Sanctuary was. Dina looked at her trail finder one more time, then at her commband. The time and coordinates were correct, but there was nothing here.

She looked around her, at the ashen rock figures, the white sunlight, and the gray dust that whirled in tiny eyes around her like rings of smoke. She studied the shy, midday shadow that she and the skimmer made. What a lonely place, she thought.

Places aren't lonely, only people.

Dina looked up. A man on a skimmer cruised toward her from the west. The man wore a weather suit with a full hood, but Dina knew it was Rayn. The white hawk hood was the same one he had worn when she first met him, but more than that was his Voice. As always, it was unmistakable. Rayn slid his skimmer to a casual halt, dismounted, and strolled up to her as if he had all day. Soft, heather suede boots reached to just below his knees, the long fringes at the cuffs sashaying in counterpoint to his easy strides. "Follow me."

Dina dismounted and followed the man to where a rocky overhang provided shade. Two rocks in the shade served as seats. She wondered if the formation was natural or man-made.

"Natural, believe it or not." Rayn pulled two bottles from behind the rocks, opened one, and sat down. He held the second out to her. "Here."

"I have my own. What is this place?"

"Save your water. Skimmers have been known to break down in the desert. This is Kathedra Kap."

"Mine is cold."

"Suit yourself, but take one of these to replace your own."

There was no point in arguing further. Dina palmed the nose of plastic offered by his outstretched hand, returned to her skimmer, deposited the bottle he had given her, and pulled out one of her own. She returned to the overhang.

Rayn nodded toward the smooth rock next to him. "Have a seat. The stone's cool."

Dina stared at the stone bench and then at the mirrored mask-eyes. "I'll stand."

He laughed, and the muffled sound gave her chills in spite of the heat.

"If you're afraid of me, perhaps you shouldn't have come."

She squirmed out of her hood and jacket, already sticky with sweat, and opened her bottle. She shook her head to loosen the strands of hair plastered to her face, tilted her chin, and swigged the cool water. Taking a deep breath, she dropped her gaze and eyed Rayn. "Fear has nothing to do with it."

He tugged at his hood, quickly freeing the long hair that clung to the sides of his face in damp ribbons, and when their gazes locked, neither spoke.

Sit.

Dina blinked, and almost as though the heat had dizzied her, sagged to the bench next to Rayn. She thought it was the tawny eyes that held her in thrall and tried to look away. Why was she rational except when she looked into those eyes?

A sly smile flirted with the corners of Rayn's mouth, and he turned away with a low chuckle.

She frowned. "Are none of my thoughts safe from you?"

"Don't raise your hackles. I'm not probing you. But your thoughts are so...surface, so transparent, it's as if you're talking to me. I can't help hearing them."

"You have me at a distinct disadvantage. I blamed myself for losing my temper with you, but I see it would be impossible to win any sparring match with you."

"You're not a *dens*, but you're clearly gifted. A novice, is all. That doesn't mean you can't sharpen your skills."

"So *I* can be an arrogant..."

"...manipulative, son-of-a-bitch like me," he finished. "Right."

"No thanks. You and I have nothing in common, and I prefer to keep it that way."

One side of Rayn's mouth pulled down, and he leaned toward her to shrug off his jacket.

"We have more in common than you think," he breathed, almost in her ear. He had nothing on under the jacket except a cooling vest. The loose web of fibers snared her gaze and did nothing to hide the tanned skin, the hard, lean muscles of his torso, or the dark hair that glistened with trapped beads of sweat.

In spite of the vest, heat radiated from the man's body in a wave that assaulted every one of Dina's senses. She could almost taste his scent on her tongue, cool and hot at the same time. She shook her head. No, she had nothing in common with this animal.

"Hardly." Why was she sitting so close to him?

The smile flicked again. "All right. Let's find some common ground. Let's agree for now that I'm a dangerous, good-for-nothing, reprehensible creature so we can move on to other topics. Why did you want to see me...so badly? And the truth this time, please."

"That, you surely must know. You seem to know everything else."

Rayn gave her an impatient look that said "enough of this."

Dina sighed and relented. "All right. You know that in the past seven months eight miners have been killed." Dina paused, and when Rayn nodded, she continued. "The local officials haven't been able to learn the killer's identity. My partner and I were asked here to further the investigation." She hesitated again, and drew a deep breath. "I believe there isn't anything that happens in this desert that you're not aware of. I need any information you have regarding these killings. There's no reason to believe that the killer will stop, unless he's caught."

Rayn's eyes seemed to bore into her, and for a moment, he said nothing. His features displayed no emotions, but the intense gaze and slight muscle twitch in his jaw spoiled the mask of total impassivity. The muscle twitch was an involuntary movement Dina had noticed numerous times in Jon's face. *When he's upset*, she thought.

When Rayn replied at last, his voice was bland. "I don't know who the killer is. The only thing I can tell you with absolute certainty is that the killer is not one of my people."

Damn! "I can't believe that there isn't something you know. You have a very efficient and organized band of men and women. Practically an eye and ear behind every rock. Something that might even have seemed insignificant to you may help me."

"I can't tell you what I don't know. I think you overestimate my powers just a little."

Dina gave her head a single shake, sending her hair flying over her left shoulder. "What? The all-knowing *dens* telling me that *I* have overestimated his powers? I don't think so. You wanted the truth so badly, why don't you give it yourself?"

"I realize you believe I'm lying, but in fact the killer has confined his deeds to the mines. I haven't seen anything, and none of my people have reported anything. It's true that a few ex-miners have joined the *Dailjan*, but they're simple men, frightened by what happened, and seeking only a safe existence. I probe everyone who joins the *Dailjan*. If the killer were here, or if anyone had any information about the killer, I would be aware of it, believe me."

Dina took a quick, deep breath and looked away in frustration. "It doesn't make any sense." She looked back at Rayn. "Would you allow me to interview those ex-miners?"

"I'd have to discuss it with my men. They weren't happy yesterday to have the law inside Sanctuary."

"It would just be me. Not Rzije, not the AEA." Dina paused. "DeStar, will you help me?" Her words surprised herself.

"Somehow, I don't think you mean help you with the questioning of the ex-miners."

She hesitated again. What was she doing? It was as if someone else were speaking the words.

"Ah...no. I mean, will you help me with the investigation? With your knowledge of the desert, and your...abilities, you could be invaluable to me."

He appeared to study her. "Ten minutes ago you said you would rather...what was it? 'Choke on the dust of this planet' than ask me for anything. Now you not only have questions, you want my help. And yet, I sense your request is sincere. What changed your mind?"

She kept her eyes on him and didn't reply, mostly because she didn't have an answer, but partly, she had to admit, because he fascinated her. She told herself it was because she had never

seen a *dens* before. She took in the full mouth, then followed
the clean, angled lines of his jaw to where the exodite stud
flashed at his ear. Below the cheekbones, shadows delineated
the smooth planes of his face. How could a *dens* look like this?
He was so different from any of the likenesses she had ever
seen of them. Not exactly handsome in the same way Jon was,
Rayn nevertheless possessed an irresistible quality she couldn't
quite understand.

Dina sucked in a quick, deep breath that caught in her throat.
The matter at hand, girl! The investigation, of course. She had
to do everything and anything to further the investigation. But
somehow she sensed that there was something more, but
something she couldn't, or wasn't prepared to, put into words.
She felt confused, and it scared her. Her mind had always been
so clear. But not now. She wondered if the *dens* was playing
with her mind. Damn him! How was she ever to know?

"I'm sure you know the answer to that better than I do."
Her answer left a sour taste in her mouth.

Rayn did understand it better than she did. It was his power.
His helping her was not a suggestion he had planted in her
mind. Even so, his power had influenced her. It seduced people,
even the strong-willed and clear thinkers. And while his plan
of seduction had originally involved a sexual conquest, nothing
more, he had to admit to the pleasure he felt at her unsolicited
request. He had given her but a tiny taste of his mastery of the
mind, and already she wanted more. *And you will keep coming
back for more, little girl, no matter what your feelings for me
are.*

"Give me a day to think about your request. Call for me
tomorrow."

"One day. No more." She pulled on her jacket. "By the
way, when I called you earlier today, was I projecting enough?
I wasn't sure if you could hear me."

"You were, in fact, shouting. But you're forcing it. You're
using your conscious mind too much. Back off on the ego and
try to let your instincts take over."

"I'm not sure I know how to do that."

"Just don't try so hard. Your powers, as I said, are strong, but your techniques need mastering."

She hesitated and looked down at the hood in her hand, as if examining it.

Rayn sighed. Too easily he picked up her thoughts. She didn't want to learn anything from a beast. Well, she needed mastering. In more ways than one.

"I'll think about that, too. I'll give you my answer tomorrow."

She scrunched the hood. "I suppose I should thank you for seeing me," she said dryly.

"Here. You'll damage the oxygen feed." Rayn stepped closer to her, untangled the headgear from her grasp, and standing close enough to feel her heartbeat, raised his arms over her head to position the hood. "Don't thank me," he whispered, his hands frozen above her. His eyes held hers for a brief moment. "You'll soon be cursing my very existence. Believe me." He eased her hood on, his hands gliding over her shoulders before she shook him off and ran to her skimmer.

***

Rayn was troubled that night, more troubled than he had been in a long time. All he could think about was the lightning storm named Dina Marlijn. *Honesty,* he thought bitterly. He had demanded it of her, but it was the last thing he could give of himself. She had truly caught him off guard today. He wanted her—that hadn't changed—and his hunger for her submission was keener than ever, but he had been totally unprepared for her request for help. The rules of the game would have to be changed.

He had no doubt she would play her part. As strong and independent as she was, she would come to him, investigation or no investigation. His power would lure her, power that even held in check would draw her like an animal to a waterhole. Her instinctive need to connect with him, as much as she would try to fight it, would override all else, even to the point of destruction. She would willingly risk her identity, her pride, even her career, everything she was and everything she had. She, with her request for help, had significantly upped the ante.

He had been primed for a quick liaison in the desert, not

for destroying her. Not that he wasn't capable of it.

He stood by one of the entrances to Sanctuary. This was normally his favorite time of day, as the low sun turned the seemingly colorless desert into a shifting kaleidoscope of blues, purples, burgundies, and gold. He turned toward the east, away from the sun, but tonight his eyes didn't even notice the bands of aqua, shell pink, and blue that melted into each other above the horizon.

He turned back to the west as the sun eased itself into the cradle of the hills and snuggled into their depths. The desert glowed with *merkwia*, the brief twilight of Exodus, and for a moment a halo of lemon yellow crowned the far-off mountains of the western Chayne. Above the yellow the sky gleamed a phosphorescent green, and higher still, the clear blue sky was already deepening to its shade of night. Rayn saw none of it.

The private, well-hidden entrance was one only he and a few well chosen comrades knew about. Even distracted, he sensed Alessane gliding up the corridor behind him. He felt her full breasts against his back as she pressed herself to him and slid her arms around him. "Star...you haven't eaten. What's wrong?"

For someone with no telepathic ability, Alessane was surprisingly intuitive. He thought for a moment how to answer her. He didn't like to lie to those close to him, and he mused that it probably wouldn't do any good anyway. Alee would know soon enough, if she didn't already, that their unusual female visitor was the cause of his moodiness. He was saved from having to answer as Alee did it for him.

"It's the woman, isn't it?"

Rayn lowered his head and placed his hand over hers, squeezing it gently.

"What do you see in her? She's ill-mannered and skinny. You saved her life, and all she did was insult you."

Rayn smiled. "Alee...eavesdropping at your listening post again?" He knew it was a habit Alee had, and Rayn could never bring himself to scold her too harshly.

"I was curious."

"I'll bet you were. Well, you don't have to worry. I don't

think I'll be seeing her again."

Alee laughed, and her laughter was gentle and soothing to his ears, like distant wind chimes caught in a soft breeze. "Star, for someone as knowing and intelligent as you are, you say some stupid things."

She sighed and released her hold on Rayn. Without another word, Alee padded softly back down the corridor.

Damn. Rayn opened his eyes, and the faces of the rocks were dark.

SEVEN
THE HOT TOUCH

Dina.

She was in her room, tired, but unable to sleep. The single word, as always, was liquid in her mind, trickling downward in a runnel that gave her chills. This time, though, the chills ran deeper, triggering sensations that seeped into her very core. She was annoyed by the uncontrollable feelings. She fought for control in every aspect of her life, and this was a battle she didn't want to lose. But she couldn't deny the arousal his Voice stirred. Above all, though, he surprised her. She hadn't expected an answer this quickly.

Yes, DeStar. She instinctively started to turn to the west, toward the Voice.

I cannot help you.

Her head froze in mid-turn, and her parted lips widened. This was not the response she had expected. The anticipation she had felt at hearing his Voice evaporated like steam, and her anger, always close at hand where Rayn was concerned, roiled up. *You mean won't.*

As you wish.

Why not?

To be close to me is too dangerous. As I have no knowledge to impart to you regarding your killings, there's no reason to risk that danger.

I'm willing to risk it.

But I'm not.

She had to think quickly. She couldn't let him end things this way. She had to see him again, had to convince him somehow to help her. What would change his mind? What could she appeal to?

DeStar, let's at least discuss this face-to-face, tomorrow.

No. The matter is closed.

Rayn... She used his given name without even realizing it. She waited, but there was no response. *DeStar, I know you can hear me. I won't give up on this. I'll keep calling you day and night until you answer me and agree to see me. Rayn...*

This has to work, she thought. She waited a moment, then called again. *Rayn.*

Meet me tomorrow at Kathedra Kap, same time.

This time she shivered at the hollowness of his voice.

***

Dina arrived the following day at Kathedra and chose to wait in the shadow cast by a crooked tor. She shaded her eyes and studied the harsh curves of the windswept formation. This was not a good idea. She laughed underneath her hood. That had to be the understatement of her career. It was not only not a good idea, it was foolhardy and downright dangerous. It wasn't like her to be reckless. What was she doing alone in the desert seeking help from a *dens*? She shook her head.

Rayn had almost certainly already lied to her. Everyone lies to the law. All the time. Even those with nothing to hide. It was a given that all law enforcement officers dealt with. Even if it wasn't, a *dens* would be the last person to tell her the truth.

Yet she had come. She had to try. The man was a passkey to all that went on in the desert, and she, with her ability, was the only one who could turn him. DeStar would never cooperate with Jon, and as for the AEA...She laughed again. They weren't even aware of the existence of the *dens*. They would never be able to successfully negotiate with him. Negotiate. That's what she would have to do. She would have to find something the *dens* wanted, and then she would have to make him believe she could provide it for him.

A rogue thought broke away from her stream of consciousness. Would she still be here even if there were no investigation? She didn't want to think about that. She didn't want to think about the allure his eyes and voice held, a temptation that was undeniable even if the man hadn't had the power to compel.

There was an investigation. Moreover, she couldn't rule him out as a suspect. Could this man have murdered the miners? She had run his name through her computer, and as expected, had turned up nothing. She had to try to find out more about him, had to try to elicit his cooperation. She waited and watched the sunlight sparkle off the mica chips embedded in the granite.

He'd come. He needed this as much as she did. Being late was just his way of exerting control. She shifted her seat on the skimmer and pulled on parts of her weather suit. In spite of the shade and her cooling vest, portions of the tunic jacket were sticking to the sweat on her body. *Krek.*

Come, now. Is that any way to greet someone whose help you profess to so badly need?

Damn! She turned around slowly and focused her gaze on the place she knew him to be. First she didn't see him, hidden in the shadows as he was, but she kept staring until he stepped forward into the light. She removed her hood, preferring to look at him eye to eye.

Rayn walked toward her with a slow, easy gait and followed her into the shade. He ran a hand through his dark hair, but it fell stubbornly back into his face as it always did. He finally looked at her, but said nothing, waiting. His eyes were narrowed to golden sparks, and Dina noticed deep creases between the thick brows. No smile curved the sensuous mouth, not even one of arrogant amusement.

Why did he have to be this way? Well, two could play. Her mental guards were raised, but she wondered if they were of any use against a *dens*. Her guards, her psychic shield, was nothing more than the programming of her own mind, reinforced by practice over the years. Her shield had served her well, but she had never tested it against a creature of this power. She simply didn't know if she'd be able to protect herself from unwanted energy of the magnitude a *dens* could generate.

"Thank you for meeting me," she said in her most professional tone.

"Let's not go through this again. Why did you insist on seeing me?" he asked, without preamble.

"Why? You know why."

"I told you I can't help you. And you obviously think of me as little higher than an slug on the evolutionary scale. That doesn't leave much, except curiosity. The non-*dens* are always curious."

His stubbornness was aggravating, but as an enforcement

agent, she was used to dealing with aggravating humans. Except that she didn't know how human he was. "I'm curious, but that's not why I wanted to see you, and you know it."

"Forgive me. Yes, I do know why you sent for me. Because I can touch you in a way no one else can." One brow hitched upwards, as if his own words surprised him.

Dina was surprised as well. Honesty was the last thing she expected from a *dens*. She didn't try to deny his statement. "And you? Why did you come? At our first meeting you told me I have nothing you need." She wondered how truthfully he'd answer this time.

He cast his gaze away from her face and ran his hand through his hair again. His eyes studied the knurled, ashen rock behind her, then flicked back to her. "I have my reasons."

So much for honesty, she thought, with renewed bitterness.

"So you want the truth? Tell me, whose truth do you want, yours or mine?" Rayn's expression hardened, and his eyes seem to glitter. "You see me as a creature driven by the need to control, possessing powers the extent of which you can't understand and have no defense against. Therefore I'm nothing but a calculating beast to you, capable of committing any and all crimes, including murder and mayhem. That's the truth as you see it. Am I right?"

The venom in Rayn's tirade caught Dina off guard, but its content was surprisingly close to her true feelings for the *dens*. So close she couldn't bring herself to deny it. "Yes, you're right. But it's not just my truth. Your description of the *dens* has been borne out in documented events time and time again."

"'Documented events.' Tell me, does so much hate and distrust on your part stem from your reading or viewing of 'documented events?'"

"No, of course not. Any feelings I have regarding the *dens* stem from personal experiences."

"Ah, I see. Then that, of course, justifies your feelings. Aside from myself, have you ever even met a *dens*?"

Gods, but he was aggravating. "No." She bent down and picked up a small black, metallic rock. "But I don't have to stand in a meteorite shower to know where this came from."

"Answer one question. If it's 'no,' then you and I can both get on our skimmers and go our respective ways, with no reason to ever see each other again. Are you willing to learn 'truth' from another point of view? Mine?"

Her eyes locked with his as she contemplated her answer. The gold sparks became molten, trapping her, holding her, as if, in letting go, she would be carried on a current to a place she had never been. She shuddered and looked away, afraid his eyes could compel her even if his mind didn't.

She considered his words. Gone was the cool facade he had shown her inside Sanctuary. The passion in his voice now betrayed a deep need. *Good*, she thought. He wanted something from her. She knew it. Dina knew what she wanted. Perhaps a bargain could be struck after all. She swung her eyes back to his.

"'Truth.' Don't make me laugh. You didn't meet me here to be understood. I say again, *dens*, what do you want of me? Why did you come here?"

Rayn laughed, and the echo that rebounded off the rocks seemed to mock her. "You are afraid of me. Don't deny it again."

"And what would I be afraid of?"

"Touching my mind." The mouth, as quickly as it had exploded in laughter, settled back into a sensuous curve.

"For me to touch your mind would be sheer stupidity. Common sense is not fear."

"Then we are at an impasse, are we not? As I said, we have no reason to continue this meeting." He took a step away from her, as if to leave.

She couldn't let him go. Not without getting what she wanted. "Yes, we do. You can answer the damn question. What do you want?"

"I want you in my head." The sound of his voice was more a purr than words.

She could feel her own blood. It raced through her body, thundering in her ears, flushing her skin. "No."

"That's the deal. Take it or not."

"What will you do for me in return?"

"I'll cooperate with your investigation. I'll give you access to Sanctuary and to my men for questioning."

The reality of his 'deal' slapped at her. She took two steps backward and felt the smooth, wind-ravaged rock press against her back. She hadn't anticipated this. *Inside the mind of a dens.* She had been lying when she told him she wasn't afraid. Could he sense her fear? Surely he must, as fear was the most easily detected of all emotions.

"Well?" A small smile tugged at a corner of his mouth.

The bastard was enjoying her discomfort. Hell, he was probably getting high off her fear. She wouldn't back down. She wouldn't go running back to Aeternus with her tail between her legs. If she did, she would have gained nothing but humiliation.

"How do I know you won't try to compel me or destroy part of my mind?"

"You don't."

"You sure know how to sweeten a deal," she said, a mock smile on her lips.

He arched his brows. The gesture widened his eyes, making them appear warm and harmless, and his smile grew to match the openness of his gaze. *The experience will be sweet enough.*

She closed her eyes and shivered. A dark part of her soul found the Voice seductive, and an equally dark part of her consciousness yearned to touch the mind that could generate such a Voice. She had to do it. She had no choice if she were to get what she wanted.

"All right. But in return, you let me interview the ex-miners in your band. You give me access to Sanctuary, and you give me the cooperation I ask for. And if you do anything to mess with my mind, so help me, I'll find a way to bring you down."

"Agreed," he said mildly. He paused, his features relaxing a little. "Tell me exactly to what degree your ability extends. Tell me also if you've ever...interacted with anyone else who has the ability—not a *dens,* I know, but perhaps another telepath."

She took a deep breath. This was something she simply hadn't discussed before. "I've probed minds, never deeply, just enough to pick up thoughts...well, emotions really, that are close to the surface. I've never interacted with another telepath, have never received anyone else until I heard you in the mine."

He raised one eyebrow. After a moment he replied. "Come. There's more to Kathedra Kap than I've shown you." Rayn circled the outcropping and led the way to a good sized cavern, its entrance cleverly hidden by the shade of a large overhang.

Inside, Rayn removed his tunic, again revealing a cooling vest over his otherwise bare chest. His tanned skin stood out in sharp contrast to the white diamond pattern of the vest, and Dina could see curls of silky dark chest hair both above and below the front edges of the vest. Snug fitting trousers were tucked into the soft heather boots.

Dina felt the wash of heat to her already sun-warmed face as her body reacted to the physical attraction her mind had been trying to deny since her first meeting with Rayn. She was thankful for the disguising spots of sunburn on her cheeks and nose, and just as quickly despaired, realizing the futility of hiding anything from this creature, even traitorous thoughts that she buried as deep as she could.

As Dina stripped off her outer weather suit as well, Rayn went to the back of the cave where several cooler units were recessed into the floor and returned with packaged cleansers and drinking water. He tossed her several of the packets and handed her a large bottle of water.

This is dangerous, she said to herself over and over. She knew she should simply get up, put her suit back on, and leave. It would be the smart thing to do. But even as she told herself there was still time to escape, she picked up one of the packets and tore it open.

Her thoughts were directing her to put a stop to this, but her body seemed strangely detached, as if it had a mind of its own, and she mirrored Rayn's motions of rubbing the cold cleansing cloths over her exposed skin. The cloths, with their scented cleansers, removed the stickiness from her body and refreshed her with the clean fragrance of mint, but she still felt as hot as when she had been sitting outside the kap. Pulls of the cold water quenched her thirst, but did little to cool her.

"Sit here," he commanded, motioning to the cushions

against one wall. Dina obeyed, her heart pounding. Time was running out. She occupied herself with adjusting the cushion just so, and making herself as comfortable as possible. Rayn sat next to her, facing her. He looked at her and waited until she met his gaze. Time was up.

"Lesson number one. To be close to me is very dangerous."

As hot as she was, a tiny shiver bit the back of her neck and skittered down her spine, like a newly hatched creature. Born of fear, or something else? Was he probing her mind, or merely picking up her thoughts? She had not felt his mind touch hers. "I know that."

She was close enough to him to inhale the cool mint of the cleansing cloths he had just used, and she realized the sharp fragrance was the scent she had detected during their previous meetings. Cool mint mingled with hot male flesh. It was as intoxicating as sweet mocava laced with Cygian brandy.

"No, you don't. You don't know what I'm capable of. I could burn you in less than a minute without even touching you physically."

"Burn?"

One corner of his mouth cocked, almost imperceptibly. "That's what we call it. It can happen on either the sending or receiving end. You've probably never probed anyone deeply enough to experience it. The mildest is a kind of sensory or emotional overload and produces involuntary physical responses, no permanent damage. More severe burns can cause loss of memory, insanity, a catatonic state, or death. Those more experienced aren't as susceptible to burn because they've learned how to handle the feedback. You, as a novice, would burn very quickly. If you were smart, you'd put your weather suit back on and leave now."

"Are you trying to scare me, or just trying to absolve yourself of any responsibility if I'm injured?"

"I take full responsibility for whatever happens. I just want you to be aware of all the possibilities, good and bad."

"A *dens* taking responsibility. That's good. All right. I understand that this is everything I've been trained to avoid, but you saved my life. I suppose it wouldn't make sense to hurt me now."

The corners of his mouth lifted in a wry smile, noticeable this time. "Are you saying you trust me?"

"Hardly. Get on with it."

"It's a beginning, but you are going to have to trust me enough to obey my commands." It was an order, not a question.

Annoyed, she nodded nevertheless. "Tell me what you want me to do."

"First, there's one more danger, perhaps the greatest of all, that I should warn you about. Thus far, with the exception of the two of us in the mine when you were trapped, all you've experienced is the cold touch. One-way communication. The hot touch, two-way communication, done with the wrong partner can be a horrible experience. It's like an invasion, a kind of rape. The hot touch done with the right partner, on the other hand, is supreme ecstasy, for there's no more intimate experience in the galaxy."

He paused and closed his eyes.

She drew a ragged breath, and tried not to think about the ache that had been building since he sat down next to her.

His eyes opened and speared hers. "I'm not quite so arrogant to believe I would be such a partner for you, given your distaste for me, but it's something to be aware of. The hot touch, with the right partner, can create a bond which is nearly impossible to break, and if broken, has devastating consequences. As I'm here illegally and you'll be leaving as soon as your investigation is complete, our chances..."

"Never mind the rest. I'm not about to bond with a *dens*. Can we just do this?"

He reached out a hand to her face, but she reared back.

His fingers froze, but he didn't pull back from her. "You're going to have to let me touch you. The physical contact makes the mental connection easier for novices."

She glared at him, but eased her head back toward him. His fingers moved again, lightly tracing the frame of her face until his fingertips rested at her temple. Dina shivered at the light touch but didn't move.

"You'll have to touch my face as well," he breathed.

She raised her right hand and skated the tips of her fingernails along his cheek.

"Touch me, Dina."

She tilted her hand, the palm as well as the pads of her fingertips pressing against his skin. The physical reaction was immediate. She tried to jerk her hand away, but he whipped his free hand up and held it over hers, preventing her retreat.

It was like nothing she had ever felt. His skin was hot, and yet she felt a cool breeze flow over her hand and along her arm, a breeze that carried cool blue sparks with it. The sparks landed on her and pricked her with a taunting heat that was almost painful. A chill ran through her, but at the same time, she felt warm, about to break out in a sweat.

Her hand twitched under his, sudden fear like a lit match in her palm, ready to burn her.

Trust me. Gently he wrapped her hand in his and brought it to his temple, forcing her palm back against his skin. *Relax.*

The tension in her body eased as she obeyed the gentle, compelling command, and she realized what she was feeling. His aura. She had never felt an aura like his before. Her own had always been nothing more than visualization. Power that could produce an aura detectable by the senses generated fear, but her fear was held in abeyance by his will. The ache that started forming deep inside her intensified, and it was all she could do to keep from shaking. What was happening to her? She hadn't even started probing him yet.

"You can feel me, can't you?" His question was a feather, borne to her on the cool blue wind. He released her hand, and this time her trembling fingers stayed put.

She knew what he meant, and there was no point in denying it. It was all she could do to nod.

"I'm impressed. Not many can, even this near to me. You know what it is." The statement was soft, but there was no hint of a question.

A tiny nod was again her reply. The blue lights, like cool fireflies, skimmed over her skin, not biting now, but teasing in their slow flickering dance.

"Your power, your protection. Your aura." The words were

barely a whisper. She shivered again, and the blue lights seemed to jump with the goosebumps on her skin. She glanced at his face. His head was tilted back, and the mesmerizing eyes were closed. His lips parted, and as they did, the web of lights melted into a solid film of blue flame, a phosphorescent glow that seemed to shimmer just above her skin. She could feel her heart pounding in the silence.

Rayn cracked his eyes open. "I know the word of a *dens* means nothing to you, but you have nothing to fear from me today. I promise you that." The soft words made the promise, but there was an edge to the smoothness of the voice that made the back of her neck prickle with warning.

The small hairs on Dina's arms felt the burning of the sheet of blue flame, but then as quickly as it had appeared, it shimmered, broke into thousands of sapphires, and was gone. A bead of sweat slalomed down her spine in agonizing slowness. She swallowed to relieve the dryness in her mouth, but her pulse hadn't slowed and swallowing was difficult.

"Dina, you must relax. Come on, slow your breathing." He waited, then strengthened the command. *Relax. Slow your heart rate.* She shuddered, but her breathing quickly became less ragged, and the pulse in her throat quieted to a slow, steady beat. "Good. I'm going to open my aura for you. My mind is open to you. Send out the smallest, narrowest probe you can, and go slowly. If I tell you to pull out, do it. Ready?"

It was all she could do to dip her head in assent.

Thought is the Creator. The Creator is energy. Unleashed, this energy can never be destroyed. The mind can never die. The palpable Voice seemed to condense inside her, prodding the shiver to again stretch its legs and scurry up and down her backside. *Go ahead.*

Dina closed her eyes and sent out a tiny probe. She was inside the protection of his aura and could feel the blue walls enclose her, sealing her off from the rest of the world. There was nothing else but him. She advanced slowly, as if she were blind and entering a strange room for the first time. Suddenly his mind was there, and she touched it, the lightest of contacts, like a single whisker brushing skin.

She felt emotions first, pain and longing, and they were so strong it was as if the pain was hers. Surprised, she started to pull back, but immediately felt him with her. *It's all right. Go on.* She heard his voice so clearly she didn't know if he had spoken the words or not. It was as if he were next to her, not quite leading her by the hand, but with her every step nonetheless.

She continued, and felt one emotion after another—yearning, desire, regret, and then, unexpectedly, an emptiness, which affected her even more than the pain had. She started to shake uncontrollably.

You're starting to burn. Back away...now, Dina! She retreated to the edge of his mind and waited. *You're all right. No harm done. Steady your breathing and try to relax. I'm right here. I'm not going to let any harm come to you.*

His voice soothed her, and her breathing returned to normal. *I'm okay, now,* she projected.

All right, try again. This time you'll know what to expect.

She sent the probe forward again and skirted the pain and emptiness as much as possible. She felt strength, a strong spirit and a strong will. Then strangely, amid the pain, she felt peace. Not a total, encompassing peace, but a small corner of tranquillity, satisfaction, and joy. It was like a nirvana, an idyllic landscape too good to be true. She lingered there, under a spell.

She could feel him next to her. *This is what keeps me alive. Without it, I would die.*

She began to shudder again.

Come, it's time to go. He stayed with her as she retreated once more. She retracted her probe, and he shook her gently with his free hand. "Dina, open your eyes and look at me."

She did, and it was like awakening from an erotic, drug-induced hallucination. Everything was possible, but nothing was real. She could feel sweat on her forehead, and her breath came in hard gasps. She blinked her eyes, trying to adjust from the images of the mental journey to the image of his face. When she was able to focus on the eyes that were so close she could almost see her reflection in them, they were as alive as a molten river of gold. She now had an idea where the current led, and it was a place both frightening and thrilling.

He stroked her face with the back of his hand, not having removed it when the mental contact was broken. "I know what you're thinking. That you're on dangerous ground. And that you like it."

She swatted his hand away. "I was on dangerous ground the moment I met you. Or should I say the moment you invaded my mind my first night on this rock. I hope you enjoyed yourself, because it's all you're ever going to get."

"It hardly satisfied me, but I enjoyed it, yes. So did you. Denial would be pointless."

She ignored his statement. "You'll give me your cooperation now."

He grinned again. "I'll do what I can. But I make no promises."

Her anger flared, and she was glad, for it dissipated the sexual arousal she could still feel deep inside her. "You bastard. You told me you'd cooperate. You told me you'd give me access to Sanctuary."

"And so I will, but I won't promise my men will talk to you." All traces of his smile were now gone. "Your partner is a fool to allow you to come into the desert alone."

Dina bristled at the criticism against Jon. "Somehow I think you had just a little something to do with that, didn't you?" When Rayn didn't answer, Dina continued. "My partner trusts me. And he knows you won't hurt me."

"And how does he know that?"

"Because if you do, he'll hunt you down and destroy you."

Rayn laughed. "I won't hurt you. But your safety is not because I'm afraid of your revered partner. If he had all of eternity, he couldn't touch me."

Dina's defense of her partner was automatic. "You arrogant, egotistical..." She raised her hand to slap his face, but he blocked her arm easily and tightly grasped her wrist.

"There are others in the desert who will hurt you. Remember that." She yanked back her arm, but he held it securely, releasing it only when she yanked a second time. She quickly jumped to her feet and, grabbing her jacket and hood, was at the cavern entrance before he grabbed her again. *Damn it, Dina! Control your emotions and listen to me.*

She stood still, feeling caught, hating the feeling, and hating him.

I can't protect you every moment.

"You, protecting me? That's a laugh. But you're right about the fool. Only it's me, not Jon. I shouldn't have allowed myself to come here. Let go of me." He released her, and she sprinted for her skimmer.

Rayn knew why she had called for him to meet her, had known all along. The moment she arrived he had read it in her face and eyes without even having to touch her mind. He was very good at reading humans. No different from any of the others, she had hated him for what he was, yet was drawn to him.

But she was different.

Because of that, he had started the game. Because of that, he would have her, and her "truth" be damned. *Truth,* he thought, the word bitter in his mind. She would never understand his truth.

He watched her go, his brows furrowed. He wasn't worried that she wouldn't return because he knew she would. He had touched her in a way no one else ever could, and there was no drug more addictive, no promise more seductive than that. He had felt the heat from her body and had easily sensed her reaction to him. A strange mixture of sexual attraction and wonderment, spiced with a healthy dose of fear. His need to dominate her had flared in that moment, and the control he had exerted to tamp that flame had been considerable.

A muscle in his jaw moved, and he felt a corner of his mouth turn down. *So, little girl, you feel caught, do you?*

EIGHT
AN ACCIDENT?

Dina arrived in her room, checked her computer, and found a message from Jon saying that he was at the mines. She was glad in a way because her mind was still teeming with countless conflicting thoughts and emotions, all seeming to crash into each other. Rayn. All the racing thoughts had to do with Rayn.

The hot touch had been...there was no word to describe it. It was unlike anything she had ever imagined, and more intimate than anything she had ever experienced. The closeness she felt with Jon, the love she felt for her family, the sex she had had with her long-ago lover—nothing came even close to the union she had shared with Rayn.

As intimate as the touch had been, though, there had been no union of souls. Far from it. She wondered how many, if any, of the emotions he had presented to her had been true. She feared they had been nothing but a collage of lies, just like his words. The picture he had shown her was like a carefully drawn landscape, detailed and colored to represent reality, but a picture just the same. He had wanted to evoke just the right response from her, she was sure of it.

Mind probes were supposed to reveal true thoughts and emotions. What she had touched had been too pretty a portrait. Noticeable by their absence had been malice, greed, selfishness, cunning, and the craving for domination that the *dens* were famous for. Granted, her probe of Rayn had not been deep, but the fact that he had been able to bury so many of his true feelings so completely bespoke both an artifice and a power that chilled her.

She laughed. He had wanted her to see "his truth." Well, she saw it all right. His truth was that he was nothing but a sandman. He wove dreams and alluring fantasies that were sugared with the promise of sexual rapture, but none of it was real.

If only she could probe deeper into his mind... No. That was one temptation she mustn't give in to. It was too dangerous.

The quicksand of his mind would pull her deeper and deeper until...

Dina didn't even want to think about it. She shook herself and tried to redirect her thoughts to more practical matters. Rayn had to know more than he admitted. He had to. He was covering for someone, but who, and why?

Her mind shifted gears, and she thought back to the cave-in at the mine. Perhaps she would remember more this time. There was some distance now from the event, in terms of time passed and emotions calmed, so she hoped the memories would surface clearly. She closed her eyes and visualized every detail she could, starting from her leaving Hrothi's office.

She remembered the tour of the mines and her refusal of an escort back to Aeternus. Foolish, that. She remembered exiting Dheru and feeling a wave of heat wash over her. Funny, the heat hadn't given her a headache before. Suddenly she had felt a desire to view the abandoned tunnels of Kewero Kel. She knew she should go back to Dheru for an escort, but felt an overpowering urge to continue. She had been quite alone and almost two decbars from Dheru when the ambush had come.

She couldn't remember the details of the man's appearance, just that he had seemed fairly tall and had been covered from head to toe in a desert suit the color of mist. He hadn't spoken, but she had nevertheless felt a terror unlike anything she had ever experienced. She had felt small and helpless against him, and when he had grabbed her and stripped her of her commband, she had the sickening feeling that he could have done anything he wanted with her. She had heard laughter as he pushed her into the tunnel and stunned her with his rez gun.

Next, Dina tried to think objectively about the attack. The killer, assuming her attacker and the killer were one and the same, obviously knew the mines. And the killer could have known she was at the mine, having seen her arrive. But how could he know she would decide to tour the abandoned sections on her own? It was as if everything that had happened had been perfectly orchestrated.

Fool! It *had* been. She was embarrassed that she hadn't guessed it sooner. After all, her first theory had been that the killer was a *dens*. She hadn't just decided to tour the abandoned tunnels, she had been compelled to do so. She was sure of it. That would explain her headache and the fuzzy memories. He wanted her out of the way, and he wanted it to look like an accident. But before she could congratulate herself on her deduction, another possibility came, unbidden.

The killer was a *dens,* and so far, the only *dens* she had encountered was Rayn DeStar. What better way to ingratiate himself with her and gain an inside track on the investigation than to stage an attack and rescue? Another chill washed over her, this time of horror as she remembered the attraction she had felt for someone who was very possibly a cold-blooded killer.

She tried again to think logically about DeStar, which was always hard. He had very conveniently been nearby when she needed help. He was about the same height and size as the killer. It seemed unlikely there would be a second *dens* living in the desert. Even if there was, DeStar, if he had been telling her the truth, would have admitted such to her. DeStar, the desert chameleon, a killer. Dina needed to clear her mind.

A strident tone from her commband brought her quickly to the present. It was an emergency signal and could come only from Jon. *Gods...* Fear, like a hammer striking an anvil, sounded a heavy thudding in her ears, and the pounding repeated itself, over and over.

"Jon, can you read me? Jon, please respond!" *Come on, come on, come on...*

"Dina...medical help...accident...between the...and the fifth way..." came Jon's voice over the commband, but the transmission was weak and breaking up.

"Jon, I can't read you. Say again, where are you?"

"...distress beacon..."

Dina sprinted out of her room, cursing each second that passed while she waited for the lift down to the storage bay. She still heard the pounding, but ignored it as she tried again to raise Jon on the comm.

"Jon! Jon, we're responding. Can you read?" The only answer was a whine of static, as if nothing was on the other end except an open transmitter. She squeezed into the lift before the doors were fully opened, and shouted the verbal command to take her to the bay.

Time seemed distorted, and seconds were pulled and twisted into a web that caught and slowed everything in its path. She wanted to scream at the needless waste of enduring the retina scan and identification check, but managed the procedure smoothly in spite of the annoying pounding that had not stopped since she had heard Jon's voice on the comm. She powered her skimmer on, retracted the braces, and keyed the sequence to open the bay doors in a series of rapid-fire movements. The skimmer comm activated, she tried again to resume contact.

"Jon, we're coming. Just hang on! Jon, do you read?" No words came in answer.

Dina raced the skimmer the short distance to the AEA Center, her tunnel vision allowing her to see little except the narrow stretch of road immediately before her. She was blind to the sunlight bouncing balls of fire off the glass-fronted buildings, the pedestrians alongside the road who turned and commented on her speed with everything from curses to smiles, and the other vehicles, which braked or swerved to avoid her.

The string of seconds continued to stretch into heavy moments, but she was at the AEA Center in actual quick time and maneuvered her skimmer to the hover deck. The large AEA hovercraft were much faster than skimmers and could home in on the beacon signal just as easily. As she arrived, a hovercraft was already powered up, and the Commander, Khilioi, and Dr. Lumazi were already boarding. Katzfiel waved to her impatiently.

"Come on, hurry, get in!" he said, grabbing her arm impatiently to jerk her inside. The hovercraft gained speed smoothly and quickly, and the way stations sped by so quickly Dina lost count. All she could think about was Jon. *Please let him be all right... Gods, don't let this happen again...*

The next heartbeat took her back in time, and she remembered every vivid detail of *that* night. The Glacian night she would never forget. The hours of standing in the frigid weather, feeling none of the cold, came back to her, and she relived the unreality of a hundred puffs of frosty breath, bobbing incessantly in the night air, while her friend breathed not at all. Agents interviewed; technicians scanned, measured, and recorded; supervisors consulted; and media hovered, all moving like a swarm of ants in a pattern not recognizable to outsiders. She had waited helplessly at the scene, unable to leave until released by her superiors, unable to do anything except watch the methodical process unfold. The cold, mechanical processing of death.

But nothing in the sheer number of personnel or state of the art technology could change what had happened. Her friend, her partner, had been transformed, in an eyeblink, from a warm, strong, intelligent woman, to a lifeless piece of evidence. Dina shook her head to shatter the image. She couldn't endure it again. She just couldn't.

"He's just up ahead," said Katzfiel, and as he said it, Dina could feel the hovercraft decelerating. It settled to a stop, and Dina could see that Jon was on the desert floor, his skimmer on top of him. She ran to him, followed closely by Katzfiel and Khilioi.

The doctor followed with her medical equipment and yelled, "Just hold on, don't move him!"

Dina and the others moved back to give the doctor room. She knelt by Jon's head and carefully removed his desert hood. His eyes were open, but he looked dazed, and his face was deathly pale and covered by a sheen of sweat. His mouth was open and he seemed to be panting, sucking in short, shallow breaths, as if he couldn't get enough air. The doctor felt his pulse and quickly looked up to Dina.

"Get a blanket from the hovercraft."

"A blanket?"

"He's gone into shock. Get it now!"

Dina sprinted back to the transport, her ears and mind still tuned to the doctor's words.

"It looks like his leg is fractured. When I give the word, I'm going to need all of you to lift the skimmer off him."

Katzfiel, Khilioi, and the others positioned themselves, and when the doctor said "now," they raised the skimmer. Dr.

Lumazi and one of her medical assistants dragged Jon out from underneath the machine. He was given oxygen, an intravenous glucose and salt solution, and his leg was immobilized. His weather suit having been partially removed, partially cut away, he was covered, loaded onto a portable gurney, and conveyed to the AEA Medical Center.

While Dr. Lumazi and her assistants worked on Jon, Dina paced in a small waiting room. Now that she knew he wasn't seriously injured, her mind began working on the possibilities. Her first thought was Rayn. Rayn didn't like Jon, that was clear. In fact, Rayn's last words had been...not quite a threat, but very nearly. Would Rayn go so far as to hurt Jon? Would Rayn think that without Jon he could do as he wished with her? Damn him! Conceited, contemptuous *dens*!

Anxious moments later, the doctor came out. "He's awake, and he's asking for you. Don't worry, he'll be okay. He's a strong man, and even more importantly, a fighter," she said, smiling.

Dina peered tentatively around the corner of the doorway and was relieved to see him alert yet relaxed. "Well, you slacker, how does it feel to be the one laid up?" Dina asked, not quite able to suppress a grin.

"Not so bad, considering the alternative," he replied, his smile small, but big enough to show the dimple next to his mouth.

"You don't look so bad, either. Is it painful?"

"Not any more. They gave me a healthy dose of painkiller."

"How's the leg?"

"A simple fracture. A very slight one, but quite a bit of bruising. I think the bruising actually hurts more than the break."

His smile had still been in place, but she couldn't help her own from sagging when she thought about what he had gone through. "Jon, what happened?"

He shook his head. "It happened so fast there was no time to react. The skimmer suddenly lost its cushion of air. The front went down, hit the sand, I went flying over the top, and the damn thing came crashing down on me. I would venture to guess it was no accident. The skimmer was either tampered with at the Visitor Center, or while I was at the mines."

"No one except personnel with a sec level four clearance have access to the skimmers at the Center. But at the mines, just about anyone could have fooled with it," she said.

"So it would seem," he replied slowly. "Listen, I'll be all right, but they're going to hold me overnight just to keep an eye on me. There's no point in you hanging around here. Go back to the Visitor Center. I want you to check the maintenance log on my skimmer and also check the access log to the storage bay back to our arrival. If there are any mechanics on the storage bay log, make sure that it's a different mechanic who checks out my skimmer. And call Hrothi. Have him check his surveillance footage from the time we had our skimmers parked there yesterday. If you find out anything, keep it to yourself for now. I'm beginning to trust fewer and fewer people around here. Just don't go into the desert alone, and please, please, be careful."

His concern for her touched her deeply. She ran a hand through his thick hair, mussing it playfully. "Yes, boss," she said, smiling. "See you tomorrow."

He winked at her as she turned for the door.

Dina returned to the Visitor Center and pulled up the information Jon had requested. There was nothing remarkable in any of the logs. The skimmer had been fully checked just prior to their arrival, and the access log showed that besides themselves, only Khilioi, the stores officer, and one mechanic had visited the storage bay since their arrival.

Dina left instructions with an AEA sergeant named Hrugaz that Jon's skimmer was to be checked thoroughly for defects or tampering, but that under no circumstances were Khilioi, the stores officer, or the mechanic who had logged into the storage bay to be allowed near the skimmer.

Hrugaz nodded his understanding and held his recorder as if it was the most important thing he had done this day. He was short for a Glacian, with a ruddy complexion and thinning blond hair. Nothing in his quiet demeanor or plain features impressed her, but at least he didn't question any of her orders. She told Hrugaz that she wanted a full report as soon as the skimmer was checked, and he responded with a "yes, ma'am" that was happily devoid of sarcasm or arrogance.

Dina then contacted the stores officer and the mechanic on the log to set up interviews for the following day. Finally she contacted Hrothi, and waited for his return call. It came quickly. The surveillance footage presented negative results.

Feeling frustrated and restless, Dina decided to go to the Crown. *Merkwia* had passed, and the sky was as dark as the deepest water on Glacia. The brightest of stars glittered clearly overhead, but thousands more were hidden by the many lights of Aeternus, as brightly lit as a holiday decoration. The air was pleasantly cool, so Dina wore a jacket and evening pants which were warmer and cut to a much tighter fit than the loose trousers designed for the midday desert heat.

She tried not to think about DeStar, but images of him refused to leave her mind. She cursed silently, not sure if it was directed at him or herself. She had been foolish to meet with him alone, and even more so to allow him to perform the hot touch with her. He was at worst a ruthless killer, at the very best a manipulating liar. How could she, of all people, knowing full well what he was, have allowed herself to get so close to him?

She entered the large, crowded hall and, debating which room to enter first, looked at the various signs. Each tried to beckon customers with light, color, and design, but none drew the eye like the sign for the Furnace. The brightest of all, with neon colored flames, it had lights that blinked on and off in sequence so rapidly that the flames realistically appeared to flare, throw sparks, and dim, only to begin their dance anew. Every time the door opened, Dina could hear the beat of the music above the voices of dozens of patrons, proof that this was, indeed, the place to be.

Just not for her to be, at least tonight. She knew she wouldn't be able to think in a place like that, but couldn't decide on the solitude of the Oasis or the casual coziness of the Mocava Cave. Afraid that the Oasis would trigger feelings of sadness and regret once again, Dina chose to enter the Cave. She sat in a private booth and ordered a tall glass of sweetened, iced mocava.

Logic pointed to Rayn as the number one suspect. He could have easily sabotaged the skimmer. She thought about her other investigative tool, her ability. Normally she trusted her intuition and the information she gleaned from her mind probes, but intuition was dangerous where Rayn was concerned. What she had experienced with him during the hot touch was completely different from the impression she had received from the killer, but she didn't trust her feelings about Rayn any more than she trusted him. Just because she hadn't felt the true terror inside his mind that she had felt in the presence of the killer didn't mean Rayn was innocent.

Yet somehow she wanted him to be innocent. Why, she didn't know. If the lying rogue was somehow blameless, there had to be another *dens* in the desert. Improbable as it seemed, she had to at least consider the possibility of a second *dens* on Exodus. As she sipped the cool, sweet drink, she found herself actually wanting to consider the possibility. She resolved to confront Rayn the next day and wrestle some truth out of him. She took her time finishing the drink and, when she did, she left the Cave. Outside in the cool, clear air once more, she drew a deep breath, and for the first time that day, her mind was at peace.

Given the events of the past few days, she wondered how long the peace would last.

NINE
THE RAINSCAPE

DeStar.

I've been waiting for you, came his immediate reply.

Conceited, ill-begotten *krek. So you think I need you so badly...* Damn, that wasn't the way she wanted to word her reply.

Yes I do.

She tried to ignore that and to not be drawn into a war of words she was bound to lose. She tried instead to concentrate on the case. *I need to ask you questions about the investigation.*

Fine. Ask away.

I would prefer to speak to you in person.

And why is that?

Because this is business, and I don't do business this way.
That's right, she thought, stick to business.

Come to Kathedra.

She hesitated, remembering her last visit to the kap, but couldn't think of an alternative. She didn't want to travel as far as Sanctuary, and she couldn't risk being spotted with him in the city. *I can be there in an hour.*

Until then.

He again drew out the parting two words so that they undulated seductively in her mind, like a lure on the end of a line, and Dina was beginning to hate his way of saying good-bye.

She arrived at Kathedra in a little less than an hour. Though it was morning, it had been a particularly hot ride, and as soon as Dina set the parking braces on the skimmer, she couldn't wait to remove her hood and wipe the sweat from her face.

Rayn was already waiting for her in the shaded entrance to the cavern, leaning casually against the rock with his arms crossed over his chest. "The gods hung the sun out today, didn't they?"

He had already shed his outer gear, including his cooling vest, and it irritated Dina to see that he wasn't even sweating.

The bastard was already putting her at a disadvantage.

A corner of Rayn's mouth twisted, but he kept the rest of his face neutral. "Come on in. Help yourself to some water and make yourself comfortable." As he said it, he dropped his arms, putting one on his hip and the other against the gray stone. He didn't move aside for her, and to enter the kap she was forced to step past him closer than she would have wanted. Not close enough to have to touch him, but close enough for her nostrils to fill with his scent.

Dina tried not to look at his bare chest, but did anyway, noticing the odd-shaped pendant he wore around his neck on a heavy gold chain. The pendant, a lustrous creamy color, stood out against his tanned skin and was the same color as the snug ivory pants he wore tucked into the heather boots. From the pendant her eyes followed the funnel-cloud of dark, silky hair downward. The line of hair narrowed as it split his abdomen and disappeared beneath the waistband of his pants. She was already regretting his choice of location, having much preferred to meet in a public place. This was first and foremost a business meeting, and she didn't welcome the distractions of his half-naked body.

Catching her glance, he asked, "What's the matter?" in an innocent tone that belied the look in his eyes.

Damn him. He was baiting her again. She was embarrassingly sure that he knew every thought in her head. *Stick to your questions, girl!* "Nothing. Let's get on with this."

"I'm at your service." The velvet-lined voice was softer than ever, and he whispered the four words almost as a caress. Rayn gave her his exaggerated bow as before, but this time almost in slow motion. "Help yourself to whatever you want."

He followed her inside, dropped down, and lounged on the ground as if it were the most comfortable spot in the world. He leaned on one elbow and studied her.

Dina closed her eyes for a moment, trying to ignore the now familiar throb of yearning that threatened to build, and went to the cooler unit to retrieve a cleansing packet and bottle of water. It was better than looking at him. She asked her first question while her back was still turned to him. "Who else lives in the desert?"

"There are others. There are lots of caverns in the Chayne and Wiara. Over the years, men and women have left Sanctuary to live on their own. Some wanted independence. Some just weren't sociable. Some didn't agree with my way of doing things."

"How do they survive?"

"Basically the same way we do. Without my...gifts...with a little more difficulty, perhaps. Some also have a little further to travel for supplies, but they get by."

Dina finally turned to face him. His hair looked clean and shiny, but it was far from groomed, and fell to cover the hand that supported his head. One long strand just to the right of the point of his widow's peak fell over his eye and curved seductively like the beckoning of a crooked finger.

She wanted to throw something at him. The pose was just too deliberate. It was all she could do to keep her voice level. "There's a possibility, then, that the killer could be living this way, in one of these caverns?"

Rayn hesitated only briefly. "Yes."

"Do you know all of these people, and where they stay?"

"Most. Probably not all."

Not wanting to look at his face or chest, her gaze shifted. The flat, tanned stomach, divided by the narrow trail of dark hair, and the well-worn leather pants that hugged his hips and thighs were no improvement.

"How long have you been here?"

"I think you're smart enough to deduce that I arrived during Ranchar's reign, aren't you?"

Though she was becoming more and more irritated with his brief answers, she pushed on. "Yes. Are there other dark outworlders here?"

Rayn raised himself to a sitting position, and Dina could sense the shift in attitude. It was not for the better. He let his head hang forward, causing more of his hair to slide in front of his ears, darkening the shadow over his face. His eyes looked up from beneath his dark brows, and the lines in his face hardened. The come-hither pose was gone, replaced by the look one animal gives another when defending his territory.

"I realize you consider me to be in this unflattering category, but who else do you mean?" The same hard edges that had formed on his face slid into his voice.

She met his gaze head on. She had nothing to apologize for. "*Mantis.* Shapeshifters."

He was slow to answer. "I don't know of any shifters. There was a *mantis* here, but I heard the *angwhi* captured him." He drew out the old Glacian word.

"*Angwhi?*" She knew the word referred to a snake-like creature, but she was surprised by his use of the Glacian word.

"Katzfiel. Your AEA and its pack of half-trained dogs."

Dina took a deep breath and decided to play her high card. "But there are other *dens* here." She stated it as a fact, not a question.

Rayn continued to stare at her, his face unchanged. "What makes you think that?"

"I know it's no match for yours, but credit that I do have something of a brain. I didn't just decide to take a stroll around the mines. I didn't stumble into that tunnel by mistake. I was driven there. Compelled to go there. Only a *dens* could have done that. I believe the same being who tried to kill me in the tunnel is the killer we're looking for. I believe the killer is a *dens,* and I believe that you know a hell of a lot more than you're telling me."

His face still showed no emotion, but his eyes seemed to flatten, looking past her. The way he looked reminded Dina briefly of Katzfiel's face when he donned his mask of impassivity. On the Commander, the look made her uneasy. On Rayn it frightened her. Finally his eyes blinked and shifted slightly, focusing again on hers. "I'm flattered you don't think I'm the killer."

"Oh, I haven't ruled you out."

The muscle in his jaw twitched. "Congratulations. You have it all figured out. Case cleared. This interview is over." He rose to his feet easily, the grace of his movements ever apparent.

"Rayn, I need your help!"

"No, you don't." He was already putting on his cooling

vest and jacket.

Dina scrambled to her feet as well. "Oh, that's right. 'One does not argue with Star.' Well, I'm not a little camp follower, worshipping at your feet. How can you be so irresponsible with your power? What you do with that power determines whether you prevent this world, or any other, from being scarred by crime and violence, or whether you promote that scarring. You have a choice, and you have the power. You can make a difference."

"The idealistic little Bureau agent. Save your preaching. Glacian morality means nothing to me."

"How can it mean nothing? He's a killer! You know who he is and where he is, and if you don't help me, you're as much to blame for what's happening as he is."

Then do your damnedest and send your vaunted boyfriend to arrest me. The deceptively smooth voice scratched the words painfully into her mind as he passed her on his way to the cave entrance. Dina winced and could only stare in disbelief as he tugged his hood on and vaulted carelessly onto his skimmer. Before the machine stopped rocking from the impact of his mount, he had it powered on and the throttle wide open. He was gone from sight before she could think of a reply to his final remark. She sat back down in the cavern and lowered her head, supporting her forehead with her hand.

Damn him! Damn all dens! She would stay in the cavern until she composed herself. No, she thought, not a good idea. She wasn't safe by herself in the cavern. Funny how she didn't worry about her safety when Rayn was near. Letting out a sigh of frustration, she quickly put on her jacket and hood, and in one fluid motion, slid onto her skimmer and brought it to life.

Rayn watched her from the crest of a nearby mound, then moved to his skimmer and followed her as far as the Albho Road. He wondered what she would think if she knew that all their "meetings" were carefully planned and timed so that he could monitor her passage from the Albho Road through the Wiara to Kathedra Kap.

***

That evening Rayn left Sanctuary through his private

entrance, and climbed to an overlook that gave him an unobstructed view of both the Chayne Gwer and the Ghel Mar. *Merkwia* would soon descend, a soft blanket putting the desert to rest for another day, and he wanted to make sure he wouldn't be disturbed, even by Alee. Alee. What was it that she had said to him? *Oh, yes.* "For someone so intelligent, you say some stupid things." *She was right.* He had been stupid.

He should have known Dina would realize, sooner or later, that the killer was a *dens*. He'd been foolish to think she wouldn't figure it out. He could, of course, compel her to 'forget.' Hell, he could compel her to forget she had ever met him.

The game was getting complicated. What did she want? Did she really expect him to betray a countryman? The idea of betrayal was, as always, a bitter taste in his mouth. He closed his eyes and breathed a silent curse. None of the alternatives were appealing. The only thing that Rayn knew for sure was that his neutral stance was quickly coming to an end. *And someone will die because of it.*

Rayn opened his eyes and looked down at the Ghel Mar. The quartz sand of the desert floor shimmered like a giant pool of quicksilver. *Like a mirror*, he thought, *like the road after a heavy rain.*

The long-ago memory instantly surged to the forefront of his mind, and when next he blinked and opened his eyes, he saw the slender youth, older than a child but not yet a man, standing alone next to the roadway. The heavy downpour had just ended, and the boy's long, dark hair hung in wet ropes around his face. The boy looked down at the murky puddle and saw the wavering upside-down world; saw the buildings and vegetation, signposts, and vehicles.

How like his own world, the boy thought, and yet how different. The boy imagined entering that tempting doorway to a second world, where objects were familiar, but where perhaps life would be different. If things were upside-down, perhaps he would still have his brother. Perhaps trust would be a thing reciprocated, instead of betrayed. And the hate...perchance the hate would be replaced by respect.

The boy stared and dreamed of plunging into the depths of the reflection. To fall endlessly down...how pleasant that would be. The last hope for escape, one quick step was taken. Wrinkled water, hit stone. He was forsaken.

The boy shed not a tear, for it was not the first time.

Rayn blinked, and still no tear was cast.

Much had changed over the years, but never that.

TEN
NO ACCIDENT

Two hours after Rayn left his perch above the Ghel Mar to return to Sanctuary, Dina entered the Opaline Oasis. She discovered a private, softly padded chair next to a decorative water fountain cast to look like a pond filled with aquatic animals. The fountain was surrounded by large potted plants, all real, and gently gurgling water tumbled down a miniature waterfall into the pond. Dina found the sound soothing.

Well, she thought, *now that I've confronted him with the truth, now what?* What could she possibly say to him that would convince him to help her? She thought back to earlier in the afternoon when she had been in her room studying every computer file she could bring up on B'harata and the society the *dens* lived in.

Though it should have been obvious to her, it took a while for Dina to realize that one of the major differences between B'haratans and Glacians was the value placed by society on morality. Dina was a Glacian, as were Jon and most of the settlers on Exodus. Glacian law and mores placed a relatively high value on morality, believing the protection of others was paramount.

B'haratans, on the other hand, placed a higher value on prudence, the protection of oneself. Only days ago her first and only reaction would have been to think of B'haratans as selfish bastards. But now, for the first time in her life, she wished she could truly understand the *dens,* could know what they wished for, what they dreamed of, what motivated them.

She wished she could have hours and hours to talk to Rayn without the verbal swordplay and innuendo. If he could only be honest with her, and she with him, how much she could learn! She would have to try to talk to him again tomorrow. Time was getting short, however. Jon was objecting more and more to Dina's forays into the desert, and Minister Chandhel was keeping a constant pressure on for progress on the case.

Progress! She almost laughed. Her interviews from earlier in the day had netted no new information. The stores officer had claimed not to have touched any of the skimmers, and the mechanic stated he only went to the bay to retrieve a tool he had left the day before. Dina had pulled up personnel files on both men from her computer, but there was nothing in either man's background or work history to raise any flags.

Worst of all, the report on Jon's skimmer had been inconclusive. Dina had personally interviewed the mechanic who had submitted the report, but got nothing from the session but a headache. The mechanic had complained about the poor quality of the skimmers and the fact that the sand and dust of the desert were constantly wreaking havoc with the machines.

She had gone back to the Medical Center to report all her findings to Jon, but his mood had been as foul as the intakes the mechanic had bemoaned.

Dina closed her eyes and heard the soft rhythm of the water as it constantly flowed through the fountain, burbling to the top, then down the stepped waterfall, finally to trickle and splash into the pond. Her thoughts drifted back to Rayn.

That was what his voice reminded her of. Water flowing down a stream...lazy and easy on the surface, strong and turbulent underneath. Suddenly she had an idea. Why wait until tomorrow?

She closed her eyes, and a quick countdown brought her mind to the Road of Time. *Rayn, can you hear me?* She projected as she had before, knowing her projection was strong enough, but there was no answer. She knew he was angry with her, but was his anger such that he wouldn't talk to her at all?

Rayn, please. I apologize for this morning. I know apologies don't mean anything to you, but I need to speak with you as soon as possible. Rayn, at least answer me.

Dina tried for several minutes more, but still received no acknowledgment. Worried now, the fountain no longer seemed soothing. Dina arose and quickly left The Oasis.

Back in her room, she made a quick plan to rise extra early the next day and again attempt to contact Rayn. Failing a response, she planned to ride to Sanctuary and make her plea in person. Sleep, however, did not come easily that night. When her fatigue finally forced her to succumb, it wasn't to restful slumber, but dreams that tormented her with images more vivid and disturbing than even her troubled daytime thoughts had been.

She was in the tunnel, and it was as dark as a killer's soul. There was something on top of her, crushing her, and she couldn't breathe. She pushed against the weight, but the oppressive heaviness remained, suffocating her. She strained to reach beyond it, and suddenly a faint light appeared above her. Encouraged by its promise, she shoved harder at the mass, and as the brightness grew, she could see at last what was pressing against her. It wasn't stone or sand, but a body—a man's body, lifeless and cold.

She saw the face and woke up with a violent start.

Dina's heartbeat pounded in her ears, and she felt chilled and damp, this time not with the sweet sweat of arousal, but the cold sweat of fear. She scrabbled off the bed and ran to the bathroom, splashing water on her face, but the final image of the dream was so vivid in her mind's eye that she couldn't stop her heart from threatening to burst from her chest. Gods, what was happening?

The last image she had seen before the dream broke had been of Rayn's eyes staring at her, dull and brown, all traces of gold leeched away by death.

She circled the room. Trying to sleep again would be futile. She looked at the time. It was still three hours before dawn. Dina suddenly knew that the only thing that would keep the fear at bay was action.

She took a shower, dressed in a desert suit designed for cooler temperatures, then recorded a message for Jon on her computer that he would receive upon awakening. In the message she stated her destination and her fear that something at Sanctuary might be amiss. She promised to send marks and a full report as soon as possible. Dina knew the chance was good that Jon would come after her, broken leg and all, after receiving a message so ominous and vague, but she didn't care. By then she would know what had happened.

She descended to the storage bay and checked her skimmer carefully for supplies, including a second desert suit for the later, hotter temperatures. Though in a hurry, she remembered to carefully check the intake on her skimmer like the mechanic had showed her.

Once on her machine, she slowly made her way to Ghe Wespero, where many of the *mercari* were already setting up shop for the day's business, although *agherz*, the Exodan dawn, was still an hour away. By now she was a familiar sight to many of the *mercari*, who were quick to send appreciative glances her way, even covered as she was in the desert suit. She knew she was especially noticeable this morning, though it was still dark out. Her evening suit had reflective strips built in, and she wore no hood, only a clear eyeshield for protection.

One of the *mercari*, whose stand was in the enviable position of being directly adjacent to the gate, waved his arms at her and called out. Impatient to be on her way, she nevertheless slowed her skimmer to find out what the man wanted.

"Please, miss. I have a message for you. Please, it's very important."

Something in the man's urgent tone made her jerk her machine to a halt. "What is it?"

"Here." The man held out his hand to Dina, and when she reached out her own hand, he dropped something into her palm, whirled, his tunic billowing out behind him, and melted into the pre-dawn darkness. Dina looked down at the scrap of folded paper, opened it, and frowned. She flicked on the reading light at the edge of her windshield and held the paper underneath the narrow beam of light, her hand trembling.

"Come to KK as quickly as you can. G will meet you there." The note was signed "AS."
She wasn't sure who "G" was, not having met all of Rayn's men, but it didn't matter.

She set her finder for Kathedra Kap via the Albho Road and accelerated her skimmer, quickly leaving the gate behind. More than ever she feared something terrible had happened.

She knew she shouldn't assume the worst, but tried to prepare her mind for Rayn's death. *The dens dead.* Why should she even care? He had saved her life, yes, but he had also lied to her. She still didn't know what he wanted with her. And what did she want with him? He was an outlaw, a thief. Not of money or goods, but of free will. Wasn't that the most horrible crime of all?

The bright beacons of the way stations were like friendly buoys on a dark sea, but she passed their brightness quickly, and the darkness soon enveloped her again. As she approached the final way station, the pinpoint of light on the dark horizon made her think of the hot touch. As the light grew larger, the circle of brightness shimmered with the promise of warmth and safety. She was home, sang the light. Home.

But the beacon, as she passed, almost blinded her, pitching her into an emptiness that was beyond black. She shuddered, and a cold chill washed over her. She tried not to think of the hot touch, but concentrated on the red glow of her trailfinder.

The coming of *agherz* restored dimension to the desert, and as the night sky rolled back before her, the horizon line reappeared. She turned off the Albho Road, and dawn bloomed behind her, lighting up the low, snaking dunes of the Wiara. She was thankful for the light, and by the time she reached Kathedra, the Exodan sun was beginning its daily ascent in earnest. She slowed her skimmer and brought it to a smooth stop in front of the cavern.

She drew her rez gun and, with the skimmer still powered on, called out. "Is anyone here?"

She heard her voice echo faintly, and then the stillness of the early morning desert returned, as if nothing had disturbed it. She waited, and just as she was about to call out again, a tall man stepped out from the interior of the cavern.

He was heavy with muscle and wore his dark hair pulled back and tied behind the crown of his head. Dina recognized him at once as the man she had first seen speaking with Rayn inside Sanctuary. He held his hands up to show he carried no weapon, then strode slowly toward her skimmer. He stopped several bars from her and spoke in a low voice.

"I am T'gaard Kai-reudh and a friend of DeStar's. Mistress Alessane asks you to come with me to Sanctuary."

"I remember you, Gaard. Tell me. Is he dead?"

Gaard blinked at the rising sun. "As of last night, no. As of right now, I don't know."

"Let's go. I'll follow you."

As Gaard trotted to his skimmer, parked just out of sight behind a rock formation, she struggled to take a deep breath, but the gritty air caught in her throat. Dina trailed Gaard as he wove his way southwestward along the base of the Chayne through the serpentine canyons, and after seemingly half the morning had passed, they arrived at the now familiar entrance to Sanctuary.

There were several hooded men posted around the entrance, and all but one stood as still as sentinels as Gaard and Dina parked their machines and hurried inside. One had preceded them inside, and before Dina got past the first chamber, Alee met her.

"Thank the gods you're here, and sooner than I hoped," said Alee, grabbing Dina's hands.

"Alessane, where's Rayn?"

"Come." Alee turned and led Dina to the inner chamber. There, on a low bed, lay Rayn. Dina moved quickly to the bed and sat beside him, automatically checking his respiration and pulse. His shallow breathing alarmed her, but she kept her features relaxed for Alee's sake.

"What happened?" she asked Alee, who had crumpled to her knees next to Dina.

"Last night, before the sunset, he left. I don't know where. He returned *al-merkwia*, but he was in a strange mood. He didn't want to talk; he didn't want anything." Alee's voice started to break. Dina could see that she had been crying and had probably had no sleep. She put a hand on Alee's shoulder and urged her gently to continue.

"I finally convinced him to have something to drink. It was a *yegwa* drink. I make it for him all the time. It's my own recipe, but somehow...last night, it was poisoned. I don't know how. He got sick. We did everything to counteract the poison, but he passed out. I didn't know what else to do. I sent Gaard to the city to leave a message for you."

"Alessane, I'm not a doctor."

"I know, but you're an off-worlder. You may know things we don't. But it's more than that. There's something between you and Star, something I don't understand. He wouldn't talk about it, but I felt I could trust you. There's no one else outside of Sanctuary I would trust."

"Thank you, Alessane. I'll do what I can."

"I'll leave you with him, but I'll be in the next room. Call for me if you need anything, or if..." Alee's voice trailed off.

Dina nodded, and as Alee padded out of the room, she turned back to Rayn. She reached her hand out gingerly to touch his face. She felt no aura, nothing. That alone scared her. But at least his skin was warm. He was alive.

It was strange to see him so helpless. He was such a powerful man, yet like this, he was no different from any other. She tried to think what to do. She had to reach him. But how? What did she know of the subconscious mind? She knew it does not think, does not rationalize, reason, or know good from evil. It just does what it's told to do, unquestioningly. It takes orders, like a good soldier. An idea came to her.

She thought back to when she was trapped in the Kewero tunnel, and suddenly she knew what she had to do. She had to do for him what he had done for her.

Glad for the privacy of the chamber, she stretched out on the bed next to Rayn. Remembering his words about physical contact making the mental contact easier, she lightly fingered the contours of his face, from the widow's peak to his temple, down along the line of his jaw to the hint of a cleft below his mouth. She couldn't resist running the pad of one fingertip across his lips, but was unprepared for the response in her own body to the warmth and softness of the sensitive skin. Her breath caught, and she struggled to clear her mind, returning her fingers to his temple and closing her eyes tightly.

She steadied her breathing and sent out a narrow mind probe. Touching an unconscious mind was the eeriest sensation she had ever experienced. There was a blackness, cold and empty, but far from the stillness she expected, it was the dark of a storm, uncaring and violent. She felt caught in a vortex that sucked at her and threatened to wrestle away all control. Dina felt herself start to hyperventilate, and recognizing the onset of burn, wisely retreated to the edge of his mind. Slowing her breathing, she waited, knowing she would have to probe him deeper than she had ever probed anyone before. Ready again, she projected the energy of her mind into his, determined to find the life she knew was still there somewhere.

This time she knew what to expect and pushed beyond the chaos of blackness. She sensed the involuntary functions of respiration and heartbeat at work, like steady machines that work as well in the dark as in the light, but she couldn't find *him.* She edged deeper still, until at last she sensed a small area of light, of life. *Rayn, can you hear me? I'm here with you. Don't you dare die on me, you bastard. Come on, take my strength and hold on to me. I won't let you go.*

She felt the area of light pulse brighter. Encouraged, she continued, willing her strength to him, compelling him to live. She lost track of time, and weariness finally forced her mind to relax. She slept, her body still pressed to his, her mind still coiled around his.

She heard the voice, far away, and frowned. It wasn't Rayn's voice.

"Dina, wake up, please..."

Dina turned toward the musical plea, opened her eyes, and saw Alee's concerned face above hers. "What is it?" she asked, still trying to pull her mind from Rayn's.

"Your partner's here. Gaard and the others are keeping him at the entrance, but your partner is threatening mass destruction if we don't produce you immediately."

Dina couldn't help smiling. Dear Jon, coming to her rescue, when he himself was barely out of the doctor's care. Self-consciously, she slowly unwound herself from Rayn's side and arose from the bed. "It'll be all right. I'll talk to him."

Alee looked at Rayn. "How is he?"

"I think he'll be okay. He's a hard kill. I'll be back after I talk to Jon."

Dina made her way deliberately to the first chamber inside the compound entrance, where Rayn's men had graciously allowed Jon to stand to get out of the sun. She recognized Gaard, as well as Kindyll Sirkhek, Trai Morghen, and Raethe Avarti, the last three from their holos in the AEA files. In addition to the four she recognized, there were four others she didn't know.

Of all the men, Gaard, a Dreinen, was the tallest, taller even than Jon. All the *Dailjan*, however, were young and physically fit. All wore stern expressions, and all of them kept their eyes on Jon. They carried no weapons, but Dina didn't doubt for a moment that any one of them would lay down his life for Rayn in an instant.

Jon was surprisingly calm, but Dina caught not only winces of pain in his face, but muscles twitching in his cheek, a sign that Dina learned months ago meant Jon was exerting himself to control his temper. She sensed the composed exterior was due to the audience they had. She had no doubt things would be different once they were back at the Visitor Center.

"Just what are you doing here? I told you to stay out of the desert." His eyes, as well as his voice, softened as he took in her appearance. "Are you all right? You look terrible."

"Thanks. Yes, I'm fine. Just tired. Jon, I had to come."

"What happened here?"

"Someone tried to kill DeStar. He was poisoned last night. He's still unconscious."

Jon's brows arched. "Gods, who's going to be next? I take it you think our killer is to blame?"

"I would assume so. I haven't been able to question anyone yet. We've been busy trying to keep DeStar alive."

The raised eyebrows folded into a frown, and Jon shuffled his feet, trying to take as much weight as possible off the leg encased in the lightweight cast. A line of sweat trickled down each side of his face. "I don't understand your role here. You haven't had any special medical training, have you?"

"Not really. I've been providing..." She halted, fishing for words Jon would understand, but none came to her tired mind. "...support," she finished lamely.

Jon laughed, but it was a sound more of pain and disbelief

than humor. "Are you serious? Support? As in 'moral support'? Dina, the fact that he was poisoned makes him no less a suspect."

The eight men surrounding Jon shifted their stances, and, while not yet aggressive, the shift signaled a palpable change in the atmosphere of the room.

Dina's attention slipped to the *Dailjan*. The eight pairs of eyes, however, were riveted on Jon, not her. "All the more reason to keep him alive," she replied, willing strength and steadiness into her voice. A confrontation with the *Dailjan* was the last thing they needed.

"We'll talk about that later. Are you done here?"

"No. He hasn't come around yet. I'm staying until he does."

Jon shook his head. "No, Dina. We have an investigation."

"This *is* the investigation." She was pushing, and she knew it. For the first time ever, she felt at odds with Jon. She didn't like the feeling, but neither would she back down. She was not going to leave Rayn.

"Be back before the sun goes down. And be prepared for some explanations." Jon eyed each of the *Dailjan* one more time, then left the compound.

Though he had tried not to let it show, Dina could see that he was favoring his injured leg and was in a good deal of pain. She stood for several moments more, her thoughts on Jon. Her expression gradually softened. This was her partner who had risked himself to come to her rescue. It had been hard to contradict him, but he had left her with no choice.

At last she blinked, and realized that four of the *Dailjan* were still standing next to her, watching her. She studied them, one by one, getting her first really good look at the men around her. They had all been nothing more than faceless, hooded beings before now.

Kindyll had a young, boyish face and was lean and muscular. His long, sun-streaked, blond hair was held at bay by a wide headband. Dina had a feeling that behind the boyish features was a man whose years and experience far overreached his appearance.

Trai was stockier in build, with short, dark hair. He stood

closest to Dina, and as she appraised him, he turned to her and met her gaze. He had a rugged, yet handsome face and cornflower blue eyes, one of which winked at her before he turned away again.

Raethe had shoulder-length, sandy hair and was the tallest and most muscular of the Glacians present. His features were strong and regular, but there was a hardness to his expression that was missing from the others. Raethe, who had good reason to bear a grudge against Mother Lode.

Another thought came to Dina. Rayn had obviously been covering for someone. One of his own people perhaps? Did that person fear betrayal?

Dina returned to the inner chamber where Rayn lay. Alee was washing him, and Dina could see that his clothes and bedding had been changed.

Alee spoke as Dina knelt beside her. "Why don't you refresh yourself and get something to eat and drink? I'll be finished in a few minutes."

She had referred to Alee in anger as a "little camp follower," but it was clear the young woman loved Rayn and would do anything for him. Dina smiled and nodded. It didn't make sense. B'haratans were supposed to be so self-centered, yet the affection and loyalty Dina saw in the *Dailjan* for their leader seemed to be extraordinary.

But was it?

She went out to where the *Dailjan* had parked her skimmer, took out the extra desert suit she had packed along with a bottle of water, then entered the chamber adjoining Rayn's. She washed, changed into the extra suit, and drank long from the water she had brought in. She refrained from eating any of the food Alee had laid out. Although Dina suspected the poison had been specifically targeted at Rayn, she didn't want to take any chances.

As she turned to leave the chamber, her eyes caught a soft gleam from the table. Dina stared at the object. It was a pocket knife. A very special pocket knife, with a handle of black pearl. Her knife.

Dina retrieved a small container from her belt and carefully slid the knife into the container, careful not to touch it with her fingers. It was the knife she had carried in her utility belt the day she was attacked in the abandoned Kewero tunnel.

She stood a moment, forcing her tired mind to think. The killer had taken this knife. Now it was inside Sanctuary. Had the killer lost it, and had it been found by one of Rayn's people? Unlikely. Had the killer left it here, or had the killer given it to an accomplice, one of the *Dailjan?* Dina decided it would be prudent for now not to mention the knife to anyone. Perhaps latent prints could be lifted from it.

She took a deep breath, stepped quietly into Rayn's chamber, and leaned against the wall next to the doorway. Her eyes lingered on Alee, who was still kneeling beside Rayn. This was his lover, thought Dina. How must she feel to see another woman lying next to him? Dina continued into the room before too many emotions could seize her. She sat down, and Alee looked at her, shyly returning Dina's smile.

"I do think he's better. His breathing is easier, not so ragged," said Alee.

Dina nodded. "Let's the two of us get some air. I think we could both use a break. One of the men can sit with him for a while."

Alee's smile widened, and she rose easily to her feet. The two women sat in the shade near the entrance to Sanctuary, where they caught a slight breeze, but it, too, was hot and provided little relief.

Dina shifted her position, uncomfortable all around. Did Alee resent Dina's intrusion into the life she and Rayn shared? Meaningful words failed her once again. "Gods, it's hot today. How can you stand it out here every day?"

"'The desert burns, but is no more blood-hot than man,'" said Alee, a wistfulness softening her voice to little more than a song on the wind. "Rayn told me that when I first met him. I used to complain about the heat, too, but after he said that, I never complained about it again." She turned to Dina. "Thank you for coming. I suppose I should be jealous of you, coming into his life like you did. Maybe I am. But I knew from the first day you were here that you'd have something with him I could never have. I'm trying to accept it. It's not easy, but what else can I do? And I'm grateful for what you did today."

"I'm just here conducting an investigation, then I'll be gone. He's very lucky to have you," said Dina, her voice gentle.

"I think you're fooling yourself, just like he tries to fool himself. For someone so wise, sometimes he's awfully thick-headed."

"And stubborn," Dina added, her smile growing.

"And overbearing," said Alee, laughing.

"He is that." Dina paused, and her face grew serious once again. "I'd better go sit with him. I don't have much time before I have to leave."

Alee nodded, and the two women embraced before Dina returned to Rayn's side. She settled next to him and studied the face before her, so young-looking and so vulnerable. Her fingers brushed the side of his face and trailed down his neck, catching on the gold chain and sliding down the smooth links to the pendant that rested over his heart.

She lifted the pendant and examined it closely for the first time. It was oval in shape, but with a round cut-out off to one side. The oval stone was a shimmering, almost iridescent cream color, and mounted inside the cut-out area was a round golden cabochon stone unlike anything Dina had ever seen. Deep within the golden stone was a silver star that shifted when Dina moved the stone back and forth to catch the light from different angles. Dina wondered where Rayn had gotten the pendant and why it was so important he never took it off.

Running her fingers up to his face once again, she stretched her mind out to his as she had done before. This time she found the small area of light much quicker than before. Did it seem larger and stronger now, or was it her imagination?

Rayn, I'm here. Everyone's here for you. Alee is here, and Kindyll, Trai, and Gaard. They all need you...

She continued talking to him with the voice of her mind, compelling him to live, until, as before, her mind finally relaxed from sheer exhaustion. Half-asleep, but still mentally connected to him, she suddenly felt that she was no longer alone. A cool ripple of air flowed over her face, and behind her eyes she saw a dome of midnight blue, the color of the sky between *merkwia* and true night. Her eyes fluttered, she sat up, and, holding the side of his face, stared at him. "Damn it, Rayn. You no-good, conceited, arrogant, *krek*...wake up! Come on, tell me you hate me. Tell me I have nothing you need. Tell me..."

"Enough shouting, little girl. I can hear you," he breathed, opening and focusing his eyes on hers. She sank her head to his chest in relief and felt his left arm slide over her, holding her to him. It was an impulsive move on her part, but it felt good, and she didn't protest his embrace.

After a moment she lifted her head and drank in the life in his eyes, as if they were a potion she couldn't get enough of. "How do you feel?"

"How do you think I feel? Like I was kicked in the gut and thrown off the top of Chayne Berg." His voice was so soft that she wasn't sure she would have heard it without her ability.

"I'll tell the others," she said.

But his left hand was still on her arm, holding her. "You do realize my men are going to look upon you from now on as a goddess. All of their immeasurable strength and loyalty will be yours."

"Ummm. And what about their leader? How will he look upon me?"

"Why, little girl, we're just even now," he said softly, releasing her arm.

Dina frowned. "Don't call me that. I'm not little, and I'm not a girl." At any other time, his teasing would have brought a tart rejoinder, but there was no bite to her protest this time. "Rayn, I know you want to see Alessane and the others, but I have to return to the city soon, and we have to talk before I go. I need to know exactly what happened to you."

"Ah, the return of the stalwart investigator."

"Rayn, this is serious."

He regarded her soberly. "Yes. This is very serious. Go, then. Tell the others. We'll have time before you leave."

Dina told Alee that Rayn was awake, and the news spread quickly through the compound. During the next hour, in which there was much quiet celebration, several of the *Dailjan* approached Dina to speak to her privately.

Kindyll Sirkhek was the first to seek her out. "Thank you, my lady, for what you have done. My heart and arm are yours," he said, bowing his head to her.

Dina looked into the boyish face and saw strength and kindness, but there was also a sadness apparent in his hazel eyes. Dina remembered from the AEA file that Kindyll had no family to return home to after the completion of his guild contract. She placed a hand on Kindyll's arm and smiled up at him. "Thank you, Kindyll. That means a lot to me."

Trai was the next to speak to Dina. "DeStar has good instincts about people. The first day he brought you here, I wondered. But no more. If I can ever be of service to you, it would be my honor."

Raethe, who said very little, and Gaard, who said even less, each managed to catch her eye, and when they did, they nodded to her in turn. Somehow, those little acknowledgments meant more to Dina than the flowery pledges of the others. Would a guilty man catch her eye? Could one of these men have betrayed Rayn? She was about to quickly probe their minds when Alee glided up to her and whispered that Rayn was ready to see her in private.

"Rayn, there's so much we have to talk about. But first things first. What happened last night?"

He shook his head slowly. "I'm not sure. I left the compound for a few hours. When I returned, Alee made me one of her 'power' drinks."

"'Power' drinks?"

"That's what she calls them. She's something of an herbalist. She makes various teas and cocktails with different herbs, depending on my mood or a perceived want she decides needs remedying. The drink she gave me last night was a *yegwa* cocktail. Water, juice, *yegwa* powder, and gods know what else. She said I looked sullen. *Yegwa* is a relaxant and a mild anti-depressant."

"Does she make these drinks for any of the others?"

"She tries, but most won't drink them. Alee's concoctions are definitely an acquired taste."

"Where does she get her herbs? Surely she doesn't grow her own."

"She grows some desert herbs, but most she buys from one of the *mercari*. I've known the man for years. He sells good quality products. Alee refuses to buy herbs from anybody else. I find it hard to believe he would sell her tainted goods."

"What happened when you drank what Alee gave you?"

"I don't remember all of it, other than I got sicker than I've been in a long time. And I remember yelling at Alee like a madman."

"Rayn, I'll have to question her."

"She didn't intentionally try to do harm to me. She wouldn't. This I know."

"Even so, I have to talk to her."

"Whatever you say, Agent Marlijn." The grin Rayn attempted manifested itself as more of a grimace of pain.

Dina took a moment to wipe the sweat from his face with a cool cloth before she left to find Alee. It didn't take Dina long, as the girl was in the next chamber, waiting to see Rayn. Dina took her gently by the arm.

"Alessane, I know you're anxious to talk to Rayn, but I need you to show me where you made this drink last night."

Alee led Dina to a nearby chamber that felt cooler than the others. Numerous airtight glass jars were crowded onto shelves that had been constructed against one wall. "This is where I do my food preparation. It stays nice and cool in this room, and there's ventilation through that passageway there."

"Tell me what happened last night after Rayn returned," Dina asked.

Alee took a deep breath. "He was in a strange mood, like I told you before. He didn't want to talk, didn't want anything to eat or drink. I hate it when he gets so moody. I finally talked him into a *yegwa* drink."

"Show me what all you put in the drink."

Alee pointed out a jar of *yegwa* powder, a jar of lecithin granules, and showed Dina the cooler that held the juice and water.

"I'll have to take a sample from each of these to test."

Alee nodded, and Dina continued her questioning. "After you finished preparing the drink, did anyone else have access to it before you gave it to Rayn? Did anyone else come into this room? Take your time and think carefully."

Alee sat down and closed her eyes. "Yes, Raethe came in and started poking around for something to eat. I gave him some sweet bread so he'd stop bothering me."

"Anybody else?"

"I don't think so. I did hear a commotion out back, but when I went to look, it was nothing. The wind often plays tricks with this passageway." Alee nodded toward the narrow tunnel that wound its way upward to the outside.

"So you left this room for a while before you gave Rayn the drink?"

"Only for a minute." The tears started welling again in Alee's eyes. "I don't know who here would want to hurt Rayn." Two glistening trails painted the girl's face. "He thinks I did it, doesn't he?"

"No, Alee. He doesn't."

Fresh pearls of moisture continued sliding down the wet tracks. She nodded her head in stubborn opposition to Dina's words. "Yes, he does. You didn't hear him. He yelled at me, accused me. The whole compound heard him."

"What did he say?"

"He wanted to know what I had given him. He said I was trying to poison him, then he came at me. I thought he was going to hurt me, but he got sick. Raethe and Gaard tried to hold him so we could give him water, but he wanted to fight everybody. It was awful. I've never seen him that angry, that violent."

"Alee, listen to me. Rayn knows you didn't intentionally try to hurt him. I think he was drugged. Is there any of the drink left that he didn't finish?"

"No, he threw the glass against the wall. I cleaned up the mess."

"One more question. Does anyone here 'dance with shadow?'"

Alee stared at Dina, her dark eyes as round and shiny as

the glass eyes of a doll.

"Alee, I know you know what I mean."

"It's not against the law."

"I know that. Just tell me, please."

"Rayn doesn't allow it. He says that any desert rat who needs to 'play with shadow' in order to escape the hardships here doesn't deserve to be a *Dailjan*."

Dina couldn't suppress a small smile. Rayn, an outlaw who had broken gods know how many laws, taking a moral stance against the dark pills commonly called "shadow." Widely accepted as sedatives and anxiety relievers, few people cared about the "shadow dancers," those who took large quantities in the hope of simulating the effects of intoxication. Even fewer spoke of the deaths that resulted from toxic levels of "shadow." After all, it was an industry worth millions.

"But 'shadow' is available from the *mercari*, isn't it?"

Alee nodded. Dina collected her samples, then took a walk through the narrow tunnel that led to the outside. She looked closely at the ground outside but saw nothing of interest and, checking the time on her commband, returned to Rayn.

"Rayn, time is so short. I wish I could do a more thorough investigation, but I can't. I don't have any proof, but I think you were given an overdose of 'shadow.' But that's not all we have to talk about."

He sighed as he studied her somber expression. "Yes, I know. Your partner and our safety are also on your mind."

He never ceased to surprise her, even aware as she was of his considerable abilities. "Now were you reading me, or was that just a good guess?"

"Guess? I never guess."

That drew a small smile. His good-natured arrogance was expected. Gods, she had even prayed for it earlier. "Jon was here several hours ago looking for me. He wasn't happy I was here and told me to be back before sunset. He wants a full accounting tonight. I think whatever spell you put over him is wearing off."

Rayn raised an eyebrow. "Spell?"

"Don't be coy. You know damn well what I mean. Jon

would never have allowed me these trips into the desert alone day after day unless he had been, shall we say, 'influenced' to do so."

"It was necessary, was it not? Besides, you came to me of your own accord, didn't you?"

"Yes. But, please, let's address the problem. After tonight, I seriously doubt Jon'll allow me to come here alone, regardless of what arguments I put forth."

"Communication between us isn't a problem. You should realize that. We can be together every hour of every day, if need be."

"Yes, but..."

"No, I don't think you understand. Do you know what a 'link' is?"

"No, I guess not."

"You were doing it earlier, with me, although you probably weren't aware of it as such. A 'link' is more than just telepathic communication. It's when two people intertwine their minds, creating a connection which cannot be broken unless the parties intentionally break the connection. A mind link can be maintained over distance, for any length of time. It's more than just 'talking' with your Voice."

He paused. "Let me give you an example. I can be here, and you can be in the city. If we are linked, even without words, you will feel me with you. It would feel exactly as if I were standing right next to you in your room. The link can even be maintained while we're sleeping. It's not an unpleasureable experience." The promise of an alluring smile teased both the corners of his mouth and his eyes.

Dina shook her head. "Ohhh, no. No mind links."

"Dina, don't tell me you're still afraid of me after all this."

"I'd be a fool to ever stop fearing you."

"Then would you prefer I compel your partner again? I can make the command strong enough that he never interferes with us again."

"No!" *Damn him!* She had vowed she wouldn't touch his mind again, but she needed him too much to let him go now. And she wouldn't let him foul Jon's mind. "All right. But for communication only. None of your...mind sex."

Rayn laughed, reaching up to brush back a slim strand of hair that had whipped across her face and caught in the sweat above her lip. She brought her hand up to push his away, but she was too slow, and he snared it, entwining her fingers with his. "How can you say that, little girl, when you know you'd enjoy it as much as I would?"

She shook her hand to untangle it from his. "Rayn, we don't have time for this."

He sighed. "Very well. But you'll need more experience with the hot touch first. You've probed me, but you have yet to allow me to fully enter your mind."

"But there's no time."

"Then we'll have to do it right now."

"You're not strong enough yet."

"I'm strong enough," he said quietly. "Come, Dina. You're out of excuses, unless you want to tell me again that you don't trust me enough to touch your mind."

Trust again. She swallowed hard, took a deep breath and looked away. She had regretted their previous hot touch episode. And yet, she had also thought about what it would be like to have him inside her mind, not just his words, or his voice, but *him.* She remembered how she felt when she was trapped in the tunnel, and he was in her head, commanding her to live. But then he was only helping her, not examining her every private thought and emotion. There would be no hiding anything from him now, and he would most certainly discover her paradoxical feelings toward him.

But there was a more practical danger. She would be giving him full access to her mind. She knew it was well within the ability of a *dens* to destroy free will temporarily. Could he imprint her mind somehow in a way that would make her his minion permanently? If he did such a thing, would she even know it? Servant to a *dens.* It was a sobering thought.

"Dina, look at me." It was not a compelling command. It didn't have to be.

She turned to search the desert eyes, wondering if she would ever be able to explore them without feeling like she was stepping into a sinkhole.

"You're smart to be cautious, Dina. But I wouldn't do anything to hurt the person who just saved my life. That's the truth. And I won't force anything on you." He gave a short, self-deprecating laugh. "If I wanted to, I could have, easily, long before this."

She considered his words. Was it the truth? She knew that control was paramount to a *dens*—the "all" in all things. Was her submission his gratification? Did she dare subject herself to such a being? And the so-called bond. Was it possible, after all, to bond with someone she had such an ingrained hatred for? Could the unthinkable happen? And if it did, what part of her would be sacrificed to him? Was there more to the bond than he had told her?

Too many questions, and no way to enlightenment except to do this. If nothing more, it would answer her question of how much she really needed him. If his touch felt like the invasion or rape he had warned about, then she would know that her need for him was as false as he was.

She prayed she would survive the enlightenment process.

Her eyes focused on his. "All right. Let's do it."

"Can you handle the intimacy? You'll never be closer to anyone than you will be to me now."

She paused. The sobering thought to end all. She gave a small nod of her head. "I know."

"No, you don't. Be sure, Dina."

She was never more unsure of anything in her life. "I'm sure."

He held his eyes shut, then slowly opened them. He directed her to sit facing him, as before in the cavern at Kathedra when she had first experienced the hot touch with him. "I don't need to physically touch you, but I'll leave it up to you if you want me to or not," he said.

His hand on her face was little compared to his mind inside hers, so she nodded her assent.

He laid the back of his hand against her cheek and skimmed it downward in a soft caress. *You have an aura, too. A silver one. Did you know that? Silver is very feminine, very regenerative and intuitive. You've done well for yourself.*

Her lids felt heavy, and she let them slide shut, shuddering as she did so, but she said nothing. She tried to feel him, but a cool whisper of air, like satin cloth being pulled over her skin, was all she felt. Was he holding his power in check, or was his power diminished by his physical ordeal? His fingers moved to her temple, and gently rested over her pulse point.

Lower your guards for me, Dina.

It was harder to do than she thought it would be. For so many years she had not only kept her guards up, but strengthened them so that it was more than just habit, it was self-preservation, her fortress behind which she was safe. Behind the walls she had erected, she was free to be herself, and if that freedom was akin to freedom within prison walls, she had never thought about it like that. She knew only that here was the one place she was protected. Yes, it was hard to lower her shield. She tried, but couldn't do it.

Dina, open for me. I know it's not easy, but it's the only way. I won't hurt you. I promise.

She forced the remaining guards to drop. She had never felt more naked or vulnerable in her life. Panic started to well up, and she fought to control it.

He felt her alarm and stood patiently at the edge of her mind. He had to let her wage her own small battle with herself before she could admit him.

After a few moments, he felt her panic subside and sent in a narrow probe. *It's all right, Dina.* He felt her fear first, her doubts about him strangely intertwined with desire. He had suspected as much so was not surprised. He next felt her pain and loneliness, and while he expected this, he was amazed at their magnitude. It explained the fortified mental guards. Did she realize what bitter prisoners she was housing behind those walls?

He lingered, trying to assuage her loneliness by his presence. With one hand on her temple, he kept his other hand lightly on her neck, over her carotid artery, monitoring her pulse. He felt her relax slightly, although her pulse still raced.

He moved on and felt her pride, strength, independence

and will. In a small corner of her mind, normally well protected, he felt her love. He knew he should press forward, that these were her most private feelings, but he couldn't. He wanted to know who she reserved this feeling for. He thrust the probe deeper and felt the overriding love for her father. On a different level he felt the love she held for her comrades. There were no names associated with these feelings, except one. She loved Jon.

Surprised, he backed away gently. There were, of course, no feelings here for him. He felt her agitation increase again, and she started to shake. He knew there were only seconds left before he would have to withdraw completely, as she was starting to burn. He moved quickly to those feelings that were closest to the surface, her fear and desire of him. He wanted to know the extent of both.

Her fear, held now in abeyance, had many layers, and would take time to examine. Her desire for him was not much easier to read. The physical hunger was strong, yet somehow tentative, as if she were a young girl unused to her own sexuality. He dug deeper, and unburied a need for him that was more than just physical. A thrill ran through him, and he loitered, feeding off her want, pulling it to him, wrapping himself in it.

She gasped and shuddered violently, and he pulled out of her mind. He held her head, and gently drew her to his chest. She started to hyperventilate.

"Dina, listen to me. Listen! You're all right, but you need to control your breathing. Try to relax and slow your breathing. It's okay, just a natural reaction. It'll pass. All you need to do is relax."

She heard the commands. They were given slowly, in a soft voice, yet were no less compelling than if he had shouted at her. She fought to control her breathing, and after a couple moments, succeeded. But no sooner than she did, she started crying. Embarrassed, she tried to stop the tears but couldn't.

The hot touch had been so overwhelming, so far beyond and unlike anything she had ever experienced or imagined, that the flood of resulting emotions was more than she could handle. His touch had been a gust of cool, fresh air in an airless vault.

She had laid all her treasures bare to him, and he had washed every one of them in a cleansing blue light, a light that was alive with his power. It calmed her, cooled her, and anesthetized her pain until all she could feel was him. His essence, his power, blocking everything else out.

But it was too much, too soon. Crying was the only outlet available, and Dina, who had never cried in front of any man save her father, covered her face with her trembling hands. If she had been thinking, she would have realized the futility of hiding anything from this man, but her mind was on automatic, fully occupied with bailing the excess emotions lest they drown her.

Rayn made no attempt to stop her, or to say anything more to her, but continued to hold her close, caressing her. His aura enveloped her, a steel-blue armor protecting her.

Within the temple of her hands the tears cleansed her face and diminished only when the torrent in her mind abated. Slowly, tentatively, Dina moved her hands from her face to Rayn's chest. She emptied her mind of all the conflicting thoughts and emotions and concentrated instead on what was before her. She slid her right hand up his chest, feeling the soft hair, warm skin, and hard muscles. She trailed her hand down, then up again to feel the well developed pectoral muscles. She fingered the silky hair and traced the narrow ribbon downward to the waistband of his trousers.

Rayn sensed her motions were only partly spurred by physical desire, that for the most part her body was still on "automatic pilot," doing its best to give Dina's mind a chance to recover from the overload of the hot touch. Rayn also knew that he had probed her longer and deeper than he should have, and that the resulting burn was the product of his selfishness. He tolerated her explorations, but he paid the price in his own body's powerful and uncomfortable responses.

He couldn't remember ever wanting to possess a spirit as much as he wanted this one. His control slipped, and the dark armor sparkled and ignited into molten blue flames, waiting to flare, ready to consume. He could take her now, easily.

He felt her cheek against his chest, soft and wet. Fresh

tears smudged his skin.

A long B'haratan oath broke the silence. He couldn't take her like this. Rayn could endure no more. He gently took her by the wrist and pulled her arm away from him. The flames were sucked back and were gone in an instant.

"Dina. Can you hear me?"

She nodded, but seemed dazed, as if she didn't know where she was.

"Talk to me if you can." He tried to keep his voice neutral. B'haratans didn't apologize. Why did he feel the need to do so now?

She took a deep breath. "Sorry. I'm not one to cry. It was just so overwhelming."

"I understand. I should have prepared you better, but there wasn't time. I won't ask you any questions about it now because you'll need time to assimilate everything. " Rayn eased her away from him, and Dina regained her seated position next to him.

She wiped the last of the moisture from her face. "Rayn, we haven't even talked about our safety. It seems obvious the killer is after both of us now."

"We'll talk about that later. For now, just be as careful as you can, even in the city. The killer has invaded the mines and my compound. There's no reason to believe he won't come after you in Aeternus. If you should come into the desert again, don't come alone. Call me first, and I'll arrange an escort for you, preferably myself, of course. You understand?"

Dina nodded. "There's something else. Something I haven't mentioned to anyone. When I was cleaning up in the next chamber, I found a pocket knife on the table. My own knife, which had been taken by the man who attacked me in the tunnel."

Her implications were crystal clear to him. "Dina, I don't know how your knife got here, but my people did not try to kill me. They did not kill the miners, and they didn't attack you in the tunnel. This I know with absolute certainty."

"But..."

"Dina, if you trust me at all, trust my people."

She let out a sigh of frustration and was silent for a moment. "The 'link.' Will I be able to do it with you after today?"

"You should be able to, with a rested and composed mindset. Go back to the city now, talk to your partner, and try to relax. Don't worry about whatever the outcome with Jon is. We have the ability to overcome just about anything. Remember that."

Dina, her eyes half closed, inclined her head forward again.

"You look exhausted, as well you must be. You're in no condition to ride a skimmer all the way back to the city. I'll have Kindyll ride you back on one of our two-person skimmers, and Gaard will follow on yours. You'll be perfectly safe with them, I promise. Gaard is a most formidable individual. And don't be taken in by Kindyll's youthful charm. He's...well, he's bested in strength only by Gaard and Rae, and surpassed by no one in heart. You've earned the undying loyalty of both of them, I think."

She smiled. "Yes, I know."

He touched her face one last time. "Go, then."

He watched her go, his face serious. As soon as Dina left, Rayn considered his next course of action. His people were shaken by what had happened, and some, he knew, had been badly frightened. Frightened people could not be trusted. A semblance of order, at the very least, was crucial, so he issued orders for increased surveillance and started preparations to move the band to a new location. As he spoke to every man and woman in turn, he carefully probed each mind. It was paramount now to know the extent of loyalty of each member. For what was to come, he would need absolute trust, the kind even a compelling command couldn't equal in staying power.

Trust. He thought about Dina and the events of the day. Had what he had done worked? Would she now cease to suspect him? More worrying was what it had done to him. But among the doubts was one certainty. There was no question now in Rayn's mind where his loyalty lay. Loyalty and betrayal. It seemed he could never embrace one without the other. A page had turned, and nothing would ever be the same. Except that.

Late into the silence of the night, he fell back against the bed's headrest, exhausted, succumbing at last to a deep sleep. His final waking thought, as it had been countless nights on B'harata, was that death had been cheated for one more day.

ELEVEN
THE SANDMAN

Gaard and Kindyll dropped Dina off at the Ghe Wespero just as the sun sat balanced on the edge of the horizon. She waved good-bye to her new friends and lingered at the gate to watch the sun gild the mar with streaks of golden fire.

So much had happened in such a short period of time that Dina half expected the world itself to change, and was almost surprised not to see the giant orange ball roll down a crazily tilted horizon. But the far-off Wiara clutched at the dying sun and pulled it slowly to its bosom. The sea darkened, the breeze cooled, and Dina was suddenly aware of the late hour. The *mercari* closed their shops for the day, and traffic at the Ghe slowed to a languid few making their way into the city.

Dina felt totally drained. She wanted nothing more than to sleep for hours but knew she couldn't put off the meeting with Jon. First things first, though. She stopped at the AEA Center and handed over to the chief technician the knife and samples she had collected personally, with instructions to give the results only to her. At the Visitor Center, she took a shower, put on a fresh outfit, then knocked softly at Jon's door.

"Come in."

Dina took a deep breath and, as Rayn had instructed, tried her best to relax. She opened the door and stepped into Jon's room, noticing, as always, his appearance. Jon'sT-shirt was wrinkled, and strands of his light brown hair drooped along either side of his face. His usual easy-going, companionable expression was gone, replaced by a look of stern concern. He sat with his injured leg supported and a tall glass in his hand.

"Are you all right?" he asked.

There was a flatness in his voice Dina had never heard before.

"Yes, just tired. How's your leg?"

"I'll live. If you want anything to drink, help yourself."

Dina's mouth felt like she had swallowed a mouthful of the Albho, so she poured herself a glass of ice water before sitting down opposite Jon.

"How's the situation at the *Dailjan* camp?" he asked.

"DeStar regained consciousness. I think he'll be all right. No one else was affected by the poison attempt."

Dina waited for the thunderclap she feared would come, but Jon's voice stayed level.

"Dina. Why were you there all day?"

"Jon, DeStar is the key to our entire investigation. He knows who the killer is, and the killer, in turn, knows that. It's the reason the attempt was made on DeStar's life. It was critical I try everything in my power to help save his life."

"What evidence do you have of any of this? Has DeStar disclosed the killer's identity?"

"No, not yet."

Jon twirled the tumbler on top of the table, skating the bottom on the circle of condensation that had formed under the cold glass. "Has he promised he will?"

"He'll help me. I'm sure of it."

Jon raised cool green eyes to hers. "You didn't answer my question."

Dina concentrated on her breathing. Jon's questions were exasperating, though not unexpected. "No, he hasn't promised me anything. He only regained consciousness shortly before I had to leave. There wasn't time."

Jon paused, even holding the glass still. "'No time.' Dina, when someone is attacked, isn't the first question you were taught to ask is 'who did it?'"

"Jon, the situation is more complicated than that."

He expelled a deep breath, leaned his head back, and stared at the ceiling. After long heartbeats of silence, his head bobbed forward again, and he sent the glass spinning.

"No doubt. Dina, here it is. You've had four days to meet with DeStar, and you've made just as many trips into the desert. Trips alone, which I never should have allowed you to make in the first place. For all that time spent, you have absolutely no information to give me regarding the killer's identity, whereabouts, or motives. And by your own admission, you don't even have a promise by this man to tell you these things."

"I've probed his mind. He'll cooperate. I just need more time."

She could feel the frustrated restlessness in Jon and knew that if his leg wasn't hurting him, he'd be pacing back and forth across the small room. Instead, Jon closed his eyes and shook his head.

"Dina, I wish you could hear yourself. Ever since you met this man, all your good sense and training seem to have eluded you. You've put yourself at risk and have nothing to show for it. And now this so-called poisoning. Do you have any real reason to believe the killer is the same person who poisoned DeStar? There could very well be some members, or ex-members, of his band that bear a grudge against him. Do you have proof that DeStar was even the intended victim?"

Dina had no answers to any of these questions. In fact, she had asked herself many of the same questions. What could she say?

Jon nodded. "I thought so. Is DeStar a dark outworlder?"

It was the one question that Dina had been expecting. She met his eyes and did not hesitate. "I don't know what he is. All I know is that he's the key to everything. I don't know what to say to you to convince you of that."

"Some information and evidence would go a long way in convincing me. I need more than just your gut instinct, and I certainly need a hell of a lot more than DeStar's hunches."

Dina couldn't believe she had heard that. Not from Jon. Not from the one person who had trusted her. The companionable closeness she had always had with Jon seemed light years away, and the ease she usually felt with him was gone, replaced by a sudden tightness in her chest and an invisible fist that squeezed her by the throat.

She fought back with her own anger. "Just when did my instincts stop being an asset to you? When they don't agree with yours? Or is there more to it than that?"

"Your instincts cease to be an asset when you allow yourself to be influenced by the people we're investigating, that's when." The last two words were fairly spat out, and absolute quiet followed their utterance, as if both parties realized that tired tempers were taking control of the discussion.

Jon paused, and Dina watched as he closed his eyes, leaned his head back, and ran his hand through his tousled hair. She knew he had allowed her every benefit of the doubt and more latitude than he would have allowed another junior officer. But she also knew that his patience was at an end and that she was not likely to win this battle. Every line in his face told her that he had had enough. She listened to the long sigh that accompanied the fix of his baleful stare on her.

"Dina, listen to me. This is the bottom line. You will make no more trips alone into the desert. If DeStar is to be questioned further, we will do it together. Do you understand?"

"Yes."

"I hope so, because this is not a suggestion, it's an order. Do you understand that?"

"Yes, sir. I understand."

"Good. Now go get some sleep. We'll talk more tomorrow morning. Meeting at the ninth hour, mark zero, okay?"

Dina could only nod, relieved that the ordeal of this meeting was over. Back in her room, she, like Rayn, fell immediately into a chasm of deep sleep.

***

Rayn woke early the next morning and was relieved to feel that some of his strength had returned, but he was even more thankful that his mind felt clear and strong. The first order of business was arranging for the safety of his elite—Alee, Gaard, Kindyll, Trai, and Raethe.

They would be moved to a new location immediately. The other *Dailjan* would be moved later, to a secondary location. Rayn already had several caverns in mind that had been discovered long ago and stocked with basic supplies. It was something he did on a regular basis, the scouting and provisioning of new caverns, and Rayn knew almost every rock comprising the Chayne and Wiara. He issued orders to everyone to begin packing necessities immediately. The elite would be moved that night under cover of darkness.

***

Dina also awoke early the following morning, feeling more

tired and irritable than she had since landing on Exodus. She decided to call Rayn early, before her morning meeting with Jon. She sighed, not knowing what bothered her more, that she had lied to Jon, or that she was worried about a *dens*.

Jon. She had not only argued with her partner, she had intentionally lied to him. It was something she never thought she would do, but when he had asked if DeStar was a dark outworlder, she hadn't wavered. She would not betray Rayn to Jon or any other officer. *Four days*. After only four days she was at odds with the best friend and partner she had ever had and aligned instead with a *dens*, a creature she thought to hate more than anything in the universe. The hate she had hosted for so many years...where had it gone?

Rayn.

I'm here.

How do you feel?

Weak, but stronger every hour.

I'm glad. What I feared, has happened. Jon has forbidden me to go into the desert to meet with you again.

It's just as well. It isn't safe here. I'm moving my people out of Sanctuary.

Rayn, I need to see you. Not right now, of course, but...soon.

I understand. It will be soon, I promise.

*Rayn...*She didn't want to let him go yet, but didn't really know what to say to him. She had always been so self-sufficient. This strange need was new territory and a little frightening.

Dina. She shuddered as she felt him caress her cheek. *Dina, you'll get through this. I'll be as close to you as that. Until later.*

She opened her eyes and was shaking. How could he have done that? He was decbars away, and yet she swore she had felt his fingers on her skin, warm and gentle. It had been real. But how?

She spent a few more minutes clearing her mind. She would see Jon soon and knew she would need her concentration for whatever interviews or research he had in mind for the day.

He was cordial enough at their meeting, yet Dina still felt that she had lost a good measure of his trust and respect. Jon was convinced that the motive for the murders involved either the mines themselves or Mother Lode Mining Consolidated. Just before his accident he had been at the mines for the complete tour he had missed the day Dina was attacked. He had interviewed both the miners and administrative Mother Lode personnel at length.

Jon's new assignment for Dina was to meet with Mother Lode's resident lawyer and review all the legal contracts in place between the company and the Synergy. Though some of her colleagues may have felt it to be a boring assignment, Dina was actually glad for it.

She thought it was a good idea, first of all, and second, it would give her an opportunity to put some of her schooling into practice. She had taken several courses in interplanetary law and one in legal contracts. The mining rights on Exodus were a highly sought after prize, and there was a lot of money at stake. Finding a legal loophole could very well explain the motive for the killings.

Dina met with Mother Lode's senior on-planet attorney, Faitaz Chukar, high inside the impressive Mother Lode structure. A light probe at the beginning of their meeting revealed the contempt she was so familiar with, but rather than let herself be upset by it, Dina decided to turn it to her advantage.

She tilted her head to the side and knotted her brows. "Mr. Chukar, could you help me, please? I'm not familiar with some of this terminology."

The man smiled, the broad curve of his mouth against his pale skin in perfect harmony with the exquisite waves in his ash blond hair. "Of course, Miss Marlijn. I understand how difficult legal documents are for a lay person."

Dina smiled her thanks broadly in return. She thusly viewed file after file, asking numerous questions which Chukar seemed only too happy to answer. While she discovered some very interesting facts, she was disappointed to learn nothing ground-shattering in importance.

On her way out of the building, she ran into Rum Ctararzin, Mother's Operations Manager.

"Agent Marlijn! How nice to see you. You're making

progress on the investigation, I hope?"

"Yes, sir, we are. I'm sure you understand that I can't discuss any of the details of that progress with you at this time," Dina replied with a pleasant smile.

"I see." His dark eyes said otherwise. "I hope you found my colleagues here to be helpful."

"Yes, Mr. Ctararzin. Very helpful, thank you."

Ctararzin dipped his head to her, and her smile broadened as she took a perverse pleasure in the man's condescending acknowledgment.

Dina left the Mother Lode building and made her way back to the Visitor Center, where she had dinner with Jon and gave him a report on her findings.

"The contracts are very complicated, and there are a good number of them. Quite a few were changed when Exodus changed administrations. I haven't looked at any of the old contracts yet. I'll try to view them tomorrow. Anyway, everyone understands the basics. The Synergy has territorial rights over Exodus. This includes all on-planet resources as well as the planet's value positionally in the system. The one valuable resource so far discovered, of course, is the exodite."

She paused and took a sip of hot mocava. "Mother Lode Mining won the mining rights by virtue of submitting the highest bid. But they run a very efficient operation, so even with the amount they pay the Synergy, Mother still turns a tidy profit. Where it starts to get complicated are the conditions under which either Mother Lode or the Synergy can legally break the contracts. If Mother Lode can prove gross negligence on the part of the local administration directly affecting mining operations, Mother can break the contracts. The suit currently being threatened would fall under this purview."

She took another sip of the sweet drink. "The Synergy, in turn, can break the contracts if Mother fails to make their payments or is found guilty of fraud. The previous set of contracts expired earlier this year, and the current set runs for five more years. At the end of the contract period the Synergy has the option to automatically renew the contracts or to accept new bids from other mining companies."

"If Mother's profits are high, why would they intentionally want to break the contracts, especially after just renewing them?" asked Jon.

"Have we verified Mother's financial statements for the past few years? Perhaps they're not really making as much as they contend."

"I've seen the current numbers, but it would be a good idea to view all the statements, current and past, in detail. When you finish with the contracts, I want you to dig in to their finances."

Dina nodded. "There could be a lot of possibilities, depending on Mother Lode's true state of affairs and that of the mines. We should try to arrange for a current Synergy survey of the mines' potential."

Jon smiled at her, the first he had bestowed on her since before she made yesterday's trip to Sanctuary. "Another good idea. I'll follow up on that tomorrow. You did a good job today, Dina. That's the kind of work I expect from you."

Whereas in the past Dina would bask in Jon's praise, she merely nodded. They ended their evening meeting soon after, and Dina returned to her room. She looked out her window and saw that the dying sun would soon perform its final act before the curtain of *merkwia* fell. Done with work for the day, she thought again about Rayn.

Rayn.

I'm here, Dina.

Is everything going well?

So far. How about you?

Things went better today than I expected. And I appear to be back in Jon's good graces, at least for the time being.

Rayn was silent for a moment. This was a woman who was in love with someone else. He couldn't blame her or himself. He had known from the start that this was a relationship headed for disaster—had known in his heart it was wrong— yet had allowed it to develop anyway. No, he thought. He hadn't just allowed it, he had pursued it. Pursued it for reasons she would never understand.

Rayn?

I'm glad it went well. I told you it would.

I suppose you're busy with your move. I shouldn't have bothered you. Her Voice faltered, just a little.

Rayn heard it. *Dina. Don't ever hesitate to call me, ever. Whatever the reason. Or even if there's no reason. Do you understand that?*

Yes, I understand.

I doubt you do, yet. Are you off Rzije's leash for the day?

He doesn't have me on a leash. And, yes, I'm done for today.

Rayn smiled at Dina's defense of her partner. She was as loyal to Jon as his men were to him. *Go to the Crown two hours from now.*

What for?

Ever the questioning mind. When are you going to start trusting me?

I don't think you'd like me if I didn't have a questioning mind.

You're right. And I don't think you'd like me if I wasn't imperious. Go to the rec hall.

Yes, Rayn.

Until later.

For once, his sign-off was devoid of guile or mockery. Dina sighed. He was such a hard man to understand. Well, she thought, perhaps that was part of the attraction. Maybe someone would meet her there with a message. Rayn seemed to have friends all over.

After resting for an hour, she rose, showered, and dressed. She left a message for Jon on the computer as to her destination, then left at the appointed time. Numerous admiring male glances and two separate offers to escort her wherever she was going came her way as she walked toward the Crown. She politely refused the offers and continued, ignoring the attention directed her way. She entered the rec hall and started for the Oasis, but halfway past the Furnace, she stopped so suddenly the man behind her bumped into her.

He's here, she thought, puzzled. He hadn't called to her, she was sure of it. She opened the door and saw a neon sign on one wall that urged patrons to "Come out of the desert into the

Furnace!"

The room was overflowing with bodies and noise. The constant ebb and flow of the people who were on their feet made it difficult to tell if they were dancing or merely coming or going. Peals of laughter, voices that strained to be heard, and the clinking of glasses skipped off the surface, while the undercurrent of music flowed steadily. The light level was that of a starlit night, and the numerous neon wall sculptures, mostly in the form of flames, pulsed and danced in counterpoint to the undulating bodies on the floor.

Dina didn't have to look around. She knew exactly where Rayn was. She wove her way patiently toward the far end of a long, curved bar where men and women were standing or sitting, enjoying drinks and each other's company.

Well, you said you wanted to see me.

She squeezed her way through to him, smiling, forced by the crowd to stand close enough to him to count the links in his neck chain. He was dressed in tight, mahogany-brown pants the same color as his hair and a loose, long-sleeved white shirt. She looked into his eyes and her breath caught.

"I didn't think you meant like this. You never cease to surprise me. How did you get into the city?" As soon as she asked, she knew the answer. "Never mind. Are you safe here?"

"Relatively safe. It's dark and crowded. If any *angwhi* come in, I'll spot them."

Even through the music and noise, Dina had no trouble understanding Rayn, even using spoken words. "And give them the...what do you call it, anyway? When you 'influence' someone?"

"*Dher*. It literally means 'to muddy.' An especially appropriate word, since my homeland on B'harata is known for its almost ceaseless rainfall."

"Do you miss B'harata? Do you miss the rain?" She wasn't sure why she asked him about the rain, except that it was one of the few features of the place she knew about.

"I miss certain things, the rain being one, yes. The rain on B'harata can be fierce, but it can also be soft. Soft, pure, and very alive. When I was a boy, it used to dance for me, sing to me, tell me stories." He paused, and his eyes took on a strange, wistful glaze. "This place...this place takes the tears and sweat of the gods and dries them to crystal shards that do nothing but bite and sting. This place is dead, Dina, in spite of the fact that all you Glacians do your best to dress it up. This whole city is made to look like a box full of glittering jewels, but it's just window dressing for a dead world."

She had never heard him talk like this. "What's wrong with turning a dead world like this into something productive and beautiful? I thought you liked it here. You chose to come here."

"As you say. A lot of worlds are closed to me, Dina. Sometimes it's not so much that I choose a place, but that a place chooses me. And, yes, I've tried to make the best of it."

"I'm not sure I understand."

"To one who is trying to escape, little girl, the destination is often not as important as the mere fact of getting away."

"Don't call me that. Escape? From what?"

"That's a story for someday." The music had slowed and was softer, and several couples were dancing closely. *Come, dance with me.*

As she heard his telepathic voice in her mind, she felt a warm runnel of pleasure trickle down her spine and coalesce into a pool of liquid fire deep inside her. *I...uh...don't dance.*

Why not? Everyone dances.

It was embarrassing, but there was no point in trying to hide the truth from Rayn. *I've never had anyone to dance with.*

Well, you do now. Come.

He led her to an unobtrusive corner of the dance floor and gently pulled her to him. She became aware first of her heart pounding in her chest. Next, she felt the heat from his body and inhaled his particular scent. It was like that of the desert at *merkwia*, she thought idly, a combination of the heat and vastness of the day, and the cool energy of the night. She knew it was his power, as tangible as the mountain mint fragrance that he wore. The latter was, ironically, grown in the city greenhouses, not the mountains, but it was sold by the *mercari* and was a popular cleansing scent with the desert dwellers. It was a scent she would always associate with Rayn.

She slipped her arms tentatively around his neck, still uncomfortable with being so close to him. His hold on her was sure, but not so tight she couldn't breathe, and their bodies moved in tandem to the music.

Relax.

The single word was like thick velvet being rubbed over the most sensitive spot on her body. She shuddered in his arms, and, as if the shudder had been a key to unlock a hidden door, his power immediately poured over her, a cool river of life force. It was hard for her vision to register color in the dim light of the club, but behind her eyes danced blue lights of every hue and shade. It was like thousands of cut and polished sapphires, iolites, and exodites, caught in the same current of power, rolling, twisting, and flashing their brilliance at her, almost mesmerizing her.

She wanted nothing more than to melt against him, and yet a small voice of caution warned her of the danger.

Rayn, don't.

Don't what, T'anga?

You know very well. Don't pull me under. That's what you could easily do, isn't it?

Of course. But you have nothing to worry about. I have a leash on it.

She moved her hands to his shoulders, ready to push away from him if his hold became too fast. *Not tight enough.*

You weaken my control, Dina. Don't you know that?

She dug her fingers into his shoulder muscles. *Pull it back, Rayn.*

I wouldn't hurt you.

Pull it back!

He loosened his hold on her just enough for her to see his face, and the cool current receded to a trickle, sliding over her skin in a teasing zigzag.

He lifted an eyebrow. "Better?"

She responded with a lift of both brows. "If and when I want to take the plunge, I'll let you know."

"Perhaps you just don't like being reminded of what I am."

All she could see in his eyes were reflections of the neon

flames. "I don't forget what you are, Rayn, ever."

A small smile tugged at the corners of his mouth, but the smile had no connection to his eyes. He eased her head to his shoulder as he tightened his hold on her again. She made no move this time to resist him. He didn't answer her.

The music ended, and he whispered into her mind before he released her. *I look forward to your taking the plunge, little girl.*

She tried to shove him away from her. "Don't call me that. I hate it."

His hand caught her waist, and the cat smile widened. "One more dance, and I promise."

A new song began, and she studied his face as he reeled her back to him for the last dance. The dark hair, worn loose, was smooth and shiny, but as usual had a mind of its own and fell forward to frame his face. His eyes, focused somewhere over her shoulder as if in thought, continued to glow with flickering light. Her gaze lingered lastly on the sensuous mouth that fascinated her, now but a breath from hers. She wondered what it would be like to kiss that mouth, and as the thought passed through her mind, Rayn's eyes shifted and locked with hers.

You know everything I think and feel, don't you, dens. This last was thought to herself, not projected at him, but she wanted to see what his reaction would be.

Do you really want me to answer that?

She stared at him, hardly able to breathe, and he leaned forward and gave her her wish. It was a soft kiss, warm and sweet, but teasing, lasting only a heartbeat before he pulled back. His body infused hers with heat, but the small ribbon of cool power floated down her spine and reminded her that it was still there. *Gods*, she thought, no one had ever kissed her like that before. The strange mixture of hot and cold made her feel faint, and her heart caught in the back of her throat.

The last notes of the song faded away, and Rayn led her back to their seats, no longer touching her. Dina tried to compose herself, but it was too crowded and noisy to practice any of her usual relaxation or visualization techniques. She settled for briefly closing her eyes and counting backwards from five to one. She still had so many things she wanted to ask him, and time was so short. He ordered a Mocava Lava for her—iced mocava with mint and alcohol added—and a Mirage for himself, a sweet, creamy drink mixed with a generous dose of *uisque*, a potent, but tasteless alcoholic liquor.

"This morning you touched my cheek. I felt it. How did you do that?"

"It's not as hard as you might think. The mind is the most complex and powerful tool in the universe. I had touched your cheek physically on several previous occasions, so I knew you had the memory of it. I simply instructed your mind to retrieve that particular memory so you could relive it. There are other ways to induce people to experience sensory feelings, but memory recall is the easiest."

"Tonight, when I arrived. How did I know you were here? You didn't call to me, yet I knew exactly where you were."

Rayn hesitated, but only for an instant. "Our minds have touched. Your thoughts are attuned to mine. Your awareness and sensitivity have increased more than you realize. Like it or not, it means that when we're close physically, you'll be able to sense my presence. Just as I can sense yours."

Dina looked away. Attuned to a *dens*.

"This bothers you," he stated.

She couldn't deny it. "There are so many things about you I don't understand."

"You will."

She looked at him. "I still have a job to do, and obligations to the IIB and Jon. I still have to find the killer and prevent him from committing more crimes. I still need your help."

He stroked her hair. "You'll have it, *T'anga*. I promise." He paused. "I have to go. I have to move my people tonight. All is in readiness. They await only my return. Are you generally free from your work and Jon at this time?"

She nodded. "Yes, our meetings are usually finished by *merkwia*. Can you come here again tomorrow?"

"With luck. Call me as you did this evening." He threw his head back and quickly downed the last of his drink. "Go on.

I'll wait for you to leave before I do."

All-knowing dens, she thought to herself. If he was any good at anticipating and satisfying her needs, he would know what to do right now.

I do know. But I can't do it in a room full of people. So this will have to suffice for now. He held her face and drew her slowly to him until he could claim her mouth with his in a slow kiss that was not quite as soft as the first one had been. By the time he released her, she was shaken to her toes.

She left the Furnace with a wide smile on her face.

She didn't see the smile slowly fade from his.

TWELVE
THE BOND

Perhaps she was overtired. Perhaps it was her preoccupation with the events of the past few days, or that Rayn was simply on her mind. Whatever the cause, she dreamed again of his death and woke with a start and the memory of sightless, ash-brown eyes fresh in her mind's eye.

Dina tried in vain for an hour to quiet her mind so she could fall back asleep, then finally surrendered to the questions that refused to let her rest. The last dream had presaged the attempt on Rayn's life. Was he in trouble again? She knew she shouldn't care, but she did. She had to know if he was all right. Yet she hesitated calling him in the middle of the night. He was probably either still moving his people, or exhausted from the effort. What excuse could she give for such an intrusion? It didn't matter.

Rayn. Her projection was tentative.

No answer.

Dina tried to rationalize. He was probably asleep. Or otherwise occupied. A disturbing vision of Rayn making love to Alessane swooped into her mind. As painful as the picture was, it was preferable to the image from her dream. She had to know.

RAYN.

I hear you, Dina. Is something wrong?

She sank to her bed. Now that she knew he was all right, she was at a loss as to what to say to him.

Dina?

No, nothing's wrong. Are you...busy?

She had almost asked if he was alone. Embarrassment washed over her as she envisioned the possibility of being inside his mind while his body was making love to another woman. The thought mortified her.

His reply was light, and she could almost hear laughter in his words.

As a matter of fact...no. The others are asleep.

There was a pause, and when next Dina heard Rayn, his tone was solemn.

Dina, don't tell me nothing's wrong. What happened?

It was just a dream.

Dina, I know it's more than that. I can feel your terror. Do you want to talk about it? Is that why you called me?

She should have known she couldn't hide anything from Mr. All-knowing, damn him. When she hesitated, he continued.

Listen, Dina, nightmares are nothing to be ashamed of. You were almost killed. It would be strange if you didn't have nightmares.

She took a deep breath. *The dream wasn't about being killed.*

What then?

You.

Dina, I'm not going to hurt you. I wish you could believe that.

Dina shook her head and stupidly realized Rayn couldn't see the gesture. When she spoke to his mind it was easy to forget he was decbars away. But now she was glad she wasn't face to face with him, because she knew she wouldn't be able to physically speak the next words.

I was running across the desert, then something, like an explosion without the bang, knocked me down. I was on the sand and couldn't breathe. A heavy weight was on top of me, suffocating me, and I pushed and pushed, but...

She paused, and Rayn didn't try to rush her.

Finally I saw what the weight was. It was you. You were dead, and your eyes were...

Listen to me! Lower your guards and let me in.

But her mental shields, instinctively raised and fortified with her fear, stubbornly stayed put.

Lower your shields and let me in.

She obeyed this time, having no choice. Her shields were no match for the compelling command of a *dens*.

I'm here, Dina. I'm alive. Hold me.

He was instantly with her, in her room, right beside her. She reached out for him, disoriented, but felt only the cool air before her and a damp sheet beneath her.

Just relax. Link your mind with mine. Slow your breathing.

As she relaxed, she chided herself. It was foolish to think he was actually in the room with her, but with the link in place and the lights off, his presence was so strong she no longer thought about the absurdity of it. She lay on the bed, and he was beside her. She felt his body heat, his strength, and as she concentrated on her breathing, even imagined she could inhale his scent. Neither spoke for a long time.

Rayn, I didn't tell you this before, but I had the same dream just before you were poisoned.

And I survived, didn't I? And I will continue to do so. It's what I'm best at. So don't think about the dream any more.

She closed her eyes. *Stay with me. Talk to me. There are so many things I've wanted to ask you about.*

Yes. Asking questions is the one thing you're best at. Ask away.

Why do you keep saying you 'escaped' from B'harata? What did you do there?

Do? On B'harata there's an old saying that you thrive, you survive, or you die. I survived, but I didn't thrive. My mother used to tell me I was born two hundred years too late. She said I would have made a good spiritual teacher, but nowadays few care about spirituality. I did various jobs, but nothing I did seemed to make a difference. I never fit in with those around me, not even members of my own family, and as the years passed, I became more and more dissatisfied with life. I was foolish enough to think I could find happiness elsewhere in the galaxy.

She smiled. *Foolishness is not confined to the young.*

Oh, but I was very young, by B'haratan standards, when I left.

What was it you were so dissatisfied with?

He hesitated. *You wouldn't understand. To you, we're all nothing but ruthless puppet-masters, are we not?*

If I still believed that, I wouldn't be here with you now, like this.

For a few moments he didn't reply, and just when she

thought he wouldn't, his words poured into her mind.

It's been long held by the dens that the advancement of the self brings advancement of society. But I'm a traditionalist. I believe the mind is a road with forks that bring choices, force decisions. But the modernists believe the mind is but a place to be fortified and made invincible, a stagnant fortress quivering with every weapon they can bring to bear. My brother Ryol is a modernist. He sees me as weak and without goals in life. Bitter laughter filled her head.

Maybe he's right. Even now I don't always know what it is I search for. All I know is that I won't live the lonely existence my brother does.

She didn't understand his talk about roads and fortresses, but she understood loneliness. *But this outlaw life, with no one to connect with...surely it's been lonely.*

It has. I've been waiting a long time for someone like you, Dina.

Is that why you visit the spacedock every time a ship comes in? How did you do that, anyway?

I don't bother with cargo ships, only those carrying passengers. The bond between the physical body and the astral body of a dens is very elastic. I merely project my etheric self to the spacedock. Distance is of no matter.

She didn't understand. *But I could see you.*

Yes. It was a wonderful surprise, was it not? Of course, I couldn't answer your challenge, so I had no choice but to return to my physical body.

She remembered the moment and her reaction to the experience. Her mouth turned down. *It was hardly a 'wonderful surprise.' I thought I had spacefever.*

Laughter again filled her. *Try to get some sleep now. I'll stay with you until dawn.*

She snuggled down under her sheet. Rayn's presence was a warm cocoon of safety around her, and she had no more nightmares that night.

Dina woke the next morning just before *agherz* to the lingering scent of mountain mint and the feel of Rayn's arms around her. If the light hadn't automatically brightened to reveal that she was alone in the room, she would have sworn Rayn lay beside her. It was an unnerving experience, but she couldn't deny the pleasure it brought. All too soon, though, they unlinked and he parted from her, promising he would see her later that evening.

Agherz was still an hour away, but Dina dressed quickly, wanting to make the most of the time she had before her morning meeting with Jon. She felt so energized she couldn't stand still, so she checked her skimmer out of the storage bay and cruised through the city toward Ghe Wespero. As early as it was, there was a throng of people on the streets, making their way to the marketplace or to their jobs. Dina stopped her skimmer near the *mercari* alongside the gate.

She sat perched on the machine and watched the sun awaken the city.

The vault of heaven over the Albho was still in the grip of night, but the sky behind Aeternus slowly paled. Gradually the gray brightened to blue, and clear washes of pale pink, coral, and sulfur yellow announced with the flourish of color the coming of the day. The structures of the city sat humbly crouched in the semidarkness, waiting for their lord to touch them with his fiery wand, transforming them into his treasured jeweled minions.

Aeternus glowed with *agherz*, and the golden god drew himself up and lit the desert. Dina looked to the west, where the Albho Mar stretched as far as she could see in any direction. True to its name, the Albho glittered in the early morning light like a sea of frost. The procession of huggers rolling west towards the mines raised billows of white dust in its wake that hung over the mar like mist.

Dina felt unusually strong and wondered why this was so. She would have to ask Rayn about it. *Ask Rayn.* A man whose real name she didn't even know. A man with no standing, an illegal alien who lived a nomad's existence in an untouched land. How could her life have changed so completely? So quickly?

The path of her existence had been, for all her adult life, if not always upward, at least foreseeable. In her control. She had worked hard to achieve her professional standing, and her personal life, well, if not exciting, had been stable and safe. Now it was as though the gods had taken control and, with a tiny push, had sent the entity known as Mondina Marlijn tumbling down a steep declivity, to land only They knew where. She had joined minds with a *dens*. Her career was in jeopardy. Her future was uncertain. She should be in despair, but she wasn't. She should be weak with confusion, but she wasn't. She felt *strong*.

A tingle on her arm reminded her of the hour. She looked at her commband and sighed. It was time to meet with Jon. On her way back, she stopped at the AEA building and spoke to the lab technician. He was pleased to tell her that one latent fingerprint lifted from the knife had come back on file. She swore softly when she looked at the report.

"Were there any other good prints that didn't come back on file?"

"No, sorry, the rest were too smudged."

"What about the samples I dropped off? Any toxins present?"

He shook his head. "Nope. The granules are a phosphatide, namely lecithin, the powder is from the *stricumthys* shrub plant, commonly called *yegwa*, and the rest is *pirus* juice and plain distilled water."

Dina thanked the technician and secured the knife and his report as evidence, hoping she wouldn't need them. She hurried back to the Visitor Center for her meeting with Jon.

Dina spent the morning as she had the day before, going over the hard copy contracts with Faitaz Chukar. She particularly requested the contracts that had been in place between Mother Lode Mining and Ranchar's administration. As she looked over the files, her brows drew together. Something was missing.

"Mr. Chukar, forgive me, but is this file incomplete? I seem to get lost after subsection 59, paragraph 4."

The man frowned, not a hair of his golden hair out of place. "I don't see how the file can possibly be incomplete, but let me take a look. To what exactly are you referring?" He leaned over her, his flowery cologne almost choking her.

She pointed out the missing section, and Chukar shook his head. "I don't understand it, but it seems you're right. Let me see what I can do."

He returned moments later with the missing section. "My sincerest apologies, Agent Marlijn. A clerical error, nothing more."

She flashed Chukar her prettiest smile, and he returned a slow smile of his own.

Krek, she thought.

She particularly looked for any defeasance within the contracts. In the afternoon she met with Chukar and Quay Bhelen, Mother's chief financial officer. Dina examined in detail the company's expenses, assets, production numbers, sales figures, and in-house geological surveys. Her request for certified copies of various documents was met by no resistance by the Mother Lode personnel.

Her evening meeting again went well with Jon. She summarized her findings and the ideas she wanted to pursue for the following day. "Jon, do we have background checks on all of Mother Lode's on-planet administrative personnel?"

"We should have. I've gone over most of them."

"I want to go over all of them again, very carefully. And I want your opinion on all of the high-ranking Mother Lode officials we've met so far," she stated.

He frowned, but nodded and gave her his opinions of Hrothi, Ctararzin, Chukar, and Bhelen. "I'm not sure where you're going with this, Dina. We need evidence, not opinions."

"You'll get it, don't worry."

She seemed to have her partner's trust once again. A rueful smile accompanied her departure from his room. Jon was probably just thankful not to be hearing a request to interview Rayn. If he only knew.

As soon as she was back in her own room, Dina called to the man who had been most on her mind all day long.

Rayn?

At your service.

She closed her eyes and shivered at the soft stroke of his

voice inside her mind. *Can you come to the city?*

Two hours. 'Til then.

This time she couldn't help shivering at his final words. However he had done it, it had felt exactly as if his lips had pressed against hers and had breathed the two words into her open mouth.

Dina could barely sit still. A nap such as the one she had taken the previous night was out of the question. She decided to head to the Crown early. She showered and dressed carefully in leggings and a matching jacket of a gray-blue color she knew complemented her eyes. Was she dressing purposely to please a *dens*? She shuddered at the thought, then dismissed it. She always tried to look her best. She topped off the outfit, as always, with her exodite ring and twisted it for a moment before entering the obligatory message to Jon on her computer. She hoped he wouldn't question her desire to visit the hall two nights in a row.

The streets were almost as crowded as they had been when she had ridden to the Ghe Wespero to witness *agherz* only hours before. She again warded off offers of escort and entered The Furnace.

She didn't sense Rayn's presence, but she was about an hour early, so didn't expect him to be there yet. She ordered a Mocava Lava and settled back in her seat to people-watch. She was hardly inconspicuous herself, however, and soon had young hopefuls settling down next to her. The first left when she said she was waiting for someone, but the second was more persistent.

"I'll accept that," said the young man. "But in the meantime, until he arrives, I could keep you company. Look at it this way. With me sitting next to you, you won't have any really obnoxious men coming up and bothering you," the hopeful quipped, a grin on his young face.

He wasn't bad looking and had an unsophisticated kind of charm, so Dina decided to humor him for a few minutes. When she didn't ask him to leave, he started telling her about himself. Dina half listened, concentrating instead on feeling for Rayn's approach. The young man finally noticed that she was watching the crowd more than she was watching him.

"Say, what does this friend of yours look like? I could help you keep an eye out for him."

Dina turned to him and probed his mind lightly. *Krek,* she thought. He just wanted to know what kind of men she was interested in. At that instant, Dina knew Rayn had arrived and was approaching the entrance to the club. She decided to have some fun with the young man.

"Well, he's not very tall. He has unkempt brown hair, oh, and he walks with a limp. Poor soul, he's not much to look at, but he really knows how to treat a lady." Dina smiled to herself as she probed her admirer's mind and picked up his shock and confusion.

A moment later, a man dressed in leather pants the color of the moon and a long taupe duster hobbled toward Dina. The young man's eyes widened as Dina stood up, put her arms around the man's neck, and kissed him full on the mouth. Over Rayn's shoulder Dina could see the man hurrying away.

"'Not much to look at?'" Rayn directed at Dina, one eyebrow raised.

The kiss had been a game, but had left her knees ready to buckle. She ignored his teasing question and tried to return to safer ground, dropping to her seat at the bar. "Are your people moved?"

He nodded. "There's no guarantee they'll be safe in the new location, but it's the best that can be done right now."

She took a deep breath. "Rayn, I need you to help me understand what I'm feeling."

Rayn shrugged out of the duster and sat down beside her. A white T-shirt covered by a cream-colored leather vest showed off his tanned forearms and biceps that filled the short sleeves of the shirt. The gleam of his pendant drew her eyes to the vee of the shirt's neckline, and Dina's eyes lingered on the dark hair that curled around the star-stone. She raised her eyes to his only when he spoke again.

"What are you feeling?" he asked with a softness that gave added meaning to the question.

Dina twisted in her seat and felt her face flame. She was

trying to be serious now, but he seemed intent on continuing the game. "I'm afraid you know only too well, but what I wanted to ask you about is the energy and strength I feel."

"That doesn't sound unusual."

"What I felt today was. I felt powerful. And a freedom I can't describe."

Rayn hesitated, ordering another Mocava Lava for her and a Desert Rain, a cocktail made from *uisque* and a pale dry wine, for himself. He drew a deep breath. "It's part of the bond. The shared life force."

Her hand froze halfway to her glass. "Bond? What are you talking about?"

Rayn took a long swallow of his drink before he turned his eyes on hers. "Everything in your life, and in mine, will be different from now on. You and I have bonded, Dina, against the odds. It's an invisible force that connects us. Like it or not, it means you'll feel a powerful need for me, mental and physical. It's how you can sense my presence, and I can sense yours."

It was her turn to hesitate. She had wanted him to be serious, and he had obliged only too well. *Bonded to a dens? Was it possible?* She didn't even want to think about the possibility. There were more pressing issues.

She pushed her drink away. "Rayn, if this is true, then help me. Tell me who the killer is. I know you know who he is."

Rayn looked away, and she could tell from the glints of light reflected off his eyes that his gaze shifted more than once, from the far wall, to his drink, back to her. At last he nodded.

"Gyn T'halamar. And you're right, he's a *dens*. We didn't come here together, and I didn't know him on B'harata. I came here first, during the early part of Ranchar's reign, and Gyn arrived about eight months later. I've run into him several times. We made an agreement to leave each other alone. I have nothing he wants. He scorns me for wanting to live in the desert with people who have nowhere else to go. He believes I'm a fool and that my powers are ineffectual. He thinks I left B'harata because I was too weak to survive there. I let him believe what he wants. And he certainly has nothing I want, so I leave him alone."

"Do you know where he is?"

"I've come across some of his abandoned camps from time to time. I favor the south face of the Chayne, which looks upon the Ghel Mar, but he favors the north face, which faces the Pur-Pelag. I don't know exactly where he is now."

"Do you know why he's killing miners?"

He drew his brows together. "My guess would be that someone's paying him."

Dina nodded. "Who do you think it is?"

Rayn shook his head. "I don't know, but it's somebody with more than just a few credit chips in their pockets."

Frustrated, she played with her glass, twirling it on the bar. "How can we stop him?"

"You can't. At least not without considerable risk."

"Can he be reasoned with?"

Rayn brushed his hair back from his face and rounded his eyes at her. "What do you think?"

She sighed. "Based on the difficulty I've had reasoning with you, I guess not. If he's being paid, can we pay more?"

He shook his head again. "You can't trust him enough to bargain with him."

Dina sighed. "Why wouldn't you tell me any of this before?"

Rayn looked straight ahead and took a sip of his drink before answering. "I had a number of reasons, not the least of which was the safety of my people. The moment I allied myself with you, they all became targets."

"So now what? What happens to us?"

He gave her a sideways glance. "Well, I can do a lot of things, but seeing into the future is not one of them."

"What happens to two people who bond, and then are separated forever?"

He shook his head slowly. "I once heard that it's like losing a limb. That you can still feel it, still feel the bond, even when the person is gone. Feeling someone who's no longer there...it affects people differently. Some can no longer function in society. Some take their own lives. Those are extreme examples, but it happens."

Dina stared at him.

He shrugged. "It's not always that bad. It depends on how strong the bond was, and how strong the people involved are."

"This bond with us...is it strong?"

He looked at her and merely nodded.

"Have you ever bonded before?" she asked.

He looked away again. "No."

"You speak of the bond as if from experience."

He studied his drink, finally taking a large swallow. "My mother and father had a strong bond."

"What happened to them?"

"My father was killed."

"And your mother?"

"I was young. I have two brothers. She survived for our sake for a number of years."

"I'm sorry."

"Don't be. There's no 'sorry' in our vocabulary." He paused. "You're not angry with me." It was a statement, not a question.

"I can't afford the luxury of anger right now. There's too much to do. Besides, it happened. Maybe it was meant to happen this way. And yet..."

"What? You still don't trust me, do you?"

Did she trust him? She certainly hadn't in the beginning. So much had happened, and so much had changed for her, but had enough changed? "We're not going to be together, are we? As you said, you're here illegally and I'm just here on assignment."

"Dina, the future's not certain. But you didn't answer my question. Or maybe you did."

"I can't lie to you, Rayn. I can't even try. I'm not sure about many of my own feelings, and I'm even more unsure about yours. We're so different."

"Not as different as you think."

She shook her head. "This 'bonding' and 'life force.' They're hard for me to understand. And there are things I need that you may not. You'll have to accept that."

"Very well, little girl, I accept it."

She exhaled a huff of air. "How many times have I told

you not to call me that?"

"I'm at least twice your age. Did you know that?"

"No. You look no older than I do."

"B'haratans age slowly. Anyway, to answer your question, believe me when I tell you I'll do everything in my power to satisfy your needs. And I won't leave you. Is there anything else you need right now?"

Dina again felt heat rush to her face. She tried to think about T'halamar instead. "Rayn, I can't tell Jon about T'halamar. Since he's forbidden me to see you, I can't very well tell him you gave me this information."

"I'll send a message to your partner, asking to see him. I'll tell him the same things I told you."

Dina nodded. "I don't think finding T'halamar will be a problem. The AEA has aircraft equipped with heat sensors. It shouldn't be hard to locate a single man in the desert. Are there any others that live alone that you know of?"

"There may be one or two, but I don't know of anyone who prefers the Pur-Pelag to the Ghel Mar except Gyn."

"Pur-Pelag?'

"The fire basin, named for the red rock there. It's north of the Chayne."

Red rock. She didn't think she had seen any red rock, had she? And yet, the picture in her mind seemed familiar. "Is there anyplace else besides the Pur-Pelag that has red rock?"

"Not that I've come across. It's a unique geological feature confined to that one basin, as far as I know. Hot as hell, and so dusty that you can't breathe without choking."

Dina looked past his shoulder, her brow furrowed.

Rayn gave one shoulder a slight shrug. "Sandstone is soft. That's why no one else lives there. Why?"

She shook her head. "Never mind. Our problem will be what to do with him when we find him. Is there anywhere else we can meet from now on? I think Jon will get suspicious if I tell him one more time I'm coming here *al-merkwia*."

"Meeting should not be a problem. I have a confidante who has a room near here. I'm sure he'll let us use it for a couple hours."

"All right. Rayn, I have one more favor. Is there a way I can interview Kindyll and Raethe? They both worked in the mines. They may be able to give me information that miners currently in Mother Lode's pay are reluctant to give."

One corner of Rayn's mouth went up. "You certainly have asked me for quite a bit tonight, haven't you?"

"Well, it's the first time you haven't been an uncooperative, arrogant, son-of-a-bitch," she countered, smiling.

"Touché, little girl. I'll talk to Kindyll and Rae, but I doubt they'll refuse you. It's getting late. You'd better be on your way."

They both stood, but Dina made no move to leave, contemplating instead the soft vest that hugged Rayn's torso. At the open neckline, the oval pendant glowed even in the darkness, as if it needed no other light source but Rayn. She idly fingered the leather lacing and fringe that hung down the middle of the vest.

What now? Trying to think of yet one more thing you need from me? came the soft whisper into her mind.

She shuddered, closed her eyes, and once again felt the physical yearning that bloomed when she heard his Voice. She opened her eyes and raised them to his. She thought to hold his eyes, but felt caught instead by the amber gaze, open and vulnerable to him as she had never felt to any other man. It was a disquieting feeling at the very least. She was sure he knew exactly what she was thinking, and yet she wasn't at all sure what was in his mind. She knew he was aware of her desire and need for him, yet his needs were a mystery to her. It was exasperating.

"Damn you. Tell me, am I forever to be at the disadvantage with you?"

"Your skills will increase with practice."

"But I'll never be your equal, will I?"

"Does that bother you?" he asked softly, a brow lifted.

"Of course."

"Well, think of it this way. You're one up on me in the looks department."

She smiled, her hands still on his chest. His talk about

destruction had worried her, and she was glad his light-hearted repartee had returned. Her questions about the second *dens* answered, she felt like teasing him again. "Can a *dens* make love without burning his partner to death in the process?"

He laughed. "You don't orbit an issue, do you?"

"I'm an investigator, remember? We're trained on how to conduct an effect investigation."

His laughter abruptly died, and his eyes seemed to burn into her. "Love making without the ingredient of trust is a dangerous concoction."

"Maybe I do trust you. Are you going to answer my question, or not?"

He studied her for a moment. "No, I don't think I will. I'd either disappoint you or ruin the anticipation of discovery."

Dina pouted. "You were right before. I don't trust you. I don't even know if I like you."

His mouth twisted, and a small grin crinkled the corners of his eyes. "You like me. Come on, time for you to go. But it wouldn't be fair to let you leave without a little of what you want." He took her face in his hands, bent forward, and kissed her lightly, slowly deepening the kiss until she could feel all the heat she had seen in his eyes. "Tomorrow, then."

She fought to keep from shaking as he released her. Somehow, her teasing always backfired. "You'll contact Jon right away?"

"Yes, and I'll talk to Dyll and Rae. They're legal, so they can come to the city to see you."

Rayn...thank you. She kissed him quickly once more, then turned and wove her way through the crowd to the door, fully expecting to hear a parting admonishment in her mind to the effect that it was not the B'haratan way to thank someone. But all she heard on her way out was the rhythm of the music and the underlying heartbeat of the crowd.

***

Rayn sat alone at the bar for a quarter hour and ordered another Desert Rain. He had done it.

When she had first told him her nightmare had been about him, he had feared something new had happened to cause her to suspect him. Certainly she had bristled at his display of power the day before. His body had tightened in frustration at the thought of slowing things down with her, until the details of her nightmare assured him that the seeds of trust were still there.

And just now she had accepted everything he had told her. Surprisingly, she had embraced the idea of the 'bond' with little argument. Her doubts would mean nothing now. From here on in she'd be ruled by more than just her logical mind. Much more.

He scanned the crowd, both visually and with his mind, and picked up a rainbow of colors and emotions, but no danger. Rayn downed his drink, slung his jacket over his arm, and unobtrusively threaded his way through the press of bodies.

Outside, the night air hugged him with cool arms, and he sucked in a long breath. She was his. And she was ready.

THIRTEEN
REVELATIONS

The following morning, Dina was gliding over the rippling sands of the Albho Mar next to Jon. True to his word, Rayn had left a message for Jon to the effect that if Jon was willing to come to Bhel Kap, Rayn would give him information regarding the identity of the killer. Bhel Kap was the storage cavern Rayn brought all would-be *Dailjan* to for interviews. Since the location was already known to the AEA, Dina knew Rayn was not disclosing anything new by bringing them there. Although the invitation included both Jon and Dina, it had been delivered to Jon's room at *agherz*.

As the bands of sunlight and shadow passed beneath Dina's skimmer, she wondered how Rayn would divulge the killer's identity without disclosing his own. Jon was sure to ask questions. Maybe Rayn would use the *dher* on Jon so he'd remember only what Rayn wanted him to. Funny how she had would have been outraged at that idea only a few days ago.

Bhel Kap was east of Kathedra Kap, where the gray spires of the Chayne melded with the white dunes of the Wiara, but Dina kept that information to herself. As they approached Bhel, slowing their skimmers, Dina felt Rayn's presence inside the wide cavern entrance. Jon, always aware of the possibility of ambush, signaled to stop their skimmers some distance from the entrance, using a long ridge of rocks as cover. He scanned the area with a life detector and picked up one signal at the cavern entrance.

"Is he there?" Dina asked innocently.

"It would appear so," Jon replied. "DeStar. Show yourself," he called.

Rayn stepped from the cavern, and sparks of sunlight flashed off the narrow sunshield he wore in place of a hood. Dina and Jon approached him slowly on their skimmers, and at the entrance, parked the machines, removed their hoods, and stepped into the shade of the cave mouth. Dina looked around, but the cavern housed only one hugger, one skimmer, and a few supplies.

"Help yourselves to water," said Rayn, removing his jacket and sunshield. He wore only a cooling vest above his trousers, and his hair was tied back with a leather thong. The sharp widow's peak was thus accentuated, and seemed to rivet Dina's attention to his face. His eyes were narrowed, and a day's growth of beard made his face look dark and forbidding.

Dina, what I tell your partner may shock you. Even if it doesn't, remember to look appropriately surprised.

Gods, Rayn, what...

"All right, DeStar, let's get to it. Your message said you know the identity of our killer."

"And so I do. He's my brother."

Dina, perplexed, looked at Jon, who hadn't so much as raised an eyebrow.

"Literally, or figuratively?" asked Jon.

"Does it matter?" Rayn's voice was already betraying a boredom with Jon's questions.

"It matters."

"Very well. Figuratively, then. He's my countryman. His name is Gyn T'halamar, and he's a B'haratan, from the Deorcas Tron system, what you so derisively call the Dark Star."

"He's a *dens*, then. I thought so. As are you," Jon stated.

Dina didn't have to pretend to be surprised. What was Rayn doing?

Jon turned toward Dina. "Why didn't you tell me?"

Before she could formulate an answer, Rayn spoke. "Don't be too hard on your partner. She had no way of knowing. She's a telepath, yes, but a mere child in the telepathic world of the *dens*. She could no more read me or T'halamar than she could fly."

Jon spent a moment more looking at Dina before shifting emerald eyes back to DeStar. "And how do you know T'halamar is the killer?"

"He and I have been in this desert a long time, and our paths have crossed on numerous occasions. He's a cold, remorseless man. It's well within his ability and nature to do what was done."

Jon barked a short laugh. "That's no proof. What would be his motive?"

"He wouldn't concern himself with what he would consider to be lower life forms if there wasn't some considerable profit in it," said Rayn, eyeing Jon steadily while he emphasized 'lower life forms'.

Jon ignored the insult. "What does he need out here with money?"

"He has power. Wealth is second only to that which he already has. You think he plans to stay on this rock forever? You forget—we have long life spans. A few years on this sand heap is like a blink in time for us. With enough of a fortune and his considerable endowments, he can go almost anywhere in the galaxy."

"Everything you've said about this man applies just as well to you. What is there to prevent me from believing you're the killer and that this T'halamar is a myth?"

"Absolutely nothing. You're free to believe as you wish," came Rayn's cold reply.

"Am I?" Jon stared at DeStar, all traces of his casual, easy-going demeanor gone. His handsome face was hard, and his eyes, squinted, glowed like green ice shards. DeStar returned Jon's stare just as unflinchingly, his full mouth untouched by derision or arrogance, his brown eyes as dark as day-old mocava.

Dina looked from one man to the other, and a chill passed through her. Her life had become so tightly interwoven with these two men that she felt every word between them almost as a physical blow.

"Your mind is your own and will remain so, as long as you don't cross me. I'm not your enemy, but I can be a formidable opponent. It is best for all concerned," Rayn said, his eyes resting on Dina's, "that you remember that."

Jon's eyes fairly blazed at the implied threat against Dina. "I won't be so veiled in my speech. Touch her, and you're dead."

Dina could stand it no longer. "Jon, DeStar, please..."

"You're right. He's not worth it." Jon grabbed Dina's arm and quickly turned her to the cavern entrance. "Come on. We won't find out anything more here."

Rayn...

Trust, Dina. It'll be all right. I'll come to the city later with Dyll and Rae. Until then.

Outside the kap, Jon pulled his hood over his head. "Arrogant bastard," he breathed, loud enough for Dina to hear.

"Hey, I'm the one who has no love for the *dens,* remember?"

"Yeah, well, all I can say is that it's no wonder they're universally despised as a race. You're not to see him alone, understand?"

"I know. You told me that already."

"Just reinforcing the idea."

"As if it'd need reinforcing after that cheery meet."

They rode back to the city in silence, thoughts of Rayn stealing from her concentration. She hoped he knew what he was doing. He had asked for her trust. It seemed she had no choice now but to give it.

Back in Aeternus, Dina and Jon met in his room after a quick clean up and change of clothing. As Dina entered the room and sat down, Jon handed her an iced mocava.

"Well, what do you think? Is DeStar our killer, or you believe his story of a second *dens?*" asked Jon, sitting opposite Dina.

"His arrogance irritates me no end, but I'm inclined to believe him. DeStar is right. I can't read him or the killer the way they can read me, but when I was attacked at the mine, I could sense a blackness, a darkness of the soul I didn't feel the times I was with DeStar. I don't have any proof, Jon, just instincts. My instincts tell me that DeStar is telling the truth."

Jon sighed. "All right. We'll leave it at that for now. Assuming this T'halamar does exist, any ideas on how we can apprehend him?"

"No. And since we don't trust our resident expert on the *dens,* Mr. DeStar..." Dina let the thought trail.

"No."

"No, what?"

"The man is dangerous. Never mind he's egotistical, manipulative, and overbearing. He's downright dangerous. He's got his own agenda, and you can be sure it doesn't match ours. He'll spin you a web of lies and half-truths and have you believing every word of it. You're not to contact him."

Dina raised her hands in a gesture of surrender. "Hey, I agree with you. One hundred percent."

"Let's forget about him for now. We seem to make more progress on this case when we're not wasting our time on Rayn DeStar. What are your plans for today?"

"I'm interviewing two ex-miners. I think you're right about Mother Lode being at the heart of all this, and I'm hoping that ex-miners will be more forthcoming with inside information. Current guild members haven't been very helpful. They know if they say the wrong thing their job and guild status are in jeopardy."

"Sounds like a good idea," Jon remarked. "I haven't had any luck arranging for a new independent survey of the mines. It appears there aren't any qualified surveyors on Exodus now. Mother Lode apparently ships them in only when they're needed, and we don't have time to do that. Have you started on the company financial records yet?"

"Yes."

"Good. Keep at it. Meet back here at the usual time. Where are you having your interview with the ex-miners?"

"I don't know yet. I'm waiting for a message from them."

"All right. Let me know. I should be here."

Back in her room, Dina was anxious to talk to Rayn. She wanted to ask him about the morning meeting with Jon, and she wanted to ask him about Gyn. Gods, there were a thousand things she wanted to ask him.

Rayn?

I'm honored you're still speaking to me.

Dina sighed. First she had had to put up with Jon's display of loathing and anger, and now she had to put up with Rayn's attitude. *What are you talking about?*

Your partner has a strong, how shall I put it? Dislike? Distrust? How about good old-fashioned 'hatred.' Your partner has a 'hatred' for me. I thought he might influence your feelings.

He tried. My feelings are my own.

You don't have any doubts about that?

No.

He hesitated, as if he had been about to say something. When he did speak, it was on a new subject.

Dyll and Rae are on their way. They should arrive at the city within the hour. They'll wait for you at the Oasis. They're legal, but they don't have any security clearance. However, if you can think of a better place for the interview, let them know. I'm sure they'll willingly follow you anywhere.

Rayn. You're not jealous of your own men, are you?

I should be. I trust my men, but I've seen how you pick up men and dangle them from your fingertips.

She steamed. Somehow, as always, he had taken her thrust, parried it, and riposted.

Now don't sputter, little girl. I trust you, even if you don't trust me.

The 'little girl' is not sputtering. She hated it when he called her that, but even piqued, she felt an overpowering need to see him. *When can I see you?*

For the first time that day a smile was reflected in his Voice. *When your interviews are over. Until then.*

Dina tried to redirect her thoughts. If she thought about Rayn all the time, she'd go crazy. While she changed clothes for her meeting with Kindyll Sirkhek and Raethe Avarti, she thought about the questions she wanted to ask them. She put on the rose-beige desert suit she had worn the day she had first met Rayn. Strange that she thought more about Rayn than the attack when she recalled that day. Almost absentmindedly, she fingered the suit, which had been repaired and cleaned, and remembered how his Voice had felt inside her mind, so intimate, yet so chilling, like the stroke of a cold hand. She sighed. So much for trying not to think about Rayn. She left a message for Jon regarding her destination, and in twenty minutes was on her way to the Crown.

As she entered the Oasis, she tried reaching out with her feelings to see if she could detect the presence of others the way she could detect Rayn's presence. Nothing. She walked slowly through the rooms and saw the fountain she had sat next to the night she had tried calling Rayn, the night he was poisoned. The seat was unoccupied, and she continued on until she saw the two men sitting in a secluded corner. Both rose upon seeing Dina.

"Thank you both for coming. Please sit," greeted Dina in her most professional tone.

"It's our pleasure to help you any way we can," replied Kindyll. The words might have sounded rote coming from someone else, but Kindyll's forthright hazel eyes and genuine smile told Dina the words came from his heart.

She told them she preferred to question them separately regarding the mines and the surveys, and they agreed without question. Raethe rose, stated he would wait in the Mocava Cave until Dina sent for him, and took his leave.

"Kindyll, how long ago did you leave Mother Lode's employ?"

"About six months. My contract ended just after Dais was killed. It was the perfect opportunity to get out without breaking my contract. Others weren't so lucky."

"Were you a friend of Dais'?"

"Sure. All the desert rats knew Crazy Dais, and everybody liked him. He'd been working the mines here longer than most, so he had a lot of know-how. He was respected. When he was killed, it was more than just a shock."

"How rich is the gem-bearing rock? Are the mines playing out sooner than expected?"

A frown drew Kindyll's golden brows together. "How did you manage to find that out? It's Mother's best kept secret."

"Then it's true."

The eyebrows lifted. "Yeah. Kewero was the richest, but it's almost played out now. Dheru, for all it's size, doesn't yield much. And Sawel, well, Sawel is mostly for show. It's too bad."

"But the Synergy survey that was done prior to renewal of the contract was a positive survey, wasn't it?"

He gave a short laugh. "Sure. It always is. Synergy surveys are a joke. See, the Syn has a big investment in this colony. They want to get everything out of the mines they can. So their surveys always show more potential than there actually is. If not Mother, some other company will bid for it. Mining companies know about the Syn surveys and that they're taking a huge risk when they put in a bid. But sometimes the lode is there, and the risk pays off big."

"But this time Mother Lode signed off on the Synergy survey. Why would they do that if they know for sure the survey's not accurate?"

Kindyll shook his head, and blond strands of hair curved into his eyes. He brushed them back. "That I don't know. A dispute over the survey would have pretty much guaranteed that Mother would not be awarded renewal of the contract."

"Wouldn't that be preferable to renewing the contract knowing the mines will play out before the end of the contracted period?"

He shrugged. "You would think so, and I would think so, but then, we're honest people. Can't say the same for the Company. Who knows? Maybe someone on the Mother survey team made a legitimate mistake. Even with all their technology, no one shrouds their secrets better than the ancient earth."

"What if the sign-off to the Syn survey was intentional, not a mistake?"

"Well, then, the mines play out, and Mother loses money. Even without profits, they have to pay rights to the Synergy."

"Unless they can find a way to break the contract legally."

Kindyll tried to digest that. "I suppose. I don't know much about the contracts."

"What if it could be proved that the sign-off was a fraud?"

"You mean done on purpose and not a mistake?"

"Right."

"Well, that would be pretty difficult, I think. All the Company surveyors are off-worlders. Normally, that is. Dais was on the survey team this last time. But he's dead, so he..." Kindyll stopped. He wasn't an investigator, but Dina could tell by his broken-off sentence that he understood the import of his words.

She finished the thought for him. "So he can't tell anyone that the Mother Lode survey was a fraud. How did he get on the survey team?"

"One of the off-worlders got sick, and they needed a replacement. Dais had a lot of experience, like I said, and had even done some surveying on past jobs."

"There was nothing in his file about his being on the survey team, and nothing in any of the interviews."

Kindyll shrugged again, a small lift of his lean frame. "I told you. The Company is a close-mouthed lot."

"Thank you, Kindyll. You've been more help than you can imagine."

"You're welcome, ma'am. I don't know what I would have done if Rayn hadn't taken me in. With everything that had happened, the job had soured for me. Even without the murders, it was nothing but politics. You could never trust anyone. The port was closed, but even if it had been open I don't have any family to return to on Glacia. I would have probably just spent my contract bonus foolishly, feeling sorry for myself, if not for Rayn. I would do anything for him."

Dina felt a wave of affection for the man with the young face and the old eyes. "Kindyll, I never had a brother, but if I did, I'd want him to be you." She reached over and gave him a quick hug. Unprofessional, she knew, but she was doing a lot of unprofessional things these days.

She sent him to get Raethe, who returned and folded his long body into the seat next to Dina. He was tall, about Jon's height, and with Jon's coloring, but there the resemblance ended. Jon was like a well-cared-for hunting dog, while Raethe was like a lean, hungry wolf, all wariness, sinew, and muscle. Dina still didn't feel comfortable with Raethe, in spite of Rayn's faith in the man.

"Why was your guild membership revoked?" she began.

He looked away, then back at her, and gave a slight shrug of his head. "One of the bosses caught me bad-mouthing Mother one night in the Furnace."

"What were you saying?"

"I don't remember all of it. I'd been drinking, but they claimed I was talking about yield, or the lack of it, I should say. Discussing yield is a big no-no."

"Who were you with in the Furnace at the time?"

"Quite a few of the rats were there. I don't remember who exactly."

"Was Kilist Marhjon there?"

Rae hesitated, cocked his head, then lifted his brows a little in resignation. He looked her right in the eye. "I have a feeling, Miss, that you're asking me questions you already have the answers to."

She ignored his remark. "Marhjon testified against you at your hearing, didn't he?"

"Kil was my friend. He testified because they put pressure on him. He didn't want to lose his job. He had a family. I didn't kill him, or any of the others." Raethe's voice raised slightly with the denial but was still under control.

She redirected her questioning. "Do you remember seeing a knife at Sanctuary, a small, black pearl inlaid pocketknife?"

"I remember seeing it and wondering whose it was. It didn't look familiar." His voice dropped again.

"Do you know where it came from?"

"No."

"Did you touch it?"

He nodded. "To pick it up and look at it."

Dina drew a long breath and turned away. She had been probing Raethe as best she could while questioning him. She had detected no guilt, fear, or discomfort, but a strength and sadness so profound that it touched her deeply. When she turned back to Raethe, it was with new eyes.

"Forgive me, Raethe. These were questions I had to ask."

"I understand. I've been through grilling a lot worse, believe me."

"I need your help, if you're willing to give it."

The shaggy mane merely rose and fell.

Dina continued questioning him, and he confirmed what Kindyll had told her about the mines playing out and how the surveys were done. She thanked him when she was finished, but didn't hug him the way she had Kindyll. One doesn't hug a wolf.

After Sirkhek and Avarti left, Dina sat alone in the Oasis.

It was still early in the afternoon, the hottest part of the day, but Dina had to see Rayn.

Rayn, where are you?

At a friends' quarters in the city. He gave her the coordinates, and she was there ten minutes later.

As he let her into the small room, her eyes met his, and her heart skipped a beat.

Come to me.

Half out of her jacket, she tugged at the remaining sleeve and threw the jacket to the floor. His power flowed over her like a midnight desert zephyr, dark and cold. Half a step later she was in his arms, trembling, her own wound tightly around his neck, as if he were a haven, not the storm itself. He kissed her, longer and harder than before, not a teasing kiss, but one that conveyed his need for her, until she moaned into his mouth. He released her slowly, but his power retracted in a heartbeat, and when she looked into the amber eyes, she thought she saw pain. The stillness she felt in the room felt unnatural.

"What is it?" she asked quietly.

"Nothing." He turned away and sat down, then leaned forward and rubbed his temples with the heels of his palms.

From the moment she had first probed his mind, she had suspected he lived with a kind of hurt she didn't understand. She wondered if it was something he would ever willingly share with her. She knew it wouldn't do any good to press him, so she sat on the floor next to his chair and waited. Finally, he spoke, but it was only of the day's events, not what she really wanted to hear.

"Yes, Dyll and Rae were very helpful," she replied to his inquiry. "I'm convinced that someone, or perhaps more than one person, at Mother Lode is responsible for the killings. It's going to be difficult to find out who, though, and even more difficult to prove."

"So am I a marked man, or did your partner believe me?"

"I don't think he's decided yet. Rayn..." She didn't know what to say.

He didn't respond, but sat with his head tilted to one side and supported by his right hand. Dina looked up and studied his face, thinking that if she had a thousand years, she would never tire of gazing at the features. His hair was still tied back with loose strands falling forward from either side of the widow's peak, and he hadn't shaved. His appearance had a dark look which seemed to match his mood. Only a moment ago, fast in his arms, she had been as close to him as a lover. Now she felt far away from him.

"Rayn. Tell me more about your life on B'harata," she asked, not really expecting him to answer.

As usual, he surprised her. "I was a misfit growing up. I wasn't aggressive, and I didn't practice the arts, so to speak. I much preferred to sit and watch the colors of the rain. I'm sure my father and my brothers were disappointed in me, thinking I was weak, but my mother understood. She knew I was strong, and she knew where my strengths lay. She was my defender. Anyway, I had but one friend, Tiryl. We were inseparable for a long time."

"What happened?"

The wistful look on Rayn's face hardened. "Tiryl made new friends as he got older. I wasn't part of their group. To prove himself to his new friends, he set me up and tried to do what he could to harm me, in the usual B'haratan way. By using his mind to overpower mine. One of my older brothers, Flyr, was with me, discovered what was happening, and saved my life. Tiryl died, and his friends exacted their revenge by destroying Flyr instead of me."

"I'm sorry." She knew "sorry" wasn't in the B'haratan vocabulary, but she didn't know what else to say.

"After that I vowed I'd never be betrayed like that again. With my father's help, I started developing my talents. I spent every waking moment practicing and honing my skills. My father was pleased, but I think it made my mother sad, in spite of the fact I was now able to defend myself. One night I overheard my mother praying. She said, 'My Raynga, don't let him be deliberately cruel. This boy I love so well, don't change him that much.' No matter how long I live, I'll always remember her words."

Dina didn't know what to say or do. Her experience with

men in this type of situation was almost non-existent. She wasn't sure what she would do to console a Glacian male in these circumstances, much less a male of a completely different culture. She untangled herself from the floor and moved to the back of his chair, then put her arms around his neck and laid her cheek against the side of his head. She closed her eyes and could detect the faint scent of mountain mint in his smooth hair. He brought his hands up to hold her forearms, and they stayed like that, neither of them speaking, for a long while.

At last Rayn gently removed her arms from around his neck and rose. He ran two glasses of iced mocava, carried one back to her, then walked over to the small window and stood looking out.

Dina knew she should be asking Rayn more about Gyn, but all she could think about was how much she wanted him. She set the glass down without taking a sip.

"Rayn."

"Um."

Dina sensed she was in trouble. Rayn still seemed distracted, hardly aware of her presence. She proceeded anyway. "I want an answer to my question."

"What question?"

Gods! Alee was right, she thought. For someone with his powers, he could be awfully dense. How could he possibly be unaware of her desire for him? No, he couldn't be unaware. She took a deep breath. "What question? The question I know I haven't been able to hide from your probes, Mr. All-knowing, since the day I met you. Can you make love to me?"

He turned and looked at her, his face hard to read, then took a long swallow of mocava before replying. "I warned you might be disappointed by the answer. Are you prepared to face that?"

Why was he playing games? She couldn't imagine being disappointed by him. "I hardly think that will be the case," she retorted, unable to keep the dryness from her voice.

"What makes you think you know anything about the subject, much less how I make love?"

The question stung more than the sharpness in his voice.

"You're right. I don't have a lot of experience with men. But I know how I feel, how you make me feel, when I'm close to you."

He set his drink down on a nearby table. "Tell me about your first lover," he said, almost casually.

Had her declaration completely gone over his head? "You're changing the subject. I want to be with you. I want to take the plunge." Why was he being so obstinate?

He blinked. "What?"

"I told you I'd let you know when I'm ready. Well, I'm letting you know."

"You're not ready."

The dispassionate reply angered her. "You seemed to think so two nights ago in the Furnace."

"I was playing with you. Tonight there are no games."

"No games? Then don't talk in riddles." But his words did more than frustrate her. They hurt, too. She knew their two encounters in the club had involved a healthy dose of flirting on both sides, but she also had thought there was more between them than that. She wished fervently she had had more close relationships with men. Did he really feel she wasn't ready for him, or did he have no desire for her? She didn't understand her own feelings much of the time, and she certainly didn't understand how men felt. Then again, she thought, all the experience in the universe would never prepare her for dealing with one stubborn B'haratan.

He turned away from her and paused, his head bent, one hand absently rubbing the stubble on his chin. He walked in a slow circle until he was once again facing her.

"Look at me and tell me what you see," came his soft request, stripped of any nuance of command or compelling power.

"Why? I thought you said no games."

"It's not a game," he said patiently. "Just look at me and tell me exactly what you see."

She stared at him. Without the long hair framing his face, she concentrated more on his features. The lines were perfect. From the high cheekbones and strong jaw to the straight nose and full mouth, it was as if an artist had worked to find just the right balance of beauty and masculinity, sensitivity and strength. The golden eyes not even the most talented artist could have rendered. They were a gift from the gods.

Even so, her frustration colored her response. "I see a man who's too good-looking for his own good, with hair the color of mud after a rainstorm, eyes like dirty snow, and a body that won't..."

The rest of her description was cut off by his laugh. "That'll do."

"So? What was the point of that?"

His face fell back into its somber cast. "You didn't say 'I see a *dens* who's too good looking for his own good.' Why not?"

She shrugged. "You can't tell a *dens* by their appearance. They look like any other human."

"But you know I'm a *dens*."

Dina didn't know what to say. She didn't know what he was getting at. What did this have to do with her wanting him?

"You forget," he continued. "You told me not long ago that you don't ever forget what I am, but you do. I'm different from human males. My physiology is different from yours."

"You make love to Alessane." It was almost an accusation.

He closed his eyes, but hesitated only briefly in answering. "She's not a telepath."

Dina didn't know why those words should hurt so much. She had known from day one that Alessane had been his lover. "So?"

"Your being a telepath complicates things. And there was no bond with Alee."

She shook her head. "I still don't understand what you're trying to tell me."

"I'm simply saying you're not ready. Trust me on this."

"Then teach me. Show me, talk to me," she pleaded.

"First tell me about your first lover. "

Gods! He was stubborn. She could either storm out or talk about what he wanted to talk about. She chose the latter, but it was a difficult subject for Dina to discuss. She was silent for a moment, letting the memories surface, trying to fish out the right images and words. "It was eight years ago. I was in school. I didn't have many friends, and no boyfriends."

At that, Rayn raised an eyebrow.

"Oh, plenty of men expressed interest in me, but it wasn't really *me* they wanted. They wanted a pretty face or a nice body to show off to others, or just to make love to. Back then I didn't know if my telepathic ability was a curse or a blessing. Most times it felt like a curse. It seemed like every time I probed someone, all I picked up was selfishness or dishonesty. So I rejected all the offers that came my way."

She drew a deep breath and slowly let it out. "Then Daar came into my life. He was a guest speaker in one of my classes. The day he gave his lecture, he never took his eyes off me. After the class he asked to have lunch with me. He was older than the others, and I thought he was different. He seemed genuinely interested in me."

"What happened?" Rayn asked softly.

"We were lovers for several months. I adored him. I thought he cared about me, too. He told me he did. He was so attentive to my needs. No one else had ever been. I was ecstatic. I had finally found someone who cared for *me*. And then..." She stopped, not wanting to continue. Dina looked at Rayn again and wanted to curse him for demanding she talk about this.

"I trusted him as I had never trusted anyone before. Then he decided he was going to quit his job and start a business partnership with a friend of his, Erel. I had never liked Erel, and once, while Erel was visiting, I probed him. I picked up dishonesty and deceit. I tried to warn Daar later that his friend lacked the integrity for a partnership, but Daar laughed at me. Finally, to save him from ruining himself with this man, I told him the truth. The truth about my ability and the truth of my knowledge of Erel."

The hatred, so close to the surface, was like a wild beast jarred from a comfortable sleep, selfish, demanding, and unseeing. Her throat constricted with the emotion, and it was hard to get the words out. She looked away from Rayn.

"But instead of being grateful, Daar was furious. He

demanded to know how often I had probed him over the course of the relationship and to know what I had read. I tried to explain that I didn't probe people on a regular basis, but it didn't matter. He called me filthy names. Names I don't want to repeat. He ended the relationship immediately. I continued to see him at the university, but he ignored me completely every time, not even acknowledging my presence."

"How can you hate the *dens* so much after having been a victim of the same prejudice that's been directed at us?" Rayn's soft, controlled voice was gone, replaced by a low utterance which guttered with emotion, but Dina barely heard him.

She looked again at Rayn, and this time saw the *dens*, not the man. The beast that had been roused demanded satisfaction, and she turned it on the creature she saw.

"Don't you see? There would have never been any prejudice against me if it hadn't been for you! The names he called me were all derogatory terms for your people, your planet. It's because of you that my life has been the way it has."

"And you think that if there were no 'Dark Star,' no *dens*, that your Daar would have welcomed your admission that you could read minds? That he would have understood? Accepted you? Continued to cherish you the same way he had before?" Rayn replied, his voice louder but still hoarse.

Another time she would have heard the pain in his voice and considered his statements, but not now. "His hate wouldn't have been so automatic. He wouldn't have spit on me as if I were a lit match that would burn him."

He took a step toward her. "Dina, listen to me. I've been around a lot longer than you have, and I've traveled to many worlds, including your Glacia. It's a fact that most people without the ability have a hard time understanding and trusting those of us with it. It's the same with any trait that's vastly different from our own. Would you trust a shifter?"

"No...but..."

"And why wouldn't you trust them? In point of fact they're not a violent people. But they're hated and feared nevertheless because others don't understand them and don't take the time and trouble to do so."

She shook her head, barely feeling her eyes glaze over with unshed tears. "But Daar would have had a more open mind if not for the *dens*."

He moved another step closer to her. "You don't know that. Daar was a fool."

She blinked, not seeing Rayn at all, but visions of the past. "Damn your contempt, damn all of you who think you know everything. You don't understand."

"What don't I understand?"

"What others suffer because of you..." Her voice dropped as she tried in vain to control the anguish that flooded her. She felt him brush her mind and she repelled him as best she could. "No! Stay out of my mind."

"Something's wrong, Dina. What are you trying to hide from me? I can feel your hate, but it's not for a broken love affair that ended years ago. It's hot, and very fresh. I can feel it. You don't hate the *dens* because of Daar. He was a long time ago, but your pain is recent. You've nurtured this hate. *Why?*"

But she only shook her head again, staring beyond him. "Damn you all to the Void!"

He grabbed her arm with one hand and her face with his other, forcing her to look at him. "Tell me. Tell me what happened to cause you this much pain."

She closed her eyes. "You killed Roanna."

"What?"

"She was killed eleven months ago. Roanna was killed by a *dens*. It was senseless. She just wanted to question him— wasn't even going to take him into custody. He compelled her to turn her weapon on herself. She was my classmate at the Academy and my partner. My best friend. There was no reason for her to die, no reason...the *dens* just kill...and now it's happening all over again."

Rayn wrapped his arms around her and held her close, and she had no energy left to fight him.

I'm so sorry, little girl. He rocked her gently, and the rancor that gripped her gradually loosened. His mind pressed hers, and the hate fled. She dropped her guards, and he advanced, but she felt no compelling commands, no power unleashed on her. He simply held her and waited.

At last, she moved her head and looked at him. *I know you're not like that. I know that every world, every race, has killers, it's just that...*

I know. And I do understand. What happened to my brother was just as senseless. It's no easier when it's one of your own kind.

He held her at arm's length and retreated from her mind. "And you trusted Daar."

She nodded. "I wouldn't let myself form any relationships after that."

"Tell me. Is Daar the reason you can't trust me, or is it that you just can't bring yourself to trust a being like the one who killed your partner?"

"I don't know if I can trust anyone."

"Anyone other than Jon," he added, the voice soft once again. "Now I know why you're so protective of him."

Dina locked her eyes with Rayn's for a long moment. "I don't have a relationship with Jon. He's my partner and my friend, and that's all."

"And what do we have, Dina?"

"What do you want from me, Rayn? My trust? To what end? All we appear to have is a physical attraction that's obviously going nowhere."

He let go of her and stepped back. "It's getting late. He'll be calling for you soon."

Dina didn't want to leave, especially like this. Her anger had drained, but not her longing. If anything, the outburst of emotion had fueled her hunger. She wanted his answer to her question. "Rayn...I need you."

"I know you do, Dina, I know. Come here."

She went to him, and he placed his hands on either side of her face. *Reach out to me, and wrap your mind around mine.*

She slid her hands up his chest, and stretched her mind out to meet his. With the link in place, he dipped his head, and kissed her, slowly at first, tantalizing her. Dina gasped. This was like nothing she had ever experienced or imagined. It was as though all her senses were heightened, as if she were inside the kiss, feeling it from the inside out. Her entire existence was his mouth on hers—hot and soft—as if all the heat of the desert was in his kiss. She started to shake, and he pulled away from her. *It's burn. Release the link slowly and take deep breaths. Come on, do as I say.*

Dina took a deep breath and shuddered. She pulled back from his mind, as he had commanded, and tried to slow her breathing. She realized her heart was pounding, but hadn't been aware of it until now.

"See? I told you loving me wasn't easy."

"Not easy, perhaps, but worth the struggle, I think."

He laughed softly, and she was glad she had lifted his dark mood, at least for a moment.

"Rayn, I have to ask you one question about T'halamar before I go. Can he use the *dher* on more than one person at a time?"

"No. He has to make a one-on-one connection. But if you're thinking of capturing him by using a large force against him, remember this: You'll likely be successful, but only after you've suffered casualties as well. I don't think you want that."

"What alternative do we have?"

"Come on, you'd better be leaving."

Reluctantly, she picked her jacket up off the floor and turned toward the door, but she paused before opening it. "Tomorrow?" she asked quietly, still facing the door.

Tomorrow.

***

He stood, long after the door silently closed behind her, and thought about the irony. She had been ready for him, but he hadn't been able to do it. He had brought her here to take her, to satisfy the growing need that threatened to overwhelm him, but found himself fighting to put her off instead.

He sagged to the bed. The game with her was over. He couldn't make love to her and risk having her discover what he really was. Not yet. There was too much at stake.

He thought about her final question. There were alternatives. Not all the games were over.

FOURTEEN
GYN

Dina awoke at morning twilight again the following day, and with the energy of the awakening sun, dressed quickly and rode her skimmer to Ghe Wespero. Quite a few of the *mercari* greeted her warmly as they plied their trade. She returned their greetings and looked first to the east, at the silhouetted structures dark against the glow of *agherz*, then at the shimmering Albho.

It was a warm morning, and all she had put on for the weather had been a narrow sunshield. As the sun began lighting sparks off the buildings, Dina could feel the blood pulsing through her temples.

After all of yesterday's disclosures, she needed to think, but it was too crowded and noisy at the marketplace. She fired her skimmer to life again and headed west across the mar. She had no specific destination in mind, only knew that the sand sky above and desert sea below beckoned her onward.

At the fifth way station she slowed her skimmer and pulled to a stop in the shade of the small structure. Something wasn't right. Parked in the shade, she felt warmer than she had in the sun. She dismounted, but realized too late that she was not alone in the shadow.

Dina stared at the man who stepped from around the corner of the building. She started to pull her gun, but quickly thought better of it. If this man was who was she thought he was, the most dangerous place for her gun to be was in her hand. He was imposing in every respect. Not quite as tall as Jon, she guessed he was a little taller than Rayn. Like all the desert dwellers she had seen, he was without a trace of fat, all sinew and hard muscle. His hair was black and hung straight to the middle of his back. Eyes that were as dark and glittering as oil snared her, and features sharp as a dagger held her. His chest was bare, but he wore loose white trousers, black leather boots, and black leather bracers on his forearms.

"Who are you?" Dina's voice felt small and weak to her

own ears, but the man apparently had no trouble hearing her.

"You haven't guessed? Ah, yes you have. I should have been disappointed in you if you hadn't. Gyn T'halamar, late of B'harata, currently of the Pur-Pelag. Do you know what that means? The Fire Basin. I like that. I like living in the Pur-Pelag. Only the strong can survive in the heat of such fire."

A red glow flowed outward from the man, and it was disconcerting, even for someone like Dina, who had experienced tangible auras before. The man appeared to be burning, yet there were no flames. The aura colored his trousers crimson, and his hair the color of dried blood. Dina's heartbeat throbbed in her head, making it hard to concentrate. She knew she was at this man's mercy, and that even if she called for Rayn's help, there was no way he could arrive in time to save her from whatever T'halamar had in mind. "What do you want of me?"

"You're afraid of me. That's smart. Fear is what helps us to survive. Yes, even the *dens* cannot afford to become complacent. But I didn't bring you here to hurt you."

The hot-coal glow flared around T'halamar, but aside from the heat, Dina couldn't feel his power on his skin. He was holding it well in check, yet he wanted her to be able to see it.

"You tried to kill me in the mine."

"It was not I who tried to kill you. I brought you here to warn you about the man who did."

Dina's heart continued to pound like thunder that presaged a storm. This was not what she had expected, and her mind was having difficulty focusing on what he was saying. She wondered if he would use the *dher* on her. Thus far she felt no invasion of her mind, but she had no doubt he could do whatever he wished with her.

She swallowed, but it was a dry swallow, tasting of fear. "Why are you killing miners?" Her question was hardly more than a whisper.

"I didn't kill the miners any more than I tried to kill you. If you think about it, you'll realize who did." He paused, and a smug smile of satisfaction twisted his mouth. "Ah, so you do know. Yes, DeStar, as he calls himself. You want to know why? Because he realizes it was a mistake to come here, but he wants the means to go elsewhere. So he sells the only marketable thing he has—his ability."

Dina's gaze felt trapped by the man's impenetrable eyes. Had her own thoughts truly betrayed Rayn? She couldn't be sure, knew only that she didn't want to believe it.

His voice, smooth and deep, continued. "Have you not wondered how DeStar just happened to be so at hand when you needed help? He has been manipulating you since he met you."

"I don't believe you," she whispered.

"Of course you don't. He's used a number of parlor tricks on you, I'm sure. But he has lied to you, hasn't he? Quite a few times, no?"

Rayn had lied to her. She couldn't deny that. He had denied knowing who had been responsible for the murders. A necessity, he had said, to ensure the safety of his people. What else had he lied about?

T'halamar laughed softly, a strange sound, like molten lava sliding over the earth. Her skin crawled with sweat.

"He is what is called on B'harata a *spithra*, after a small creature, which, unable to overpower its prey, uses cunning and trickery instead. The *spithra* lures its victims into its lair by emitting an attractive scent, then slowly binds the hapless one to the lair one strand at a time. The victim doesn't even know it's caught until it finally finds itself completely bound by spun threads, nearly invisible, but with the relative strength of the hardest metal in the galaxy."

Dina's skin felt fevered, and she shivered at the same time sweat broke out on her brow beneath her hood. This couldn't be true. Not Rayn.

"I'm a loner. What better scapegoat could DeStar come up with than me? Think about it. You'll find what I say is the truth. It's not too late, if you want to save yourself."

Dina closed her eyes. She tried to probe the strange man before her, but without success. She felt her effort easily repelled, as if she were a small child trying to hit a grown man.

"Go now. If you like, ask him if what I say is true. Just be prepared to hear more lies."

She didn't move. She couldn't believe he wasn't going to hurt her.

He laughed again. "Go. I have no hold on you, and no desire to harm you."

Dina looked up again at the piercing gaze in the arresting face. The aura was gone, and all she saw was his normal coloring, the deeply tanned skin and jet black hair. His eyes glittered back at her, far too alive. She turned and fled, vaulting onto her skimmer and accelerating back to the city at top speed, still afraid he would come after her. During the ride back to Aeternus she tried not to think about Gyn or Rayn, allowing instead the mesmerizing ribbons of light and shadow over the desert waves to occupy her mind. She wanted to wait until she was back in her room, where there were no distractions and no danger, to sort out her feelings.

Less than an hour later she was in the Visitor Center, taking a warm shower and still trying to hold back the stream of images and emotions that flowed into her consciousness, then ebbed, only to be replaced by other, more disturbing impressions.

Finally, when she was clean, refreshed, and dressed, she tried to organize her thoughts. Gyn had said some of the exact same things about Rayn that Jon had said to her. That Rayn was manipulative and just a little too handy when she needed rescuing at the mine. Was her inability to be objective about Rayn blinding her from obvious truths?

She had been increasingly clearer and clearer about her feelings for him. But were her feelings to be trusted completely? She had been wrong about Daar. Perhaps she was wrong about Rayn, too. How could she know?

Solid proof. She needed proof that Gyn was the killer and that someone within Mother Lode Mining was behind the killings. What she needed was an insider. Someone in the Mother organization who knew what was going on and was willing to help her.

She would need Rayn's help again, and help from Kindyll and Raethe, but she hesitated in calling Rayn. Dina didn't know whether or not she should tell Rayn about her encounter with T'halamar. If she didn't, she was taking a risk, because so far there hadn't been anything she had been able to keep from him. But if she did tell him, how would Rayn respond? A harder decision was what to tell Jon. She had violated Jon's direct order by going into the desert. She had been compelled to do so, she was sure, but how could she make Jon believe that? Dina decided to wait to talk to Jon until after she had seen Rayn again.

It was still morning, the sun not having yet ascended to its highest celestial post. She took a deep breath.

Rayn.

Dina...what's wrong?

How did you know?

Just tell me.

I need to see you. It's important. And I need to talk to Kindyll and Raethe again.

I'll send them to Bhel Kap. Come up the Albho Road and wait for me at the fifth way station. I'll meet you there and escort you to the Bhel. How soon can you leave?

No, not the fifth station, anyplace but there.

What's wrong with you? All right. Make it the fourth station, but make sure you wait for me. I don't want you coming all the way alone.

I'll wait.

Dina changed into a lightweight desert suit and half an hour later was at Way Station No. 4 with Rayn. This station, not as large at No. 5, was nothing more than a storage cache, providing food, water, supplies, but no shelter.

"Dina, tell me what's happened."

"Not here. Someone might come."

"I don't care. Tell me."

Dina took a deep breath. "All right. I know I can't keep anything from you anyway. I met T'halamar."

Rayn let loose with a long string of profane expletives. Most were in B'haratan, but Dina didn't need to understand the language to know that Rayn was more than upset. "Tell me all of it."

"No, Rayn, not here."

He stood a moment in frustrated silence, then nodded. "At

Bhel, then. Dyll and Rae are waiting there."

Moments later, while Kindyll and Raethe waited near the cavern's entrance, Rayn took Dina deep into the kap's shadowed interior, and she told him everything, including Gyn's accusation that Rayn was a *spithra*. Rayn's expression was controlled now, but cold. Dina thought she preferred the anger of the storm to this dreadful appearance of calm.

"Do you believe any of what he told you?" Rayn asked, his eyes unreadable.

"I considered what he said, but no, I don't believe him."

"Dina, I need to probe your mind. As thoroughly as I can without burning you. I have to know."

She knew it was dangerous, knew that Rayn would have no trouble reading her doubts about him, but also knew that she had no choice. She needed his help. With a small dip of her head, she consented. They sat on the cavern floor facing each other, as close as lovers would sit, hip to hip. Dina closed her eyes as she felt his hand on her face and his mind reaching out to hers. No current of power flowed over her this time, no teasing blue lights or sensual cool wind. This was business. He held his power thoroughly in check. She opened her mind to him, and once again experienced the wonder of the hot touch.

When it was over, they were both silent for a moment. Dina spoke first.

"Rayn, could T'halamar have placed any commands in my subconscious without my having realized it?"

"Given his powers, probably. I didn't detect anything foreign, but it's possible he planted something deeper than my probe reached. All I can do is try to counteract anything he may have planted with commands of my own. Hopefully, given our bond, your subconscious will naturally obey my commands over anyone else's. You want me to do this? Or, should I say, do you trust me enough to allow me to do this?"

So her contradictory feelings were clear to him. Dina realistically had expected little else. She searched his eyes for his reaction to her doubts, but in the darkness of the kap they remained unreadable.

"If I let you do this, what happens to me? Does it bind me

more to you? Does it give you more power over me?"

He shook his head slowly. "Your will is, and always will be, your own. This is for protection only."

She looked as deeply into his eyes as she could, but saw nothing but their dark beauty. She knew she was taking a risk allowing anyone to compel her, but nodded her assent. Better Rayn in her head than Gyn. If Gyn had indeed manipulated her subconscious, she would definitely need Rayn's help.

Rayn touched her face again, and she shivered in spite of the heat. A moment later he broke the contact, and she looked at him quizzically.

"I didn't feel anything."

"No, but it's done. Now tell me, what do you need from our friends over there?" Rayn inclined his head toward Kindyll Sirkhek and Raethe Avarti.

"I need someone inside Mother Lode who's willing to help us. I need to know from them if they can suggest anyone to me. Also, I know that you have a network of...shall we say 'eyes and ears' in Aeternus. Perhaps one of them might be able to help me. I need to know who's corruptible and who's not. Not just inside Mother Lode, but inside the AEA, Aeternan Administration, anywhere."

Rayn raised an eyebrow. "Network?"

"Rayn, don't deny it. Please, I need your help."

He smiled and touched her face again, letting the back of his hand trail slowly down her cheek and the length of her neck. "You shall have it, little girl. You shall have it. It's true that I have some, shall we say, 'sympathizers', in Aeternus, but word would have to be spread very carefully and discreetly among them. It's possible one or more of them are working both sides."

"All right. I understand." She shivered as his hand lingered at the base of her neck. Damn the investigation, she thought, there were so many other things she would rather be doing with this man. One side of Rayn's mouth turned up in that smug half-smile that made Dina just want to slap him. "Damn you, DeStar."

His smile faded. "You'll get your wish, little girl. Go on,

now. Go talk to my boys. They look anxious to be off."

Dina waited a moment longer, wishing she could read his eyes, but as he stepped away from her, shadows beneath his brows were all that met her gaze. Finally, she nodded, and turned toward the entrance of the cavern. She sat with the two ex-miners and explained what she needed.

Raethe, a man of few words, was surprisingly forthcoming. "Hrothi is plumb as they come. Believe it or not, he testified in my behalf at my revocation hearing."

Kindyll nodded. "He took Johnter's killing real hard. They went way back together."

"How did Hrothi react when Mother signed off on the latest Syn survey?" asked Dina.

"He was livid," said Kindyll. "I overheard him damn to the Void everyone from Nastja to Ctararzin to Hwa-lik."

Dina considered the names Kindyll had mentioned. Ctararzin was Mother's Operations Manager and Hwa-lik was the company's top on-planet official. "Who's this Nastja?"

"Rukhyo Nastja. He was in charge of the survey. He's an off-worlder and gone now. He left before the killings started and the port was closed," said Kindyll.

"Convenient. Do you think Hrothi would help me? At the possible expense of losing his job?"

Raethe answered. "He might. A lot of people are surprised he still has his job at all, considering what's happened."

"That's right. After Dais was killed, some of the miners were already calling for his resignation," added Kindyll.

"No," said Dina, "I have a feeling that Mother needed someone to take the fall. They won't dispose of him until they're done."

Raethe's eyes flicked to Kindyll's, and the two seemed to exchange a silent understanding.

"Who else inside Mother do you know?" Dina pressed the two men. "I need someone inside I can trust, and I need to know who might be part of the conspiracy."

"Conspiracy?" asked Kindyll, shifting his gaze back to Dina.

"I wouldn't doubt it," said Raethe. "There aren't any I would trust except Hrothi. Like I said, he was more than fair with me. About the only one who was."

Dina nodded, and her gaze idled on the man before her as she tried to think of more questions. He was a good-looking man, but with his long, shaggy mane of sandy hair, his wary, stern visage, and the coiled strength of his body, he never failed to remind her of a wild animal.

He tossed his long hair back, and Dina's attention focused on Rae's right shoulder. Naked from the waist up except for a cooling vest, the bright design stood out against the tanned skin. A yellow and orange sun—half its face peeking above a horizon line—shot long, thin rays outward and upward.

Raethe saw where her gaze was fixed, and shrugged. "It's just a tattoo."

"It's beautiful. Did you get it here on Exodus?" The rising sun had reminded her of the *agherz* she had witnessed the past two mornings.

Raethe laughed, a rare sound for him. "No, it's nothing to do with Exodus. Most of the desert rats have them."

"I don't understand."

"Miners are a superstitious lot. *Agherz*, not just on Exodus, but wherever we're working, is a special time of the day for us. Almost sacred, you might say. It symbolizes the hope of the new day, hope that this day will be the day the biggest and best stones are found." He shrugged again. "Sounds silly, I suppose, but it helps keep us going."

Dina was silent for a moment, looking again at the hard features. The soul of a poet and the courage of an untamed beast. And yet he lost his job because he made the mistake of drinking too much. "Hmmm, interesting. You say a lot of the miners have these?"

"Sure. Dyll's got one, too."

Kindyll pulled the front of his vest apart, and Dina could see the stylized yellow and black design, quite different from Raethe's, yet clearly a rising sun, on the center of his chest.

"So...anyone with a tattoo like this is a miner..."

"Or ex-miners, like us," finished Kindyll. "It's a Guild thing. You won't find them on Company dogs like Ctararzin or

Hwa-lik."

"No, the only tattoos they would have would be money chips or credit symbols," said Raethe, and they both laughed derisively.

Dina smiled with them, but something was niggling at her mind. *Ex-miners...*

"Thanks, both of you. You've been a big help. If you think of anything else that might help me, let Rayn know."

They stood, and Dina returned to Rayn.

A rare smile lit his features. "I hope you realize what a tribute to you that was. I've never seen Rae fawn over anyone that much—not even Alessane when she brings him a plate full of warm sweet bread."

Embarrassed, Dina couldn't think of a reply. She resorted to a playful "*Krek*," as she knocked him gently on the shoulder, smiling herself.

But the light-hearted moment was brief, and Rayn left to instruct the two ex-miners to return to camp.

By the time he returned and they were alone once more, her serious face was back in place. "I should go. I want to set up an appointment with Karsa Hrothi, head of security at the mines, as soon as possible," said Dina, not really wanting to leave.

"I don't like you going into the desert alone."

"I won't go alone. Either Jon will be with me, or maybe we can arrange for Hrothi to meet us in the city," she replied.

"I don't trust Rzije. If you can't meet Hrothi in the city, call me."

The silence of the desert was absolute. Dina could hear her own heartbeat, and it felt as if with every beat the distance between them increased. Why was it that every time she wanted to get close to Rayn another barrier rose? She crossed her arms. "Jon is my partner. I trust him with my life."

Rayn didn't reply at once, but took a deep breath and bent his head, hands on his hips.

Dina waited, her eyes persistent in trying to read his features, but all she could see were the dark strands of hair curving from the widow's peak to the center of his forehead and the crescents of black that his downcast eyes painted against his tanned skin.

Rayn looked up, his head cocked to one side. "He can't protect you the way I can," came the soft response at last.

"No, no one can ever do anything as well as you can, can they?" Dina turned and strode toward the entrance, leaping onto her skimmer. *Damn him!* How could her feelings for him be so crystal one moment and so muddled the next?

As quickly as she moved, however, Rayn was an easy match for her. His skimmer was a shadow to hers as she sped southeast, weaving her way between the rock warriors of the Chayne and the sand creatures of the Wiara, engaged in their eternal battle in the sun. Dina was aware of Rayn's presence, even as she stared straight ahead, and knew there was nothing she could do or say to deter him from escorting her. She expected him to call to her as they rode, but the silence continued, broken only by the low hum of the machines.

On the Albho Road, the mountain gladiators left far behind, she sped by the way stations, and still Rayn rode beside her. And still there was nothing but silence, sun, and sand. Finally, when Dina passed the first way station, she felt Rayn's presence slip away from her and, turning her head, saw that he had stopped his skimmer there. Turning her attention back to the road, she continued toward Ghe Wespero alone.

***

Rayn sat and watched her, kept company only by the questions that haunted him.

Two hours later he returned to Keneko Kap, where his "Elite" were encamped, but gave only a brief greeting and perfunctory instructions before ascending to Berg-Frij, a small cliff high above Keneko Kap. It was Rayn's newest place of *m'riri*.

It was an old B'haratan word meaning "reflection." The ancients had believed, and had taught, that the keys to a successful, prudent life were discovered through rituals of self reflection. Over the years, however, the teachings of *m'riri* had become twisted, misunderstood, and largely ignored. It had been the weight on the scale that had balanced the power of the *dens*.

But in modern times on B'harata, the scale had tipped increasingly toward power. The result was a world peopled with those eager to dominate and control, with no regard for the journey that takes them to their destinations. The quick path of violence was all too often the only road taken.

Rayn's mother had practiced *m'riri*, as best as she understood it, and had tried to teach Rayn. But it had been a difficult concept to grasp as a child, and as he grew, he too, like so many others, spent his time perfecting the arts of the *dens* instead. It wasn't until his mother was ill and near death so many years ago that Rayn had listened at last, and understood, if just a little.

As he gazed now upon the Sea of Glass, he heard his mother's words in his head. *Remember the m'riri, Raynga. It will not fail you, ever, wherever you go, whatever you do. It will guide you and keep you safe, and it will bring you peace. You are strong with the dens, and for that I am glad. It will keep you alive. But for life, Raynga-cha, for life, you need the m'riri...*

He had tried, and still tried, but the true *m'riri* was as elusive as a cool breeze during the devil hour. Too often he sought escape in the reflection, as he had as a child, instead of understanding. And too often he had tried for peace, for life, and had gained little, and that at great price. Why was the price always destruction? Why was the B'haratan way always destruction?

And now his attempts at escape had brought him here, to a desolate and primitive colony, and to a life-force named Dina. But thus far nothing had changed. The more he reached for order and life, the more he summoned chaos and death.

Rayn sat in the shadow of a small overhang on the cliff and stared at the endless shimmering moiré of the Ghel. How could he hold on to that life-force without destroying her?

What does T'halamar think about when he gazes upon the red dust of the Pur-Pelag? What would Dina think if she knew the real truth? Does T'halamar ever contemplate his life? Does she know what I'm doing to her? Am I so different from him? If I destroy her, or if Gyn destroys her, what's the difference?

Three hours later, the *m'riri* gave him an answer, but embedded stubbornly in the answer, like a crystal in a rock, was another question. Was he strong enough?

FIFTEEN
THE VOW

Dina stood inside her room and listened to the soft whisper of the door gliding shut behind her. She longed for an old-fashioned, manually operated door she could slam, and imagined one instead in her mind. The mental wham, however, did little except remind her that her headache was not going away.

She took a deep breath of the conditioned air and stripped off her desert jacket, letting it slide to the floor. *To the Void.* She was tired of Rayn's arrogance. She unfastened her cooling vest and shrugged it off her shoulders, her muscles so tight she could barely turn her head.

She was tired of Jon's orders. Her trousers were next, collapsing the tent of white diamonds the vest had made on the floor. She was tired, too, of Katzfiel's and Khilioi's disdain. She took refuge in the shower, having further littered the floor with her T-shirt and undergarments. And she was tired of hearing the laughter of the black souls behind the killings.

She jutted her chin forward and stood perfectly still, letting the jets of water pelt her skin with revitalizing coolness. The water reminded her of Rayn's power, cool and cleansing. Well, she had her own power. They all thought she was weak, but they were wrong. The curtain of water soothed her, and she silently vowed she would bring down everyone involved. She thought about Karsa Hrothi, twisted her exodite ring, and was confident her vow would not be broken.

A verbal command raised the temperature of the water, and only when she felt the warmth melt the remaining knots in her neck did she turn off the water and exit the shower. Dina looked at the layers of yellow and white strewn on the floor like wilted flowers and smiled. Eager now to make progress, she picked up the mess and dressed in a fresh outfit.

Her hair still damp, she called Jon and met with him in his room. She told him what the ex-miners had said about Hrothi, and added what her own research had uncovered.

Jon nodded. "I agree. My impression of Hrothi when we met him was that he was a forthright man. I also agree that we should try to meet with him here, not at the mines. I'll try to set up a meeting right now." Dina listened in as Jon called Hrothi and made an appointment for early the next morning at the Visitor Center. She was disappointed at the delay, but it couldn't be helped.

Back in her room, she tried to think about something other than Rayn. She ran a glass of chilled juice and, to distract herself, had the room computer run the time line she had constructed of the dates of every relevant incident she had discovered. Every day she had entered new dates in, and every day she ran the time line, hoping to pick up on some previously missed connection. She sat and watched as the computer projected a visual time line across the length of the room, its machine voice announcing the various incidents in chronological order. Dina had set the time line to begin just over a year ago.

"3.135.2. Miner Raethe Avarti is found by superiors talking about low yield in The Furnace," stated the computer voice, as the appropriate date on the visual was highlighted.

"Two months later, 3.135.4, the Synergy survey of the mines is completed. One month later, 3.135.5, Avarti's guild membership is revoked, and he joins the *Dailjan*. Also during this month, an anonymous tip leads to the apprehension of the *mantis* Xuche by the AEA. One month later, 3.135.6, the Mother Lode mine survey is completed, and Mother Lode signs off on the Synergy survey."

Dina gave a verbal command to the computer to stop running the time line. *Xuche.* Dina had dismissed thoughts of him when it was discovered he wasn't the *Uz-Dailjan*, and she had only asked Rayn about him briefly. But there he was, right in the middle of things. And found on an anonymous tip. Why? And by whom? And why at that particular time? Dina stared at the blank wall and mentally threw the glass of juice at it. Why hadn't she thought to investigate Xuche more thoroughly? Jon had viewed the initial report. She returned to his room where Jon was sitting at his computer, his leg propped up.

Dina balanced on the edge of the bed and leaned forward.

"Jon, I'm curious again about the *mantis,* Xuche. It's too coincidental that he was found when he was. Who submitted the AEA report on Xuche?"

"Katzfiel himself."

Dina swore. "I knew it. I think Xuche is our link between the desert and Aeternus, and I think Katzfiel's dirty."

Jon leaned back and put a hand in front of his face. "Whoa, Dina, hold on a minute. Where did that conclusion come from?"

"My instinct, Jon."

He raised both brows.

"Okay, okay, I know. You want more. But don't you think it at least deserves looking into?"

"Perhaps, but let's not go accusing anyone when we have no proof."

"Where's Xuche now?" asked Dina.

"He was deported as a dark outworlder. He was found eight months ago, when the spaceport was still open." Jon paused. "So what do you propose we do? If you question Katzfiel, do you expect him to tell you anything other than what's in his report?"

"No. But I still think it's worth a shot. It should be interesting to see what a mind probe on him reveals."

"What do you expect to pick up that you failed to on previous probes?"

"I won't know for sure until we talk to him, but I sensed a real fear before. Fears are powerful emotional programs. Those programs are interpreted by the inner self as goals to be achieved. If the fear is strong enough, maybe I can gain some insight into his motivations. Or, if he lies, that should produce a stress that's easily detectable."

Jon sighed. "All right. But I'll do the questioning. We have to proceed very cautiously here. Katzfiel has a lot of clout."

Dina nodded. "I was going to suggest you conduct the interview. It's clear he has a poor opinion of me. Can you set up a meeting for as soon as possible? I'll just need a few moments to review the Xuche file."

Jon gave Dina a pointed look, telling her in no uncertain terms that he would do it, but his way. He contacted Commander

Katzfiel, who agreed to meet with them at the AEA Center in one hour.

Dina had no time to waste. She returned to her room and brought up the computer file on Xuche. There wasn't much in the report other than what Jon had told her. As she viewed it, she dictated questions to the computer, and mentally kicked herself again for not having asked Rayn about Xuche in detail. If she knew the true facts regarding Xuche before going into the meeting with Katzfiel, it would be a big advantage. Dina checked the time. She could still call to Rayn and ask him about Xuche. If she could swallow her pride.

The image of Rayn's face as she had walked out on him earlier came into sharp focus. Why did he have to display such a contempt of Jon just because Jon doesn't have the power of the *dens*?

She stared at her computer. No. She wasn't going to run to Rayn for help every time she had a question. If she did, it would only justify his disdain for them. She saw again the controlled features in her mind, but the image dissolved, and all she could see were his eyes. The strange golden eyes. What had been behind them? Pain? Or something darker?

Dina went into the bathroom, splashed cold water on her face, and shook her head. She couldn't afford to think about Rayn now. She would need all her faculties sharp for Katzfiel. She dried her face, swiveled onto her bed, sat cross-legged, and ordered the lights to dim.

She took a moment to seal her senses from any distractions, then imagined herself on Glacia, gazing at a late afternoon sky, the crisp, clear air magnifying the clarity of the aquamarine hue. She saw the color on the backs of her eyelids, pure, crystal, ice blue. A watersky blue she had never seen anywhere but on Glacia. The color of the full moon on a winter night. She took three deep, slow breaths, then let her body go limp as she exhaled. She counted backward from twenty to one, and recited one of her inductions. *I am calm. I am relaxed. I am comfortable, and am ready to move to a higher state of consciousness. My awareness expands, and my perception widens. I see all.*

Satisfied that her mind had reached the proper mental state, she nevertheless wished she had had more time. In answer, she heard a tiny voice in her head tell her she would have had more time except for her preoccupation with Rayn. Annoyed, she pushed the guilt aside, printed out her questions for Jon, and knocked at his door.

Jon looked at the questions and nodded. "Okay. We'll see how it goes, but I don't think it'll be pleasant. Whatever you do, keep your mouth shut and let me do the talking."

"Yes, boss. I'll sit quietly like a good girl, but he's going to get the most thorough mind probe I can muster."

"Just make sure your expressions don't give you away. If anyone here knew you were a telepath, there'd be hell to pay."

"Don't worry about me. Besides, I don't think there could be much about Katzfiel that would surprise me, except maybe to find out he was a choir boy as a child."

Moments later, Jon and Dina sat with Commander Katzfiel in his office. Katzfiel's expression, as always, was stern. His hair—short, severe and cut flat across the top—reflected the harsh angles of his cheeks and jaw line. Only the restlessness of his liquid silver eyes, like transparent fish, relieved the severity of the straight lines comprising his other features. Dina didn't like his eyes. Their unusual color notwithstanding, they were cold and unyielding, taking in everything, but giving nothing back. She glanced down at her recorder, pretending to adjust it, while she sent out a probe to Katzfiel.

"Now then, Agent Rzije. Just what is it about the *mantis* Xuche that merits a personal meeting with me? And how is this person, long gone from Exodus, connected to your murders?"

Dina thought briefly that the ill-disguised contempt of the man before her now rivaled even the arrogance of DeStar. She glanced at Jon and knew that a similar thought was running through his mind.

"Just routine follow-up, Commander. We believe the killer to be a denizen of the desert, and since Xuche lived in the desert, there's a good chance he had contact with the killer. There's a possibility Xuche might have said something during your interview with him that would be helpful to us."

"Xuche was found and deported before the killings even started. Everything he told me is in the report."

"Who took the anonymous tip that led to Xuche's apprehension?"

"Corporal Khilioi recovered a written note delivered to this building's entrance by a young boy. We found the boy who made the delivery. The offspring of one of the *mercari*. He could only tell us that one of his father's customers gave him the note along with a chip if he would deliver it. Frankly, I don't quite see where all this is going."

Dina continued her probe as Jon asked for details of Katzfiel's interview with Xuche. She felt the contempt that was obvious even without the probe, and skirted those feelings, hoping to touch other, less apparent emotions. She felt hatred, then what she was hoping to sense. Fear.

The fear, while sufficiently hidden from normal observers, was clear to Dina, and quite strong. She probed the area of fear as thoroughly as she could, trying to locate an association for the dread. He wasn't afraid of Jon and Dina. Then she touched it. Failure. There it sat, as deep-seated as the trunk of an ancient tree, its roots firmly entrenched in its host.

Dina looked at the Commander's face while he explained, with exaggerated patience, that Xuche had claimed to be the *Uz* but refused to name any of the other *Dailjan* or to divulge the locations of their encampments. He was very good. The man didn't sweat, and his fluid gaze continued to support the facade of cool indifference.

Since Dina knew Xuche had lied about being the *Uz*, she doubted any of his other statements were true. But why had the *mantis* lied? Or was he indeed someone else's puppet?

Katzfiel made a gesture of checking the time. "Really, Agent Rzije. It's getting late. I fail to see what this has accomplished. There isn't anything I can tell you that isn't in my report. I do have other pressing matters to attend to."

Jon gave the Commander his most charming, innocent smile, complete with dimples and smile lines emanating from the green eyes. Dina briefly wondered how many opponents had been conned by one of those smiles.

"You've been more help than you know, Commander. We appreciate your time, and apologize for any inconvenience our meeting may have caused. We'll see ourselves out."

Jon and Dina rose, and as they exited Katzfiel's office, Dina glanced backward over her shoulder. The Commander sat at his desk, his right elbow propped on the smooth desktop, his fingertips lightly drumming his jawbone, as if he were sending a message which begged an answer. The black pupils, strangely enough, didn't dart around the room, but floated in their liquid sea.

Back in Jon's room, he dropped to his bed, stretching his injured leg before him. Dina relayed her findings while she ran two glasses of ice water.

"Contempt, hatred, nervousness, stress, fear. The contempt was most surface, the fear buried the deepest. He fears failure, but failure of what, I'm not sure. Was he lying? I don't know."

Jon took the water from Dina and sipped at it thoughtfully. She sat at the computer, making room on the table amongst the paper files for her glass.

Finally, he set his water down and looked at her. "Dina, listen to me. You know I value your ability and what it can do for us, but I think the time has come for you to put it aside. Personally, I, too, have a pretty strong dislike for just about everyone we've met on this rock, but we can't let those feelings dictate our investigation."

"Jon, my ability is more than just liking or disliking someone."

"I know, but I really want you to look beyond it and concentrate on solving this thing logically. You're a good investigator, Dina, I know you are. Don't let your ability be a crutch."

"Jon..."

"No, no arguments, Dina, please. Just do as I ask, all right?"

She fumed, but what could she do? She gave Jon a curt nod. "I'll be in my room."

Moments later, she sat, frustrated, and thought about Jon's words. Proof. Jon wanted proof. As valuable as her ability was, proof was the one thing it couldn't provide. Maybe he was right. She certainly wasn't making much progress as it was. Dina took a deep breath, cleared her mind, and had her recorder replay the conversation with Katzfiel. She heard his final words, leaned back, and closed her eyes. Of course. Why hadn't it struck her before?

She sat at her computer and issued commands for file retrieval, but before she brought up the file she wanted, her head started to throb relentlessly. She ordered the computer to pause. She needed to rid herself of the headache. Her mood had been blackened by Katzfiel's and Jon's words, and she wouldn't be able to make headway until she was able to think clearly.

There was so much to think about. Rayn, Gyn, Hrothi, Katzfiel, Xuche. The names were like puzzle pieces drifting through her mind. They teased her, the pieces touching, then breaking away again, daring her to bring order to the chaos. The throbbing in her head bloomed. She needed fresh air.

Dina left a message for Jon that she would be at the Cave. Donning a suit with an attached cloth hood, she pulled the hood up and put a pair of narrow sunshields on. Thus attired she was able to walk to the Crown undisturbed. Dina sat in the Cave and ordered a mocava, but as she sat sipping the drink, the petals of pain behind her eyes continued to unfurl. Maybe the peace and quiet of the Oasis would be better.

She swigged the remainder of her drink and hurried next door, anxious for the relief the peaceful room promised. There were few people inside, and Dina wound her way to the fountain with the waterfall and aquatic animals. As she drew up next to the fountain, a man stepped out from behind the cover of several of the tall, potted plants. His long hair hung loose down his back but was braided with a fine silver chain on either side of his face.

"Well, young lady, have you thought about what I told you?" he asked.

Dina stood frozen. The pounding of her heart replaced that in her head, and was so loud that the happy burbling of the fountain seemed far away. She tried not to panic. This was a public place. Surely T'halamar wouldn't try anything here. She cast her eyes quickly from side to side. To her consternation, there was no one else in sight.

"Well?" he repeated.

"Yes, I thought about what you said."

"But you haven't changed your mind, have you?"

There was no point in lying. "No," she said.

"Then let me give you something else to think about. Let me tell you what I'll do to your friend DeStar if he even so much as thinks about making a move against me."

Dina stood motionless, vaguely wondering if he were compelling her to stand so still. Energy started to well from the man's body, thick and viscous, like body fluid. It crawled over her skin, hot and suffocating, and Dina thought she would faint. She closed her eyes, but saw nothing but a blood-red pool behind her lids. Not sure if she preferred that to looking into his eyes, she opened hers.

"First I'll show him how much stronger I am than he is. I'll have him groveling at my feet until he acknowledges my superiority and begs for mercy. Then I'll tell him what I'll do to you when I'm through with him. I'll paint him a very detailed picture of the two of us, you and I, and of all the infinite ways you will please me. Oh, and I want you to start thinking about that, too. Because when I'm done with DeStar, rest assured I'll come for you. This is a promise, from me to you, and from me to him. Tell him that." The words were very slow and deliberate, as if he wanted to make sure she heard and remembered every one.

"You're mad," was all she could whisper.

He responded by broaching her mind swiftly and sharply, and she gasped, helpless against his invasion. Silent laughter filled her head.

"DeStar is more useless than I thought. He hasn't even begun to satisfy himself on you, has he? I, on the other hand, want you very much. And you, everything you do for me will be of your own accord, because you will know that never will you find another man who can satisfy you as I can." The black eyes danced before her, and she saw nothing else.

His flow of power over her abated, but in its place she felt a fabric of fear weave itself around her, as if with each word he spoke new threads spun out to her. She tried to shake the fear, tried to shake her head and say "no," but she couldn't get the word out.

"After DeStar fully understands the way it is, and the way it will be, I will put him out of his misery."

"You can't...kill him." Dina's voice was low and hoarse. The four words had been a struggle to voice. The fabric tightened around her and drew her closer to him. She took a step forward.

The full mouth twisted. "Oh, I don't think I'll kill him. I just may leave his body intact, although it would give me great pleasure to destroy that, too, but I'll definitely destroy his mind, bit by bit. I'll erase his memories so that he won't know you, this place, or who he is. He'll be like a child in the desert."

Again Dina tried to shake her head, and her mouth opened, but no sounds came forth.

He released his power to flow over her once again, and she cried out. She felt as if she were standing inside a funnel of flame. The violence and heat spun around her, and she felt a suction pull her closer to him.

"You feel it, don't you? The promise of power. It pulls you." The low voice dropped to a whisper.

She took another step forward. She was horrified, and yet...the tanned face was not unattractive. The angles were sharp, the nose narrow and straight, the jaw line almost square. The dark eyes beckoned like jewels.

Dina took two more steps, her face now only a handbreadth from his. She tentatively put a hand to his face and stroked his cheek. His skin felt hot. She jerked her fingers away. She moved her hand to the side, trailing her fingers down one long braid to his chest, bronzed and smooth. She ran her fingers over the contours of his hard muscles. She was more afraid than she had ever before been.

Was she being compelled? Surely she must be, for she couldn't stop. What of Rayn's commands, instructing her to respond to no one but him? Was Gyn that much stronger than Rayn? Just what had Rayn injected into her mind? Or was she doing this all on her own?

"You want me, too, don't you?" he asked quietly.

She looked up at the eyes that flashed like obsidian. Did she?

"Don't you?" the man repeated.

"Yes," she replied, surprised at her answer. He leaned down and teased her lips with his own, until hers parted for him, admitting his hot tongue. His kiss was hard and insistent. As he continued kissing her, he ran his hands upward from her waist. She hadn't put on a cooling vest due to the evening hour, so when he cupped her breasts in his large hands there were only two thin layers of clothing between his skin and hers.

"True power is an intoxicant, is it not? Admit it. DeStar has not this power, will never have it. And he will never make you feel like this." She felt her body react and tried to pull away, but couldn't. The arousal she felt was both unwelcome and uncomfortable, yet increased when he ran his thumbs over her nipples, teasing them to an almost painful hardness. He dragged his mouth from hers, but kept his large hands on her breasts.

"Yes...just imagine how it will feel to have my mouth where my hands are now. But we will leave that for another time. When you come to Detour, you'll have all of me, and I will have all of you."

"Detour?" was all she could ask.

"My humble home. If you want to visit the Void, take a right hand turn at the Wiara." T'halamar's laugh was short-lived and bitter. "Go now. Tell DeStar what I told you. And remember, no *spithra* will never be able to satisfy you the way I can."

The energy flow retreated. Dina found her legs and ran out of the Oasis. Back in her room she cleansed herself as thoroughly as she could, but still felt dirty.

How could she have walked up to T'halamar and allowed him to kiss her like that? She had been compelled to go to the Oasis, she was sure of that part of it. She had been compelled to kiss him, too. There couldn't be any other explanation. Yet there had been no denying her body's reaction to his kiss. How was she going to hide this from Rayn?

She thought of Rayn, and his cooling aura, and suddenly she thought no more of her embarrassment. Rayn's power was no match for Gyn's. She knew it. Gyn's aura shouted masculinity, aggression, and power—a primary, positive force. He had easily brushed aside Rayn's programmed "protection." What other explanation could there be?

She was suddenly very afraid.

SIXTEEN
DEATH IN THE MINES

It was the eighth hour the following morning when Dina sat with Jon in his room, preparing for the meeting with Hrothi. She had not slept well, and her nerves felt frayed and rubbed raw. Her mind was anything but clear. A look at Jon did not make her feel better about their pending meeting. His long hair hung limply around his ears, and his eyes had taken on the shade of freshly frost-killed plants, dull and dark.

"Karjon, you have a priority one call from Minister Chandhel waiting."

"Now what? Computer, answer with visual," grumbled Jon, raking a hand through his hair to sweep the long strands from his eyes.

The computer image of Chandhel's somber face appeared. "Agent Rzije, I'm afraid there's been another incident at the mines. Another death."

"Another miner?" prompted Jon, when the Minister paused.

"No. It's Karsa Hrothi, Chief of Security. The area's been secured, pending your and Commander Katzfiel's arrival. There's a transport leaving from the AEA Center in a quarter hour. Be on it. I'll meet you at the mines."

"Gods," breathed Dina.

Jon swore loudly. "Get what you need from your room. Now!"

Dina returned in less than a minute, and they were at the Center in less than ten. There was a frenzy of activity on the AEA hoverdeck, as Katzfiel barked out orders to his men. The Commander spared Jon and Dina only a glance, albeit one that would wither an *anghwi*, and jerked his head toward the craft, indicating they should board. Dr. Lumazi was already aboard, as well as numerous AEA officers. Dina didn't see Chandhel. Doubtless he had his own transport.

In a moment everything and everyone was loaded, and the hovercraft ascended and accelerated toward the Albho Mar. Dina's mind had felt frozen since hearing Chandhel's voice proclaim Karsa Hrothi as the victim.

She knew she should be concentrating on what she had to do once they arrived at the mines, but all she could think about was her earlier meeting with Rayn, Kindyll, and Raethe. She had told Rayn she would be meeting with Hrothi. What had been her exact words to him? She tried to remember. She had relayed her feelings to the two ex-miners that Hrothi could be an ally. To Rayn she had simply said she was going to meet with Hrothi, but Rayn's men could easily have conveyed to him her conversation with them.

It was too much of a coincidence. In her profession, Dina had found there was no such thing as coincidence. Last night she had feared for him, but now, in the light of day, everything seemed different. She felt a chill of dread spread throughout her limbs as she thought about Rayn. She thought she had been right about him, and everyone else wrong, but was that possible?

She had allowed him to compel her. His compelling commands were supposed to have been protection against T'halamar, but they hadn't worked. Maybe it wasn't that Gyn was stronger. Maybe Rayn's commands had had nothing to do with protection. She had placed her life in his hands, and now the chill deepened to a cold fear. What commands had he really placed in her mind?

Her mind was lifted from its reverie by the sound of Katzfiel's voice. "Gentlemen, and ladies," said the Commander, nodding to Dina and Dr. Lumazi, "Here's the situation as we have it. Karsa Hrothi, Mother Lode's Chief of Security, was found one-half hour ago outside the Kewero Kel by one of his staff members, Kalyo Rhoemer. Hrothi was dead on the scene. Thus far we have no witnesses. The scene has been secured, and Rhoemer has been held in isolation pending our arrival. No one at the mines has been allowed to leave or enter. Agent Rzije, of the IIB, will have authority at the scene. Agent?"

"After viewing the scene, my partner and I will interview Rhoemer. Commander, I'll need a list of everyone at the mines, including miners, Mother Lode personnel, and any visitors. And I'll need a statement from each. Doctor, I'll need your report on the victim as soon as possible."

Katzfiel nodded and started issuing specific instructions to his men. Dina forced her mind to start working. Their scheduled meeting with Hrothi. She had to find out who knew about it. It wouldn't have been a secret. Perhaps someone had been in Hrothi's office when Jon had made the call. Perhaps he had mentioned the meeting to an associate. Dina gave her head a small shake. As much as logic told her that Rayn was involved, she found herself persisting in trying to believe him innocent.

The hovercraft settled at Dheru Kel, and its passengers assembled quickly at the entrance, where they were met by Rum Ctararzin, Operations Manager for the mines. Ctararzin escorted Katzfiel, Dr. Lumazi, Jon, and Dina to the murder site, while the Commander's men began their interviews.

Ctararzin addressed Jon on the way. "This is intolerable, Agent Rzije. We've tried to be patient, but this investigation, as has been obvious to everyone, has been a farce since the beginning."

"With all due respect, sir, we have work to do," Jon replied, not slowing his stride.

"Your work seems to be nothing more than closing the gate after the herd escapes. The Mother Lode Board will be convening tonight, and I don't think the results will be to your liking."

"Fine. You do what you have to do."

"Don't be flippant with me, young man. A report from me can break you. Both of you."

***

Thus began a long and grueling day for Dina. Though she had met Hrothi only briefly, she had liked him, and it was hard to look at the remains lying on the hard ground just outside a long-abandoned entrance to Kewero Kel.

Dr. Lumazi was with the body. The area had been cordoned off, and no one else had been allowed access to the body. Two uniformed AEA officers stood guard nearby to make certain no one disturbed the area surrounding Hrothi.

"Please, Agent Marlijn, be brief." The doctor's voice was soft, but authoritative.

Dina knelt by the body, not wishing to disturb it, and looked at the doctor, who had knelt with her. "I understand. A moment is all I need." She cast her eyes down at the handsome face, glad the eyes were closed so she wouldn't have to look at their lifeless blue depths. Dina's gaze moved downward to the partially opened mouth. As if he were trying to tell her something... Her eyes moved lower still, to where his left hand lay curled across his heart. Dina saw several lines across the back of the hand, not scars, not wrinkles, but part of a design. She gently pushed the cuff of Hrothi's sleeve upward with her gloved hand, and looked at the wrist. The colors of the tattoo remained vivid. The symbol of hope, she thought, and let the cuff slide back down the arm and over the wrist.

She knelt a moment longer and stared at the rugged face, the features a mask of stillness. Dina looked at the abundant steel gray hair, and her eyes followed the thick curving strands, which, like living tendrils, embraced his ears and blossomed into long silver sideburns that flared beneath his cheekbones. Something wasn't right.

Dina looked up quickly at the doctor, and their eyes met. Before Dina could speak, the doctor cut her off.

"As I said, Agent Marlijn, please be brief. I need to get the body back to the Medical Center as soon as possible. I can't preserve it in this heat. Perhaps you would like to accompany me? I'm sure the findings would be instrumental to your investigation."

Dina locked her gaze a moment longer with the hazel eyes that seemed so familiar. "Yes, thank you, Doctor. I understand. Let me just tell my partner where I'll be."

Later that evening, after everything possible had been done, Dina returned to the Visitor Center. She had run the gamut of every possible emotion during this day, sorrow, frustration, anger, disbelief, astonishment, and satisfaction. And it wasn't done yet.

Rayn!

I hear you, Dina. There's no need to shout.

Shout? Damn you, you arrogant krek! I haven't even begun yet. What do you think you're doing? Are you crazy?

She normally sat quietly when transporting herself to the

Road of Time in preparation for talking to Rayn telepathically, but now she paced back and forth in her room, her anger giving energy to her tired body.

If you're referring to Hrothi's murder, it had to be done. I had no choice. The situation was far too dangerous.

You could have told me about this. No, I take that back. You should have told me.

And you would have agreed? I hardly think so. Besides, there was no time.

And now I'm a part of it anyway. This will cost me my job, you know. What am I supposed to tell Jon? And the Minister? Chandhel's called for a meeting at the ninth hour tomorrow. What am I supposed to tell them?

Dina reached for her head, as if to grab a fistful of her hair, then dropped her arm in frustration.

Stall them. Blow whatever smoke at them you want to. Just make sure you do one thing. Give me time.

For what? She was sure she wasn't going to like the answer.

Hrothi's only step one. Now that he's out of the way, T'halamar and the others have to be dealt with. Did you find out who they are?

Yes, all but the middle man. But I think I know who he is. But, Rayn, we need proof. Proof. Do you understand that?

She dropped onto the edge of her bed.

You'll get it. Did our friends talk to you about Rhoemer? He's the next one we have to worry about.

Yes, but it's dangerous.

Where is he now?

Dina sighed. She was in the middle of this crazy scheme, like it or not. *The AEA Center.*

The word hasn't been spread yet?

Dina took a deep breath and held it, trying to relax. *No, I was waiting to talk to you. Just what are you going to do next?*

Hold you in my arms. Meet me at our usual spot. The rest of this has to be said face to face.

Ten minutes later in the small room of the housing complex, Dina looked at the dark shadows under Rayn's eyes and the lines around his mouth that made it appear as if a great weight were pulling at him, and this time she had no trouble reading his features. The man looked exhausted. All her anger and fears drained out of her, and she went to him without a word. He banded his arms around her, and she buried her face in the curtain of his hair, inhaling his scent, as if she could thusly draw on his strength.

"Oh, Rayn, everything is such a mess! Jon will kill me, and if he doesn't, it won't matter. I've broken so many rules and regulations that my career is finished even if I do solve this case."

He laughed softly. "The lives of countless people are at stake, and you're worried about rules and regulations?"

She laughed as well, but it was not a sound of joy or mirth.

He put his hands on either side of her head and drew her gently away so that she could see his face. *It'll be all right. Everything you need to conquer is right here,* he communicated, massaging her temple and stroking her hair. She looked into his golden eyes, as clear and intoxicating as Cygian brandy.

"It's so easy for you," she breathed.

"No, *T'anga'cha*. Not so easy. Not so easy." He held her again, caressing her gently, until she finally pulled away a little.

"You've called me that before. What does it mean?" she asked.

"Now if I told you, the word would lose it's magic, wouldn't it?"

"*Krek,*" she said, smiling.

"That's better. I told you I'd help you, and I will. Now, little girl, tell me what I can do first."

"Well, I have to know about the *mantis* Xuche. I'm sure he's involved in this somehow."

He pulled her down to sit beside him on a narrow bed. "Ah, friend Xuche. He arrived after I did, but before Gyn. I have no use for any of the *mantis*. They are all words, nothing but words. Xuche roamed the desert, trying to establish a following. There were a number of people who were attracted to the desert even before the killings started, you see. He did manage a few followers, mostly 'shadow dancers,' the weak, the easily led, and those who didn't mind living the most austere of lifestyles. In case you haven't noticed, my people don't want for much."

Dina smiled. "The AEA report stated that Xuche claimed to be the leader of the *Dailjan*."

"Either the report was falsely made, or Xuche lied. Or, he could have been compelled to say that. He was never with me or any of my people."

"Did Xuche have a connection with Gyn?" She tried to show no reaction when she said Gyn's name. He wove the fingers of his right hand gently through her hair, smoothing it away from her face.

"I'm sure their paths crossed. Everyone who lives in this desert comes across everyone else eventually."

"Did you or any of your *Dailjan* tip off the AEA to Xuche's presence and location in the desert?"

Rayn shook his head. "No. I had no use for the man, but I wouldn't turn over a fellow, what do you call us? A fellow 'dark outworlder' to the *angwhi*."

"I think I know who did. Could Gyn have made Xuche a pawn?"

"Very possible. Gyn has the ability to make anyone a pawn."

"Except, of course, you," Dina said, her smile reappearing.

"Except, of course, me."

"Arrogant bastard."

Rayn's mouth cocked up in that half smile that irritated Dina. A second later, though, the smile was gone and his brows were knitted with concern. "What about Rhoemer? If he doesn't trust us, we won't be able to take care of him."

"He trusts us, so he says. How will we get the word of his location to the right people ?" asked Dina.

"Don't tell me you haven't witnessed how quickly a rumor spreads throughout a workplace? Rae and Dyll assure me that the desert rats are infamous gossip-mongers. Don't worry, it'll be taken care of. All you have to do is see that Rhoemer is taken to an unsecured location. I want to make sure my men can get to him."

"We can't keep the AEA out completely. Are there any you trust? I haven't met any I would trust with the time of day," added Dina, her eyes flickering up and down Rayn's face.

"I believe that."

"Don't start."

"Very well. Do you know a Sergeant Hrugaz?"

"I've met him. He didn't impress me."

"You can trust him. This is his place we've been meeting in."

Before she could open her mouth to protest the secret he had kept from her, he leaned forward and took it in a slow, deep kiss.

Breathless, she pulled back and looked at him with suspicious eyes. "What was that for?"

"For what I'm going to tell you next."

Rayn told Dina of his plan to confront T'halamar himself.

"You are crazy! Rayn, don't go, please! He'll destroy you." Dina started to panic. She had a feeling that Rayn would go no matter what she said to him, but she had to try to stop him.

"No, he won't." The simple statement, quietly and confidently uttered, failed to reassure Dina.

"Rayn, no, listen to me! I know what he plans to do to you. I *know*."

Rayn frowned. "What do you mean, you *know*?"

Dina hadn't wanted to tell Rayn about her last encounter with Gyn, but now she had no choice. "I met with him at the Oasis. He compelled me to go there, and he compelled me to stay with him while he told me what he would do, first to you, and then to me. He was laughing the whole time, as if I were nothing but a toy."

The expletives that, even in a foreign tongue were becoming familiar to Dina, spewed forth, as Rayn jumped off the bed and strode to the window.

"Tell me exactly what happened." He was still facing the window, but Dina got the impression he wasn't seeing anything beyond the glass.

She shivered at the chill in his voice, but couldn't feel much worse than she already did. "There was nothing I could do against him. I couldn't even move. I had no will at all. He didn't hurt me, but he could have done anything to me, anything...or he could have compelled me to do anything. And I would have done it. No matter how degrading, how vile, I would have done it. That was the most frightening part. Not what he did, but the possibilities of what he could have done, or could do in the future. And you...he doesn't plan on killing you. He's going to destroy your mind, reduce it to that of a child's..." Her throat tightened, and she couldn't continue.

He turned to her. "Dina, now it's your turn to listen to me. You've forgotten what I am. I am exactly the creature you hated when you first landed here. My powers are considerable, and are not, and never have been, diminished by the fact that I left life on B'harata long ago to pursue other roads. I possess every one of the traits you abhor—plus a few others. T'halamar will not destroy me."

"But he will! Rayn, he was able to compel me in spite of the commands you planted in my mind to resist him. That proves he's stronger than you are, doesn't it?"

"All it proves is that I underestimated him the first time around. It won't happen again."

"Rayn, I felt his power. It was strong."

Rayn shook his head. "You felt what he wanted you to feel. I have much he doesn't have, Dina, and never will. Believe in me." In one fluid motion he was back at her side and gathered her to him.

"Then there's nothing I can say or do to change your mind."

"No."

After a time, he released her and held her chin so that she was forced to look at his eyes. "Listen, and mind this above all. Once I leave to confront T'halamar, don't try to call to me or reach out to me. If you do, you'll not only distract me, you'll hurt yourself. More precisely, you'll cause me to injure you, perhaps even kill you. My mind will be untouchable to someone at your novice level. You'll burn in an instant. Dina, do you understand? If you try to touch my mind, the burn will probably kill you."

Dina's eyes were wide. "But how will I know if you're all right? The not-knowing will be impossible."

"No, it won't. I'll contact you as soon as I can. In the

meantime you must wait."

She couldn't answer.

He shook her. *Dina. You must heed me in this. You must.*

In that instant, her mind cleared, and she felt her strength return. She looked deep into his eyes and swore she saw her reflection there, caught and held for eternity. Hate? Abhor? She couldn't hate this man no matter what he said or did.

Rayn, I'll do as you say, but I must know the outcome as soon as possible.

Oh, you'll know soon enough. When I can, I'll have my men send word. But don't come to me in person until Gaard contacts you. He'll have this with him.

Rayn put his left hand over her right, which was still behind his neck, buried deep in his hair. He moved it to his chest and closed her fingers over the pendant that always resided there. The stone felt smooth and warm from the constant contact with his skin. Dina closed her eyes and shuddered. It felt almost alive. His life, his warmth, she thought.

It's made of mother of pearl and star bharonite, from my planet. My name, my true name, is engraved on the back.

Dina looked down and examined the gleaming gems, then turned the pendant over, but she couldn't decipher the strange symbols engraved there. She searched his eyes again. They were only slightly deeper in color than the bharonite. The golden stone. *Is this where the name DeStar came from? The star stone?*

In part.

And your real name? Do you trust me enough to tell me?

When this is over. If anyone comes to you other than Gaard, or if Gaard comes to you without the pendant, don't trust what is said to you. If it should go badly, any one of my people, no matter how loyal, could be compelled to deceive you. Do you understand?

Dina could only nod. She had to know the answer to one more question before he left. *How long? How long after it's over before I can be with you?*

A couple days, maybe a little longer. "I have to go."

Dina understood that in speaking to her, he was already pulling away from her, preparing to leave. She knew she had to let him go. She mustered her dignity and prayed her throat wouldn't be so tight she couldn't talk. "Just make sure you come back." It was barely more than a whisper, but at least she got the words out.

"You have my word."

"Your word. Giving your word doesn't sound like something a B'haratan would do," she said with a small smile.

Rayn smiled in return. "It isn't. Someday you'll know that I mean what I tell you without my having to give you such meaningless reassurances."

Her smile grew.

"You need to go back and get some sleep before your meeting."

She shook her head. "I don't care about the meeting any more. And I don't need sleep half as much as you do. Promise me you'll sleep before you meet T'halamar. Rayn, promise, please."

"I promise, little girl. I'll contact you before I go after T'halamar. You know what you have to do."

She nodded.

"Come here."

She obeyed, willingly, and when she did, he kissed her again, softly and slowly.

"This is not the way to persuade me to leave."

"Shall I insult your partner? That seemed to do the trick last time."

"*Krek.* All right, I'm going." Dina looked at him one last time, then slipped out the door quietly.

Rayn, I do believe in you.

She wondered why she hadn't been able to say it to his face.

***

Nine hours later Dina sat with Jon, Chandhel, and Katzfiel in the same room they had had their initial meeting in. That first meeting seemed so distant now. Had it been only twelve days ago? Dina had felt so eager and excited then, with all the confidence in the world in Jon and herself. Chandhel had seemed so pleased that they had arrived. Now Jon looked tired and defeated, and Chandhel looked like he was ready to hang them in place of the killer. His lined face looked pinched and drawn, but the blue-green eyes blazed. Only Katzfiel looked the same as before.

Chandhel rose and wasted no time on preambles. "Agent Rzije, Agent Marlijn, the situation on Exodus has become critical. You have been here twelve days. Twelve whole days. We expected to have some results in that length of time. Not only does it appear that we do not, but people are still dying!"

Chandhel's voice rose with his last sentence, and he paused to regain his composure.

"Frankly speaking, when I was told that only two IIB agents would be sent here, and that one was, for all intents, a 'rookie,' I was quite disturbed. But I was assured that the agents would be two of the best. Thus far, my fears have been confirmed in the manner in which this investigation has been run."

Chandhel paused to wipe his face with a finely woven white cloth. "I'm told that just yesterday, only hours from the time Karsa Hrothi was being murdered, the two of you were wasting Commander Katzfiel's time asking about someone who was deported even before the killings started—someone who couldn't possibly have anything to do with all this. My associates are displeased as well, and let me just say that Mother Lode and Synergy officials are just a little more than displeased!"

A vein at Chandhel's temple popped out, and a purplish color was evident even on his tanned skin. Again he paused, this time taking a sip of cold water as he did so. "Mother Lode's planetary CEO, Jai Hwa-lik, met with me last night. He's been in contact with all local Mother Lode officials as well as the home office on Glacia. They'll be filing their suit immediately. Commander, please continue." Chandhel dropped heavily to his seat.

Katzfiel pushed his chair away from the table, but didn't rise. He turned his pale eyes to Jon. "Agent Rzije. You will tell me now what suspect information you have developed. With our help, you are instructed to apprehend this person or persons before *merkwia* tomorrow. This is a directive from the highest echelon, and it allows for no discretion or alternative action. Do you understand?"

Jon glanced down at the recorder in front of Dina but didn't look at her. He drew a deep breath and addressed Katzfiel. "Sir, please know that we understand fully the gravity of the situation. This has been a very complex case, and we've been following a number of leads. We have discovered two *dens* living in the desert, and we believe that one, if not both of them, are involved in the murders."

Dina looked at Jon, incredulous. She wanted to ask him what he was doing, but knew better than to contradict him in front of Chandhel and Katzfiel. Jon continued speaking, without so much as a sideways glance at Dina.

"One calls himself Rayn DeStar. He purports to be the *Uz-Dailjan* and lives in the Chayne Gwer. Both my partner and I have spoken to this man. The other is Gyn T'halamar, who lives alone in the Pur-Pelag. Agent Marlijn has met this man so can vouch for his existence."

"And what evidence do you have against these men?"

Jon didn't blink. "Each has implicated the other, Commander. Both have means, motive, and opportunity."

"Good. We'll meet and formulate a plan to bring these two men in for questioning before tomorrow night. Minister?"

"When your plan is set, you will advise me of such. This meeting is closed." Chandhel rose and left the room.

"Agent Rzije. Meet me in my office in one hour. You will bring ideas on how best to take these two men safely into custody," Katzfiel said, still looking at Jon.

Jon and Dina left the conference room, passing Maris and Corporal Khilioi in the anteroom. Dina met the woman's gaze, but Maris wasn't smiling. Her expression was cold, but more than that, there was a open haughtiness that had been absent before. Unlike Maris, Khilioi was smiling, but to Dina his crooked smirk was as far from friendly as the woman's contempt. The bandwagon was certainly getting emptier by the minute.

The Commander, as usual, had ignored her, but she had bigger problems to worry about than Katzfiel. To Maris and

Khilioi she gave not a single further thought. As soon as she was alone with Jon in his room, she directed her ire at him.

"Jon, how could you? We don't have any evidence DeStar is involved."

Jon took off his shirt and threw it at the bed. "Take the blinders off, Dina. We have plenty against him. What did you expect me to say in there? I had to give them something. Did you expect me to say 'oh, Minister, we believe that there is a conspiracy within Mother Lode Mining to discredit the Synergy so they can win a big lawsuit, but we don't know exactly who's involved, and we don't have any evidence.' Come on." He hobbled to the sink.

Upset as she was, alienating Jon would not further her cause. She stepped to his side to apologize. "I'm sorry. You're right. I'm just tired. What do we do next?"

"Well, you understand the *dens* better than anyone. You're going to have to help me come up with this plan. We're going to have to find a way to bring them in without allowing them the opportunity to turn their mental powers on us."

Dina thought fast. "All right. Just give me a moment in my room to freshen up." She wanted to be alone to call Rayn. The telepathic communication was so intimate that Dina felt uncomfortable doing it in the presence of others.

"One minute. Chandhel didn't give us much time. Let's not waste it."

Dina nodded, and was grateful to slip inside her room at last. She closed her eyes and tried to compose her roiling feelings. *Rayn.*

It didn't go well, did it?

No. Worse even than I imagined. Chandhel gave us an ultimatum. Jon gave up both you and T'halamar to the AEA. We have until merkwia tomorrow to apprehend you.

Dina could hear Rayn's laughter in her mind.

Rayn, this isn't a joke. The AEA has life sensors and motion detectors that'll make it easy to find anyone in the desert. And once located, they have an arsenal of weapons that will render anyone, even a dens, incapacitated. And don't think you can hide, because even if you can, what about your people? Katzfiel won't hesitate to use them against you.

I wasn't laughing because I'm amused, believe me. You're right, little girl, I won't risk the lives of my friends, but things are happening fast. You have to buy me time, today at least.

"Dina, get in here!" came Jon's voice from the other side of the door.

I don't have any clout with these people. They don't even give me credence as an investigator.

Then use your influence with Rzije to convince the angwhi to go after T'halamar first.

Rayn...

"Dina!"

"Coming, Jon." *Damn!* She took a deep breath and opened the door to Jon's room.

He frowned at her from the computer. "What's the matter?"

She tried to compose herself. "Nothing. I just don't like ultimatums, that's all."

"Neither do I, but we don't have many choices right now. We have less than an hour to decide what to do. Any ideas?"

"I think we should convince the Commander to go after T'halamar first."

"And why is that?" Jon asked.

She sat on the bed and leaned forward. "Because I really believe that he's the killer, not DeStar."

"Dina, you don't know that."

"Yes, I do. The *Dailjan* are good people. I've probed most of them. A killer wouldn't choose to live among people like that."

Jon shoved at a pile of printed reports, not seeming to care that some of them slid to the floor. "Come on, Dina. It's a well known fact that murderers throughout the ages have been able to live in society without their friends and neighbors aware of what they are."

She stood up. "Jon, please, trust me on this. If you're not going to trust my abilities, why did you choose me for this assignment?"

Jon sighed. "Okay, you win. But we're going to have to come up with a different reason to convince Katzfiel."

She shrugged and stepped over to pick up the papers from the floor. "It'll be easier to locate T'halamar. He's all alone in the Pur-Pelag. Once the sensors pick up a lone life form, chances are very good it'll be him. If we try to scan for DeStar in the Chayne, we'll pick up numerous scattered life forms. We won't have any way of knowing which one is him."

"All right. That makes sense."

The meeting with Katzfiel, while not the most pleasant Dina had ever attended, at least achieved what Dina wanted. A dawn raid was planned for the following day, and it was agreed by all to try to apprehend T'halamar first. Jon spent the rest of the day in planning the details for the raid, and for preparing the equipment needed.

Dina had her own plans.

SEVENTEEN
THE PUR-PELAG

With the help of a life sensor, it didn't take Rayn long to locate T'halamar's camp in the Pur-Pelag. It was in a small valley surrounded by orange and burgundy sandstone rocks, carved into twisting, huddled forms by wind and water over millions of years. The place had a mysterious beauty to it, but Rayn saw none of it.

He cut the power on his skimmer thirty bars from the shadowed opening in the rock, swivelled off the leather seat and, in slow, measured paces, walked toward the cavern, no weapon in hand. The only concession he made to the weather was a narrow sunshield covering his eyes.

Rayn stopped twenty bars from the entrance and waited.

A moment later, Gyn stepped from the shade of the cavern into the sunlight. His hair was pulled back and tied behind his head, and he was naked from the waist up. As he sauntered toward Rayn, sunlight flashed off the sweat on Gyn's bronzed torso.

T'halamar covered half the distance between the cavern and Rayn and halted. "Well, well. If it isn't the little *spithra.*"

"I received your message. You really didn't expect me to turn down such a charming invitation, did you?" Rayn asked mildly.

"Did you get all of my message? No? Allow me to tell you the parts that the delectable Miss Marlijn no doubt left out. The part about her opening herself so willingly to me? And did she neglect to tell you how her body responded to mine? Truly, it has been a long time since I've seen a woman become so aroused so quickly. She seemed starved for attention, as if she hadn't been satisfied for a long, long time. What's the matter, *spithra*? Unable to get the job done? Or does she simply show no interest in a weakling like you?"

A dark red current of heat flowed from Gyn, and Rayn saw the sunlight brighten the energy like candlelight through a glass of dark wine, rich, strong, and heady. Rayn felt the heat of

Gyn's power, but deflected it easily away.

"You can cut the theatrics, T'halamar. Your bad-boy display doesn't impress me." Rayn removed his sunshield and casually tossed it to the ground, refusing to let T'halamar's taunts distract him. "I hope you enjoyed yourself with the lady. She does have a beautiful body, does she not? Fortunately for her, she'll survive your crude grouping. Unfortunately for you, she has depths of beauty you'd never be able to reach had you a hundred years to try. But, alas, you won't even get the chance."

T'halamar's dark eyes narrowed and burned like black coals. "Try? Oh, I'll do more than try. I'll have her, every part of her, body and soul. And while I'm inside her, possessing her utterly, I'll tell her how on this day I destroyed you, bit by bit. Do you suppose that'll increase her pleasure? I can't wait to find out."

"It's quite apparent you've fantasized about her a great deal. Of course, that's about all you can do, isn't it? Fantasize?"

"You're about to learn differently. After today you'll wish fantasizing *was* all I could do. At least, that's what you'd wish if you had a mind left to wish with."

"Enough posturing. You don't scare me. Let's get to it. You'll find I'm not quite as easy a target as those unsuspecting miners," Rayn said.

Gyn sniggered. "They were pitiful, weren't they? I enjoyed them, but the pleasure was over much too soon. I do hope you'll last a little longer than they did."

"Oh, I assure you I will," Rayn replied softly.

The two men circled each other slowly, two creatures driven by ancient instinct to fight for domination. Rayn felt a pressure against his mind, willing him to submit. Rayn's mental guards easily blocked the suggestion, and he returned a similar compelling force toward Gyn.

Gyn sneered. "Oh, I do hope you can do better than that. Or perhaps not? It's been a long time since you've imitated a true B'haratan, hasn't it?"

Rayn felt an increased pressure at his mind, and the beginnings of pain, but still was able to block it out without a problem. "I'm more of a B'haratan than you've ever been. Tell me, how much power did it take to compel those miners to put their hands against their heads and squeeze? A whole lot, I'll bet." Rayn increased the pressure on Gyn. "And it took a big man, a big B'haratan, to accept money from the *angwhi* to do that big job, didn't it?"

Gyn advanced, his long strides eating up the distance between them. "I'll take advantage of the *angwhi* any way I can. As you should. Or didn't your mama teach you that?"

Rayn, who had backpedaled a few steps, halted. So he was right about the *angwhi*. He ran his hand through his hair to push the damp strands out of his face and brushed the sweat off his forehead with his suede armband. He knew he had to stay in control and not let any of what Gyn was saying get to him. "You take advantage of everyone you come into contact with, don't you? That's why you have so many friends." Rayn gradually stepped up the pressure on Gyn, but it didn't appear to have any effect on him.

Gyn laughed. "Your friends are your weakness. I think I'll pay another visit to them, too, when I'm finished with you. Oh, you do know that I visited once before? Your little girlfriend, Alessane is it? She gave me quite a pleasurable time. She filled your drink with poison, and then while you were writhing in agony, I filled her. Pity she misunderstood my command to mix the 'shadow' in a drink. If she had mixed it with alcohol, it would have killed you. No matter. It will be more satisfying this way. Speaking of satisfying, your little Alessane was very responsive, almost as much so as your new girlfriend. Maybe I'll have both of them together." Gyn laughed again, still advancing on Rayn.

Rayn stepped back until he was only a few bars from his skimmer, then circled to his left, putting the sun behind him and into Gyn's eyes. The pain Rayn was experiencing was considerable, but he knew how to ignore pain. "Using the *dher* on a couple of women seems to be the only way you can gratify yourself. Or did the *angwhi* who paid you get a little extra service rendered when he handed over the payment?"

Gyn's anger flared, and his mental guards dropped just a little. It was enough for Rayn to pick up a brief image of the

AEA officer who had paid Gyn for killing the miners. Keeping his own guards in place, Rayn kept the pressure on. "What, no response? Maybe pleasuring an *angwhi* wasn't so much fun, after all."

Gyn's laughter died. "I was only going to destroy your mind, but you're going to pay for that. When I finish with you, there won't be anything left."

With every step Gyn made toward Rayn, Rayn sidestepped to the left or right. "What are you waiting for? So far you're just like that *mantis* you manipulated, all talk and nothing more."

Gyn rushed him, lashing out with a powerful side kick to Rayn's chest. "And you're as ineffectual as wind through the Wiara."

Rayn, moving with the blow, caught very little of its force. He countered with a leg sweep that took Gyn off his feet. Just as quickly, though, Gyn was back up and aimed a roundhouse kick at Rayn's head. Rayn, off balance, absorbed most of the blow on the side of his head and went sprawling into the rust-colored dust of the Pur-Pelag. Gyn grabbed Rayn by the vest, pulled him up just enough to bury his knee in Rayn's abdomen, then with his right fist to his jaw, sent Rayn into the grit again. Rayn pushed aside the pain once again and rolled away from Gyn before Gyn could grab him.

Rayn, still on the ground, took a moment to catch his breath before asking, "I'm curious about something. When you attacked Agent Marlijn and poisoned me, did you throw that in on your own as a bonus, or were you hired to eliminate us? If you were hired to do it, somebody didn't get their money's worth. Not finishing me is one thing. But really. Not to be able to kill a skinny little Glacian girl is quite something else. Did the *angwhi* demand a refund for such ineptitude?"

Rayn could feel Gyn's control slipping as his rage mounted. The larger man's breathing also became more labored as they exerted themselves in the midday desert heat, but Rayn knew it was far from over. Gyn threw himself at Rayn and caught a knee in his chest for his trouble. Rayn gathered his feet like a spring and knocked Gyn backward with enough force to fell him. Both lay in the dust, and both were slow to get to their feet.

Gyn hadn't stopped applying pressure to Rayn's mind, and Rayn, though still able to keep his mental shield in place, was starting to feel the sharp stabs behind his eyes. Both were covered with streaks of red, the filings of the basin floor sticking to the sweat on their bodies.

When Gyn didn't respond, Rayn continued. "That must have been doubly embarrassing for you. First the little Glacian girl outsmarts you, then the *angwhi* insult you by not giving you the opportunity to finish the job. Not that they did any better. Sabotaging Rzije's skimmer...now that was a pretty bad idea, even for an *angwhi*. Or was that your idea?"

"I'm going to take immense satisfaction in replaying your death in that Glacian girl's mind while I use her body to the fullest." Gyn aimed another roundhouse kick at Rayn, and caught the back of Rayn's head, sending him face first into the dust.

Rayn was unable to mask the pain now. The sharp pains threatened to cut his concentration, his temples throbbed, and the pressure on his mind was almost unbearable. The heat of the Pelag was debilitating, and he was slow to gather his feet beneath him. Gyn didn't give him a chance, but kicked him in the ribs several times until he lay on his back, hardly able to move.

He looked up at Gyn and smiled. *No matter how much you torment that little girl, no matter what you do to me, you will have to live with the fact that she bested you. You, a powerful B'haratan, out-played by a little yellow-haired girl.*

And you, spithra, can consider that your final thought in life, because you're now going to die.

Gyn kicked Rayn in the ribs once more, rolling him onto his stomach. He then grabbed Rayn's hair and hauled him to his feet, grabbing him around the neck with a choke hold. *How does it feel now, spithra? Does it feel like talk now?*

Gyn maintained the choke hold a moment longer, until he felt Rayn's body go limp in his arms. He threw him to the ground in triumph, lifted his face to the sun, and raised his arms above his head, letting out a cry of jubilation.

In that second Rayn felt Gyn's mental guards drop, and he concentrated all the force he could on Gyn's mind, compelling him to put his hands on either side of his head. The look on Gyn's face changed from that of sweet victory to shock, and the cry of conquest rose to a scream as Rayn continued compelling Gyn with all of his undeniable power. He kept on the pressure, and somehow found the strength to increase the demand. Gyn's hands slowly lowered to his ears and covered them, as if trying to shut out the sound of his own scream. Rayn closed his eyes and expertly dealt the killing mental blow.

The Pelag swallowed the last of Gyn's shriek, and the dull thud of his body hitting the hard basin floor told Rayn it was over at last. He lay face down in the grit, totally spent, his head throbbing and his ribs aching, but the pressure was gone from his mind. Rayn listened to the settling of the dust as the faint breeze swirled the red powder around his head. Then, off to the east, he heard a sweet sighing, almost musical. He smiled. The wind in the Wiara was laughing.

Several long moments later, when a measure of Rayn's strength had returned to him, he rose from the floor of the Pelag and checked Gyn's body. It was indeed lifeless, the skull crushed on either side of his head and the eyes dull and dark, staring up at the sun, seeing none of the light. Rayn bent down and closed the vacant eyes. *You never did see the light, did you?*

He dragged the body into the nearby cavern and dropped it in the shade of the entrance. He gazed down at it and tried to feel some measure of compunction for killing a countryman, but couldn't. *One less bastard for this world or any other to worry about. And yet, we were not all that different, were we?* Rayn knelt down and scooped up a handful of the fine red dust. Rising, he let the dust sift through his fingers to be sucked away by the breeze, but enough settled onto Gyn's face to redden the mask of death. *The fire basin was an appropriate home for you, my friend. I hope it prepared you well for the Void.*

Rayn returned to his skimmer, bent down, and examined the small holorecorder mounted on the side. "Stop recording," he said softly.

EIGHTEEN
THE RATS' REVENGE

Decbars away from the Pur-Pelag, a man in a hooded cloak kept a silent vigil in front of one of the many Aeternan housing complexes. He had watched, a fat smile hidden beneath the collar of his cloak, as two AEA officers had escorted the Mother Lode security officer from the AEA Center to his quarters. The officers had gone in with Kalyo Rhoemer and, after almost an hour, were still inside.

The man outside waited and watched, and his anger smoldered with the fanning of time, consuming his earlier satisfaction. *Bumbling fools*, he thought. Why hadn't he gotten the word about Hrothi? It should have been his decision. And as if that wasn't bad enough, he fumed, the job had been botched. Karsa had lived long enough to give a dying declaration to Rhoemer. But Rhoemer was smart. He knew to keep his mouth shut, knew not to cooperate with the AEA. And now he would ensure that Rhoemer's mouth stayed shut for good.

The man allowed himself a small smile. If only the AEA had intelligence half as thorough as his, they might solve a case now and then. Not that he was complaining. They had made it only too easy for him.

At last, his patience stretched almost to the snapping point, the man saw the two officers leave, weaving down the street, slapping each other on the back.

Worthless idiots. Probably stayed for a few drinks while on duty. The man snorted. Perhaps they had eased his task after all.

He entered the building and took a lift to the sixth floor, the hood of his cloak and wide sunshield concealing most of his face. The corridor stretched before him, silent and empty. He stood outside Rhoemer's door and listened carefully. The smooth hum of a recycling unit and the sound of running water wafted to his ear.

He sounded the soft chime.

"Who's there?"

"It's just me, Kal. I wanted to make sure you were all right after yesterday's ordeal."

"I'll buzz the door. Hold on."

A second later the door slid open, and the man looked inside before entering. The corners of his mouth lifted. This would indeed be easy. The figure at the sink, his back turned, swayed back and forth, as if humming a tune to himself. A dirty blue robe covered his stocky build and hung nearly to the floor.

The strong smell of alcoholic beverages hung in the air of the small room. The man in the cloak wrinkled his nose. "I want you to know, Kal, how sorry I am. How very sorry. I know how close you and Karsa were," he said softly.

Kal stood with his head bent forward and nodded, his short brown hair bobbing, barely visible, above the robe's collar.

Perfect. The man in the cloak raised his arms and, like a striking snake, instantly had his victim helpless.

A glass fell and shattered.

Kal tugged desperately at the cord tightening around his neck. He sank to his knees, then bent forward and tried to pull the assailant off balance. The man in the cloak moved to the side to regain his leverage and gave a renewed yank on the cord. He would not lose the game now.

Out of the corner of his eye he saw a giant of a man step from behind a tall bank of cabinets. Releasing the cord, he scrabbled backwards, away from the giant, but his boots skittered on the broken glass. He whipped out an arm to the counter for support and realized too late that he had provided a perfect target for the giant's fist. The blow to his unprotected face sent him sprawling to the floor, and the explosion of pain scattered all thoughts of victory.

Sergeant Hrugaz, Dina, and a uniformed Mother Lode security officer rushed in from the adjoining room. Hrugaz grabbed the would-be assassin and hauled him to his feet, yanking the hood down.

Dark red hair hung over dazed eyes that darted between the man in the robe, who he suddenly realized wasn't Kal, and the security officer. "You!" His cruel mouth twisted, and he spat at the officer. "Desert filth!"

Kalyo Rhoemer grinned at his boss in return. "I prefer 'desert rat,' myself."

"On behalf of the Interplanetary Investigation Bureau and the AEA I place you under arrest, Mr. Ctararzin," Dina said as she took Mother Lode's Operation Manager into custody. "The charge is attempted murder."

The man in the robe still knelt on the floor, rubbing his neck. He looked up to see the big man hold out a hand to him. Trai Morghen grasped the outstretched hand and allowed himself to be hauled to his feet. "Thanks, friend," he said, winking one blue eye.

Gaard nodded in return, and a rare smile lit his stoic features.

***

As Ctararzin's ill-fated vigil began in the city, three other men stood in the desert, considering their own destiny.

At the entrance to Keneko Kap, Rayn gave a package and final instructions to Kindyll and Raethe to meet the man and woman at the Medical Center. "They're expecting both of you. They'll know what to do. Stay in the city as long as this takes."

Kindyll nodded, his face serious. "Rayn, you know I'll do this, but..."

Rayn cut him off with a hand to Kindyll's shoulder and a look that brooked no argument. Kindyll nodded, and Rayn looked away, then back to his friend, seeing into the compassionate hazel eyes and knowing the man meant only the best.

"If she sees this recording, she'll know I'm alive. For now that's enough. I'll meet with her in person after this is all over. She'll understand," said Rayn. "The two of you are the only ones I can trust with this. I'm asking you to trust me, too."

Rayn picked up Kindyll's quick thought that she might understand, but he didn't. Understand he might not, but trust he did. This stronger thought lapped the previous one, and though Rayn didn't need to hear Kindyll's next words, he was touched nevertheless.

"You don't have to ask for trust. It was earned long ago."

Rayn smiled and shook the lanky young man's shoulder

gently. "Thank you, my friend. I wouldn't have been able to do this without you."

Raethe stood next to the two men, slouched against the rock wall, his eyes studying the hard ground. He hadn't said anything, but Rayn knew he, too, could be trusted implicitly. Rayn turned to the tall man. "Rae..."

"Listen, Rayn, you don't have to say anything. There are two people I would do anything for." Raethe tossed the package Rayn had given him from his left hand to his right. "Our friend is one, and you're the other."

Rayn met Raethe's eyes for the length of a heartbeat, then simply nodded. "Be off, then."

The show was about to begin.

NINETEEN
THE WITNESS

Soon afterward, *merkwia* performed its nightly dance of color, but missing from its audience were several very perplexed and busy individuals. Priority one calls had gone out to Minister Chandhel, Commander Katzfiel, and Jon to meet Dina and Dr. Lumazi at the Medical Center. Preparations for the dawn raid on the Pur-Pelag had come to a sudden but tentative halt as the news was received that one killer was dead and another was in custody.

An emergency meeting had been called for the eighteenth hour, but Dina had been at the Medical Center, answering a request from the doctor that she come as soon as possible. Dina had all but flown there, fearing the worst. She had been on edge all day, not knowing the outcome of Rayn's confrontation with Gyn, and even the satisfaction she had felt in trapping Ctararzin hadn't diminished her feeling that something was wrong.

The cryptic news that the killer was dead hadn't helped her, for Gyn had declared his innocence to her all along. If Gyn had defeated Rayn, Gyn would naturally proclaim that "the killer was now dead."

But as soon as Dina's eyes met those of Dr. Lumazi, Dina knew Rayn had prevailed. She silently thanked whatever gods had been listening to her plea for Rayn's safety.

"Doctor, how much do you know about the *dens*?"

Jalena Lumazi gave her a wan smile. "Considerably more than I did two days ago. I know their reputation and what they're capable of. But I also know that Rayn DeStar does not deserve to be called a 'dark outworlder.' Rather than my trying to explain what happened, I want you to watch this holo. It's quite startling and graphic, and unlike anything I've ever seen. I should warn you, though. Both these men allude to liaisons with you, liaisons of a sexual nature. The others will be seeing this holo very soon. I thought it best for you to see it first."

Dina's heart pounded as she viewed the three-dimensional

recording. It was an eerie feeling, almost as if she were right there in the Pur-Pelag watching the scene play out. By the end of the holo, the kaleidoscope of emotion left Dina's knuckles white, her throat tight, and her mouth as dry as the fire basin itself.

She paused for a moment to clear her throat. "It's true I've developed a close relationship with DeStar in the past few days. I've only met the other *dens,* T'halamar, on brief occasions. The first time he tried to kill me. The other times he used what's called the *dher* to try to convince me that Rayn was the killer, not him. He also tried to make me believe I was attracted to him. I never accepted any of his illusions. That was all that happened."

Dr. Lumazi raised her eyebrows. "Chandhel, Katzfiel, and your partner will be seeing this recording shortly. Some of them, not understanding the *dens* and how they operate, may believe the worst of you."

Dina shook her head. "As long as Rayn's alive, it doesn't matter. Thank you. I'm more grateful than I can ever express."

The doctor's smile widened. "You're welcome. Oh, and DeStar left this for you. The meeting will be starting shortly. You will assist me?"

"Of course."

"I'll leave you alone for a few moments."

Dina waited for the doctor to exit the room, then opened the note. It was hastily scrawled and brief. There was nothing personal in it, not even an assurance that he was indeed uninjured, just a reference to the name of the AEA officer who had contacted Gyn, the name Rayn had plucked from his mind before he killed him. She nodded. It all fit.

The eighteenth hour struck, and Dina entered the conference room to join Chandhel, Katzfiel, and Jon. The men were talking among themselves, speculating on what unknown developments had transpired. When Dina sat down next to Jon, he looked at her with his brows drawn together.

"Why did Dr. Lumazi want to see you?"

"You'll see in a moment."

Jon opened his mouth, but had no time to protest her evasive answer.

The door slid open, and Dr. Lumazi appeared. A heartbeat of silence was followed by all the men talking at once.

"Gentlemen. If I can have your attention, please." The room became hushed, and the doctor continued. "Thank you. I realize this is all highly irregular, but be assured that what I have to impart to you is of the utmost importance. If you will please reserve your questions and comments, we will be able to make rapid and orderly progress."

The doctor paused and, satisfied with the continued silence, proceeded. "Earlier this evening, as you all know, Rum Ctararzin was taken into custody for the attempted murder of Kalyo Rhoemer. What most of you don't know is that the man who committed the actual murders at the mines has been located, and he himself has been killed. There is evidence of both his crimes and his death. I also have knowledge of those persons responsible for hiring this killer, one of whom is Ctararzin."

The undertone of voices started to swell, and the doctor held up her hand for order. "Gentlemen. Please save your comments." As the murmurs died away, she continued. "As you all know, there have been two *dens* living in the desert for some time. Your assumption that one of them was the killer is correct. I'm now going to show you quite a remarkable holo. Please remain silent. Play recording."

Dina watched again as the scenes played out. Knowing what was on the recording, she flicked her eyes toward Jon several times. He didn't look at her, concentrating instead on the images. His expression didn't change, but Dina caught the telltale twitch of a facial muscle more than once. The end of the recording was met with utter stillness.

Jon lowered his head and buried his face in his hands, but Dina felt the eyes of the other two men squarely on her.

Finally, Chandhel spoke. "Doctor, how do we know this T'halamar is truly dead? The *dens* are known for tricks."

"I have the body. You will be free to view it later," said Dr. Lumazi.

Jon lifted his head. "Who are these *angwhi* they spoke of?"

"Agent Marlijn? If you would?"

Dina rose and joined the doctor at the podium. "Just as we insult them by calling them 'dark outworlders,' they insult us by calling us snakes. By *angwhi* they are specifically referring to the AEA."

"They implied T'halamar was hired to murder the miners by an *angwhi,*" Jon stated. "But no one was named. A derogatory term like *angwhi* could in fact refer to anyone. How does this bring us closer to the people who ordered the hits?"

Dina returned Jon's glare with a steady look. "I have a statement from DeStar in which he names the person who contacted T'halamar and made the arrangements for both the murders and the payment. There is no direct evidence against this contact, but a good deal of circumstantial evidence. He's a bit player in this drama. I feel if he's confronted, there's a good chance he'll try to cut a deal by giving up other more important players."

Chandhel spoke next. "Doctor, with all due respect to your abilities as a highly regarded physician, just how is it that you came into possession of this holo? You're not an investigator, nor have you been active in this investigation to the same extent that Agents Rzije and Marlijn and Commander Katzfiel have been."

"I was approached as one who could be trusted. In addition, my skills as a physician were required in order to keep one of the witnesses alive."

"What witness? DeStar? Where is he now, anyway?" asked Jon.

"No, not DeStar. He's still in the desert. Even with all the help he's provided, he fears apprehension as a 'dark outworlder,'" replied Dina.

"You still didn't answer my question. What witness?"

"And which one of my men is supposed to have been involved in this?" asked Katzfiel, who, to Dina's surprise, had been speechless since the playing of the holo recording. There was absolute quiet, as everyone waited to hear the answers to both questions.

Dina accommodated them. "The witness is in the next room.

He'll come in shortly and tell you his story in his own words. The AEA officer who contacted T'halamar is Corporal Khilioi."

Everyone started talking at once, until Chandhel's voice rose above the others. "People, please! We'll deal with Khilioi later. Let's hear what this witness has to say."

"Yes, ladies, if you would," said Katzfiel, and Dina took pleasure in the fact that he was acknowledging her at last.

Jon could only stare at Dina incredulously.

Dr. Lumazi nodded, and pressed a key before her. "Gentlemen, if you would please join us now."

The door slid open, and three tall men entered the room. Two were lean and tanned, with long hair that fell to their shoulders. One had a wary look in his eyes similar to that of an animal taken from his domain and placed in a strange locale. The eyes of the second were just as keen, carefully studying each of the people in the room.

The third man stood between the other two, and though he lacked the taut, vigilant air of the desert dwellers, his sky-blue eyes showed strength and intelligence. The new arrivals waited, greeted only by stunned expressions and stilled tongues.

Jon leaned back and ran his hands down his face.

Chandhel, in a surprisingly even voice, finally broke the silence. "Indeed. Sir, we are all appropriately astonished and, I might add, gratified to see you well. Please introduce us to your associates and proceed with what I am sure will be quite an amazing story."

The man with the gray hair and azure eyes looked at Dina and nodded his head toward her. "Agent Marlijn already knows these two men. Gentlemen, I'd like to introduce two friends of mine—Raethe Avarti and Kindyll Sirkhek. I've known both of them for quite some time. They worked for me and did their jobs well and with integrity. Through circumstances beyond my control, they left the employ of Mother Lode Mining some months ago and are now part of the Desert *Dailjan.*"

At the term *'Dailjan,'* the eyes of those seated flickered like fireflies to the others in the room, then just as quickly landed once more on the speaker.

"In doing what they did, they not only gained a freedom

those of us still in the grasp of Mother can only envy, but they probably saved their own lives. I will be forever grateful to them for saving mine, and for giving me the push I needed to reach for that same freedom. I am ashamed to admit I needed that push, and only hope that what I do now will atone to some small extent for my having held my silence for so long."

With that, the three men sat at the conference table, Karsa Hrothi between the two *Dailjan*.

Hrothi continued. "First, let me satisfy your curiosity regarding my obvious state of good health. Two days ago, Agents Rzije and Marlijn requested a meeting with me after Agent Marlijn interviewed my friends here and learned I might be willing to impart sensitive information regarding Mother Lode. A few hours after agreeing to this meeting, I was contacted by Avarti, who requested to see me immediately at a *Dailjan* location in the desert. Raethe described it as a life-or-death situation. Out of respect for the working relationship I had with him before his guild membership was revoked, I went. Before you ask how I could go into the desert alone, not knowing for sure that Avarti wasn't associated with the killer, I can only say that maybe I was tired of playing things safe."

Hrothi paused and looked at the people before him. All eyes were riveted on him. "In any case, I did go, and met with Avarti, Sirkhek, and a man named Rayn DeStar. They told me they feared for my safety and felt my upcoming meeting with Rzije and Marlijn could provide the catalyst for my demise. Believe me, the same thoughts had gone through my own mind many times. We talked about what could be done and decided that the best way to keep me from being killed was to fake my own death. For this I needed more than just the help of the *Dailjan*."

Hrothi took a sip of water, then continued. "I needed someone at the mines I could trust, and I needed Dr. Lumazi. We knew we could trust her. She's a distant cousin of Kindyll Sirkhek. The other person we chose to trust was Kalyo Rhoemer, one of my assistants. I've worked with him a long time and know him to be an honorable man. So my 'demise' was carried out with the help of a drug which slows heartbeat and respiration, simulating death. Rhoemer's job was to secure the scene and make sure no one came near enough to me to detect the truth. Dr. Lumazi's job was twofold—to confirm my 'death,' and to whisk my body away to the Medical Center before anyone else could examine it."

"Now to the beginning of the story..." Hrothi spent the next few hours detailing a story of greed and corruption that began eight years before, with the administration of Avvis Ranchar and the granting of the first mining contract on Exodus to Mother Lode Mining.

He told how the colony was a boom, with Kewero Kel rich beyond expectations, how Mother Lode's profits were the highest in years, and how for two years, Mother's highest placed on-planet personnel, including Ctararzin, Hwa-lik, Chukar, and Bhelen had made more money than they knew what to do with.

But Kewero wasn't as deep as they thought, and it wasn't hard for the 'top four' to see that the profits probably wouldn't continue for the length of the contract. But, Hrothi explained, the ousting of Ranchar and the changing of the administration provided an opportunity too good to let pass.

The contracts were changed with the new administration, and when they were, conditions were added. Most notably the condition that Mother could break the contract if negligence could be proved. Hrothi stated that he didn't think the four knew at that point what they would eventually do, but the loophole was now in place for that time in the future when it would be needed.

And that future was not long in coming. For several years, to be sure, a status quo prevailed. Dheru was opened, exodite was mined, profits continued, and no one spoke about yield.

But as the blue veins of pegmatite became harder and harder to locate, the four began to worry. They were used to the wealth this planet had gleaned for them, and they didn't want to give it up. Simply not bidding at the end of the five-year contract and closing up shop was never an option.

The new Synergy survey, done ten months ago, was a positive one, as always, explained Hrothi. Mother took their own survey, and bid on the new contract. But the catalyst was

Dais Johnter. He was put on the survey team at the last minute to replace an outworld survey member who had taken seriously ill.

But Dais didn't do as he was supposed to. He didn't keep his mouth shut. He started talking to anyone who would listen how the Mother Lode survey was a fraud, that the mines were almost played out and didn't hold any future. At that point the decision was made fairly quickly. Johnter would be silenced and would also provide the groundwork for a negligence suit against the Synergy.

T'halamar, the perfect killer, was hired, and Johnter was indeed eliminated.

Hrothi, who had, in his silence, condoned the actions of the others up to that point, was burning with anger and frustration, but knew to keep his mouth shut. The alternative was to end up as Dais had. So in a silent, impotent rage, he stood by and watched as one by one, his miners were killed. No one would care about one dead miner, you see, he had said, but numerous dead miners, that was another story.

Mother could easily point the finger at the Synergy and say that the Synergy was not only inept in not stopping the crimes, but to blame in the first place for allowing dangerous 'dark outworlders' entry to the colony under Ranchar's lax administration. They had an excellent suit against the Synergy, and if they had won, the settlement would have been for far more than the mines, even in their most productive days, could earn.

And two lone IIB agents, what could they do?

TWENTY
THE LIGHT AND THE DARKNESS

The next day was a frenzy of activity, as Khilioi was taken into custody, Ctararzin was interviewed, and attempts were made to verify the rest of Hrothi's story.

Dina's satisfaction, however, was blunted not only by her worry about Rayn, but by Jon's reaction to her involvement in Rayn's scheme to fake Hrothi's death. Jon wouldn't speak to her beyond what was necessary, and, when he did, his eyes were cold and hard. Every chilling glance he gave her promised there'd be hell to pay when this was concluded.

As Dina left the Visitor Center following another meeting, an AEA officer approached her. "Agent Marlijn."

Dina couldn't remember the young officer's name and glanced quickly at his name badge. "Yes, Officer Drukelez?"

"I've a message for you. There's a man waiting for you now outside Ghe Wespero."

"Who is it?" But as Dina was asking the question, the officer was already turning and striding away. Could it be Gaard?

She felt her heart pounding as she hurried back into the Visitor Center and keyed access to the storage bay. She already had her sunshield on and decided not to waste time putting on a full weather suit. After all, she wasn't going much beyond the city. She powered on the skimmer and slipped it through the bay before the doors were fully opened.

She passed between the columns of the Ghe and left the noise and the bustle of the *mercari* behind. As she cut back on the skimmer's throttle, her chest felt tight, and she struggled to breathe. It wasn't the atmosphere, but her emotions. She tentatively brought the skimmer to a stop, and as she did, felt her heart slam against her chest like a prisoner raging against the confines of a cell.

She closed her eyes against the glare of the sun. Rayn would tell her to relax and slow her breathing. She tried to as she squinted and scanned the area, but all she saw was the mar, glittering like a field of frost caught in the sunlight, melded to the white-hot sky, and all she heard was her blood in her ears.

Then she saw him, standing next to his skimmer about twenty bars to her right, almost invisible in his silent, stock-still stance. She turned her skimmer and nudged it forward slowly, powering off the machine several bars from where he stood. She sent out a light probe and verified quickly that it was indeed Gaard.

Dina took a deep breath and watched as he strode up to her. The undulations of the heat shimmer gave a mystery and grace to his movement and softened his appearance. As he stood before her, though, he looked as stoic as ever, straight and motionless, his only concessions to the desert a narrow sunshield and a cooling vest. His hair was tied back in its usual long ponytail, and his powerful tanned arms, bulging with muscle, gleamed with sweat. He uttered no greeting and made no sign acknowledging Dina.

She waited, knowing Gaard would talk to her in his own good time, and that it would avail her naught to try to hurry him. Dina felt the sun sear the skin of her neck and face, and she became very aware of the stillness of the desert.

"He's alive, well, and will contact you soon," came the low, masculine voice at last.

Dina closed her eyes and waited. The words were stated with no emotion, but Dina knew that behind the expressionless mask was one of Rayn's most loyal and steadfast comrades. Even though Dina knew Rayn was alive, it reassured her to hear Gaard say it. *The pendant.*

She forced her eyes open. *The pendant, Gaard, show me the pendant.* She knew Gyn was dead, knew that no one else could compel Gaard to betray her, but she still wanted to see the stones that meant so much to Rayn. It would be the final sign that all was well with him. She dared not ask Gaard for it. But what if he just forgot it? *No, Gaard doesn't forget, and he doesn't make mistakes.* She could feel pearls of sweat slide down her chest between her breasts and down her back along her spine. She hadn't bothered to put on a cooling vest.

Then, without a word, Gaard reached out his left arm and took hold of Dina's right hand, raising it to waist height and turning her palm to the sky. As he did this, his right hand dipped into a trouser pocket and pulled something out. He placed the article in her palm, and curled her fingers over it gently.

They stood a moment like that, both of his large hands cupping her small one. As Dina studied his face, she thought she saw his mouth soften a bit, almost into the promise of a smile. She wished they didn't have the sunshields on, as she would have liked to have seen Gaard's eyes.

"Thank you, Gaard."

He nodded once in acknowledgment, squeezed her hand lightly, and released it. He turned slowly and walked away from her, his image again wavering in the torrid air current. He mounted the skimmer, powered it, and sat for a long moment, looking in her direction. The heat rollers steadied, and Dina had a final clear view of him before he turned and was slowly secreted by the dancing waves of light and heat.

Dina watched him disappear, then shifted her gaze downward. Her fingers opened slowly, like the petals of a flower unfurling, and there in her palm, like the flower's pistil, winked the golden star.

***

During the early evening of the third day following Rayn's battle with Gyn, while Dina curled on her bed, trying not to think and not to feel, she heard the Voice in her head.

Dina.

Something was wrong. She didn't know how she knew, but like so many feelings she had had lately, she was absolutely certain she was right. *Rayn? Are you all right?*

Come to Kathedra as soon as you can. I'll be waiting.

Rayn, wait... She waited, but there was no reply. Dina bounded off the bed, pulled a cooling vest from the room cooler, and quickly put on a weather suit. She rinsed her face and was headed for her skimmer within two minutes. Her hair was loose, but the narrow sunshield she opted for instead of the full hood kept it somewhat in place. Within the city proper she impatiently kept the speed of the skimmer down, but as soon as she reached the gate, she gave the machine full power.

Her mind raced at an equal speed, trying to guess what had

happened to Rayn. *Damn Gaard for not telling me more!* Had Rayn been injured after all? That would explain the three days—perhaps he had needed time to recover from injuries. But Gyn had wanted to destroy his mind, not his body. Perhaps Gyn had succeeded in breaking down Rayn's mind to some extent. As she ran through the possibilities, she felt her chest constricting again, and her breathing became labored.

The ride to the kap seemed endless as she crossed the Albho Mar, the faltering sun turning the desert sea from mirror-like facets of silver and midnight to those of amber, mauve, and purple. The rush of warm air on her face stung, but she no more felt it than she took note of the collage of evening colors.

There was only her destination ahead, symbolized by a glowing red dot on the skimmer's trail finder. The red glow, built into the windshield, was like a promise, and led her on. The tiny red sphere pulsed and grew, until Dina, recognizing the unmistakable outcropping of rock, slowed the skimmer to a hover. Even in her haste, though, Dina's habit of caution persisted.

She searched the entrance of the cavern, but saw nothing. Almost immediately, he stepped from the shadow into the honeyed sunlight and took several uneven paces in her general direction.

Dina all but dropped the skimmer to the ground and ran toward the cave, straining to see, but the low sun was behind him, casting him in a silhouette as black as the Void. The feeling of wrongness persisted, and her fear leapt with her strides. He almost appeared to be staggering.

She pulled up and came to a dead stop, unable to see his face, frightened suddenly that he might be disfigured somehow. Would she be able to accept that?

"Come ahead, Dina. It's all right." The words were stated as if by rote, and did nothing to reassure her, but she took one tentative step after another until she was an armslength away. She could see his face now, shadowed, but visible. To her relief she saw no injuries, but his eyes were dark and his mouth unsmiling.

She pulled her sunshield off, crammed it into her trouser

pocket, then opened the front of her weather jacket. His eyes, flat as his voice, followed her every movement. She reached underneath her T-shirt and cooling vest and pulled the pendant to the opening at her neck.

She closed her eyes briefly and clutched the stone tightly, feeling its smoothness and warmth, then pulled the chain over her head. She took one more step closer to Rayn and was vaguely aware of a strange taste in her mouth. Rayn dipped his head forward so she could reach over him to place the chain around his neck, and the realization that she had bit the inside of her lip was quickly swept away by the encompassing familiar scent of sweat, leather, and mountain mint. He lifted his head while her arms were still around his neck, and her heart slammed so hard it seemed deafening in the desert silence.

She fought for control but lost. Sinking her hands into the dark hair tangled by wind and sweat, she pressed herself against him and willed him to return the embrace. He did, but strangely there seemed to be neither joy nor passion in him as he held her.

For the moment, she didn't care. She concentrated on what she had—the warmth of his body against hers, his hard strength, the feel of his thick hair between her fingers. He was alive.

He held her as long as she needed to be held, until her curiosity finally compelled her to release him. She leaned back, her hands still on either side of his face, feeling the sweat-soaked strands of hair at his temples.

Unable to look into his eyes, she bent her head and moved her hands down to the pendant. She moved her fingertips across the stone to his bare skin, feeling the hard muscles and damp curls. Even in the shadow, she could make out the shifting silver star in the golden stone.

She finally worked up the courage to speak. For now, spoken words would have to do. His blank eyes did nothing to invite the intimacy of telepathic communication.

"For three days this kept me alive. I know how important this is to you. I'm glad I could give it back." She paused, but when he said nothing, she continued. "I know what this is. It's a mother-and-child pendant. The mother-of-pearl is the mother, and the bharonite, the star stone, is the child. The golden star. That's you, isn't it? You're the child, the golden star, Rayn DeStar."

She looked up, and Rayn's battle for control of his emotions began to break through the stiff facade. His lips parted, and as his eyes glanced at the evening sky, then away to the rocks, then back at her, she could see they gleamed with moisture. A drop of sweat slowly zigzagged down the side of his face.

In that instant he looked more vulnerable than she had ever seen him.

"Rayn, talk to me, please." Her plea was a rough whisper.

He looked straight into her eyes. "The light and the darkness."

"What?" This was not what she expected.

"You're the light, and I'm the darkness."

"I don't understand what you mean." The fear, which had subsided a little while he had held her, started to well up again.

He released her completely. "You were right about me when you first met me. I'm everything you hated and feared. I just destroyed a man, totally, without showing any mercy during the act or any remorse afterwards. And he a countryman. No, more than that. This far from home, a brother."

"Rayn, *he* was the killer. He would have destroyed you, without mercy or remorse, then me, then would have gone on killing. You were the only one on this planet who could have stopped him."

He turned away from her, studying first the desert floor, the gray dust soaked to a deep golden coral by the dying sun. He shook his head and raised his eyes toward the sky. Struck by the light, the eyes became amber jewels in a face of bronze. She saw his adam's apple work. "It's more than that."

He paused, drew a ragged breath, then continued. "From the moment I met you, I've done nothing but lie to you, deceive you, and seduce you."

Dina felt as if she had just had all the wind knocked out of her. Of all the things she had feared to be wrong, this was not one. She shook her head in denial. "No, that can't be so. I probed your mind. I felt what you were feeling."

He gave a small, bitter laugh. "Your present emotions make you forgetful. If you remember, you didn't trust me. You were right not to. What you did that day for the very first time I've been doing for decades. I knew I could hide anything I wanted from you with laughable ease. When you first asked me for help with your investigation I knew about T'halamar. I'd known about him for a long time, just as he knew about me. I was afraid if you found out about him, it would just serve to reinforce everything you already believed about the *dens*. And I had other plans."

Her mind was spinning. Rayn's words took on a surreal sound, as if he were speaking in an alien tongue. "What other plans?"

"In the beginning I tried to resist you. I told myself it was wrong to destroy you." He shook his head. "But I couldn't stop. It's in my blood. From the moment I saw you on the spacedock, I wanted to possess you, seduce you into coming to me."

He still wasn't making sense. "But why the whole seduction routine? Why not just compel me?"

He laughed again, an empty sound. "The *dher* is only a challenge when used on another *dens*. There's no sport in using it on someone like you. And the conquest, the sport, is everything to a *dens*."

"But I did come to you willingly! All you did was give me all that mumbo-jumbo about *denzen* physiology and my not being ready for you. You didn't seem the least bit interested in making love to me."

"By then I found myself caring too much about you to hurt you any further. The deception was part of the plan. Falling for the light wasn't."

"What are you talking about?"

"Everything about you is light. Sometimes like lightning. Either way, I tried to catch it. When I could, I fed off it. I bathed in it. I saw reflected in you the image of the man I wanted to be. The B'haratan that doesn't kill. The *dens* that doesn't lie. But the more I bound you, the more I became what you hate."

She swung her head slowly back and forth. "Light?"

"Your youth, innocence, strength. You clarity of purpose and the clarity of your ideals. And, yes, always, your beauty. You have no idea how much I wanted you."

She was still struggling to grasp what he was saying. Wanted? Past tense? Didn't he still want her?

"Rayn, you gave to me, too. Your strength nourished me. Your will, your power, made me feel warm and alive. Whenever you left me or disconnected a link, I shivered with cold. Do you know that the first day I met you, after you had rescued me from the mine and conveyed me to Sanctuary, I felt a chill when I let go of you and got off the skimmer? And I hadn't even seen your face or heard your name at that point."

She searched his eyes for the answers to her questions. As in the past, she felt herself caught and held, transported to a place beyond physical reality. It was the bond. The bond led her through twin golden tunnels to a place where her answers were clear. The bond was the truth of her feelings. *Wasn't it?* She was suddenly afraid again.

"Rayn, answer this. Did we really bond?" she asked, in a whisper.

He closed his eyes, and his hesitation gave her his answer before he spoke.

"It only exists between one *dens* and another. With you there's no such thing. That was part of the seduction, part of what a *spithra* like me does. You see, Gyn was right about me all along. Gyn and your partner both. They both saw me easily for what I am." His reply, like her question, was barely audible.

She waggled her head again, as if her persistence in denying his words could change them, but all she succeeded in doing was to whip strands of hair into her eyes. The bond existed, she knew it did. She pushed the hair out of her face. "But I knew where you were without seeing you. And I could feel your presence without hearing you."

"Mind tricks. Some simple, some complex, but all very practiced. I've been doing this for many years."

Dina still couldn't believe what she was hearing. "No. I *know* what I feel."

"Listen to me. Every time we met, I sent you a 'ping.'"

"A what?"

"One of the *spithra's* best tricks. A mental equivalent of tossing a stone at you. I touched your mind very lightly, just enough so you were aware of my presence."

"Don't keep saying that word, *'spithra.'* "

"You're right. It's not a nice word. But it's what I am. The deception is over, Dina. You have the truth now that you so badly wanted. It's time now...to let you go."

She looked around, desperate for the sight of something familiar, but there was only her skimmer, the rocks, and Rayn, all bathed in the red-gold light. "I refuse to believe any of this."

He stroked her hair, set aflame by the dying sun. "I'm sorry, little girl. I really am. I've never said that to anyone."

She reached up and slapped his hands aside. "Well, it doesn't make me feel any better to be the first to hear it. I'll tell you something. I don't care what words you say to me. As you've told me time and again, words are meaningless. I know what I feel when I touch your mind, and whatever you say about the bond being nonexistent, I feel it. So go ahead and tell me again how you've just been using me and how you don't care about me." *It won't matter because I know you would die a thousand deaths for me, and that no man will ever love me as you do. You told me you wouldn't leave me. I believe that, no matter what you say.*

He drew her to him again and held her, but this time she felt his longing and desire in every part of his body. He held her like that for a long time, not speaking, but communicating with his hands, stroking her hair and caressing every curve of her back.

She held him fiercely, until, at last, as if drained of all strength, he sank to his knees, dragging her down with him. They knelt on the desert floor, supporting each other for moments that lost all meaning except that they were together.

Finally she pulled away from him just enough to see his face. Her fingers followed her gaze, and she felt the tears on his cheeks. Wondering briefly if they were hers or his, she looked into the golden eyes. They gleamed with moisture, but there was no shame apparent in the release.

"How can you want anything to do with me after knowing the truth?" His spoken voice was so low and pitted that she heard it more with her mind than her ears.

She still cradled his face, wiping away the wetness with her fingertips.

"Your truth, not mine." Dina's reply was no louder than the brush of her fingers against his skin, but she knew he'd hear her just as easily as she had heard him. The corners of her mouth tilted toward the sky. "Just tell me one thing. Do you want me as much as I want you?"

His eyes locked in a union with hers that caused a troupe of shivers to dance down her spine, and he shook his head slowly. "No. No, I'm not going to tell you. You know that's not what I do. I'm going to show you."

He rose to his feet, pulling her up with him, then effortlessly scooped her into his arms. She wound her own around his neck, and he carried her easily into the depths of the kap, where he set her gently down on one of the mats.

Touch my mind.

She stretched out her mind, like a hand straining upward to grasp what had never before been within reach, and when her mind touched his, it was as though a door, long locked, was sprung. A cool, fresh wind flowed through the portal of his mind and danced around her, a celebration of life. She laughed and wondered how she had ever lived without this joy.

Let me into your mind, flowed the wordless whisper, borne on the wind. *Let me be one with you.*

It was not a compelling command, yet a fine trembling shook her as she welcomed him into the depths of her mind and soul.

Stay here. He rose, reached into a cooler unit, and brought out several packaged cleansing cloths, tossing a couple to her. *This is the desert way.* He stripped off his cooling vest and knelt on the mat facing her, his knees enclosing hers. She stared at him, her mouth dry and her pulse racing, as it always did when she was close to him.

Well, little girl?

She blinked, reached down for one of the packets, tore it

open, and slid out the scented cloth saturated with waterless cleanser. She smiled. Mountain mint. She lifted her eyes and drank in his face, the face she never tired of, and with the mind link in place, experienced him in a way she never had before. Not only were her own senses heightened, but she could feel every response in him.

She folded a corner of the cloth around her index finger and started at the top of his head, by the widow's peak, touching the arrow of dark silk that so intrigued her. From the point a thick strand arced in a lazy crescent that embraced one golden eye. She looked into his eyes, and fell in, seeing nothing else, seeing everything else. In their amber depths she saw the Road of Time, the windings of the past crisscrossed with the promises of the future. The endlessness of the ripples of the Field of Forever dizzied her. She closed her eyes and leaned forward. He closed his.

The cool current of air around her shimmered and melted into a blue flame, and heat flared, licking at her, chasing all else away. His passion, his longing were so deep she felt the beginning of burn, both on her skin and in her mind.

He brought his hand up. *Slowly, little girl.* His hand held hers, and gently guided it downward. She opened her eyes to his, and the sparkle of a smile lit them.

She resumed her exploration of his tanned face, from the cheekbones down the clean lines of his jaw to his chin. She touched the corner of his mouth, and his lips parted. The full mouth that could mock, tease, or make her feel like all the heat and wonder of the desert was in him when he kissed her. His eyes were portals to his soul, but his mouth was the doorway to his sensual self. His warm breath was a whispered invitation, and the provocative half-open mouth beckoned her. Unable to resist, she leaned forward and melded her lips with his, moaning when the sensations wrought by the link engulfed her. The softness enticed her, his strength snared her, and his need held her. The blue flame sucked at her, and she felt nothing except his heat, surrounding her, drawing on her, almost devouring her.

Too quickly, though, she started to fight for air. Rayn broke the kiss, raised his head, and holding her hand, guided it again, slowing her down, lest she burn.

I'm sorry, little girl. I'll try to control it.

His energy flow abated a little, and she nodded, drawing a long breath that was shaky with need. His eyes never left hers as she next concentrated on the muscular neck, using the cloth with one hand and running her fingers through his hair with the other hand, combing the sweat-soaked strands off his face. She then cooled his chest, smoothing the cloth over the hard pectoral muscles on either side of the lustrous, cream-colored pendant. His skin was so hot it felt fevered, and she could feel his heart beating, strong and fast, almost in tandem with hers. She held the pendant with her free hand, absorbing its heat, and with the cloth, followed the narrow trail of dark hair downward to the waistband of his trousers.

Letting the cloth slip from her grasp, Dina ran her hand lower still, until she could feel the hard evidence of his physical desire for her. She felt that desire increase with his sharp intake of breath and the rise and fall of his chest, and in her mind she felt the echo of his emotional need for her, just as powerful and turbulent. His energy poured over her again, like a thousand wicks trimmed low, waiting to burst into flame. It was controlled, just barely.

Her own control fragmenting, she hesitated, her face against the hot flesh of his chest. His heartbeat, amplified by the link, thundered in her ears, the sharp scent of mint filled her nostrils, and her mind failed her, unable to hold the torrent of emotions flooding it. She was drowning, and she started to gasp for air, as if the flames around her had consumed all the oxygen in the kap. Her floundering mind caught his name and held on.

Rayn...Rayn... I'll burn.

I just may burn along with you, little girl. I've never wanted a woman the way I want you.

He shifted position, and drew her away from him. *Unlink your mind from mine, or both of us will go up in smoke.*

She hesitated, reluctant to let go of the promise of magic she had yearned for and waited for.

Gods, Dina, I want this as much as you do, but if we

continue with the link you'll self-destruct. Trust me, please.
There'll be another time.

She nodded and slowly unwound her mind from his. She still felt his passion, as well as her own, but at a lower, more manageable intensity.

He gave her a moment, then gently brought his arms up between them, pushing her away just enough to undo the front of her cooling vest. She dropped her arms, and he slipped the vest off her shoulders. Running his hands down her side to her waistband, he jerked the hem of her T-shirt out of her trousers, and, with one fluid move, pulled the shirt up and over her head, revealing a snug, no-nonsense desert bra.

Rayn reached for a fresh cleansing cloth, and with it, caressed her face, her neck, her
shoulders, and her arms, lingering at the hollow at the base of her throat and the soft underside of her upper arms. She felt the cool dampness of the cloth acutely, even without the link, and shivers of cold and pleasure skittered across her skin wherever he touched her.

When he drew the cloth over her breasts, still covered by one thin layer of cloth, she thought she would jump out of her skin. She shuddered at the cool touch and arched her back to demand more of the sweet punishment.

But the cloth was just to prime her, not punish her, and already he was painting her flat belly with swirling wet strokes, raising designs of goosebumps in its wake. She squirmed, and he deftly undid her desert trousers, just as handily easing them down off her legs. She gave a kick and launched the trousers to the floor.

He stroked her long legs down to her ankles, then slowly dragged the cloth in lazy circles upward again until he reached her thighs. She parted her legs and, when he touched the soft skin of her inner thighs, she trembled again with prickles that shot up and down her spine and a meltdown that started pooling in her center. When his bare hand moved higher and cupped her between her legs, her body jerked, not in fear or revulsion, but in sweet agony as the meltdown accelerated.

Rayn... The word was a plea, brimming with the need she

felt in every part of her body.

I know.

He tossed the cloth aside and, raising his right hand to her face, smoothed the damp strands aside. His fingertips grazed the side of her face, tracing a line from her temple, across her cheek, and along her jaw to her chin. She closed her eyes. Her skin prickled with sensation wherever he made contact. *You make me feel so alive.*

That's a start, but I'm going to take you far beyond alive.

He copied her movements of a moment before, and with his index finger planted next to the corner of her mouth, he moved his thumb and rubbed it lightly over her lips. Her lips drew slowly apart, and he leaned forward and took her mouth as she had claimed his.

His lips were neither teasing nor gentle, as when he had kissed her in the past, but drew on her as a thirsty soul in the desert pulls on a flask of water. She moaned, and even without the mind link, all she was aware of was his mouth—hot, hard, and insistent, tugging at her, tasting her, tantalizing her. She buried her hands in his hair, and falling back to the mat, wrapped her legs around his hips.

He released her mouth and pulled the bra up and over her breasts and head. When Rayn stripped her of her clothes, it was as if she awakened from hypersleep, as if the clothes had been the chrysalis of a sleep pod, sloughed off after many years. She blinked and experienced a freedom and clarity that thrilled her. In the low light of the cavern her vision had never been more clear. She had no doubts, no questions, no fear. Her body and mind were one. Her prison walls had tumbled, and even as her physical need drummed through her body, the realization hit her like a crystal bright sky after a storm.

Rayn was above her, his long hair hanging forward, the golden eyes gleaming, and the pendant twirled slowly in space just above her. She watched it catch the light as it moved, the mother stone glowing, the star stone winking.

I love him, she thought, *the star who traveled so far across the galaxy to burn for me.*

Only because you set me on fire, little girl. The torch is all you.

Though the link was broken, her mind still stretched out to encompass his every thought and draw them as deep into her heart as she could, tucking them like a precious trove into a hidden, guarded niche. As her mind reached out to his, her body thrummed. A freedom, yes, but not a release, not yet.

Gods, Dina, you're more beautiful than I imagined, and believe me, I have a good imagination.

Dina smiled, her eyes half-closed in anticipation. She reached up, slid her hands around his neck, and pulled him down to her. She felt first the warm stone as the chain and pendant pooled in the well between her breasts, then his hot mouth and even hotter tongue.

He cupped her breast from underneath, pushing it gently toward his mouth, and his lips and tongue cherished the soft flesh surrounding the pink peaks. The sensitive skin of her breasts magnified the sensations rendered by the different textures of Rayn's face. His soft lips kissing the inside of her breasts, his rough, wet tongue scoring circles of fire around her aureoles, and his scratchy two-day growth of beard rubbing the tender skin to even greater sensitivity all drove her higher toward the mountaintop she aspired to.

She arched into him, but while he played every curve and swell, still he was careful to avoid the demanding hard buds. Her fingers dug into the ridged muscles of his neck and shoulders, and she writhed beneath him, but still he denied her. Instead, he slid one hand down over her flat stomach to her one remaining piece of clothing, her desert shorts. He moved his hand lightly over the soft material until his hand was between her legs once again. He began to stroke her, gently at first, then with more pressure, until she responded by pushing hard against his hand, begging for more.

Rayn, please... Her hands tugged at him, pulling his head down to her as her mind pleaded with him to end her torture.

He slid his hand inside the shorts, and at the same time, touched the tip of his tongue to one nipple. She threw her head back and bit her lip to keep from crying out. He repeated the touch, holding the contact longer this time, then wagged his tongue back and forth over the peak, hardening it even more. She arched again as much as she could, her breasts, full and thrusting, demanding still more. He touched his lips to the nipple, then kissed it, then combined tongue and lips to tease it. She thought she would scream.

When he finally took the nipple deep into his mouth, her body shuddered, then relaxed. As he suckled her, his fingers probed deeper and deeper, caressing the honeyed folds, teasing her hard bud of desire. The meltdown continued, robbing her of air, robbing her of her senses, leaving only naked desire.

She began pulling fiercely at his trousers, trying to undo them. Releasing her for a moment, Rayn accommodated her, first pulling her shorts off, then divesting himself quickly of his own trousers and shorts. He stretched the length of his body alongside hers. Wrapped together, their hands and mouths explored each other, not slowly this time, but with urgency. Sweat sheened his body, and his hair was plastered in wet strands to his face. She pushed it back, and her own curtained both their faces. He buried his fingers in her hair, and his touch made her feel more treasured than if his hands had discovered a chest full of gold coins.

The clarity of just moments before was gone, shattered by their need, and the individual sensations spun and blurred together with ever increasing speed. When he began stroking her again, probing her folds until his fingers were inside her, she cried his name aloud, over and over.

Shhh, T'anga'cha, the waiting is over.

He quickly straddled her, positioned himself, lifted her hips, and drove into her. She bowed against him. Nothing Daar had done to her had even remotely been like this. She had thought she had loved Daar, but that had been nothing like this. As Rayn began a slow rhythm of powerful thrusts, each deeper than the one before, she knew with a certainty that he was touching her in places Daar had never reached. But it was so much more than that. Now she kept no secrets, no longer pretended to be someone she wasn't. This was a true union of more than just body. This was the power of the suns and moons and stars, the vastness of space, the heat of the desert. It was the joy of music, the peace of the rain, the quest for light.

It was her mind mirrored in his, and his in hers, so that she no longer knew if the emotions she felt were her own or Rayn's. And it didn't matter. They were as one, link or no link, bond or no bond.

Their joined bodies were perfect complements to each other. His hardness to her softness, his power to her resiliency, his hunger to her bounty. But there was no darkness. The only complement to the light was a soul that sought his way by turning to the brightest flame he could find...a lightning storm named Dina.

At long last, he plunged into her one last time, the hardest and deepest thrust of all, and she held his body as closely and fiercely as she held his thoughts in her heart. He moaned against her, and shuddered with his release.

As the blanket of night descended on the Kathedra Valley, there was no darkness at all.

TWENTY-ONE
SOUL OF THE NIGHT

They slept for a while, blankets and the heat of their bodies warming them, but soon the deep chill of night penetrated the depths of the kap. Rayn woke Dina with a soft, lingering kiss. The shivers that gamboled down her body this time, however, were due as much to the cold night air as to the sweetness of his touch.

He quickly rose, lit a lantern, and returned to Dina with two warm night outfits. He tossed one to her. "Here. Put this on. We're going outside."

"Are you crazy? We'll freeze."

Rayn laughed. "You forget. I'm a master at desert survival, day or night. You won't freeze. I promise."

"*Krek,*" she said, smiling, quickly pulling on the soft thermal pants and jacket. She watched as Rayn did the same, then nodded his head toward a heat blanket that he had pulled out of storage.

"Take that and follow me."

"Don't we need a lantern?"

His only response was a soft laugh.

Rayn picked up a couple cushions and a second blanket and headed out of the cavern. There was no need for a lantern to pick their way across the desert floor. Foraii and Egnis were just rising, and their beams flooded the small valley with a soft, luminous glow.

The desert floor glinted like marcasite, and the shadowed tors sat crouched, attending to their eternal sentinel duty. Rayn chose an even spot on the desert floor and dropped the cushions. He nodded to Dina to put the blanket down, and he arranged the comfortable bedding.

"I want you to experience the desert at night. It's something you'll never forget."

"As if I would ever forget this night," said Dina, smiling.

Rayn motioned for Dina to get under the blanket then joined her, adding his heat to that of the cover. She sat cradled between his legs, her back against his chest, his arms wrapped around her. He rubbed his cheek against her hair.

"Magnificent, isn't it?" he whispered into the strands. When she shivered he tightened his hold even more.

Dina leaned back against him and raised her eyes. The celestial show was indeed magnificent. Millions of glittering stars were mounted like jewels to the black velvet backdrop. Like millions of exodites, she thought, flashing all the colors of the rainbow. Some stars were bright and white, some pulsed with a red glow, some gleamed with a bluish hue, and some were the pale yellow of *agherz*. She tried to pick out specific stars. "Can you see Deorcas Tron?"

"Of course. But don't you mean 'Dark Star?'" he countered.

"No. I don't think I'll ever call it that again."

He buried his lips in her hair and kissed her above her ear, then pulled an arm out from under the blanket and pointed to his right. "There. The large, bright yellow star just above that diamond shaped asterism. See it?"

She nodded. "It's not so dark, is it?"

She felt the smile in his voice as he answered. "No," he whispered, "not so dark. Sister stars, you know, yours and mine. A double star, bound for all eternity, but no one on Glacia ever wants to acknowledge any relationship."

"Someday they will, Rayn. Someday."

They sat like that for a long time, not speaking. Dina drank in the magic of the night, warm in Rayn's arms, feeling a peace she had never in her life known. *If only this night could last forever*, she thought.

It will. Up here. It will last forever, no matter what happens in the future. Remember that.

She shivered again, as if she had just seen that future.

***

He made love to her as Foraii and Egnis descended toward their daytime lair, slipping behind the watchful tors.

Her soft kisses on his eyelids were like the birth of *agherz* depositing cool pearls of dew on the naked rocks, and the power of his emotional response to her simple gesture nearly overwhelmed him. He took her mouth with his and felt her shudder, and though it was not quite the shudder of acquiescence that signals surrender to his power, a wave of sexual gratification surged through him nevertheless. It was a trait bred deep into the *dens*, the sexual pleasure that domination brought, and Rayn couldn't have changed it, dismissed it, or ignored it if he had tried. But as he held her he also felt her longing for him, her yearning to reach the end of the tunnel of loneliness she had been trapped in so long, and suddenly the importance of her desires washed everything else away. He pressed his mouth against the soft curtain of her hair, silvered by the beacons of the night.

Link with me, Dina. I want you to experience this. He felt her thoughts and emotions embrace his, and this time Dina was able to maintain the mind link without burning. As his mouth and hands worshiped her, he felt her perception of all she used to know shatter. He stayed with her, and together their minds journeyed to a dimension where two souls truly became one.

Dina had never experienced anything like it, yet she felt no fear. He was with her, and she knew he wouldn't let her come to harm. There was no Voice, not even in her mind, yet she knew what he wanted her to do, and she obeyed him without question. She released rational thought, released her traditional five senses, and reached out for feelings and sensations she had never before experienced. Her perception was heightened, yet she lost track of time and space. She knew not if they made love for minutes or hours, if moonlight or sunlight bathed them. She felt weightless, floating, her tunnel vision so narrow all she knew was the heat, strength, and passion that cocooned them as they spun faster and faster. She saw nothing except a dome of black sky behind her eyelids, against which burst blooms of colors so vivid she had no names for them, and heard nothing save a roaring in her ears, as if an ocean surrounded her, suspending her, blocking all else out.

At long last, his body still merged with hers, the spinning slowed and the roaring subsided, and she felt buoyed on a calm sea, drifting. Thought returned, and her first was wonder at which work of art had truly been more magnificently wrought by the gods, all the stars in the heavens, or the giving soul and body of one man.

They lay in each others arms and watched the creation of day. The faintest stars dimmed first as the black sky paled to midnight blue. Gradually all but the brightest white and yellow stars in the western sky were extinguished, and the eastern horizon slowly infused light and color into the dark, giving it warmth and life. The blue paled to the clarity of the finest Exodan glass, and washes of transparent yellow and red flowed from the unseen palette of the gods, tinting the horizon with blended shades of lemon, peach, and orange.

"Do you know that the miners celebrate the dawn? It's the hope that *agherz* promises with the birth of each new day," whispered Dina.

"Ummm. How did you hear of that ancient tradition?"

She smiled. "I'm an investigator, remember?" She lay with her back against Rayn's chest, his arms wrapped around her. She ran her hands up and down his forearms, feeling the muscled contours. "Actually, Raethe told me."

Rayn smiled into her hair. "Rae. Bless his heart. He was ever the lone wolf, but it was his voice that first expressed concern for Hrothi's safety, and his insistence that I do something about it."

She nodded. "You have quite a band of comrades, you know that?"

He was silent for a moment. "I couldn't be prouder of them if they were my blood brothers," came the soft whisper.

They lay silent again, watching the ball of fire breach the horizon line.

"So is it done? All of it?" Rayn asked after a while.

"The investigation?"

He nodded. "I know that Trai and Gaard helped you snag Ctararzin. Trai still hasn't stopped telling his story of how he was very nearly the ninth victim of the already infamous Mother murderer. Gaard just rolls his eyes. I've never seen Gaard so dramatic."

"Whose idea was it anyway, to pretend to have Hrothi, with his last dying breath, tell Rhoemer who the killers were?"

"Rae and Hrothi himself came up with that one. Hrothi thought that if he had to go to all the trouble of dying, it should serve more of a purpose than just to keep him alive. What happened to that *anghwi,* Khilioi?"

"As predicted, when he was confronted, he was more than willing to tell all in order to avoid being charged the maximum. He was the one who tampered with Jon's skimmer. I should have first suspected him when I saw him in the holo with you."

"With me?"

She nodded. "He was one of the undercover officers who tried to infiltrate the *Dailjan* by masquerading as a dissatisfied city worker. He recorded all those meetings. On one holo he was covered with red dust. I didn't pick up on that for a long time. Anyway, it was while on one of those *Dailjan* hunting assignments that he came upon Xuche in the desert. Khilioi, ever the opportunist, saw his chance to take into custody a dark outworlder. However, Xuche being what he is, which is basically a coward, tried to make a deal with Khilioi to save himself. He told Khilioi there was a *dens* living in the Pur-Pelag, and didn't the officer agree that a *dens* would be a much bigger prize than a *mantis.* Khilioi did indeed pretend to agree, and searched the Pelag for T'halamar, never with the intention of taking him into custody, but to feel him out as a possible killer for hire. Khilioi was always thinking how best to take advantage of a situation. The reputation of the *dens* is well known, you know."

"Yes, little girl, I know," Rayn said, stroking the side of her face.

"Khilioi and T'halamar struck a deal and agreed that it would be prudent to get rid of Xuche once and for all before he said the wrong thing to the wrong person. So Khilioi provided the anonymous tip to Katzfiel as to Xuche's whereabouts, while Gyn compelled Xuche to give a harmless story to the Commander regarding his escapades in the desert. Xuche was deported, just as T'halamar and Khilioi anticipated he would be. Katzfiel never knew the truth about Xuche, never knew about T'halamar or Khilioi. Gods, I can't believe how wrong I was about him."

"Separating fact from illusion is difficult, even for a telepathic investigator. All telepaths are vulnerable, you know, even the *dens*. We all make mistakes, little girl. Gods know I've made my share," he said, leaning forward to kiss the hollow behind her ear.

"You did the right thing with Gyn. What made you change your mind about helping me?"

"The *m'riri.*"

"*M'riri?* What's that?"

"The ancient B'haratan custom of self-reflection. My mother taught me, years ago, but I was never very good at it. Until now. I used the Ghel Mar as my meditation focus. On B'harata I used the mirror of the rain, but the Ghel was the closest thing to a rainscape I could find in the desert."

Mirror. Dina remembered the dream she had had about the man in the mirror. Another premonition? She shuddered at the thought. "So...it was through this self-reflection that you made the decision to help me and to face T'halamar on your own."

"Simply put, yes. The *m'riri* told me that I could no longer run and hide. I had to take a stand and put aside my prejudice."

She squirmed out of his grasp and turned to face him. His words surprised her. "Your prejudice?"

A crooked smile that Dina could interpret only as a smirk split his face. "Gyn was a countryman. I was reluctant to betray him, no matter what his crimes. In the beginning you were as much a foreigner to me as I was to you. A very high-and-mighty foreigner at that."

Dina's mouth dropped open. She picked up a pebble and tossed it at him. "*Me* high-and-mighty? Don't be so smug. The gods punish those who are smug, you know."

He reached for her and pulled her to him again. *The gods will just have to punish me some other time,* came his voice in her mind as his lips claimed hers again.

***

An hour later they were back inside the kap, the desert already becoming uncomfortably warm. Stretched out on a mat beside him, she faced him, her head propped by her left arm. Her right hand rested over his heart. She stared at him.

"What?" he asked.

"'What?' What do you mean, 'what?'" she replied.
"Since when haven't you been able to read every thought in
my head every minute of every hour?"

"I can't read every thought, every minute."

"The hell you can't."

"Very well. I'll rephrase. You're memorizing my face.
Tell me why. My appearance is remarkably unremarkable."

"Not to me it isn't. To me it's beautiful." Dina looked
away. "I think there's a very good possibility we'll be
separated for a long time."

He frowned. "What do you mean?"

"The Synergy is not a very forgiving entity. In spite of
all the help you've rendered, I've overheard rumors you're
going to be deported."

"Not to a penal colony, I trust?"

"No, probably back to B'harata," she replied, still
looking away.

His left hand covered the hand over his heart. "You
wouldn't come with me?

Though quietly and simply phrased, Dina could detect a
note of suspicion in the question, a fear that she would
decide she was indeed better off without him. She looked
back at his eyes. "If I could, of course. But deportation ships
are secured and don't accept ordinary passengers."

"Surely you'll have some influence as a result of
bringing the murder investigation to a successful resolution."

"I doubt I will. Especially once I resign my IIB position.
I'll just be a citizen, no different from anyone else."

"There are other options," he stated.

"Oh sure, you could use the *dher* on everyone. I would
prefer to do things legally."

"It's a long trip to B'harata. We'll be put into
hypersleep, so the journey won't be bad at all. What's really
bothering you?" he asked.

She looked down. "This is such a tiny rock. I guess I've
gotten spoiled...being able to call you any time I wished and
having you right beside me in an instant. But the galaxy is so

vast. What if something unforeseen happens? We'll be out of reach, with no way to contact each other, no way to know where the other even is..."

"Dina."

He put his arms around here, and held her, stroking her hair. She felt his hard muscles and the warmth of his skin, but when she moved her arms down his sides, he winced in pain.

"Careful, little girl, my ribs are still pretty bruised."

"I'm sorry," she whispered, frowning. "They didn't seem to bother you last night."

"Last night I had other things on my mind."

The corners of her mouth lifted at the memories, but then the smile fell. "Rayn, this is just what I'm talking about."

"What is?"

"It reminds me that you're not some god, immortal and indestructible. You're just a man."

"What happened to imperious and all-knowing? When did I become so humble in your eyes?"

"When I fell in love with you, you arrogant *krek*."

He held her at arm's length. "Listen to me. I've been around a long time. I've only been on Exodus a few years, yet in that time I've made several life friends. Friends that would do anything for me, not because I compel them to, but because that kind of loyalty has developed between us. I have friends like that on many worlds, even a few on B'harata," he added, smiling. "I'm from Sha'haran. It's one of the largest cities on B'harata. There's quite a good size Glacian population there. Diplomats, ambassadors, missionaries, all have been coming to B'harata for years, and many stayed. A community of teachers, doctors, merchants, and other providers has sprung up to support them. You wouldn't have any trouble finding a place to stay among them, and work, if you wished that. If you're there, I'll find you."

She just stared at him, not speaking.

He sighed. "You're still not reassured, are you? Before we part, if we part, I'll give you a list of contacts, people on different worlds who can be trusted, and who have the ability to find me if need be."

"If you're anywhere to be found."

"Yes, if I'm anywhere to be found. And just to make sure you don't lose this information, I'll burn it into your brain. Would that make you happy?"

"Only one thing would make me happy right now. And if you can't figure it out, then you're not the man I think you are."

She needn't have worried. He was the man she thought he was.

TWENTY-TWO
"NO GOOD-BYES, LITTLE GIRL"

The next few days sped by all too quickly. Once Hrothi, Khilioi, and Ctararzin gave official testimony, the Mother Lode house of cards quickly tumbled. Hwa-lik, Chukar, and Bhelen were all implicated and taken into custody, and each hurried to give evidence against the others in an attempt to save themselves. The decision was indeed made to deport DeStar back to B'harata, and Dina resigned her IIB commission immediately thereafter.

When Jon heard about her resignation, he sought her out and begged her to rescind it. Though her mind was made up, she heard him out, curious as to the arguments he would put forth. When he finished, she smiled and took his hand. He was a good agent and a loyal partner, and she would always love him for that, but his arguments had consisted only of "duty," "talent," and vague hints at promotion.

She brushed his mind then, something she had never done before, and she wondered no more about his inner feelings. Affection, but no passionate love. Sorrow at their parting, but no regret at any of his actions. And though he hadn't said so to her, it was clear that he didn't understand how such a level-headed woman as Dina could fall in love with someone no better than an outlaw. She had always valued Jon's opinion, and the fact that he didn't think she had made a wise choice saddened her, but his wishes for her well-being were genuine, and in this at least Dina was glad.

Rayn spent one day in the desert without Dina, saying good-bye in his own way to the friends he had made there. At *merkwia* of that day, he ascended to Berg Frij, high above Keneko Kap, and looked out upon the Ghel one last time. He sat and watched as the still sea changed colors, deepening with infinite slowness, from gold to red to purple to a deep velvet blue.

Thank you, my friend, for being my rainscape. I told Dina that this was a dead planet, but I was wrong. My apologies to you. As Rayn rose to leave and turned his head, he caught a

flash of light out of the corner of his eye from the hyaline sea.
As he descended the rocky path, he smiled to himself, turned,
and winked back at the Ghel.

***

They stood at the dock, knowing boarding would soon
commence. The final moments were carefully spent, like hard
earned wages, and Dina wondered briefly if time would ever
be a luxury for her.

"Do I have to tell you how I feel about you?" whispered
Rayn.

She looked into the rich eyes. The words were always nice
to hear, but she knew how he felt. "No."

"Good. In that case, I'll tell you. B'haratans don't use the
word 'love' to describe the way they feel about those they bond
with. I can say that I love my comrades, Gaard, Dyll, Rae, and
the others for their loyalty, for their goodness. I love Alee for
her unselfishness, her understanding. But those we bond
with...it's a need only they can fill." He paused, then continued.
"Each one of us have incomplete or empty spaces in our souls.
If we're lucky, we find one person who is able to fill all those
hollow places, fill them perfectly and completely. When I'm
with you, there's a beacon that illuminates every dark reach of
my soul. I need that. I need you. That probably sounds selfish
to a Glacian."

"No. No, it doesn't." She bent her head down and took off
her exodite ring, the one her father had given her what seemed
now so long ago. "Here. Take this. I'm sure it won't fit you,
but wear it on a chain. Look at it and I'll be with you, lighting
your way, no matter how far apart we are."

He took the ring and smiled as he tried it on his little finger.
It didn't fit even over the first knuckle. "Don't worry. It's not a
sign we don't fit. I'll wear it around my neck, in place of this."
He lifted his pendant over his head and gave it to her. "Wear
this for me, and remember that my strength will always be
with you."

She looked at the back side, where the strange markings
were engraved. "Will you tell me your real name now?"

"Raynga D'anthara."

"'The other.'"

Rayn frowned. "How did you know?"

"When you gave me the pendant before, I had my computer scan it and translate for me. Why did you change your name?"

"I always thought it was a cruel joke. 'The other of two.' There were never two, only myself. My mother used to tell me that it was a name of good luck, that it meant I was sure to meet someone I would bond with. But after I left Deorcas Tron, I took the name 'DeStar,' partly because of the stone in the pendant, and partly because I wanted to retain some identity of my birthplace. 'DeStar' is a corruption of your Glacian term 'Dark Star.' To take that name proudly was my subtle way of laughing at all of you."

Dina smiled. That definitely sounded like Rayn. It would be hard for her to think of him by any other name than 'DeStar.' "Your mother sounds like a wise person. I wish I could have known her. My mother died when I was only ten. I wish I would have known her better, too." She looked back up at him. "Will you use your true name now?"

"Yes, little girl. I am your 'other' now, like it or not, forever. And you are mine, T'anga'cha."

She sighed. "Will you please tell me what that means?"

It's B'haratan for 'child of light,' he voiced in her mind, giving her a final soft kiss.

Sergeant Hrugaz and Officer Drukelez stepped forward unobtrusively, and the Sergeant spoke softly. "Rayn, Miss Marlijn, it's time."

Rayn nodded and broke the kiss. *No good-byes, little girl. I'll see you very soon on B'harata.*

Her cheek still laid against his, she ran her hand down the side of his face one last time, her fingertips memorizing every contour. *On B'harata.*

Rayn turned and accompanied the AEA officers to the ship, not turning toward her again as he boarded, not saying anything more to her. He didn't have to. She understood.

EPILOGUE

Rayn's ship departed on time, and he was put into hypersleep for the ride home. Dina left Exodus a week later on a ship to Glacia. The parting with Jon had been bittersweet.

He had told her he would always be her friend, and that if she ever needed help of any kind, or even just a shoulder to cry on, she knew where to find him. Tears had welled up in her eyes then, and when Jon asked her if Rayn would mind if he kissed his girl, Dina laughed through the tears. She told Jon that she kissed whomever she liked, and Jon had said "that's my girl," and, brushing the tears from her cheeks with his fingers, had bent down to kiss her sweetly on the lips.

Dina arrived on Glacia in good time, and visited her father, telling him the story of the desert. Unlike Jon, Dina's father made no judgment on her decision to leave her career behind and to pursue a *dens* across the galaxy, but celebrated the joy he saw in her eyes. They sat in the crisp iceblink air, and he told her stories of his childhood while they sipped hot brews flavored from the spice trees. The leisurely days they spent together were special, and though she didn't know it, they would never come again.

The day came for Dina to board the ship for B'harata, preparations and paperwork finally complete. She embraced her father and remembered his parting words to her. "Never give up," he had said. The ship was a cargo ship, the only one available. The *Palladia* departed on schedule, and Dina was put into hypersleep with the captain, her final conscious thoughts of Jon, her father, and lastly, Rayn.

It was a long journey, but that story is yet to be told...

Don't Miss
Jaye Roycraft's
Image Series
Four Acclaimed Vampire Romances

Book One
DOUBLE IMAGE

Dalys Aldgate has been a survivor for 235 years. Life as an Australian convict had sharpened his survival skills, but the bush also bestowed him the ultimate gift of survival—a journey to the Other Side. His soul left behind, Dalys became a mirror for those still human—a polished surface upon which the living can project their fantasies, never seeing the "monster" on the mirror's other side. In present day Mississippi, "Dallas" lives a reclusive life as owner of a haunted inn while trying to forget his even more haunting past.

Ex-cop Tia Martell is now a freelance photographer trying to adjust to life "after The Job" and put the years of violence and death behind her. While on assignment to shoot antebellum mansions in Natchez, Mississippi, murder brings her face-to-face with Dallas Allgate, the coldest, yet most fascinating, man Tia has ever met. Before Tia can unravel the mystery of the man with the hypnotic eyes, a young vampire and his master, Jermyn St. James, seek out Dallas for revenge. St. James only wants Dallas' true death until he sees Tia. Now he wants her, too.

Tia's in danger from St. James, but she's in even more peril from Dallas—the man who knows death even better than she does. In their struggle for life, one of them will have to make the ultimate sacrifice. But will Dallas let Tia make her own choices, or will he bend her will by projecting her fantasies upon his…Double Image.

Book Two

AFTERIMAGE

Russian Alek Dragovich, enforcer for the Undead, is feeling the weight of his years and has yet to find the elusive affaire d'amour that would lighten his burden. Nothing, but nothing, is going well.

His position in the Directorate is in jeopardy, and even his mentor Nikolena is threatening to remove her support if Drago doesn't stop employing his unorthodox methods of resolving his cases. Nikolena gives Drago one last chance to redeem himself—to locate and eliminate a high-ranking member of the Brotherhood who is using forbidden methods to ascend the hierarchy. Still, Drago has little interest in Nikolena's schemes until this one becomes personal. When someone tries to kill him…that's personal.

That "someone" is raven-haired Gypsy Marya Jaks, daughter of a dhampir, offspring of a vampire and his mortal wife. Dhampirs are famous among the Roma for their ability to detect vampires, thereby making them perfect vampire killers. When Marya learns that Drago has deemed her a threat to the vampire community and has ordered her termination, she strikes back.

Drago, the hunter, has become the hunted, but is it Marya who truly wants him dead or Nikolena's mysterious power-hungry vampire? Drago resolves to keep Marya alive until he can learn the truth, and he must summon the strength of will to elevate himself from pawn to player in the deadliest of games.

The afterimage of Drago's neon blue eyes has haunted Marya from the first moment she encountered him in her bedroom, but will the image signify her destruction, or a bond so powerful it can overcome a legacy of hatred.

Book Three

SHADOW IMAGE

Welcome to the idyllic lakefront town of Shadow Bay, where expectation and reality are shores apart. A young woman comes to escape the pressures of the big city, and a very old creature comes to ease himself back into the world of the living…and neither finds what they imagined they would.

Shelby Cort has had enough of working for a big-city police department. Ricard De Chaux, the notorious le docteur la mort and ex-Paramount for the Undead in France, has been escaping for years and now reluctantly works his way back into human society. They meet in the small town of Shadow Bay, Michigan—Shelby as Sheriff and Ric as the new county medical examiner.

When dead bodies start to pop up in unlikely places and the killings go unsolved, Shelby comes under attack from town officials, the media, and her own co-workers. She finds an ally in the new ME, both grateful for his support and drawn by his exotic good looks.

But what Shelby doesn't know is that the killer isn't human. What she also doesn't know is that the cool, collected Dr. De Chaux is by night Doctor Death, the new Overlord of the local Undead, whose top priority is to protect his new charges. Doctor Death hides one piece of evidence after another from the Sheriff, as all the while Ric fills Shelby's off-duty time with longing and passion.

When the killer goes after Shelby and all Ric's secrets are on the line, where will his allegiance fall?

Book Four
IMMORTAL IMAGE
Coming in January 2003

The Directress Nikolena needs a spy. An illegal secret society of vampires has sprung up in Baton Rouge and is creating a small army of "aberrations," creatures that are half-human, half-vampire, and highly susceptible to the will of their masters. Led by Vangeline, a mysterious female reputed to possess great power, this society is a threat not only to the human world, but the hierarchy as well. Nikolena's past enforcier fell victim to l'amour. Needing someone who is immune to feminine wiles, she turns to her favorite new enforcer, whose motto is "no one goes Scott-free."

Revelin Scott is normally pretty easygoing. Even the snide comments of his coworkers that he's nothing but Nikolena's "new dog" don't faze the new enforcier. But when Rev is instructed to dye his hair, change his name, and go undercover, he fears the worst. When he's saddled with a young woman whose brother was one of Vangeline's aberrations, Rev knows the case will be bad. Denice Geron has information he'll need to infiltrate the society, but her disrespect and defiance test his patience to the limit.

Denice's brother Michel, infected with vampire blood, had the strength of will to resist the machinations of the société, and before he was found out and killed, he was able to relay information to his sister. Denice seeks help of the Brotherhood and is passed up the chain of command, but instead of getting what she envisions as the epitome of vampirekind, she gets "Sean Ardwolf," a cocky young vampire who looks more like a debauched rock star than Dracula.

She helps him gain access to the société, but Vangeline is more powerful than anyone imagined, and even Revelin/Sean is drawn into her web of seduction and poisoned by her tainted blood. Denice is his only salvation, but it would mean her death to help him now. A few weeks ago the decision for both would have been easy. Now nothing is easy, no one is to be trusted, and there's no going back.